FAILURE TO MATCH

BAD BILLIONAIRE BOSSES
BOOK 2

KYRA PARSI

Cover design: KNSDESIGN

CONTENT WARNING

To check the content warnings for this book, please visit https://kyraparsi.com/content-warnings/

1

"SIXTY-SEVEN FAILED MATCHES. *SIXTY-SEVEN*."

I knew it was coming, yet I still flinched when the leather folder slapped the oak conference table.

You'd think I'd be used to it by now. Alice and Mitch both seemed to be.

"How is it possible that you haven't been able to find a single appropriate match for the only client that actually fucking matters? *How*? What the fuck am I paying you three for?"

It was a trick. You weren't supposed to answer her.

"Someone answer me. *Now*."

My gaze dropped to my lap, which was a mistake. The only thing Vivian Hale disliked more than an incompetent employee was a spineless one.

Sure enough, the nanosecond I cowered, her attention zeroed in on me, her neck tugging back like a viper preparing to strike.

"Jamie," she snapped. "You've been keeping awfully quiet today. Care to chime in?"

Not even a little, no. What was the point when she wasn't willing to listen?

Still, I lifted my chin and set my shoulders back. I had my answers memorized by this point. It was just a matter of reciting them.

Here was the thing—Vivian didn't actually want an explanation as to why we'd spent the last eight months failing to do our collective jobs. She didn't *really* want to hear why we were struggling to find a suitable match for (arguably) the most eligible bachelor in North America and (inarguably) her most high-profile client.

If Vivian wanted real answers, she would have listened to us half a year ago when we'd warned her this might happen.

The only thing the CEO of Charmed Elite wanted to hear was yet another lie about how we had A Very Thorough Action Plan in place to address The Issue and were *this close* to getting her results. Because at the end of the day, failing to find a match for Jackson Sinclair would be irrevocably detrimental to the reputation she'd spent twenty-odd years building—the one that had her hailed as the number one matchmaker in the world.

The industry was small, and the Sinclairs were... well, they were *The Sinclairs*. One of the wealthiest, most influential families in the country. Money talked, and word of mouth was everything in this business. If we failed, rumors would spread that Vivian had lost her touch, and our competitors would start circling our existing clients like vultures, waiting for the inevitable exodus that would follow if Minerva Sinclair decided to take her business elsewhere.

The super fun part? Vivian was flat-out in denial. She didn't want to accept that we'd *already* failed, which was why Alice, Mitch, and I had spent the last few days brushing up our résumés instead of working. Because when this whole thing ultimately blew up, Vivian needed someone to blame. Getting fired was an inevitability.

Clearing my throat, I shot her a reassuring smile and—

"It's not us."

My mouth snapped shut, my eyes flaring as they darted to Alice.

Vivian's neck *slooowly* rotated in her direction, her glare lethal. "What?"

"It's not us, Vivian," Alice repeated calmly. Too calmly. She sounded almost bored. "It's him."

Mitch and I exchanged questioning glances as Vivian let the silence stretch, daring her to go on.

Alice wasn't deterred, though. Instead of shutting up, she lifted an unapologetic shoulder and let it fall. Not for the first time, I was convinced she didn't experience fear the way the rest of us did. Likely due to her upbringing.

I'd feel invincible too, if I had her financial safety net.

"He's impossible." She held Vivian's glare with unbothered ease. "Jamie tried to warn you this would happen six months ago, but you didn't want to hear it."

Mitch jerked beside me, kicking Alice under the table from the feel of it. He was ignored.

Inspired by her no-fucks-given approach, I sat up a little straighter. Maybe today was the day. Maybe this time Vivian would listen. "Viv, there are less than a hundred single women in the entirety of North America that meet his criteria and, as of yesterday, he's turned down sixty-seven of them."

"So?"

I thought that part was pretty self-explanatory but

okay, I could spell it out for her. "We don't really know what else you want us to do. Mitch and Alice have been working nights and weekends to find appropriate matches for his standing appointments, and I've been staying late to do damage control on the carnage of angry tears and bruised egos he's leaving behind. We're tired."

"Chances are good we'll run out of candidates before we find him a partner. It's not *us*, it's *him*," Alice reiterated. "Jackson Sinclair doesn't need a matchmaker, he needs a miracle worker. And a really good therapist, if I'm being honest."

Mitch shrunk an inch in his seat.

"*And*?" Vivian pushed. "What's our plan? How do we work around these obstacles—"

"We don't. We fire him," Alice countered smoothly.

This time when Mitch jolted, he managed to kick her hard enough to earn himself an irritated glare.

Vivian's lips twisted into a sneer-like smile as she stepped up to the table. My stomach crumpled. "Your proposed solution is to fire Jackson Sinclair as a client? Do you have any idea what that would do to our reputation? Half of our active accounts joined *after* Minerva announced the partnership at her luncheon. What do you think will happen if she takes her business somewhere else?"

They'd probably run into the same issues with him that we had. I bit my tongue; Alice didn't.

"Again, we told you this might happen, right after he sent one of his assistants to do the onboarding interview on his behalf," she said. "We *still* haven't actually met him in person."

Vivian waved a dismissive hand and started to pace again. "Not taking him on as a client wasn't an option.

And firing him now is out of the question. What I need from the three of you is a solution."

"That's the problem, we don't have one," I said. "We've tried everything short of Immersive, and that's only because he won't agree to it."

A blessing in disguise if you asked me. Not that I was senior enough to even be considered for the role, but I couldn't imagine being stuck to Jackson Sinclair's hip like that for an entire month, knowing what I did about his file.

The Immersive Coaching Package was normally reserved for our most challenging clients. They were assigned a full-time relationship consultant and dating coach who spent four weeks studying their daily life, routines, behaviors, and habits, then used the gathered data to find them a suitable match. The whole thing was very intense.

The assigned consultant was even required to attend their dates and observe them from a distance so they could "coach" the client afterward if required (which, nine times out of ten, if a client's situation was critical enough to warrant an Immersive, then coaching was definitely required).

"I'm with Jamie," Alice said. "Unless he's willing to bend on some of his criteria and spare us a bit of his time, then we're all out of ideas."

Vivian crossed her arms, but instead of lashing out, she granted us a single firm nod. "All right. I admit that his rigid schedule and expectations for a partner make this more limiting than we might like, but it's not impossible. Failure isn't an option here—it just isn't. We have to find a way to work around it."

Again, denial.

I slumped back in my chair, but Alice stood firm. If anything, Vivian's reluctance to see the reality of our situation only fired her up. "We've done everything we can with the information we've been provided. Sixty-seven women miraculously met his insane criteria, and not one of them was able to secure even a second date with him. Not *one*. Our data has to be flawed for that to happen but, again, he refuses to partake in our assessments himself, so we're stuck working with what we have. All his tests, questionnaires, and interviews were done by his staff, and some of them weren't even fully filled out. His team is dictating what information we need to do our job, and it's just not working. There's a reason we wouldn't have made these exceptions for someone with a different last name, Viv."

I was half-convinced that Jackson didn't actually want to find a partner, but I couldn't figure out why he'd waste so much of everyone's time and resources, including his own.

The sign-up fee at Charmed was a hefty seven figures, not to mention the level of initial commitment our programs required. The company catered to the top one percent of the one percent, and if there was one thing our clients had in common (apart from their incomprehensible wealth) it was that they didn't like wasting their own time. That was why they hired us in the first place—to do all the vetting and hard work for them.

"Why?" Vivian asked, her sharp gaze snapping among the three of us. "*Why* haven't they been able to secure a second date with him?"

"Your guess is as good as ours," I said.

"What does that mean?"

I edged forward in my chair. "The feedback we've been

getting from his team has been vague and confusing, so we really only have the women's version of events to work with. But that doesn't help since we need to know why *he* didn't think the dates went well."

His matches never voiced any complaints about the experience, and most of them were quite upset after being told that Jackson didn't want to pursue anything further with them.

Another thing a good portion of our clientele had in common? They weren't used to rejection, and some of them did not know how to handle it.

Vivian nodded again, and for the first time since we'd been assigned this hellish nightmare of a case, it felt like she was maybe hearing us.

"Okay," she said. "So then, there you go. That's your next step."

I frowned. "What is?"

"You need to figure out what's really happening on those dates."

There was only one way I could think to do that, but she wasn't going to agree to it. "Could we maybe sit in on one of your meetings with Minerva and see if she has any insight—"

"Out of the question."

Then I was out of ideas.

Mitch nudged at his wireframe glasses, finally deciding to take the baton. "Vivian, we're really not exaggerating. He won't even get on a five-minute call with us. And since he hasn't signed off on an Immersive, we can't exactly send someone out to observe the dates..." He trailed off when Vivian started to shake her head.

"No," she said. "Try again. He's not going to budge on

his schedule. Think of a different way. You need the data, so how will you get it without his cooperation?"

"We've spent eight months trying. He won't—" Alice cut off abruptly, her eyes going in and out of focus. She sucked in a short breath. "Oh."

Oh?

Oh, what?

But before I could ask, Vivian cleared her throat and smoothed down the front of her pleated dress. "Figure this out, and soon. I don't care what you have to do to get me results. Minerva is running out of patience and if she decides to take her business elsewhere, half of our portfolio will follow, and that'll mean layoffs. Period."

She shot Alice one last knowing look on her way out, the opaque glass door sliding shut behind her.

"Holy shit," Mitch breathed, his upper body practically collapsing on the table. "The fucking balls on you, Alice."

She glared at him. "The next time you decide to play violent footsie with me under the table, don't. You almost ripped my tights with that last kick."

"I was trying to save you from yourself. Vivian looked like she was ready to fire you on the spot when you started talking back."

Alice rolled her eyes. "She's going to fire all three of us anyway. She knew exactly what an impossible clusterfuck this was going to be from the very beginning. Why else would she assign three junior consultants to a client this important instead of taking it on herself?"

"Because we're young, ambitious, and willing to put in the long hours it requires?" Mitch tried.

"No. Because we're young, naive, and disposable."

"That's incredibly depressing," I said.

"It's reality."

I slumped in my chair with a sigh. I really didn't want to lose this job—not after I'd worked so hard for so long to get it. Charmed was the crème de la crème of matchmaking companies, so anywhere I went after this would feel like taking ten steps back in my career. Not ideal.

Before Jackson Sinclair, my professional life had been perfect. I'd loved my job, the people, the work-life balance, and even Vivian hadn't been so bad when we weren't constantly disappointing her.

I swiveled in my chair. "You know... if we get fired and have to look for new jobs, we're going to need to explain why we weren't able to find a match for a literal Sinclair." The industry was small, and people talked. It was bound to get out. "They're all going to ask."

Mitch shoved a rough hand through his hair. "I'm more worried about tomorrow night. We have no one to send to Jackson's standing appointment, and I doubt we'll find a match in less than thirty hours. If we have to pull another all-nighter and sleep here, I'm gonna lose my fucking mind. I can't do it."

"Also, how the hell does she expect us to get unbiased data on the dates?" I looked between the two of them. "Drones? Hacking security cams?"

"I have an idea that'll take care of both problems," Alice cut in. "But you're really not going to like it."

"No. Absolutely fucking not." No way. There was no way I was willing to do it.

Alice leaned in, arms flattening on the table. "Come *ooon*. It won't be that bad."

Was she serious? "You want me to go on a date with Jack the fucking Ripper and you don't think it'll be *that bad*?"

"It's not like you're going as yourself," she argued. "You'll be undercover."

"How is that not a thousand times worse?"

Not only was it a terrible idea that would undoubtedly blow up in our faces, but I was the absolute worst person for the job. I hated lying. It made my insides itchy, and the upkeep was almost always too stressful to be worth it.

"Don't overthink it," she said. "We'll hook you up with some discreet surveillance equipment and give you a solid fake profile. You'll be fine."

"You're *really* not thinking this through," I told her.

"Agreed." Mitch tapped his knuckles on the table. "Too many things could go wrong. Plus, there would be absolute hell to pay if Jackson ever found out."

Right. Exactly. "Not to mention I don't meet any of his physical requirements."

I was blonde, five-foot-seven, and twenty-eight.

Jackson Sinclair only dated brunettes between the ages of thirty and thirty-six, and they had to be at least five-foot-ten. His last match (number sixty-seven) was a former Miss World winner and current CEO of a major PR company. He'd take one look at me, turn around, and leave. Just like he had with Allison Park (number twenty-nine), who'd then spent a full hour screaming at me over the phone like it was somehow my fault.

After that, Vivian had called Minerva to ask that Jackson at least respect the one-hour requirement Charmed had for all first dates, the point of which was to ensure our clients gave their matches an actual chance.

Alice shrugged. "We'll get you a wig and a pair of platforms, put you in a dress long enough to cover your feet, and have you arrive early so you'll be seated by the time he gets there. He'll be none the wiser."

"If it's that simple, why don't you do it?" I challenged.

"I'm five years younger and two inches shorter than you, Jamie. Even if you put me in heels high enough to meet his stupid height requirement, I wouldn't be able to walk in them. Plus, you've been doing this for a lot longer than I have, you have a ton more experience dealing with clients, and you're kind of amazing at reading people."

Bullshit. "Gentle reminder that I was friends with Ria for a decade before she met your brother and didn't realize her nostril flared when she lied until he pointed it out."

They were now married—her brother and my best friend. That was how Alice and I initially met. I'd done this to her. I'd gotten her this mess of a job.

"You were too close to Ria. That's your blind spot, but it won't apply to Jackson."

"I can see his face just fine on the screen if you're wearing a camera," I said. "And he probably won't even notice your height if you're seated—"

"No," Mitch blurted abruptly. "No, uh, that's not... Jamie should do it. I vote for Jamie."

Alice frowned at him. "What's wrong with you?"

"Your torso," he responded.

"Excuse me?"

"Your... uh, it's the height thing. Even if you're sitting down, he'll be able to tell... because of your torso. It's... short," he explained eloquently.

Alice stared at him for a full, wordlessly unimpressed minute before turning back to me. "There you go. I can't do it; I've got a short torso."

Mitch's neck was purple.

"I don't care. I'm not doing it," I said. "I'm not."

"Fine." Alice let out a long breath. "Then I guess it's back to the drawing board."

Yes. Fine. Great.

We'd figure something out. We always did.

"It's not like a *bad* torso. It's just compact."

She shot him another lingering what's-wrong-with-you look before getting up. "I'll grab us coffee. We're going to need it."

Mitch deflated the second she was gone, his forehead hitting the table with a sad *thump*.

"Smooth," I said.

"Shut up."

2

"I CAN'T BELIEVE I let you two talk me into this."

I was sweating, my neck, knees, and head were itchy, and there was a solid chance I was going to throw up before I reached the table.

"*Relax*," Mitch said through the earpiece. "*It's going to be fine. Just stick to the plan.*"

"I really don't have a good feeling about this, you guys." I swallowed, my eyes darting around the rooftop patio of the high-rise apartment building.

It was beautifully decorated; I'd give him that. The curved mosaic pool was lined with ornate lanterns, pink roses spilled out of large garden urns everywhere you turned, and a candle-lit table was set up right in the middle of it all. Combine that with the clear night sky and an unbelievable view of the city skyline, and the whole thing was suffocatingly romantic.

"*Terrible or not, it's the only idea we have*," Alice pointed out. "*And you're going to do great. You know your profile inside out, you know what info we need and what questions to ask to get it, and we'll be with you every step of the way. Just stick to the plan like Mitch said and don't overthink it.*"

None of that made me feel better. And not just because I was too busy trying not to trip over the too-long skirt of my dress (which was basically a gown) to pay actual attention to what she was saying. These heels were stupidly high, and don't get me started on how hot and itchy the wig—

"*Incoming.*"

I froze dead in my tracks, my heart jumping up to my throat as I scanned my surroundings.

He was early.

Why was he so early?

He was *never* early from what we'd been told by his matches. He always arrived at 8 p.m. on the dot and ended the date at 9 p.m. on the dot.

Everything else they'd said checked out—a member of his team had greeted me downstairs, accompanied me up here while making polite conversation, and informed me that Mr. Sinclair would be joining me shortly before excusing themselves.

Why the hell was he early tonight? Did he know something was off? Had we somehow managed to fuck this up already?

"I don't see anyone," I whispered after my third full spin.

"*Shit. Sorry. It was just your reflection in the pool,*" Mitch said. "*I'm in a hypervigilant state or whatever, and your black dress looked kind of like a suit—*" He cut off with a pained hiss right before the audio went dead.

"Hello?" Panic clawed at my chest when no one answered. "Alice? Mitch?"

"*Sorry about that. Mitch has lost mic privileges for the time being. It's 7:57 so you still have three minutes until he arrives, you're good.*"

"Okay. Thanks."

"*You should sit down though. Height thing aside, it might look a little weird if you're just standing by the pool and glancing around like someone's after you.*"

I frowned. "How do you know I'm glancing around?"

"*Your boob keeps moving.*"

Right. The camera was sewn into my dress, blending in seamlessly with all the hand-sewn beads. Between the embellishments and multiple layers of fabric, this thing weighed almost as much as I did. It was also a rental and cost more than my car.

But, you know, I had to look the part to play it. None of Jackson's matches were showing up to these dates with a fifty-dollar off-the-rack dress.

I took a deep breath, my newly manicured nails digging into my clutch as I lowered into a seat at the table.

"*Less than a minute, Jamie,*" Alice said softly. "*You should stop responding to us now, just in case. And we'll keep the talking on our end to a minimum so you can focus.*"

I nodded even though they couldn't see me.

"*Fifteen seconds.*"

I smoothed out my skirt, bracing myself as my pulse kicked again. My instincts were screaming, telling me to run.

"*Three.*"

My teeth sunk into my bottom lip, my breathing growing increasingly unsteady and shallow. I should've taken the tequila shot Mitch had offered before I got into the Uber.

"*Two.*"

I shouldn't have suggested we do a countdown. It wasn't helping.

"*One.*"

I sucked in a breath.

Held it.

Held it... some... more...

The air spilled out of my lungs in an audible rush as I twisted in my chair, looking back at the double-door entrance I'd been led through.

"*Odd. They all said he was exactly on time.*"

I shrugged out of habit. "It's only been like fifteen seconds, maybe he—"

I yelped, my soul launching straight out of my body when I turned back and saw the literal giant looming over the table.

"*Shit, sorry! Your arm blocked the camera when you turned. I didn't see him come in.*"

And I hadn't heard him.

He'd materialized straight out of thin air.

"Hey," I breathed, blinking up at the broad, scowly tower of a man with my palm pressed to my startled chest. "Sorry. I, uh, didn't hear you arrive."

The man's scowl dug deeper, his pale blue eyes thinning into suspicious icicles. "Who were you talking to?"

His voice was surprisingly deep and smooth. Like smoked English whiskey and honey.

Did we know Jackson Sinclair had a slight British accent? Because it wasn't in my notes. I'd have remembered.

"Pardon?" I asked dumbly.

"You were speaking to someone when I walked in."

"Um... there's no one here."

Narrower and narrower went his eyes. "I'm aware."

I cleared my throat, blinking away from the intensity of his glare as I peeled my palm from my chest and discreetly wiped it against my dress. Then I held it out to him.

"I'm Grace," I said, forcing my lips into an unsteady smile. "Grace Lambton. You must be Jackson Sinclair."

He scanned my outstretched hand, looking for... I wasn't sure what, exactly. It was just a hand. When he finally did take it, the corners of his mouth quirked down with obvious displeasure.

It was so blatant and off-putting that I instinctively wanted to pull back. Instead, I gritted my teeth and kept my smile intact as his large, smooth hand wrapped lightly around mine. For less than a second.

Then he slipped a white handkerchief out of his pocket and wiped his fingers one by one, as though I'd coated them in grime.

My mouth fell open, my forced smile fading as Alice made a strangled noise in my ear.

"*Did he just...*"

He did.

And he did it while maintaining unwavering eye contact, almost like he was waiting for me to take offense and challenge his behavior. His eyes flicked up to the night sky when I remained silent.

Was this real? Or was he fucking with me?

A suited waiter appeared from somewhere behind me and began filling our champagne flutes with sparkling water. "Anything to drink, madame?"

"A martini," I said just as Jackson took a seat. "Please."

"*Yeah, you're gonna need it. Why's he looking at you like that? What's wrong with him?*"

I didn't know. I was trying very hard not to look directly into the biting glare being shot at me from across the table.

I'd been right. Coming here had been a terrible fucking idea.

The plan had been to wait for Jackson to speak first so we could observe how he normally broke the ice, what types of questions he asked, and how much initial interest he was willing to show his date. The one possibility we hadn't considered? Him not speaking. At all.

I sat there, fiddling restlessly with the dainty rings stacked on my middle finger, waiting.

And waiting.

And waiting.

Until I thought I might choke on the silence.

"So," I blurted, "tell me a bit about yourself, Jackson."

I cringed as soon as I said it. Even my tone came across as job interview-esque.

Then I made the mistake of meeting his gaze, which was now filled with a lot less irritation and a hell of a lot more boredom. He checked his watch, exhaled impatiently through his nose, and said, "What don't you already know?"

I blinked. "I'm sorry?"

His head tilted ever so slightly to one side, mocking. "Are you hard of hearing, Miss Pennington, or is wasting people's time simply a hobby of yours?"

The only reason I realized my mouth had fallen open was because his wintry eyes flicked down to it before narrowing again. Even Alice was stunned into silence.

"It's, um, Lambton. Grace Lambton," I corrected him gently. "Not Pennington."

He wasn't embarrassed. Nor did he offer an apology for the error.

I shifted in my chair. "I'm sorry, have I done something to offend you?"

Heat bloomed over my cheeks when he checked his watch again. Reality set in, sinking straight to the pit of my stomach, hot and uncomfortably heavy.

This was the man I'd been comforting women over for the last eight months? *This* was who they'd all been crying over? *Him*?

I'd never reached for a drink faster in my life. The martini was in my grip before the unsuspecting waiter had even placed it down. I took it right from his gloved hand with a small "thanks" and downed it.

"Can I please get another one?" I asked Henry, per his nametag.

If Henry was taken aback, he masked it well. "Of course."

"*Jamie*," Alice warned quietly. We'd agreed on one drink to calm my nerves. No more than that.

I folded my hands on my lap as I sat back. There was a long list of questions I was supposed to ask Jackson. We'd spent half the day coming up with them, crafting them in a way that would allow us to gain as much useful information as possible within the allotted hour.

Information that we needed not just to help ourselves, but to help *him*.

That was before.

"*What are you doing? Why aren't you saying anything?*"

Eight months.

I'd spent the last *eight months* being yelled at, cried to, and emotionally dumped on because of this man. And this was how he was acting on the dates? This was how he was treating all our hard work? Our eighty-hour workweeks?

Why the hell hadn't any of the women said anything?

Anger unfurled in my chest as I shot Jackson a sarcastic smile. "So. How many of these things have you been on?"

He quirked a brow. "Pardon?"

"These dates," I said, my tone clipped and dry. "I've been with Charmed for six months and still haven't had any luck. They just can't seem to get it right, can they?"

His eyes thinned again. Did they do anything else or was that, like, their whole personality?

"What? You don't agree?" I said when he didn't respond.

"*What are you doing?*"

Jackson's mouth ticked open like he was about to say something, but he shut it when Henry reappeared with a second waiter in tow.

"Belon oysters with a delicate mignonette sauce to start." He placed two attractively decorated plates in front of us, along with my fresh martini. "Chef Russo also recommends a glass of the 1996 Domaine Raveneau Blanchot Chablis to bring out the fresh flavors of the dish."

Jackson gave a nod of approval, and the bottle was opened by the second waiter.

"Bon appétit."

I barely paid attention to any of it, my gaze stuck on the man sitting across the table.

His date, Grace Lambton, didn't have a lot of dislikes. Because if she did, Jamie Paquin would have had a hard time keeping track of them. However, there was *one* item listed under the "Disliked Foods" section of her file: shellfish.

Grace Lambton despised shellfish.

Jamie loved oysters, but they made Grace want to vomit.

So, either no one on his team had actually read the information we'd sent over, or...

"*Holy shit. Is he... motherfucker's throwing the date on purpose, isn't he?*"

We were about to find out.

"Something the matter?" Jackson asked smoothly, a smug little smirk toying with the corner of his mouth.

"Not at all."

He didn't look surprised when I reached for the first oyster. In fact, he seemed to expect it, swirling his wine delicately as he watched me. The arrogant prick was used to people jumping through hoops to try and impress him, wasn't he?

What did make his expression stutter, however, was when I reached for the second oyster immediately following the first. He'd expected at least a bit of hesitation, maybe even some struggle.

"Oh my god, these are amazing," I said, throwing all dinner etiquette out the window as I went for a third.

He frowned, his lips parting slowly as his wineglass stilled mid-swirl.

I couldn't taste a fucking thing over the bitter anger simmering in the pit of my stomach. I could have been shoving spoonfuls of wet sand into my mouth for all my tastebuds cared.

When I was done with the oysters, I polished off my martini. Then the glass of wine.

I could already feel a light buzz humming under my skin, fueling the fire rushing through my veins.

"Aren't you going to eat?" I asked Jackson. He'd done nothing but stare for the last five minutes. "The sooner we're done with the meal, the sooner this night ends. I really don't want to stick around for the full hour if we can help it."

"Jamie. Tone it down."

Jackson blinked slowly, his freakishly light eyes sliding over my features like he was having a hard time reading them. Odd, since I was doing absolutely nothing to mask the genuine contempt I felt toward him. It should have been written all over my face.

"You'd like to end the night early?" he asked carefully.

Man, his voice was so deliciously deep. And his subtle accent touched every word just enough to give them an attractive little curve.

How annoying.

"Yes," I answered. "Very much so."

We'd gotten all the info we needed. If Jackson was trying to throw these dates on purpose, there wasn't anything we could do. He'd essentially wasted eight months of our lives and was about to cost us our jobs.

At this point, spending the next forty minutes with this man was about as appealing as having my eyelashes repeatedly waxed while listening to moist chewing ASMR.

It wouldn't even matter if he confessed to throwing the dates on camera because we'd get fired for violating the client's trust and tricking him anyway. There was no winning for us.

"Don't *you* want it to end early?" I asked, crossing my arms.

He studied me for a long moment then held up a

hand, presumably stopping the wait staff from delivering the next course.

"I mean, this is going rather terribly, wouldn't you agree?" I insisted when he didn't respond. "I know Charmed has the one-hour first date rule, but I won't tell if you don't."

What was confusing to me was that *he* looked confused. Did he think this was going well? Or was he just not expecting me to acknowledge it out loud?

Seriously, how the hell had not one person mentioned his appalling behavior in their post-meeting follow-up? And how had this man managed to make it through sixty-seven dinners without having at least one person walk out on him?

I was tempted.

So, so tempted.

My feet had already shifted, my fingers were already curling around the clutch on my lap, and with every silent second that ticked by, the urge became stronger. Until I couldn't hold it in anymore.

"Ripper," I said.

Jackson blinked. "What?"

"*Fine*," Alice sighed in my ear. "*Yeah, get out. We got our answer, I guess. We can just start applying for new jobs tomorrow.*"

I'd shot to my feet before she was done talking, not taking into consideration how much alcohol I'd chugged in the span of fifteen minutes. The world spun out of balance for a moment, and I started to tilt on my heels.

Jackson bolted up and reached for my arm, which backfired in the most catastrophic way possible.

I wasn't sure how it happened, exactly. One second, I was instinctively yanking back from his touch, and the next, my heels were tangled in the drag of my dress, and the more I tried to correct my balance, the worse it seemed to get.

"*Whoa, what the fuck is happ—*"

I didn't hear the rest over the deafening sound of all the water rushing against my ears.

3

I WAS HAVING A NIGHTMARE. A terrifyingly vivid nightmare but a nightmare, nonetheless. It made so much sense!

On the bright side, now that I'd realized I was dreaming, I was one step closer to waking up.

Probably right after I drowned.

I could see the warm lantern lights rippling across the pool's surface, I just couldn't seem to reach them no matter how hard my legs kicked or my arms pushed. In fact, instead of moving closer, I seemed to be floating farther and farther away. Almost like I was being dragged down by something.

The realization hit just as my heels touched the bottom of the pool.

I full-on panicked.

The dress.

Not only were the layers of fabric getting in the way of my kicks, but they were about a hundred pounds heavier when wet. It was like having an anchor wrapped around my body.

It wasn't a dream. I was about to drown for real.

I released my clutch and reached behind me. But no matter how much I flailed and fumbled, my fingers couldn't find the tiny zipper pull.

Ria was going to murder me when she found out I died while she was on her honeymoon. She'd be so pissed. I'd never hear the end of it, especially if the whole afterlife thing turned out to be real. She'd hunt me down the second she got there.

We'd made a pact eight years ago to pass away in our sleep together, holding hands, in the retirement home we'd spent a decade wreaking awesome havoc on. Like the chaotic best friend version of *The Notebook.*

And Toebeans was going to think I abandoned him. Though, to be fair, he'd probably get over it pretty quick. Ria would adopt him, and he was such a cuddle slut for her husband that he'd forget I ever even existed—

My grim train of thought sputtered to a halt when a large pair of hands circled my waist from behind. Next thing I knew, I was being pulled up, up... up...

Only to sink straight back down. My lungs were burning.

What the actual fuck was this stupid dress made of? Cement?

I twisted around (with a *lot* of effort) when my feet touched the bottom again, only to come face to face with a *very* pissed-off Jackson Sinclair. The man had absolutely mastered the art of the furious scowl.

I shook my head at him, gesturing at my dress. But before I could point to the zipper running down my back, he'd hooked his fingers underneath the sweetheart neckline of the stupid deathtrap and was *tearing it straight down the middle*. Like it was fucking paper.

He bared his teeth, his corded muscles bulging out of

his white shirt as he ripped the fabric open, right before he helped me kick my way out of it. I'd have been really impressed if my lungs weren't on scorching fire.

I shot up to the surface, my chest screaming, yelling, *pleading* for relief. And I almost made it too. I was so, so close—mere inches away from the rippling lights—when my spasming lungs caved. I inhaled and choked, my body attempting to expel the water as something gripped my waist and hoisted me up toward the lights.

I broke through the surface with a gasp. My vision was practically nonexistent, my lungs working overtime to hoard as much oxygen as possible through all the violent coughing. I flailed, gasped, kicked, trying to find something to hold on to through the blinding blur of tears, pool water, and terror. I was vaguely aware of being twisted around by an external force just before my fingers managed to find purchase against something warm and solid.

I clung to it with shaking desperation as I continued to cough and choke, and before I knew it, my heels were scraping the bottom of the pool again. This time, though, my head and shoulders were above the water.

"Bensen!"

The warm, solid thing I was now fully pressed against vibrated when the deep, husky voice barked the order.

"All taken care of, sir. The staff are on their way, and I've sent someone to notify the Ms. Harrisons. They'll be expecting you."

"Call Dr. Santos. She inhaled a bunch of water."

"Right away, sir."

I wanted to swipe the wetness from my eyes, but my fingers refused to pry open. I was holding on to fistfuls of Jackson's shirt like my life depended on it. Because it genuinely felt like my life depended on it. My panicking brain was convinced that if I let go, I'd plummet to the bottom of the pool again.

I didn't know how long we stood there, but it was long enough for my vision to clear, the coughing to subside, and my brain to calm down enough to register the fact that I was naked. The dress had been padded, so I had nothing else on except a pair of shoes and panties. Oh, and I was still pressed flush against Jackson Sinclair's chest.

Forcing my fingers loose, I stepped away and lowered myself until I was neck-deep in the water, my arms wrapping protectively around my bare chest.

Not that it really mattered. Jackson's eyes were cast skyward, fists tight at his sides. He'd let me go right after we'd made it to the shallow end of the pool, it was me who'd held on to him.

"Can you step out of the water by yourself?" he asked the stars through clenched teeth.

"Yes. Yup. Thanks."

"Bensen."

"Already done, sir."

My head swiveled toward the voice. A man wearing what looked like a stereotypical butler's uniform was standing poolside, gloved hands clasped neatly behind his back, which was currently turned to me.

"Madame, when you are ready, you'll find a fresh set of towels on the stand to your left. There are two female members of staff on standby if you require additional assistance."

"Uhm, that's alright." Color raced over my cheeks as I duck-walked to the stairs, arms still clamped over my breasts. I all but ran to the towels, my heels squelching and clicking loudly.

"I'm good now, thanks," I stated as soon as I had a towel wrapped around my torso.

Bensen didn't turn but Jackson moved, trudging out of the water in long, angry strides. Instead of going for the remaining towel, though, he pinned me with a seething glare. "Follow me."

First of all, I didn't understand why he was so pissed. It wasn't like I'd fallen into the pool on purpose. Second of all, I wasn't going anywhere with him. I needed to get my stuff from the bottom of the pool and leave before this night had the opportunity to get any fucking worse.

"No, thanks." I squelch-clicked my way toward the other end of the pool. The dress could rot down there for all I cared, but I needed to get my clutch since it had my phone (though that was probably fried anyway) and license—

My heart stopped beating when I saw it: a rippling flash of chocolate mahogany peeking out from underneath the large puddle of black fabric.

My wig.

My wig was at the bottom of the pool.

Fuck.

Fuck fuck fuck fuck fuck.

I was utterly frozen, my eyes stuck to the water as my brain scrambled. My wavering reflection stared back at me, blonde curls tied and pinned back, makeup running.

This was karma. She'd come for me.

"Your items will be retrieved by the staff," Jackson said.

At least now I knew why he was so livid.

"That's all right," I squeaked, unable to look at him. "I can just, um, go get it myself."

There was a heavy beat of silence before he said, "You think I'm letting you get back in the water?"

Too bad it wasn't up to him.

"Can you turn around?" I didn't want to jump in with the towel, and I *really* didn't want to drop it while he was still watching.

The heat of his glower continued to wash over my skin, which meant he hadn't turned away yet. And something told me he wasn't going to.

"Madame, if I may," Bensen started calmly. "Trained members of our staff are already on their way with the appropriate equipment to retrieve your items, and I can personally assure you that they will be in your possession again shortly. If you follow Mr. Sinclair, you'll be escorted to his penthouse, where the head housekeepers, Ms. Harrison and Ms. Harrison, are ready for you with a fresh set of clothes. That is unless you'd prefer to be driven home in your current state, in which case, I can have that arranged."

Bensen had a point.

As much as I didn't want to step into Jackson Sinclair's lair, there was no way I was getting into a cab wearing nothing but shoes, underwear, and a towel.

"Madame?"

Bitter regret clawed up my throat, my heart clanging heavily in my chest. "All right," I muttered quietly. "Thank you."

Jackson's hands were still balled into rigid fists when I made my way over to him, my shoes clacking unattractively with every wet step.

"I didn't realize they made heels that high," he noted bitterly, harsh eyes piercing mine with pointed judgment.

My mouth stuttered open like it wanted to respond

even though my mind was blank. When I didn't answer, Jackson rolled his eyes, turned around, and stomped away.

I had to jog awkwardly to keep up with him, my ankles bending and twisting on every third step. His legs were so long.

Six-foot-six was taller than I'd realized. His minimum height requirement kind of made sense. I wasn't justifying his behavior or anything, but I could see how this one requirement was maybe not as unreasonable as some of his others.

That and the age thing. He was thirty-five, so I guess it also made sense that he wouldn't want to date someone who was still in their twenties.

But the rest of his list was unreasonable and ridiculous.

He led us around a hidden corner tucked behind an exceptionally large set of ferns, where two uniformed men greeted us with synchronized dips of their chins and polite half-smiles before opening the double doors.

I chewed the inside of my cheek as we made our way down a sleek hallway, desperately trying to come up with an excuse for my hair.

"I collect them," I eventually said. "Wigs, I mean. I collect them, wear them everywhere."

He didn't respond.

Just continued stomping.

"I realize it's kind of a *unique* hobby to have, but everyone has something they're into that's a little weird. Some people like collecting dead animals and stuffing them, I like collecting dead hairs and... wearing them."

Nope. I should not have put it like that. The choice

made my throat curdle like it wanted to regurgitate the words in a different order. I could still fix this. I could—

Jackson stopped so abruptly that I almost walked into him nose-first, which would have been unfortunate since the man had the cushioning of a brick wall.

Five quick *beeps* later, a solid mahogany door was thrown open with dramatic force and Jackson stormed inside, immediately disappearing around the corner like he couldn't wait to get away from me.

Yeah, well, it wasn't like I adored *his* company. Just because he'd saved my life a little bit didn't mean I'd forgiven him for ruining it.

Jackson grumbled something unintelligible from the depths of his lair, and before I could change my mind and decide to walk home half-naked, two identically stout women with identical faces, identical cotton hair, and identical black uniforms with identical white aprons had rounded the corner. Their eyes widened when they took in my appearance.

"Oh dear. Oh no no no no *no*," the one on the left insisted, shaking her head disapprovingly.

"Honestly, child. You're going to catch a cold," her twin chided with a deep frown. A warm, soft hand was wrapped around my arm in an instant, pulling me inside before I could manage so much as a quick hello.

These must have been the housekeepers Bensen had mentioned.

"I knew this would happen," Ms. Harrison huffed as she guided me through the sleek apartment. It was very grey in here. Very expensive-looking and very, *very* grey.

"We have told that boy—we have told him *many a time* —how dangerous that pool is," the other Ms. Harrison claimed.

"It's the damn curves. The least he could do is cover it while he's entertaining. Not one for listening, though, is he?"

"Incessantly hard of hearing the things he does not want to, Young Master Sinclair. Always has been. Even as a wee little thing."

"Though we shouldn't say *wee*, should we? He's been taller than us since before he lost his last milk tooth. Mind you it did take a while. Just did not want to fall out. Stubborn to the teeth, Young Master Sinclair."

"I don't think that's the expression, Mabel."

"Is it not?"

"It is not."

"She knew what I meant, though, didn't she? Even his teeth are stubborn, dear. That's all I'm trying to say."

I wasn't given a chance to respond.

"We finally had to give it a little tug ourselves."

"Mistress Sinclair would have had our heads if she knew, but he never did tell her. Loyal as can be, the Young Master. Once you've earned his trust there's no getting rid of it, is there?"

"It's worrying, is what it is. There are people who will take advantage of that, you know."

"Takes one rotten apple to spoil the whole batch."

"Though the Young Master isn't very easy to trick, is he?"

"Well, he couldn't be. Not with his upbringing."

"You learn quickly when enough people disappoint you at that age."

"Born with a diamond spoon in his mouth, the poor lad."

"I don't think that's the expression either, Mabel."

"Is it not?"

"It is not."

"What's it supposed to be, then?"

"Silver spoon. Not diamond."

"Oh, well that doesn't have the same impact, does it? Though I'm not quite sure where I was going with it anyway. I've been rambling a bit again, haven't I, Molly?"

"We both have, I'm afraid."

"Why didn't you say something, dear?"

They looked up at me expectantly, waiting for my answer. I blinked between them with my mouth parted.

I was at a loss for words.

I'd been so absorbed (and confused, impressed) by their seamless back-and-forth that I'd stopped paying attention to what turns we'd taken to get to the large bedroom we were now standing in. I had one hand still clutching the towel around my body, the other cradling a bunch of items they'd stuffed into it—more towels, fresh clothes, sandals, toiletries.

Mabel (if I'd caught on correctly) placed her hands on her plump hips and frowned at her sister. "Look at us, Molly. We haven't even offered her a hot cuppa this whole time, have we? And she's still soaked!"

"Do you fancy some tea, dear? We have a pot of oolong brewing. Well, it's an oolong and pu'er mix. But Young Master Sinclair complains when we brew the pu'er by itself."

"Claims it smells like a dirty barn."

"Took us a while to get used to the stench ourselves, that's for sure. But it's mighty good for you, isn't it?"

"And he doesn't complain about much—never did."

"So, when he does, we pay attention."

"He also never drinks any of it. No matter how many

times we try to explain the benefits, it always falls on daft ears."

"That's not the expression, Mabel."

Oh my god, no. I couldn't re-enter this loop.

"I'm sorry to interrupt," I said just as Mabel went to respond. "Could I maybe get some privacy while I change? Thank you for the clothes, by the way. This is all very kind."

They beamed up at me at the same time, all dimples and rosy cheeks.

"Oh, you're very welcome, dear."

"We'll just be outside the door, then. Give us a shout if you need anything. And the doctor will be here—"

Molly was cut off by a loud bang as the bedroom door ripped open and slammed against the wall.

"What in the heavens—Jackson! You *cannot* simply barge into an occupied bedroom as you please!" Molly complained, clutching her chest.

But he wasn't paying her any attention. His eerily pale blue eyes were locked on me, and they were... murderous. That was the word. Jackson Sinclair looked like he wanted nothing more than to strangle me right then and there.

"You were *recording me*?" he thundered, tossing a handful of items onto the bed.

My heart sank to the pit of my stomach when I registered what they were. My headpiece and the camera that had been sewn into my dress. I guess I should have seen this coming. For some reason, I hadn't thought they'd notice the camera. It was small and well-hidden enough.

Molly and Mabel gaped, looking rather scandalized as their round, disbelieving eyes dashed from me to Jackson, then back to me.

"Oh dear."

"Oh no."

The wig was one thing. The headset was one thing. Separately, I could explain them. But add the camera, put it all together, and I had no excuse. It was all very incriminating, and I couldn't come up with a single reasonable lie that would make it better.

"It's not what it looks like," I tried. He probably thought I was a client who'd... well, I wasn't sure what. My heart was pounding, my nerves were frantic, and my brain was scrambling, which meant I was seconds away from making things worse. That's usually what happened when I panicked.

But before I even had the opportunity, Jackson tossed the rest of what he was holding onto the bed. My clutch, my phone, and my keycard. For work.

The one that had my full name, picture, and the Charmed Elite logo right on it. I'd brought it with me because I was supposed to head straight back to the office after our "date." Also because I was an idiot. Clearly.

"Get. The fuck. Out of my house," he spat darkly. "Now, Miss *Paquin*."

"She's... she's naked, dear."

"At least let her—oh!"

I snatched my stuff, tucked my chin, and ran out of there with nothing but a towel on.

4

VIVIAN LOOKED like she wanted to rip out her own hair and strangle me with it.

I couldn't exactly blame her, but I could say that it was unnecessary. I was already suffocating.

The three of us were standing in her office, chins tucked low like a bunch of chastised children. Well, except for Alice. While my spine had withered into a defensive slouch, her posture was kept at a normal angle, and I swear she was starting to zone out from the boredom. Probably because we'd already been here for a half-hour while Vivian yelled and slammed things down on her desk.

If I was being completely honest, Vivian's reaction didn't seem fair to me. I mean, she'd told us she didn't care how we got her results, so long as we got them. Those had been *her* instructions.

I was starting to think Alice's observations were accurate. It was becoming increasingly evident that the three of us were nothing but sacrificial scapegoats to her.

If we succeeded, she would gladly take all the credit. If

we failed... well, this. We were living it. She'd pushed us into doing something spectacularly risky out of desperation, and now she was about to fire us over it. Alice, Mitch, and I would never be able to find another job in the industry after this got out, but that didn't matter to Vivian. As long as the blame was being put on others, the damage to her professional reputation would take a reduced hit.

After all, the majority of our clients were here to work directly with her. She'd probably spin this to make herself look like the victim. She was good at that. PR was her forte.

Still, the people pleaser in me—the one that desperately needed her boss to approve of her—was weeping. And I didn't know how to turn it off.

"What in the ever-loving *fuck* were you thinking?" She kept pacing, pacing, pacing. The question was made to sound like it was directed at the group, but her eyes were drilling holes into my skull. "*Jamie*! I asked you a question!"

Normally, I'd have forced myself to meet her gaze and respond, but I really didn't have it in me today. I hadn't slept all night, my feet were sore and blistered from limping home in those cursed heels, and a good chunk of my mind was preoccupied with trying to figure out how the three of us were going to come up with fourteen thousand dollars in seven days.

Because that's how much the torn dress and bloodied, water-damaged shoes cost to replace: $13,921.32. The bill was due next Friday.

Oh, and my phone only took calls on speaker now, so I had to replace that too. But at least I'd gotten it to turn on. The overnight rice thing really did work.

Alice had offered to go to her parents for the money,

but I knew how desperately she wanted to avoid that. The whole point of her moving here was to stand on her own two feet.

Vivian scoffed when I stayed quiet. "Nothing? You have nothing to say for yourself after *ruining* this company's reputation? After tainting all the hard work, blood, sweat, and fucking tears I've put into building this brand from the ground up?" She stopped pacing, placed her hands on her narrow hips, and opened her mouth to rip into me some more. But she was interrupted by a string of soft knocks on her door.

"What?" she snapped.

Laury poked her head into the room gingerly. "I'm so sorry to interrupt, but the Sinclairs have arrived. Their car just pulled up to the building."

I glanced to my left, my pulse lurching. Mitch and Alice were as shocked as I was.

The Sinclair*s* were here? Plural? I'd assumed Jackson would send a member of his team (maybe a lawyer) to speak to Vivian on his behalf.

Vivian's entire demeanor changed. Her hands dropped from her hips and crumpled into fists, her head raising an inch as her throat worked with a swallow. Nerves. Vivian Hale was nervous.

"Fine," she said, an edge to her voice, "I'll meet them in the Rosé Room right away."

Which meant we were finally dismissed. I desperately needed a cup of coffee and a good bathroom stall cry. But just as I began to turn on my sore heel, Vivian snapped her fingers and pointed one at me.

"You," she said. "You're coming with me."

I tensed, my stomach clenching.

Alice glanced between Vivian and me, her brows drawing together. "Should we come as well?"

"No. The two of you are to head straight to the White Room and wait. Jamie and I will join you after our meeting."

"But—"

"*Now*, Alice. Before I call security and have you escorted there."

Alice gave me a look before obeying, though I couldn't tell what she was trying to communicate with it. The stress and lack of sleep had destroyed my cognitive functioning. I was barely able to think, and now I had to stand in front of the Sinclairs and go through this whole berating nightmare all over again.

At this point, getting fired would be a relief.

Jackson's aunt was, to put it lightly, an experience.

Minerva Sinclair was a tall, willowy woman with stark white hair and cutting features, and her signature "look" consisted of cherry-red pantsuits, vintage cat-eye sunglasses, and knife-sharp stilettos. Per our client paperwork, she had her personal tarot reader (Imogen) on speed dial and kept her wrinkly sphynx cat (Harry) cradled against her bony chest everywhere she went, as per the guidance of her spiritual advisor (Velma).

Honestly, if her nephew wasn't such a pain in our asses, I'd think she was pretty awesome. She had the type of old money, no-fucks-given energy you couldn't help but admire. Also, she'd literally named her hairless cat Harry, and I didn't think she'd intended the pun.

Still, even with all that going on, my eyes immediately gravitated to the figure looming behind her.

He walked into the room like he owned the whole building and everyone in it. His presence demanded my attention, from his imposing height to the perfectly tailored crisp black suit.

It was surprisingly aggravating. Irritation flamed across my chest when his frosty eyes found mine, narrowing.

See? I knew it. That *was* their whole personality.

My eyes rolled before I could stop them, and it was noticeable enough that Minerva caught it, her white eyebrows arching behind the curve of her sunglasses.

"Minerva." Vivian gave the air around her client's cheeks two swift kisses. Her brown-nosing was not acknowledged; the air kisses were not returned. "It's so nice to see you again. Come. Sit, sit. Laury's on her way with your tea. And Mr. Sinclair, it is such an honor to finally meet—"

"Is this her?" Minerva interrupted. Her crisp voice tipped with an unidentifiable accent—a mixture of French, German, and British, maybe.

Vivian stiffened, her smile wavering just slightly. "This is Jamie Paquin, the employee we were discussing over the phone this morning. That's correct."

"Jack."

Jackson Sinclair's head tilted mockingly to one side. "I'm not sure," he drawled, "her features weren't exactly memorable."

My anger flared, a rush of buzzing warmth sprinting through my body.

"Says the man with the personality of a hardboiled egg."

You could hear a fucking pin drop.

In my defense, I hadn't meant to say it out loud.

Okay, that was a lie. I'd definitely meant to say it out loud.

"I beg your pardon?" His eyes slit into challenging icicles. He wasn't smirking anymore.

I wondered what I'd need to do to get them to close all the way. It probably wouldn't take much.

"Oh, I'm sorry, are you hard of hearing, Mr. Sinclair, or is wasting people's time simply a hobby of yours?" I spat back.

Okay.

All right.

That one may have taken it a bit too far. I needed to reel it back. He deserved it, in my opinion, but Vivian was gaping at me like I'd smacked her across the face with a drowned sewer rat. This wasn't how I was supposed to be behaving. She'd brought me here to act as a good little punching bag. The silent kind that didn't talk back.

Maybe that was what Alice had been communicating with her look. She'd been trying to warn me.

Irritation swept over my skin, its claws sinking into my throat. It was an uncomfortably vivid sensation, and very new. I wasn't used to this level of frustration. I wanted to throw something. Flip the whole room off. Cry.

Minerva Sinclair peeled off her sunglasses slowly, her slim, scrutinizing eyes running over me twice.

"Sorry," I muttered to her—and her *only*—while my fingers curled into my palms. "He said that to me last night. It was unwarranted and rather rude."

Her right eyebrow arched. "Before or after your true identity was revealed?"

"Before," I said, even though Vivian was giving me her shut-the-fuck-up-this-instant look.

What was she going to do? Fire me?

Jackson's head jutted forward like he simply could not believe my audacity. "Is this your fucked up version of an apology?"

I ground my teeth, my nails digging into my palms, determined in their quest to draw blood. "Your chances of receiving any sort of apology from me were squandered the second you kicked me out of your apartment at night with no clothes and no working phone."

Vivian's soul was yanked straight out of her body. The color drained from her face so rapidly I thought she might faint. She didn't know about the pool incident. She'd heard a shortened version of the story from Minerva over the phone last night, called us into her office bright and early this morning, and refused to hear us out when we'd tried to explain.

She had no context as to why I was inside Jackson Sinclair's apartment naked. And you know what, maybe she didn't deserve any.

Minerva's face went slack before tightening again, and then she was twisting on her sharp heels and glaring up at her giant nephew. "You *what*?"

An irritated muscle worked its way through Jackson's jaw, his eyes flicking up to the ceiling like it could grant him the patience he needed to deal with my bullshit. "I didn't— It should have gone without saying that you were to leave *after* getting dressed, but you ran out before I could correct myself."

"Oh please," I scoffed, "if you're gonna do shitty things, at least have the balls to own up to them."

"*I* did the shitty thing?" he snarled incredulously as he

stalked forward. "Miss Paquin, might I remind you that you trespassed onto my property under false pretenses, disguised as a matchmade romantic interest, and proceeded to record our meeting without my knowledge or consent. Please explain how *I'm* the bad guy for kicking you out of my home as a consequence."

"All right, fine," I said. "I'm sorry for that part. I acknowledge that it was wrong. But I only did it because you've spent the last eight months refusing to meet with us. You haven't taken any of our tests or answered any of our calls or filled out any of our questionnaires yourself. One of your interns did the lifestyle assessment on your behalf, for heaven's sake. How does that make any sense when we're literally trying to find you a life partner?"

"My lack of participation in your inane methods does not excuse several illegal acts that—"

"You haven't participated in any of their assessments yourself?" Both of Minerva's eyebrows were curved now.

Jackson's lips pressed into a line so tight, it drained them of life. "Not... directly, no," he managed through gritted teeth. "There was no need. They've been provided with more than enough data to find me a suitable match."

"With all due respect, the data we've been given by your team is so limiting that there's—"

"Jamie. Enough."

The rest of my complaint withered against the chill of Vivian's tone, an apology forming in its place. But I swallowed it back. She knew that Jackson wouldn't take any of our tests himself. We'd brought it up in countless meetings with her. So how was this the first time Minerva was hearing about it?

They had two scheduled meetings a month to discuss our progress, so how had she not thought to mention something so important during any of their sixteen meetings to date? Maybe Minerva could have helped. Maybe she could have convinced Jackson to at least sit down with us for a bit.

We'd been working non-fucking-stop for eight months straight and she couldn't have done just one thing to help us out?

My frustration built and built until it reached my eyes. But I would not—*I would not*—cry in front of these people.

"You're dismissed," Vivian said.

Gladly.

But I wasn't going to wait for her in the White Room. I was going to walk straight out of here, crawl into bed with a bottle of Pinot and a pint of chocolate ice cream, and re-binge the seventh season of *Chef Wars International*. (Daniel Omori's chin dimple and three-legged golden retriever were medicine for my withered soul.)

Tomorrow I'd send Vivian my zero-weeks' notice and start looking for new jobs.

I didn't know what the hell I was going to do about the money I owed for the dress and shoes, but I'd figure something out.

"Actually, no," Minerva said just as I began to limp-march out of Vivian's office. Jackson's attention flicked to my feet momentarily, his jaw working as it clenched, unclenched.

Not only were his freaky eyes only capable of one look, but the man as a whole was only capable of experiencing one emotion.

See? The personality of a hardboiled egg. With, like, added hot sauce or something. And not the good kind.

"Pardon?" Vivian tried her best to keep her tone light

even though she was vibrating with rage. How *dare* I not act as the silent emotional punching bag she'd brought me in here to be? What else was I, the disposable employee she'd been taking advantage of over the better part of the last year good for?

"I'd like her to stay," Minerva said, still watching me as she scratched Harry the hairless cat mindlessly. He was super cute. Real ugly, but very adorable. And the diamond collar wrapped loosely around his wrinkly neck likely cost more than I was set to make this entire year.

He had it made, and he knew it per the bored, unimpressed way he was slowly blinking at me.

"I don't think that's a good idea, Minerva," Vivian tried.

Minerva barely spared her a glance. "Didn't you mention something about tea? Why don't you go fetch us some of that while this young lady and I chat? What type of tea do you normally drink, Miss Paquin, was it?"

"Jamie," I offered.

A dangerous number of crimson blotches began spreading across Vivian's face and neck. "My assistant is actually brewing—"

"Do they know what type of tea Jamie likes?" Minerva asked slowly, bright nails scraping lovingly against Harry's long neck.

"I don't think it's necessary to keep her here for the meeting," Jackson cut in.

I bit my tongue.

"Nonsense. The meeting is *about* her; she deserves to be heard. Vivian, bring the poor girl some chamomile or something. I don't want to have to ask again. She's clearly distressed, and from what little I've heard her say, I don't blame her."

Well, that was kind of her.

Jackson didn't seem to agree. His shoulders rose a rigid inch, his throat working to swallow back an argument he knew he probably wouldn't win.

Vivian left the room without another word.

"Sit down," Minerva ordered.

I listened, Jackson didn't. He remained on his feet, looming over us like one of those scowling gargoyles attached to the exterior walls of medieval cathedrals. That is until his aunt slipped him a pointed look that made his jaw tick. He lowered into the chair beside her.

"Now," Minerva started, "tell me what happened last night."

Jackson tapped his foot. "This is a waste of time. I've explained—"

"Hush. I've already heard your version of the events. You barked about it for a full hour this morning. It's her turn."

He bristled. "She's a liar and a fraud, Minerva. How can you believe a word—"

"Either shut up, Jackson, or go help Vivian with the tea."

Oh, *hell yes*.

Smug delight sprouted in my chest, easing the tension in my shoulders. I decided right then that, despite her unfortunate blood relation to the grumpiest hardboiled egg on the planet, I liked Minerva Sinclair. And I was going to tell her the truth.

After all, what did I have to lose?

"We call him Jack the Ripper," I told her.

That was probably a good place to start.

5

IT SPILLED out of me like a kettle on high heat.

I told her how he'd earned the nickname. How many hearts he'd ruthlessly stomped on to be dubbed "The Ripper" by me and my colleagues.

I told her about his insanely rigid and near-impossible criteria, and how difficult it was for us to find even *one* woman who met all the items on the list, let alone the sixty-seven he'd turned down.

I told her about the damage control line and the sheer amount of hours I'd spent comforting the women he'd turned down with such callous indifference—the sheer amount of hours we, as a team, had spent on his file.

And finally, I told her about why I'd gone undercover in the first place. About how his refusal to meet with us combined with everything else had pushed us over the edge. We needed accurate data and couldn't think of any other way to get it.

I kept my tone and phrasing as professional as I could manage, presenting her with all the facts. Then I apologized for my actions, because regardless of what my motive had been, what I'd done was still wrong.

All the while Vivian had been sitting beside me on the couch, silent and stiff as a wooden board.

"I'm not convinced Jackson wants a partner," I finished off almost an hour after I'd started. "Everything from his strict criteria to his behavior on our date indicates that he couldn't be less interested in finding someone through our services."

By the time I finally shut up, my untouched tea was cold, the pillow on my lap was permanently disfigured, and I was slightly out of breath.

But holy shit did that feel good.

It felt so, so, *so* fucking good.

I wished Alice and Mitch were here. I'd tried my best to cover everything, but it would have been nice for them to get their voices heard too. Finally, someone was listening.

After a long stretch of silence, Minerva nodded one last time. "Okay, so what would you recommend?"

"For what?" I asked.

"If we were to start over with Jackson, how would you suggest we go about it?"

"Vivian would have to..." I trailed off when she shook her head.

"I'd like to hear *your* professional opinion, Miss Paquin," she said calmly. "If you could hit rewind on Jackson's file, go back to day one, how would you handle it? What would you do differently? Assuming, of course, that you had his full cooperation this time around."

Jackson had remained silent while I talked, much like Vivian. Though I was very aware of how intently he'd been watching me the whole time.

I cleared my throat, keeping my focus on Minerva. "All right. In my professional opinion, unless Jackson is willing to enroll in our Immersive program and put in the work with a senior consultant, I wouldn't recommend he stay with Charmed. I believe we've done everything else we can for him at this point."

In my defense, she'd asked.

Vivian had died a thousand deaths over the last hour, and that last comment pulled a tortured little noise out of her. In *her* professional opinion, I was a waste of salary and benefits, and any employer who hired me after this was an idiot.

It didn't matter that I'd had a perfect streak before Jackson's file hit my desk. It didn't matter that she'd deemed me to be a "promising candidate" for the next available senior consultant position before *he* happened. It didn't matter that I'd received nothing but praise from my previous clients or that I'd been pushed to the point of burnout.

To her, none of that mattered.

Minerva's lips twitched, amused. "You think he's that dire? He needs a full-time babysitter and dating coach?"

"To be honest, he probably needs two."

She laughed, Jackson ground his teeth like he was dead set on cracking at least three molars before this meeting had concluded, and Vivian was undoubtedly making a silent vow that my great-great-great grandchildren would pay for the sins my big mouth had committed in this room today.

Minerva tapped a slim finger on her armrest. "Why do you think that's a better approach than simply having him sit down and participate in your assessments himself?"

Oh, that was easy. "Because I'm not sure Jackson actually knows what he wants. His team has relayed to us what he *thinks* he wants, but every time we've handed him exactly that, he's turned it down. Not once, not twice, but sixty-seven times."

"Makes sense," she said. "It's settled then. We'll take the package."

Jackson turned to her, thick brows slamming together. "Absolutely not. This is where I draw the line, Minerva. I won't have a stranger move into my home and follow me around like an imprinted fucking duckling for an entire month just so I have to sit through more of these ridiculous dates. We had a deal."

"Past tense," she snapped back at him, her tone sharp. "And it's no longer on the table. I asked you to *try*, Jackson."

His jaw tightened. "I have tried. I've provided almost every data point asked of me, attended every date on time, and sat through hours upon mindless hours of utterly insufferable conversation. If you only knew—"

"I'm not an idiot and I don't appreciate being treated like one. Your version of trying would not include asking the woman you're on a date with if she's hard of hearing. If it is—if that's what you truly consider appropriate behavior—then you don't deserve what you already have, let alone anything more."

His mouth shut with an audible snap. It would have been amusing if their back and forth wasn't so intense.

"You'll agree to the coaching, and you'll put actual effort in this time around. We'll speak about striking a new deal later, with significantly tighter terms."

Every muscle in Jackson's body was coiled into knots. He looked ready to explode.

"Minerva, if I may," Vivian interjected.

"You may not. We have had two meetings per month for the better part of a year and not once had you thought to mention any of this. You led me to believe that everything was running smoothly and justified the prolonged process by claiming that Jackson was simply 'a little picky, and rightfully so.' Had this been brought to my attention sooner, it would have been dealt with sooner. I told you on day one that I wanted transparency."

Vivian kept her chin up. "I apologize if you don't believe I've been transparent with you. However, Jackson does not need coaching. Revisiting some of his assessments should be enough, especially if he'd agree to just... loosen up some of his criteria."

"How would you know?" Minerva shot back. "From the sounds of it, you haven't touched his file since it landed on your desk along with the big fat check covering your overpriced fee."

"I—Minerva, I assure you I've been working just as diligently as the rest of the team to find your nephew a suitable match."

I'm sorry, WHAT?!

My mouth fell open before my brain could stop it. Everyone saw.

"We've tried doing things your way, Vivian, and it's yielded less than desirable results."

I could almost hear Vivian's blood boiling behind her perfectly polite smile. "Fine," she finally agreed. "I'll see which senior consultants are available. Even better, I'll do it myself."

"No need." Minerva waved her hand. "Jamie will handle it."

Jackson shot Minerva a you-can't-possibly-be-serious

look, and I agreed. Because she couldn't possibly be serious.

"I'm afraid that's not possible," Vivian said. "Jamie lacks both the experience and the expertise to perform the required assessments, and she's nowhere near qualified to do the coaching."

"Agreed," Jackson said, as though he knew exactly what he was talking about. Asshat. "And I hardly think it would be appropriate given what happened last night."

"Jamie, what do you think?"

Heads snapped in my direction. But, again, I chose to keep my focus on Minerva.

"I think there are a lot of other consultants that would be better suited for the job than me." Plus, the second this meeting was over, I was walking straight out of the building and never looking back. There was no way in all of hell I'd agree to do an Immersive with Jackson, even with the bonus—

The bonus.

Forty thousand dollars on top of my monthly salary. Even after tax, I'd have enough to pay for the shoes, the dress, and a new phone. The rest would help cover my living expenses until I landed a new job.

Still, I wasn't entirely convinced it would be worth it.

"But would you be willing to do it?" Minerva asked.

I shifted on the couch. "Vivian's right. I don't have the training or the experience."

"Minerva, is there a reason you're set on Jamie?" Vivian asked. "Experience aside, I have more than a handful of senior consultants who would be much more suitable personality-wise to handle the demands of an Immersive experience."

What did *that* mean?

"Explain," Minerva ordered.

"Jamie is... young," Vivian said. "And these month-long experiences can be intense. I also need to make sure that my employees are comfortable with the positions they're being put in at work."

Oh, *bullshit*!

First of all, I was twenty-eight, so not that young. Second of all, where was this so-called concern for our comfort when we'd been forced to sleep on conference room couches to meet Jackson's standing deadlines? Where the hell had it been when we'd tried to tell her, time and time again, that this *wasn't working*?

I swallowed it all back, averting my gaze.

Minerva's attention drifted back to me. "You still haven't answered my question. Would you be willing to do it?"

No. Absolutely not.

Or, like, maybe. I didn't know. Forty thousand dollars was a lot of money to turn down. Especially since I was *this close* to unemployment.

"I need some time to think about it," I said, ignoring the two sharp glares my answer earned me.

Minerva's mouth ticked with a faint, secretive smile. "How does twenty-four hours sound?"

I limp-ran straight to the White Room as soon as I was finally dismissed, while Vivian stayed back to finish the meeting.

"They want me to do an Immersive," I blurted before either Alice or Mitch could speak. "With Jackson. They want me to do an Immersive with Jackson Sinclair."

They both looked up at me from their seats around the small table, jaws going slack.

Alice recovered first. "What? Why?"

Great question.

I sank into the chair across from her. "That meeting didn't go at all the way I expected. Minerva actually listened. Well, first she asked, and then she listened. And when I was done talking, she asked me what I would do differently if we started over with Jackson's file, and— You know what, not important. What would you guys do? Would you do it?"

They both answered at the same time.

"I would."

"Not a fucking chance."

Mitch jerked back in his chair, blinking at Alice. "Wait. Did you say you *would*?"

She shrugged. "It's forty grand in thirty days."

"Right," I said. "And we kind of need it to pay for the clothes I ruined."

Mitch nudged at his wire-framed glasses. "It wasn't all your fault."

Except it kind of was. Alice had specifically warned me to be careful with the dress. It wasn't their fault I'd chugged a bunch of alcohol on an empty stomach and tripped on my own two feet. Alice had even tried to stop me from drinking too much while it was happening; I just hadn't listened.

"He's going to make your life hell if you do it," she said. "After what we saw last night, it's not going to be a pleasant experience. Especially for your first Immersive —" She cut off when the door was ripped open by a very tense, very huffy Vivian Hale. It slammed shut again behind her.

The Sinclairs were already gone, then. That was quick.

Her dark eyes zeroed in on me. "You have so much explaining to do. In what world did you think it would be appropriate to insult our biggest client right to his face?"

I said nothing. I could tell she was only getting started and interrupting her would just prolong what was already going to be a painstakingly long process.

But instead of falling into another scolding rant, Vivian placed both fists on her hips, looked me dead in the eyes, and said, "You're doing it. The Immersive."

I blinked. She was the one who said I didn't have the experience or skillset to do it, so why was she changing her mind all of a sudden?

"Minerva isn't taking no for an answer," she said. "And she won't agree to have you shadow a senior consultant either. I tried."

"But *I* could still say no," I pointed out, frowning.

She shifted on her feet, looking uncharacteristically uncomfortable. Alice and Mitch picked up on it too, if the shared glance between them was any indication.

"You could." The words scraped against her throat on their way out, almost like it hurt for her to admit. "But the Sinclairs would fire us if you did."

How was that my problem?

"I made a deal with Minerva," Vivian went on. "If you do the Immersive and are still unable to find Jackson an appropriate match, they won't take their business to a competitor. This will be it for them, which is the best-case scenario for us. It'll limit rumors, minimize damage to our reputation, and prevent an exodus. You need to do it."

Was she serious? She expected me to just smile and agree? After everything that had just happened?

I weighed my options. I could say no and tell Vivian to

shove it. Or I could agree, go through one month of hell for forty thousand dollars, and *then* tell Vivian to shove it.

"When do they expect me to start?" I asked.

"Monday, the fifth. You'll be going through an intensive two-week training program with me and Tammi beforehand. Expect to be here at six every day, sans Sunday. We'll likely need to go until eight or nine p.m. to get you prepared in time."

She said it with a straight face.

"Will I be compensated?"

"Compensated for what?"

"All the overtime you expect me to work for the next two weeks. Will I be compensated for it?"

Alice brought a subtle hand to her mouth to hide her smile, her dark eyebrows lifting with genuine surprise.

Vivian studied me for a few moments. "You're a salaried employee. It's expected that you put in a few extra hours here and there when required."

"Right. But I've—*we've*—been working overtime nonstop for eight months straight. So, unless I'm going to be paid for the additional hours, I'll be here from eight to five, Monday to Friday."

Either way, I'd be earning the same amount of money.

There was a shocked beat of silence as Vivian's forehead broke out in blotches of red.

"What's gotten into you?" she asked.

I was *exhausted*, that's what. And angry. And incredibly sick of being taken advantage of. My well was empty. Last night had drained what little energy and patience was left, and this morning had refilled it with bitter acid.

"Vivian," I said, emphasizing her name with the same lack of enthusiasm she often used with mine, "you've been taking advantage of us for months. You knew from day one that Jackson's requirements for a partner were beyond unreasonable and that his lack of direct participation would end up causing us major issues. That's *why* you assigned three junior consultants to him in the first place. You needed someone to blame after this whole thing blew up, and you didn't want to lose anyone you deemed valuable. So, excuse me if I'm not all that keen on providing you with any additional free labor."

The words flowed out of me with effortless, unrushed ease. I didn't stutter, look away, or cower even an inch. Funny what you're capable of when you have absolutely no fucks left to give.

The blotches on Vivian's face had spread down to her neck, disappearing under the deep vee of her silk blouse. But before she could open her mouth and slice into me again, I said, "I'll do it under three conditions. One, Alice and Mitch have employment immunity while I'm doing the Immersive. You can't fire them."

She laughed.

It was a dry, scraping sound that didn't even come close to reaching her eyes. "Oh please. I don't know who you think you are in this room right now, but I'm not *asking* you to do this, Jamie. You don't get to—"

"Then no." It was that easy.

She stopped, her eyes darting to Mitch and Alice before narrowing. It was one thing to have her authority undermined in private, but another thing entirely to have it happen in front of others.

"I have three conditions," I repeated. "Either all three are met, or I don't do it."

"You'll be fired if you don't," she told me point-blank.

See, that had been her biggest mistake. I'd been so acutely aware that I was going to lose my job over this file that I'd eventually just accepted it. There was no fear or shock value left in her threat.

I shrugged. "If I get fired, so does Charmed."

I had her. I knew I had her when she crossed her arms and raised her chin, looking down at me like I was beneath her.

"What are the other two conditions?"

I had to swallow my smile.

"I want half the bonus upfront." The bill for the clothes was due in seven days and their policy very explicitly stated that they wouldn't grant extensions. "And I want you to write all three of us glowing recommendation letters for future employers, which you will adhere to when they call you for a reference."

Because even if the events of last night made their way through the industry's overactive rumor mill, a glowing recommendation from Vivian Hale could potentially offset it. It was our best bet.

The room held its breath while she contemplated her options. Eventually, she caved. "Fine. You're expected in my office first thing tomorrow morning. All three of you are dismissed for the day."

It was the answer I'd expected. I knew she would agree because I hadn't left her a choice. Still, as soon as she was gone, a sense of relief, pride, and satisfaction swirled up my torso.

"Dude," Mitch breathed, his eyes wide with awe. "That was fucking incredible. Holy shit."

"Who's got the balls of steel now?" Alice said with an impressed nod of acknowledgment. "Way to go, Paquin."

It felt unbelievably good to give Vivian a tiny taste of her own medicine. To be the one who stood up for the group.

How much better would it feel when I did the same to Jackson, I wondered.

He'd put me through eight months of pure hell, and karma had presented me with the perfect opportunity to return the favor. Tit for vengeful tat.

And I had two full weeks to plot my revenge.

6

"What the hell is that?"

Those were the first words Jackson Sinclair said to me when I entered his home, two weeks after our meeting.

"It's a cat," I answered flatly. What a stupid question. "This is what they look like with fur."

His eyes narrowed. He did *not* like it when I insinuated he was an idiot—got it.

"What the fuck is it doing *here*?"

I cuddled Toebeans closer, placing a small kiss behind his twitching ear as he surveyed his new surroundings, making note of all the best butt-licking spots. I'd taken him out of his carrier as soon as we left the cab. He hated that thing with a hissing passion.

"Where else would he be staying for the next month?" I asked.

"That thing looks like it does nothing but shed," Jackson bit back.

I hummed.

He wasn't incorrect.

"Take it back outside," he demanded rudely. "I don't want it anywhere near my furniture."

Unsurprising, given the state of this place.

I looked around the living area, rigorously unimpressed by it all. Every inch of the massive space was pristinely grey, black, or white. It was all very sterile-looking. Like specs of dust were plucked straight out of the air before they could even think about settling on anything.

It didn't even feel like anyone lived here. It just looked like an insanely expensive showroom. It was really elegant and well put-together but, like... okay, for example, what was the point of having a couch that made you feel bad about using it? That thing was so blindingly white and angular I'd be scared to sit on it the wrong way.

Jackson's frosty blue eyes and sandy brown hair were the only noticeable pops of color in the room. Even his clothes were black and white. (Speaking of, who the hell wore a full three-piece suit at home?)

I offered him my best, most insincere smile. It went unreturned. "The good news is that his fur is the same shade of grey as a lot of your furniture, so it probably won't be too noticeable."

His jaw twitched. "Miss Paquin, don't you think it would have been appropriate for you to ask for permission before bringing that thing—"

"That *thing* is a *he*," I corrected, already depleted of patience. "His name is Toebeans Maguire, and I did get permission. This was all cleared with your aunt before I agreed to come here and do this with you."

The only other person I trusted to watch Toebeans for a full month was Ria and she was currently in the middle of a ten-week honeymoon with Alice's brother, so here we were.

Jackson's jaw worked unhappily, but he didn't argue. He looked like he desperately wanted to, but he forced himself to bite it back.

I didn't have a ton of insight as to what his relationship with Minerva was like, but from what I'd observed so far, she held all the cards. Her word was final, and Jackson obviously hated it.

"Fine," he managed, the muscles in his neck straining like they protested the word. "Just make sure he stays in your suite. I'll get Bensen to—"

He made the mistake of taking one too many steps forward.

Toebeans hissed, baring his tiny fangs at the approaching threat as his tail flicked with outrage. It was aggressive enough that Jackson recoiled back, brows crunching together.

"Look at that." I grinned. "He loathes you."

Toebeans didn't like most strangers, especially men. But I wanted Jackson to feel special.

"Odd," I went on. "He usually loves everyone."

"He wasn't all that fond of me either, sir." Bensen walked into the room just in time to ruin my fun. His voice was tilted with light amusement, and he shot me a quick smile before returning his attention to Young Master Satan-clair. "I wouldn't take it too personally."

I'd rather Jackson did take it personally though.

To me, Bensen said, "Your items have been taken to your rooms. I'll escort you there whenever you are ready."

"Take her there now," Jackson grumbled, eyes pinned to the big furry ball of adorableness loafed up in my arms like it was a ticking time bomb. "We'll resume our meeting after she drops the feline off."

Bensen dipped his head politely. "As you wish, sir.

Miss Paquin, if you and Mr. Maguire would please follow me."

Mr. Maguire.

I liked that.

We were led through two separate hallways, down a short set of stairs, and into… ah, yes, *of course* this place had a separate area for the live-in staff. "Servants quarters" as they were called. And *of course* Jackson would assign me a room down here.

I bit down a smile. If it was supposed to be an insult, it didn't come across as one. This space was already warmer and more homey than Jackson's side of the penthouse.

"You'll have to excuse Young Master Sinclair's mood," Bensen eventually said. "This process has not been exactly easy for him."

Right. Because it'd been a walk in the fucking park for me.

"You don't appreciate me defending him," he went on, a knowing smile tightening his cheeks as he watched me.

I shrugged. "I'm sure you have your reasons."

I was also sure they had something to do with the fact that Jackson was signing his paychecks. I couldn't fathom why he'd defend him otherwise.

His jaw shifted like he was going to say something else, but he seemed to decide against it, choosing to remain silent until we finally arrived at a set of white doors.

"Here we are." He held out a long bronze key for me to take. "This is for you. You'll find that the lovely Ms. Harrisons have stocked the suite with everything you may require for the duration of your stay with us. However, please do let us know if there is anything else we can assist you with. We are, per the direct request of Minerva Sinclair, at your full service."

I took the key—which was just shiny enough to distract Toebeans—and thanked him before twisting the door handle open.

Bensen tipped his head forward. "I'll be out here when you're ready to be escorted back."

"Oh, that's okay. I remember how to get back. You don't have to wait."

"As you wish, Madame." Another head bow.

"Actually, could you please just call me by my name?" I said.

"As you wish." And I swear his lips started to form the M before he stopped himself.

"Thank you." I offered him a smile before entering the suite which, as it turned out, was bigger than my apartment.

I mean, sure, I'd downgraded to a studio after Ria moved out, but still.

I set Toebeans down so he could sniff and wander around while I did the same. There was more color in here than I'd expected, though it was all very soft—lots of muted pinks and gentle creams. I liked it. It reminded me a little of my bedroom growing up.

This was a lot nicer, and the walls lacked all the scratch-and-smell stickers but, you know, it had some of the same comforting vibes.

"Okay, yeah," I said to Toebeans, who was carefully choosing which middle area of the upholstered bed would be best for him to monopolize. He needed to ensure my spine remained as contorted as possible while I slept. Otherwise, what would be the point? "I wouldn't mind being stuck in here for a month. Not too bad huh, cutie?"

There was a walk-in closet, a huge balcony, a small kitchenette, and even a minibar. Also, the bathroom was *swanky*. It had a rainshower, a toilet that talked, and a velvet storage bench tucked tastefully under a large window overlooking the Toronto city skyline.

By the time I left the room, Toebeans had made himself at home on top of a throw pillow he'd knocked off the couch. He hated new people but had absolutely no issues adjusting to new environments.

"You okay to be left alone for a bit, cutie?"

He yawned, tail swooshing.

He'd be fine. I was almost sure of it.

I was lost.

Like *lost* lost.

This place was a fucking maze and the harder I tried to get out, the more confusing the twists and turns seemed to get. I was positive that I'd walked through the same hallway at least four times, except each time it had led me to a different room or area. And because everything was so fucking sleek and modern and monotone, there weren't enough visual markers for me to navigate from.

How the hell had I made my escape so easily when I'd run out of here in the stupid towel? Was it an adrenaline thing?

I thought I had it. From my recollection, Bensen had taken just two left turns before we'd reached the staircase. One by the giant matte-black minimalist painting, and the other by the Bonsai tree with the twisted white trunk. I'd made it to the painting but couldn't find the tree to save my life.

There were just more hallways with more minimalist paintings and doors leading to *more* hallways with *more* minimalist paintings and doors. It'd probably only been fifteen minutes or so since I left my suite, but it felt like an eternity. I was thirsty, my wrists were sweaty, and—*there*! Yes! A Bonsai tree with a white trunk!

Except I could have sworn the one we passed by initially had a swirled trunk. I remembered because it looked distinctly like soft-serve, and it made me a little hungry. I sighed, glancing around. Maybe if I could find a member of staff or something, I could ask—

"What are you doing?"

I yelped, whipping around as my palm slammed against my chest.

"Jesus Christ," I breathed. "You really need to not sneak up on me like that."

For someone built like a skyscraper, Jackson was incredibly light-footed.

"Why are you sneaking around my property?"

"I'm not. I was lost."

His eyes narrowed like he didn't believe me. Then again, they quite literally didn't do anything else, so maybe he did believe me and that was his way of showing it.

"How'd you know where I was anyway?" I straightened the hem of my blouse, pushing my shoulders back.

He flicked his chin to something above my head. A security camera.

"They're everywhere." It was more of a warning than anything else.

I eyed him. "Define *everywhere*."

"Your suite is one of the very few places you won't find them. That's all you need to know."

"Cool." That was the only thing I cared about anyway.

And then we just stood there, staring at each other awkwardly.

Or, like, awkwardly on my part. His eerily light eyes were sliding between mine like they were convinced I was up to something.

I cleared my throat. "Are you gonna lead me back so we can sit down and do the orientation, or..."

His gaze lingered for one more breath before he peeled it away, turned around, and stalked away without another word. I hopped into step beside him without missing a beat. It wasn't hard. He wasn't exactly unpredictable.

"So," I said, keeping my tone friendly and conversational, "when I was trying to find my way back, I came across two grand pianos. Do you play? Because that wasn't included in any of the forms your staff filled out."

He said nothing.

I rolled my lips as the length and speed of his steps picked up. He wasn't going to entertain the whole small talk thing with me.

"I always wanted to learn," I told him, half-jogging to keep up with the new pace he'd set. "My parents couldn't afford the lessons back then, though. Or the piano. Or even the music sheets, really."

I waited.

Still nothing.

So, I went on, "Not that it's too late. I could just start learning now. If you know of any good teachers with decent rates—"

He stopped abruptly, twisting on the spot to glower

down at me. Predictably. "Let me make something that should already be quite clear even *more* clear. I have less than zero interest in engaging in any sort of pleasantries with you over the next month. So, unless the topic of discussion pertains directly to the—what are you doing?"

I'd whipped out my phone, opened the designated document, and was in the middle of scrolling to the appropriate section. And since I didn't want to be rude, I started speaking the words as I typed them. "Inter...personal... skills... abysmally... inadequate."

His eyes (predictably) narrowed, his shoulders (predictably) tensing. "What?" he snapped predictably.

"My evaluations." I slipped my phone back into my pocket. "It's part of the process. We'll talk about it in depth during orientation."

"The evaluation doesn't start until tomorrow, not to mention our interactions aren't supposed to be scored."

Wrong. "We started the second I stepped into your house, Mr. Sinclair, and our interactions absolutely *do* count."

His brows pushed together. "The package specifically stated—"

I waved a hand dismissively around his chest, just as I'd seen Minerva do. The skin under his left eye feathered.

"Min encouraged me to take creative control of the process," I informed him, trying my best to suppress the bubbly glee rolling up my chest. This was even more fun than when I'd told Vivian.

"*Min*?"

Oh. Right. Yes.

"She insisted," I explained, grinning up at him. "She's really nice, fantastic taste in bakeries. We've bonded quite a bit over the last two weeks."

A flash of surprise cut through his expression. "You've been spending time with her?"

"Yes. We've met up a bunch. Oh, and I'm supposed to be reporting my findings and opinions directly to her over the next month. Not sure if her team has communicated that with yours yet."

There was a solid chance he was about to have a hernia.

"She's mostly worried about you not trying," I went on. "But I feel like you already know that."

His jaw worked as his teeth ground together. "And you'll be the judge of that, then? Deciding whether or not you believe I'm putting in the effort?"

"Precisely." And he was doing a horrible job so far.

Jackson closed his eyes for a single moment, rubbing a knuckle against the bridge of his nose. Then, without a word, he turned and began walking away again.

He wasn't even willing to *pretend* to try.

How predictable.

7

IF I HAD a sleep paralysis demon, it would have Jackson Sinclair's eyes.

That was the loudest thought running through my head as he glared at me from across the living room, jaw tense like he was biting back how badly he wanted to tell me to get the fuck out of his house.

Physical demeanor in professional settings: abysmal.

"That's about everything you should expect from week one," I continue, undeterred. It wasn't like any of this was surprising. I'd had rock-bottom expectations for him, and he was simply delivering. "I'll be acting as your shadow, collecting data that will be used to find someone whose daily habits and lifestyle are compatible with yours. I suggest going about your day exactly as you normally would, pretending like I'm not there."

The more I talked, the more rigid and resentful Jackson's demeanor became. Until there were two separate veins popping out of his forehead and multiple muscles worming through his jaw.

It was a delightful sight to behold. Truly.

I hadn't felt this much job satisfaction and accomplishment in months—eight and a half of them, to be exact.

"That will take us to week two." My tone was unabashedly reflective of the fluffy delight his rage evoked in me, and we both knew it. "Which will be when we start your coaching."

His fists were white. "I don't need coaching."

"Oh, you definitely need coaching," I said without hesitation. "I can say with absolute confidence that if anyone needs a dating coach, Mr. Sinclair, it's you. That's my professional opinion, speaking from direct personal experience."

His glare was seething, but I didn't care.

He'd asked me if I was hard of hearing *and* gotten my name wrong in the same sentence, for fuck's sake. And the date had only gotten worse from there. I mean, I was pretty certain he'd been trying to sabotage it, but still. As the wise old karmic saying went: fuck around and find out.

"The coaching will be personalized to fit your specific needs," I continued, "covering all your major weaknesses, as determined by my evaluations." Which, in Jackson's case, was pretty much everything other than his physical presentation and attire. "However, if there are any specific areas you'd like for us to put additional focus on, please let me know."

Jackson's eyes flicked down to his wristwatch, his foot tapping once. Sadly for him, we still had seventeen allotted minutes left for our meeting and I didn't plan on ending it even a second early.

After all, I knew how much Mr. Sinclair *loved* punctuality. He always arrived on his dates exactly on time and ended them the nanosecond the hour was up. And it had absolutely nothing to do with the fact that Charmed had a sixty-minute first-impression requirement, which, again, had been put in place to ensure that our carefully selected pairings actually gave each other a fair shot.

"The focus for weeks three and four will depend on how the first two go. I'll still be gathering data, though likely at a reduced scale at this stage, especially since I won't be shadowing you at work anymore. If your coaching has gone well, we can move on to discreetly monitored dates. This time around, however, your partners will be selected based on my gathered data in addition to what we discuss during our sit-down interviews, a schedule for which has already been sent to your team. Our interviews will be held outside of regular office hours so they don't overlap with any other meetings you may have, and you *will* be expected to attend them all yourself. I don't accept subs."

That was the gist of it. I had all the main points covered. Good thing I had absolutely no shortage of relevant topics to talk at him about until the hour was over and he cut me off.

So that was exactly what I did—wasted his time like he'd wasted so much of mine.

I talked and talked until the skin under his eye twitched, and I could *see* him silently counting down the seconds until three, two—he shot to his feet a half-second before the big hand hit twelve and walked out of the room while I was smack in the middle of my sentence.

I rolled my lips, suppressing a smile as I picked up my phone again.

Abysmal.

Manners. Attitude. Body language.

All of it.

All of him.

Abysmal.

"I'm sorry, you're where right now? Doing *what*?"

I wiggled deeper into the stack of pillows propped up against the bedframe and almost purred. It was like being hugged by a puffy cloud.

"Don't you dare fall asleep on me right now, Jamie," Ria snapped, glaring at me through the painfully bright screen of my phone. It was incredibly sunny where she was—some island off the coast of... a country, either in Europe or Africa. I honestly couldn't keep track anymore, and not just because I was perpetually exhausted. All I knew was that they had internet access for the first time in almost two weeks.

"Sorry." My eyes were watering with the effort it took to stifle my yawn. "This bed is insanely comfortable, and I didn't sleep very well last night. Nerves and stuff."

I'd also stayed up way too late, going over my high-lighted notes from my two weeks of training with Vivian. The material hadn't been difficult, there'd just been a lot of it.

"You can sleep after you tell me what happened," Ria insisted. "Because the last time you and I talked, you were burnt the fuck out and on the brink of a legit emotional breakdown over this man's bullshit. Yes or no?"

"Correct," I confirmed. She'd threatened to fly back to Toronto in the middle of that conversation. It'd taken me almost an hour to convince her that canceling the rest of her honeymoon was a massive overreaction and completely unnecessary. Even though, selfishly, I missed her enough to almost want to allow it. *Almost*.

But I couldn't do that to her or her husband. Poor Adrien had been understanding enough as it was. The day Ria moved out, we'd cried so much that he'd felt the need to triple-check and make sure it was actually what she wanted. Then he'd offered me a permanent room in his penthouse, where I could leave all my stuff and stay over whenever I felt like it.

That was what had finally gotten us to calm the hell down. And you could just *see* the relief in his body language when her tears had slowed. He was so painfully in love with her that sometimes watching them interact was like looking directly at the sun.

They reminded me of my parents.

And that was all I'd ever wanted, you know? Ever since I was a little kid. That pure, blinding happiness that comes with finding your person. If I really thought about it, that was probably why I got into matchmaking in the first place. I fucking *loved* love, and what could be more fulfilling than helping... people... find...

"...Jamie!"

"Mmm?"

"You're dozing off!"

I forced my eyelids back open. It was not easy.

"Sorry. What were you saying?"

"Jackson Sinclair. The Immersive. Explain."

Ugh. It was such a long story, though. And I was so sleepy. It was half-past eleven and Toebeans was already curled up beside me, snoring softly.

I let out a heavy sigh. "Can it wait until we're back in the same time zone so we can talk about it over a bottle of wine? I'm dying and Satan-clair's day starts at, like, five in the morning."

She was disappointed. I knew she was disappointed because her eyes flicked away from me right away, the one corner of her mouth dipping.

I couldn't blame her. I'd been so busy with this stupid file and her internet access was so annoyingly shit, that we'd only had one or two conversations last longer than fifteen minutes in a month. The worst part? The majority of what we talked about was how I was still struggling. *That's* how much space I'd allowed my job and one stupid client to take up in my life.

The anger and resentment rooted in the pit of my chest flared again, making my mouth taste bitter.

"I'm sorry, Ree." I swallowed back the raw emotion kicking at my throat. "I know this was supposed to be our catch-up session, I just..."

"It's okay," she said with a sigh. "The time zone thing is a bitch and none of these stupid islands have any Wi-Fi. It's supposed to be on purpose, for guests to disconnect and yada yada yada, mental health. It's not your fault."

I adjusted my feet under the duvet, tucking one behind the other. "Right, but I've also just been so exhausted that... I mean, even at your wedding—"

"None of that," she said. "I don't want to hear another apology over it. I already said it was okay."

Was it okay though? Because falling asleep at your best friend's wedding reception felt very much like it stepped into *not okay* territory.

It was only for a minute, and it happened while I was waiting for her on the couch just outside the bathroom, but still. It felt very, extremely not okay to me.

I'd almost cried when she'd gently nudged me awake

and offered to take me upstairs to my hotel room so I could get some rest. Even thinking about it now made me feel like shit.

"I'll make it up to you," I promised. "When you're back, I'll make up for all the... for how I've been over the last eight months."

The Immersive would be over before Ria and Adrien were back, and I was going to quit my job at Charmed as soon as I received the second half of my bonus. And then I'd make it up to her.

To my parents.

To myself.

Ria pressed her lips together, shaking her head once. "We'll talk about this when I get home. You're doing that thing where you're being unreasonably hard on yourself, and I have *thoughts*."

I huffed a little laugh. Of course she did. If nothing else, Ria had *thoughts*. Always, and about everything. And I couldn't fucking wait to hear them. Right after I finished exacting my revenge on Jackson Sinclair.

She was going to be so proud of me, bloodthirsty as she was.

8

It was significantly worse than I thought. And that was saying something because my expectations had been *low* low.

Jackson Sinclair was the epitome of someone who had way too much money and not nearly enough self-sufficiency. I'd been shadowing him for just under three hours and I genuinely couldn't believe someone actually lived like this. He had "a person" for almost everything. It was beyond excessive.

His breakfast was prepared by his personal chef.

His workout was dictated and supervised by his personal trainer.

His outfit—which had been hand-picked in advance by his personal shopper—was laid out for him by his personal maids.

His hair was styled by his personal barber, who *also shaved his morning stubble for him*. (This one really got me.)

And finally, his personal driver drove us to his office, where his personal assistant, Savannah, was waiting for him with his morning coffee and a perfectly rehearsed briefing of his schedule for the day.

It was seamless. His team was more organized than, like, certain branches of the military, I assumed with absolutely no knowledge of the subject whatsoever.

"And this is your desk," Savannah said to me once she'd finished Jackson's briefing. "The *PA* button on your phone is linked directly to mine, in case you ever need anything. Minerva specifically requested it."

She said that last part quietly, her head dipping like it was supposed to be our little secret. The smile and wink that followed confirmed it.

Minerva had moles in the office? I couldn't decide whether that was weird or awesome. Maybe a bit of both. Jackson caught on to our hushed-toned exchange and when she left, his ghostly eyes slid to me, narrowing. Like it was all my fault.

I smiled.

He glared.

I sat down.

He stood up.

I followed suit. "Where're we goin'?"

You know when you can just tell when someone wants to punt you into a different dimension because they're just so very over your bullshit?

"I need to relieve myself," he bit out. "Or are you expected to follow me in there too?"

"Nope. All good. Have fun."

Irritation crept up his neck, and he felt the need to adjust his tie before he slammed the office door behind him. There was an ensuite bathroom less than ten feet from his desk.

He was going to *loathe* me by the time the thirty days were up.

Just thinking about it brought me an unhealthy amount of joy.

~

Normally, under these specific circumstances, I'd have been bored out of my mind. I assumed that was his plan: to bore me until I caved and went home. But man oh man did he underestimate how much pent-up resentment I had fueling my willpower.

This was child's play.

All he'd done was change his in-person meetings to virtual ones and pop in a pair of headphones so I couldn't hear what was going on. Oh, and I guess he'd marked the whole floor as off-limits to all other employees, save for Savannah. No exceptions.

Not that I could blame him for that last bit. A lot of our Immersive clients opted out of being shadowed at the office and did most of their work from home instead, wanting to keep their private lives private. But Minerva hadn't given Jackson a choice. He was free to improvise when employees asked about me (a "business consultant" was what we'd settled on) but that was about it.

I didn't know what carrot she was dangling to make him jump through this many hoops, but whatever it was, it had to be *good*.

"Is this what I can expect for the next month, then?" Jackson asked just as I was trying to decide what to do for lunch. "You're going to sit there and stare at me while I try to work?"

I kept forgetting about his accent. Not like, *forgetting*

about it, but just not fully remembering how... his voice just sort of... never mind. I didn't know where my brain was trying to go with that.

Either way, it was the first time he'd acknowledged my presence in five and a half hours, according to my watch. Pretty impressive. I knew he'd break before the day was up though. He needed me to quit, and the silent treatment wasn't going to be an effective way to get the job done.

"I'm observing, not staring," I assured him. "And the plan is to continue doing it, yes. It's kind of the whole reason I'm here."

He held my gaze as he leaned back in his chair, head slanting to one side.

"Did you have another question?" I asked politely. It looked like he might.

"I'm trying to figure out whether or not you realize how absurd and pointless this all is."

Rude. "I'd appreciate it if you wouldn't refer to my work as absurd and pointless, Mr. Sinclair."

An unfriendly spark flashed across his freaky eyes. "I was more referring to the program, but you're right, the same can be said about your profession."

I kept my smile smooth and pleasant as I threaded my fingers on my desk. "Let me guess, you think my profession is pointless because you don't believe in it."

"In what, exactly?"

"What I'm trying to sell you. Either you don't believe in love, or you don't think I can help you find it." There was a hang-up in there somewhere. I'd know by the end of the month.

He quirked a brow, studying me. "You got all that from one morning with me?"

No. I got all that from eight months of slaving away at

my job, banging my head against the wall trying to find a partner for a man who was doing his absolute damnedest to make it impossible for me.

"Am I wrong?" I asked.

The one corner of his mouth twitched like it wanted to be amused. "No. You're not wrong."

Knew it. Honestly, the man couldn't be more of a cliché if he tried.

"Great. Any decent sushi places around here you'd recommend?" I was starving.

My inquiry went ignored. "Why are you here then? If you're aware I think it's all bullshit, why waste your time?"

"Poké would be good too. Whichever is closest."

"Is it for the money?" he prodded. "The experience? A gold star on your résumé?"

"To start. Why?"

He wanted to make a deal. He'd pay me to fabricate my data, and I'd still be able to put the gold star on my résumé. In his head, it was a win-win.

"If you're open to it, I'd like to come up with an alternate arrangement," he said, searching my features for visual cues as to how his proposition was being received. "An arrangement that works better for both of us."

"No."

A pause. He clearly wasn't used to hearing that word.

"You don't even know what my offer is yet."

Oh, so he wanted to do this the long way then. I glanced at my watch. I'd allow him... six more minutes.

"Okay. What's your offer?"

"Two hundred thousand," he deadpanned. "But all of this stops. No shadowing, coaching, tests, or interviews. Though, as far as Minerva is concerned, we've done all of it and more."

"Oh," I said, "then still no."

He *really* didn't like hearing that word. "Five hundred."

"No."

"One million."

"No."

His elbows were planted on his desk now, eyes piercing mine from across the room. "Miss Paquin, I'm offering you a million dollars to spend a month *not* working," he explained slowly. In case my teeny tiny brain wasn't capable of comprehending the complexity of his proposed arrangement, I guess.

"No, Mr. Sinclair," I said, voice mocking. "You're offering me a million dollars to sacrifice my integrity and put my career at even more risk."

"Oh please." He leaned back again, adjusting his tie. "Tell me, where was your integrity when you put on a wig and lied to me about who you were?"

My skin flamed with sudden irritation. "I have no intention of striking any sort of deal with you or double-crossing my employer. And unless you want this all included in my next report to your aunt, I suggest you drop it."

I turned back to my laptop.

Integrity: nonexistent.

Entitlement: all but invented and trademarked by client—

"Twenty."

My fingers paused on the keyboard. My gaze snapped back to his. "Pardon?"

He reached into his desk drawer, pulled out a small rectangular booklet, scribbled something across the top layer, tore it off, and stood up.

Approximately five thundering heartbeats later, I was

staring down at a signed check from Jackson Sinclair. For twenty million dollars.

He slipped his hands into his pockets as he loomed over my desk, watching me.

"Slight change of plans," he said when my frying brain failed to re-establish a connection with my tongue. It wasn't until Savannah's voice came on the speaker that I realized he wasn't talking to me. "I'll be eating at Umu today. Push my one p.m. to Thursday."

"Sure thing. I'll call them and have your table prepared. Will Miss Paquin be joining you?"

"No." I could taste the smug arrogance in his tone, it was so palpable. "I don't believe she will."

And then he walked away.

9

You don't understand just how much twenty million dollars is until it's staring you in the face, threatening to better your life. You think you do, but you don't. Not really.

My whole existence flashed before my mind's eye. Past, present, and future.

My student loans? Gone.

My parents? Retired, their mortgage and line of credit paid off.

I could buy a house with this type of money—anywhere I wanted. I could travel, move somewhere warm, adopt a pony, take up surfing and sailing and the piano and whatever else I wanted.

I'd never have to worry about living paycheck-to-paycheck ever again. This little piece of paper would change my life.

I had to take it. Like, I *had* to take it. If not for me, then for Mom and Dad. It would be incredibly selfish and stupid of me to not accept this deal. My brain was trying very, *very* hard to convince me of that. Because among the pure disbelief, excitement, and shaky nerves, there was something else. Something slick, squirmy, and wholly unpleasant.

It struck me that, as life changing as this kind of money would be for me, it wasn't anything significant to Jackson. I was letting him buy me with what he considered to be pocket change, which made me weirdly sick to my stomach.

Letting my pride and ego stop me from accepting a lifetime of financial security would be a pretty stupid thing to do, though. I had to take it.

But could you sleep at night? Knowing you let Jackson Sinclair buy you like this?

Well, I mean if I could afford a really nice mattress, then yeah. Definitely.

I snatched the check off the desk and ran to the elevator. But instead of going to the bank, my feet turned right when they hit concrete, leading me straight to Umu.

I was an idiot.

~

Jackson Sinclair had his own private dining room at the most exclusive and expensive Japanese restaurant in the city. Because of course he did.

It was gorgeously decorated—lots of neutral colors, dim lights, and minimalist on-theme furniture—and cost more than my annual salary to retain. I could almost guarantee it.

The cocktail he'd been about to sip froze in the air when the waitress slid the shoji screen open. His lips parted farther. He blinked.

But I was too riled up to revel in it.

My pulse was thundering, my fingers trembling as I all but slammed the check down in front of him. "Twenty *million* dollars? Is this some sort of sick joke?"

He gaped up at me, eyebrows slowly rising. For a solid minute, the room was silent.

Well, mostly silent. I was breathing quite heavily, having stomped all the way here, and my heart was marching to a pretty violent beat against my eardrums.

Jackson continued to stare, icy-blue eyes gliding between mine. Until, eventually, the one side of his mouth lifted. "All right." His smooth accent hugged the words in a way that made my stomach swoop. "Sit down, Miss Paquin. Let's talk."

Yeah. Fuck no.

I wasn't another member of his staff. He couldn't just order me around.

"I'm booking you for a psych eval," I said. "Next week. Have your team send me your schedule and I'll work around it. You'll need a two-hour block."

His mouth did that tilting thing again. It wasn't a smile. Jackson wasn't capable of those.

"Sit," he repeated, gesturing to the chair across from him.

I rolled my eyes. "Some early coaching advice since, again, you very clearly need it—outside of the workplace, ordering people around is generally not considered an attractive quality. Neither is trying to bribe them or thinking that you can solve everything with money."

It happened again. The mouth thing.

"Okay. Since you insist, we can stand."

He rose to his feet and stalked over to me, stopping mere inches away so he could look down at me all smug. "Better?"

I crossed my arms and held my ground. Sure, I had to tilt my head all the way back to maintain eye contact, but I still had my dignity. "It's great."

"That hasn't been my experience, by the way."

"What?"

"I have yet to come across a problem that can't be solved with money," he insisted, just as the soft, clean scent of his cologne hit me. It was highly pleasant, actually. Didn't suit him at all. "Bribes have worked rather well for me in the past, and as for ordering people around... you'd be surprised."

Something about the way he said the last part made color threaten to sprout over my cheeks. I brushed it off. "Yeah, well, you can't bribe your way out of this one, I'm afraid. My soul's not up for sale."

His head slanted to one side, his cool gaze sliding over my face. "Everybody has a price, Miss Paquin. We just have to find yours."

"Okay, telling someone they have a price? Also incredibly unattractive."

"You're really not taking the money?" he asked, blatantly ignoring my sage advice.

"I'm really not taking the money."

"Why? You agreed that was why you were doing this in the first place."

"I also said I wasn't willing to put my career at risk."

He shrugged. "With twenty million you could set up your own agency. Make your own rules. I was there, I saw the dynamic between you and Valerie."

"Vivian."

"Vivian. Sure."

"Not remembering people's names is also highly unattractive," I said. "Clear indication that you're self-absorbed."

"I remember the ones that matter. The point is, if you're the one running things, you don't have to put up with management and their bullshit. In fact, you'd be paying other people to put up with yours."

"Nah, I'm good." I turned on my heel, ready to leave, but stopped when his fingers unexpectedly grazed my sleeve. "What?"

His eyes were narrowed again, but not with scorn. He looked more curious than anything else. "How much to make you go away? Seriously."

Wow. He *really* didn't get it, did he? "Unfortunately, I'm not a problem you can just throw money at."

"What do you want, then?"

"To do my job," I said. "The one you insulted this morning which, by the way, is also a highly unattractive thing to do."

"Your job entails convincing lonely, desperate people that fairy-tale endings are real. I've seen the adverts, Miss Paquin. They're shameless and grotesque. My insults were warranted."

I bristled. "Okay, see? *This* is exactly why we needed to do your personality evaluation in person. Cynical wasn't even on your list."

"I'm not cynical, I'm a realist."

"Oh please." I rolled my eyes, taking a half-step forward. "That's what assholes say to justify being assholes. You're also rude, obnoxious, arrogant, and entitled as all hell. Who the fuck thinks it's appropriate to insult someone's occupation like that right to their face?"

His lips tilted again. With sarcasm this time. "The current adverts for Charmed push the concept of soulmates, Miss Paquin. And utilizing things such as tarot to help clients find their 'one true match.'"

My temperature spiked. To be clear, the tarot thing was reserved only for the clients who asked for it. "So?"

"Do *you* believe in that bullshit? That the universe is alive and helping guide you to the *one* person you're meant to be with? Is that why divorce rates in this country are so high? Because people are being guided to their soulmates left, right, and center?"

I had never in my life met someone so relentlessly infuriating. "I believe, very strongly, that there's someone out there for everyone. And yes, maybe there's some higher power that's helping people find each other. I don't know! What I do know is that romantic love, soul-deep connections, and happily-ever-afters are all real. If I didn't believe those things, I wouldn't be doing this for a living."

"Oh, so you've experienced it then."

It wasn't until then that I realized just how close we were standing, how hard we were both breathing. I swallowed, staying put. If anyone was going to step back, it was Jackson.

"Not personally, no," I said. My luck with men and relationships thus far had admittedly not been great. "But I've seen it."

He huffed out a dry, mocking breath. It was almost a laugh.

"I have!" I insisted, even though there was no point. My mouth kept moving, fueled by my bruised ego. "My best friend is on a ten-week honeymoon with the love of her life as we speak. And my parents just had their thirtieth-anniversary last month, and they couldn't be more in love. So... there you go."

You know when you say something in the heat of an

argument, and it immediately makes you feel juvenile and stupid? Because those points sounded a lot more eloquent in my head than they did out loud.

I cleared my throat and tried again. "I've also seen a lot of success with my clients." Prior to him, that is. Back when I actually enjoyed my job and found it fulfilling.

Jackson quirked a brow, lips rolling like he couldn't believe just how childish and gullible I was.

It scraped something deep in my chest, and before I could think better of it, I said, "Bet I can prove you wrong."

I regretted it before the sentence was even out of my mouth. I regretted it even more when he chuckled. It was the first time I'd seen him fully smile, and... damn. All straight white teeth, prominent canines, and masculine charm. As much as I hated to admit it, Jackson Sinclair was hot as sin.

There was a reason so many attractive, successful women were so heartbroken over him. Well, that and all the money, power, and the most eligible bachelor in North America thing.

His personality was shit though, so most of the time it was easy to forget about his looks.

"Last chance." He slanted his head condescendingly. "Take the money."

I didn't know whether to be relieved or insulted that he didn't take me seriously enough to even acknowledge the bet. My brain said relief, my ego screamed *PROVE HIM THE FUCK WRONG. MAKE HIM WEEP FOR YOUR FORGIVENESS.*

"I'm not taking the money." I curled my fingers into my palms. They were a little too tempted to reach for the check. I couldn't risk it.

His lips were still tilted with amusement as he studied me. "Miss Paquin, a fair warning, I have no intentions of playing nice or making the next thirty days easy for you. Take the money, forge the data, and save us both the headache and time."

I shot him a wry smile. "Mr. Sinclair, a fair warning, I'm sick of your shit and half the reason I agreed to do this was to make your life as miserable as you've made ours over the last eight months. You don't scare me."

"That's what this is about? You're turning down twenty million dollars for a bit of revenge? A little *short*-sighted, wouldn't you agree?" He leaned down an inch when he said the word "short."

I was five-foot-seven.

He was built like the Abominable Snowman.

If anyone in this room should have been self-conscious about their height, it wasn't me.

I blinked up at him slowly, sarcastically. "I don't care how you spin it, you can't buy my integrity."

He clicked his tongue. "Like I said, everybody has a price."

"Oh yeah? What's yours?"

"Approximately thirteen and a half billion, give or take daily market fluctuations."

Huh. "Less than I thought."

His smirk expanded slowly as he watched me, but before he could bite back, two waiters entered the room… and promptly stopped in their tracks, their widening eyes bouncing between Jackson and me. In their defense, we were practically toe to toe.

I took two full steps back, arms folding over my chest again as I gave them my best nothing-to-see-here smile.

"Our apologies," one of them said. "We'll have the staff knock before entering the room again."

Oh, wow, no. "Not necessary. I was just leaving," I said as they placed the food down. Three stone plates of vibrantly presented sashimi, squid, and caviar.

"You can eat first," Jackson said, "the order was automatically upped to two when you arrived."

"No, thanks." My mouth was watering, my stomach was threatening to growl, but the absolute last thing I wanted to do was sit in that chair.

"You said you wanted sushi."

"Still do. But I've already dined with you once and it's not an experience I'm willing to repeat. Plus, there's a sushi kiosk at the mall two blocks down, so I'm all set. See ya."

I didn't linger long enough to hear his response.

10

TOEBEANS WAS RIGHTFULLY unimpressed by my incompetence when I finally made it back to my suite, ninety whole minutes past his dinner time. He was curled up on my sweater, tail jerking irritably as he yowled his complaints.

"Sorry, cutie." He jumped down from the bed, trotting over to stand as inconveniently in my way as possible while I fished out a can of wet cat food from its designated cupboard. "Here."

He looked up at me expectantly as I tossed the empty can, his tail continuing to whip.

"Go on. I'm looking," I reassured him, sinking to the floor.

He'd been like this since he was around six months old. Would not touch his food unless someone he trusted was there to watch his back while he ate. Ria and I took turns when we lived together, and after she'd moved out, I'd hired an on-call sitter to come in and look after him when I had to work late. Though it'd taken almost two weeks of us feeding him together for him to trust her.

"We need to figure out a new system, huh?" I scratched his fluffy back as he munched away. I had a feeling my evening schedule was going to be somewhat erratic over the next month. "I'll ask the Bad Man if he's cool with Rosie coming down here to feed you."

She'd already said she could, her fee would just be a little higher to make up for the increased travel time, which was fair.

Once Toebeans was done, I gave him all the obligatory post-dinner pampering until he got sick of my love and swiped my fingers away. *Enough, human.*

"Fine." I kissed the top of his head before getting up and stripping out of my stiff work clothes. I was starving. Not only had I skipped breakfast, but by the time I'd made it to the sushi kiosk, the lunch rush had stripped the shelves bare. I'd been left with a small pack of stale California rolls and a sugar-free iced tea.

I slipped into a pair of jeans and a grey tee, then unpinned my curls and let them fall loose from their too-tight bun before shoving them back into a much looser one.

There.

That was so much better.

"Kind of like taking your bra off at the end of a long day, but for your hair, huh?"

Toebeans chirped, and I couldn't help it. I just couldn't. I knew he'd had enough, but he was too darn cute, my derpy little meatloaf.

I bounced over to where His Chonky Adorableness was curled up on the bed and gave him more kisses, annoying the ever-loving shit out of him. He was plotting my murder so hard; it was so cute.

"Okay." *Peck*. "Bye." *Peck*. "Be good." *Peck*. "Last one." *Peck*. "Promise." *Peck*. "I'll miss you." *Peck*.

He placed his paw on my mouth after the last one and yelled right in my face.

"Mmkay. Sorry. I'll go for real now."

I pushed off the mattress, snatching my phone and keys on my way out the door. Two more air kisses to my little monster and—

"Who were you talking to?"

I screamed, my feet lifting from the carpet as my heart lurched into a panic attack.

"Stop doing that!" Fucking hell.

Jackson cocked his head, his lips twitching like my distress amused him. Heathen.

"Apologies." He did not look apologetic.

"What the fuck are you doing hovering outside my room like a creep?"

"I wasn't hovering. I was on my way to dinner and heard your voice coming through the door."

Lies. Bensen had sent me the floor map yesterday and I had the layout of this whole maze memorized. "The dining room's that way." I pointed a finger at said way. "At the other end of the apartment."

"I'm well aware of where the dining room is, Miss Paquin. This is, after all, my home. Were you speaking to yourself again?"

"None of your business."

I started walking.

He followed.

"If you want to have guests over, you'll need to go through the appropriate security channels."

"I don't plan on having guests over." Oh, except, "I may need to bring in a petsitter, though."

"For what?"

"Toebeans."

"The cat?"

You know when you're so done with someone that even the way they breathe pisses you off? Because the way Jackson was breathing right then was really pissing me off.

...

There was a good chance the hanger was setting in.

"Yes," I said. "I need someone to feed him on time when I can't."

"Petsitter is fine. Bensen can have supervised access arranged for them if you let him know."

"Great, thanks."

"How was your mall sushi?"

I stopped, glaring up at him. "Why are you following me? Our cut-off was at seven today."

"I'm not following you, I'm on my way to dinner. We've already had this conversation, Miss Paquin. Are you all right? First I catch you talking to yourself—"

"I wasn't talking to myself. I was talking to Toebeans."

"The cat?"

Oh my god. Okay. "I thought you said you had less than zero interest in engaging in pleasantries with me over the next month."

"I'd hardly call these pleasantries, seeing as neither of us finds them at all pleasant."

I crossed my arms, waiting for him to get to the fucking point.

Instead, he said, "You didn't answer my question about the mall sushi."

I rolled my eyes, and I swear I saw his mouth quirk before I walked away.

"Is this your new plan?" I asked as he—once again—

fell into step beside me. "You're going to annoy me into quitting?"

He hadn't said a word to me after lunch. Instead, he'd waited until I was off the clock.

"Perhaps," he said. "Why? Would that work?"

My stomach growled when we reached the staff kitchens and the smell of garlic and savory spices hit my nose. I also needed to talk to Bensen about getting some fridge space and kitchen access. I couldn't live off takeout for the next thirty days.

"There you are!" One of the Harrison twins (Molly, I guessed) popped out of the curved archway of the kitchen, a checkered oven mitt covering one hand. "What on heaven's earth took you so long?"

"Sorry." Jackson's head ticked in my direction. "Our new guest is rather talkative."

I blinked up at him. "I didn't realize you had a sense of humor."

"I don't," he deadpanned.

"Hello, dear," Molly said to me. "Molly Harrison. Head housekeeper. We met a couple of weeks back."

I took her outstretched hand with a smile. "How could I forget?"

"Yes, well, it was quite the memorable night, wasn't it?"

"I'd say so." Mabel appeared behind her sister. She was holding the other checkered oven mitt. "Hello again."

"Hi. I'm Jamie, by the way," I said. I couldn't remember if I'd had a chance to introduce myself last time.

"Oh, yes, we've heard all about you, Miss Paquin, haven't we?"

"We have. It's been quite the commotion around here since you turned up."

"Mistress Minerva's given us a couple of visits too."

"She's asked us to take good care of you. Talked to the whole staff."

"Hard to please, Mistress Minerva."

"She's taken a liking to you though, so you must have done something right."

Jackson snorted.

I ignored him.

"Would you like to join us for dinner, dear?" Molly asked kindly.

"Oh, she can't," Jackson cut in. He had a shoulder leaned against the wall, hands stuffed casually in the pockets of his slacks. He was still in his office attire, sans the suit jacket. "I'm afraid Miss Paquin doesn't find me to be adequate dinner company."

The sisters gaped up at me like I'd just spat on their whole ancestral tree.

"Well, that's just nonsense, isn't it?" Molly's voice was pitched high, her shoulders bristling with indignation.

"You're lovely company, dear. Any girl would be lucky to dine with you, and don't you believe a word otherwise."

Jackson preened—positively *preened*—at the compliment, smiling as he bent down and placed a quick kiss on her plump cheek. "Thank you, Mabel."

Huh.

My brows arched as I watched the unexpected interaction. It was oddly sweet.

"I stand by it," I said. "He got my name wrong on purpose and very rudely asked me if I was hard of hearing, all within the first five minutes of us meeting."

"Jackson!" Molly whipped at his arm with her oven mitt.

"Did you really?" Mabel frowned up at him.

"Not at all how we taught you to behave, is it?"

"It is not. Why would you do such a thing?"

How *we* taught you, she'd said. Interesting, seeing as how neither of them had been mentioned in any of the familial background or childhood reports Jackson's team had filled out. "*They've been provided with more than enough data to find me a suitable match*" my ass.

"How do you know it was on purpose?" he asked me.

"You're many things, Mr. Sinclair, and transparent is definitely one of them."

Two lines formed in the middle of his brows. "What?"

"Transparent," I repeated slowly. "Adjective. Means easy to perceive, and in your case, predict."

There was a long beat of silence as Jackson held my gaze. When it clicked, his shoulder snapped off the wall with force. "You think I'm… predictable."

"Highly."

"With the personality of a hardboiled egg."

I lifted a shoulder. "I stand by that too."

"Meaning what, exactly? You find me bland?"

"And generic. Not necessarily a bad thing, it just means I know exactly what I'm getting when you and I interact, just like I know exactly what I'm getting when I bite into a hard-boiled egg. Any hard-boiled egg. Because regardless of the brand, they all basically taste the same. Does that make sense?"

"Oh, dear."

I wasn't sure which sister said it because I refused to be the first to look away from the staring contest Jackson and I were locked in. His eyes were going to start narrowing in three, two… and there. See? Predictable.

"And is this all your *professional* opinion, Miss Paquin?"

Molly stepped in before I could answer. "All right,

well, I think we should all go sit down. Then, after dinner, we'll have a nice, calming cuppa. What do you say?"

"Yes, yes, let's go, m'dears. The lamb is getting cold, and this conversation isn't headed anywhere good, is it?"

"I don't believe it is, no," Molly agreed, taking Jackson by the arm. She tried pulling him, but he was rooted in the spot, his glare lethal and challenging.

"Like I said, she won't be joining us," he bit out.

I should have agreed to eat with them, technically. I needed to observe him in his natural habitat and take notes on his interactions, but I'd pissed him off enough that he wouldn't be acting as he normally did anyway.

It would need to wait.

I smiled at the sisters. "I really appreciate the offer, but I think it's best if I skip this one. The first week comes with an adjustment period for the client, and it's important that Mr. Sinclair still has some normalcy and space."

"All right," Mabel said with a gentle nod. "That's reasonable. But you will join us next week, won't you?"

He ate with them often, then. I wondered who else was frequently invited.

"Of course," I assured her.

She snatched Jackson's thick arm, pulling him into the kitchen while she muttered about her sauce needing a quick stir.

It wasn't until I was halfway down the hall that I realized Molly had lingered, the oven mitt wringing in her hands as she watched me leave.

11

Why was it that every time I spent a night somewhere that didn't have my name on the lease, my brain was adamant that the tiniest noise or movement was an immediate prequel to my violent murder? Was it an evolutionary thing? Were my ancestors really that—

It happened again, the secretive shuffle outside my room.

My comb froze midway through my damp curls, my head twisting toward the door as I held my breath. Toebeans had heard it too. His ears were twitching, gaze pinned to the door.

After a few beats, someone knocked.

I frowned. It was only ten, but still. A little late to show up at someone's door unannounced, no? Unless you were Ria.

"Yes?" I placed my comb down.

There was a hushed response from the other side, but I couldn't quite make out the words.

"I'm sorry?" I called.

"It's Molly," she whispered again, a touch louder this time.

"Oh." I got up, half-jogging to open the door for her as I stuffed my ringlets into a bun. I hated the feeling of wet hair sticking to my neck.

"Hello, dear." She was holding a silver tray with two steaming cups of pale tea and a plate full of pastries.

"Hey. Everything okay?"

She tried to give me her most convincing smile, but it twitched before it could reach her eyes. "I thought maybe you'd like a nighttime snack."

"Why are we whispering?"

She shook her head like she didn't know what I was talking about but refused to confirm it with her words.

I eyed her before stepping aside. "Come on in."

She shuffled in and nudged the door shut with her foot right away. Her voice was back to a normal pitch when she said, "Thank you. I'm sorry to—oh, hello little darling." She stopped when she spotted Toebeans, her round cheeks expanding. "Bensen wasn't exaggerating, was he? You *are* a very handsome boy."

Toebeans whipped his tail, unimpressed. He knew he was pretty. This wasn't news.

"Not too fond of strangers, though, is that right?" she asked me.

"Unfortunately not."

"Oh, well, that's okay." She straightened, wiping her hands down the front of her apron. "Neither is Young Master Sinclair. We're well used to that in our house. You can have all the space you need, Mr. Maguire, rest assured."

She wiped her hands again.

Shifted on her feet.

Cleared her throat.

"Molly," I said.

"Yes, dear?"

"Would you like to sit down?"

"Well, sure. If you insist."

I bit back a smile as she plopped down on the couch and reached for a porcelain cup, blowing on it delicately.

"So." I took a seat beside her. "How was dinner?"

"Oh, fine, fine," she answered, her tone trying a bit too hard to remain nonchalant. "More lively than usual, I suppose, but that's better than the alternative, isn't it?"

I hummed as I picked up my own cup, cooling it before sipping. Chamomile with a touch of honey. Yum. "Do you all eat together often?"

"Every night. Unless one of us is indisposed. Jackson especially, what with all the business trips and client dinners..."

"And dates," I supplied. Two nights a week for eight months added up.

She hesitated, looking away. "Well, we still set a place for him on those nights."

My brows rose. "He eats two dinners?"

"No... not quite." She suddenly seemed very interested in the subtle ribbons of steam curling out of her cup.

"You know," I said, "any conversation you and I have over nighttime snacks doesn't have to be on the record."

That got her attention. "Really?"

"Really. Also, you should know, I'm *great* at keeping secrets. I mean, it's partly because my memory is horrible, but still."

She let out a warm chuckle, her shoulders relaxing. "Wait until you get to be my age. Some mornings I'll be staring right at my feet, trying to recall if I've put on my shoes."

I smiled into my cup. "Thank you for this, by the way. I'm a big fan of nighttime snacks."

Ria had made it a thing for us. At least once a month, she'd sneak into my room with a bag full of goodies and a bottle of wine, and we'd go to town, chatting and gossiping about anything and everything.

I missed having her around so much that if I thought too hard about it, it made my throat thick.

Not that I wasn't happy for her, because I was! It was just… we'd lived together for *ten years*. Maybe that was why I hadn't complained at first when my hours at Charmed increased. The apartment was very quiet after she left. It took some getting used to.

Molly sighed. "I do apologize for showing up unannounced. Truth be told, I'm not supposed to be here. The staff has been given very specific instructions by Young Master Sinclair. We're not supposed to speak about him with you, you see. At all."

She wouldn't be the first member of his staff to break that rule. Bensen had done it yesterday when he'd defended Jackson. So, either they weren't necessarily afraid of the consequences, or whatever they were trying to achieve via these conversations was important enough to be worth the risk.

I picked up a pistachio éclair and bit into it, waiting.

"Mabel doesn't know I'm here either," she went on. "She'd never agree with me betraying the Young Master's trust in this way. She'd have my head if she knew, believe you me."

"And what about Jackson? Wouldn't he be angry if he found out?"

"Yes, I suppose he would. But it's different, isn't it?"

"How so?"

She twisted on the couch to face me full-on, her hands curled tightly around her cup. "You've misjudged him."

Her tone carried so much firm conviction that it left no room for argument. I could see it in her eyes. She believed it with every fiber of her soul.

"I can't blame you for it. Truly, I can't," she went on. "I realize Jackson's behavior has been more than a little damning, but there are so many things you don't know. And how could you, really?"

"Is that why you're here? To provide me with that information?"

She placed her barely touched tea back on the tray so she could fiddle with her apron. "In a sense. I'd also like to ask you for a favor. Well, two of them."

I finished off the pastry, nodding for her to go on.

"Not for free, of course. I'm willing to pay you for your efforts and—"

I quickly shook my head, waiting until I was done chewing to interrupt her. "Molly. I don't want your money."

She hesitated. "They're not small, these favors."

"Why don't you tell me what they are first?"

But before she could map out a way to get the words out without overstepping whatever internal moral boundaries she'd set for herself, another set of knocks echoed through the room.

Molly blinked up at me, her brows drawing together. "Who could that be, at this hour?" she whispered.

My inkling was confirmed when, without prompt, the person on the other side of the door quietly declared, "Hello, Miss Paquin? It's me, Mabel Harrison."

Color me shocked.

"What is *she* doing here? She told me she was going to bed early!" Molly hissed, scandalized by her twin's willingness to spin such reprehensible lies.

My guess was that both sisters were here for the same thing but, "Let's see, shall we?"

I got up to open the door just as Molly scuttled into a corner, hiding from view.

"Hello, Mabel."

"Hello, dear," she greeted with a wide smile. "Care for a nighttime treat? Steamed milk and honey with raspberry biscuits."

There were two cups on the circular tray she'd brought with her.

I smiled. "That's very thoughtful of you. Would you care to join me?"

Not that I'd needed to ask, seeing as how she was already pushing her way past me and into the room.

"Oh, well, if you insist."

"Mabel Harrison!"

"Ah!" Foamy milk splashed across the silver tray as Mabel jolted. "Oh, for heaven's—what are you doing here at this hour?"

"I could ask you the same thing, couldn't I?"

"*Meowrrr*," Toebeans complained, ears twitching. Ruckus wasn't tolerated in his vicinity.

Mabel started again. "Good lord, any other living thing lurking in this room that I should know about?"

"Just us," I assured her. "That's Toebeans. He's chill if you don't invade his personal bubble."

"He doesn't like strangers," Molly clarified.

"Does he not?"

Molly nodded. "He does not."

"Oh, well, we're used to that in this house, aren't we?"

"That's exactly what I said."

I sank onto the couch, grabbed my still-steaming cup, and settled in for the ride.

"You said you were going to take the teas to the library," Mabel accused her sister as she set down her ruined tray.

"And you said you were headed straight to bed!"

"Yes, well, I couldn't very well tell you what I was really up to, could I? You'd have had my head if you knew," Mabel said.

"And you'd have had mine."

"Bloody right. What do you think you're doing, going against Jackson's orders?"

"Well, I couldn't just sit back and let this opportunity pass by, could I?"

"And I could? It'd weigh on my conscience if I did, wouldn't it? Drag me straight to an early grave."

"That's the whole point, isn't it? What would he do then?"

"We can't just not do anything about it."

"Exactly why I'm here. It's well worth a shot."

"And?" Mabel looked between me and her sister expectantly. "Have we come to an agreement?"

"Not yet," Molly said, palms bracing on her knees as she sat down again.

"And why not? It's all straightforward, isn't it?"

"It is not. I was just about to tell her about Richard and how we initially came on when you barged in."

"Why does she need to know all that for? Just ask her to do the damn thing. Time is of the essence, Molly. The girl only has thirty days."

"Why don't you do it, then? If *you're* so bold."

"Well, all right." Mabel rubbed her hands together decidedly before placing them on her hips. "Miss Paquin, we need you to find Jackson a life partner."

"That's... sort of what I'm here for," I said.

Molly shook her head. "No, dear. You're here to try, but you've already given up on him. We saw your interaction earlier tonight, didn't we?"

"We need you to *want* to help him. It's the only way this will work."

My brows knit together as I looked between them. "I'm so confused. Why does everyone want this man to be in a relationship when he clearly couldn't be less interested?"

"Minerva has her own reasons," Molly said briskly.

"We're not very happy with the way she's handling it, but that's not what's important right now."

"We raised that boy, Mabel and I did."

"Hired two weeks before the Young Master was born, and we were both at the hospital when Richard Sinclair was told he finally had an heir. Watched him walk straight out of the room and go back to work."

"Our titles have changed over the years, but we've been looking after Jackson just the same, haven't we?"

"We have. We've been there since he took that very first breath, and believe you me, Miss Paquin, we've seen and heard it all. Even the things that weren't meant for our eyes or our ears."

"And we can't blame him for how it's all turned out, can we?"

"Would have left a blister in my mouth too, had I been in the poor boy's shoes."

"I don't think that's the expression, Mabel."

"Is it not?"

"No, love. It's bitter taste. Blister sounds much more unpleasant," Molly said.

"Well, then it's just more accurate, isn't it?"

"Either way, he's mistaken, dear. Or maybe misled is the better word. Or maybe—oh, I don't know. Mabel, you explain it."

"He's afraid is what it is," Mabel said boldly. "That's the root of it. Petrified of it happening to him. And who wouldn't be?"

"But we can't let it just go on like this, can we? He has us now, but what happens when we're gone?"

"He needs companionship," Mabel said to me. "Someone who understands him. Someone he can confide in."

"How else would we be able to rest? There's no other way."

"We'd be tossing and turning in our graves with worry. We can pay you, of course—"

"I already tried that," Molly said. "She won't take the money."

"Well, why not? We're asking you for a service."

I slid forward on the couch, putting my cup down. "Okay, listen, I understand what you're trying to do for Jackson. It's obvious that you care about him, and while this is all very sweet, I gotta be honest—I can't force someone into a relationship if it's not what they want. And I *absolutely* can't force them to fall in love."

There was a short pause as Molly and Mabel glanced at each other, and I had a distinct feeling they were exchanging more than just looks.

"We're not asking you to force him into anything, dear," Mabel said.

"That wouldn't work well at all, would it?" Molly agreed.

"No, it would not."

"The boy is too stubborn to be pushed into doing anything he doesn't want to."

"And love isn't something you can control, is it?"

"It is not. He can't be forced into love, but he also can't stop it from happening, can he?"

Mabel nodded. "No one can. That's what we're trying to say."

"What we need from you is to set up the opportunity. Find him someone who speaks his language, who *understands* him. Someone he can't resist."

She said it like it was just that easy. Like she wasn't asking for a miracle.

Molly shifted in her seat when I didn't respond. "We know you've had a hard time getting the information you need from him. And I assure you, regardless of what program he's forced into, it's not going to get better."

"He's already made enough temporary adjustments to skew your data. And don't get me started on the interviews you have planned."

"You won't be able to get any of the answers you really need. Not in thirty days."

Following their back and forth was sort of like watching a tennis match. They didn't even pause.

"Minerva did say that she required him to at least cooperate," I said.

"Oh, that won't matter," Mabel insisted.

"You don't know him very well yet, Miss Paquin, but believe you me, that boy is *sharp*."

"We taught him better than to lie, but he'll speak in partial truths is what it is."

"Give you just enough to satisfy your requirements, but leave out the parts that actually matter."

I crossed my arms, leaning back again. "Okay. And how do you propose I get the information I need if he's not going to give it to me?"

Molly sat up a little straighter. "Well, that's why we're here, isn't it?"

"We can't give you the information outright, as that would be a breach of trust, but..."

"But we can guide you," Molly finished. "Can't we, Mabel?"

"I don't see why not."

I narrowed my eyes at their careful tone. "Guide me how, exactly?"

If the whole twin communication thing wasn't just a myth, they were doing it right now with all the looks they were exchanging.

"Like, for example," Mabel eventually said. "When Molly needed an excuse to visit you without raising any suspicion, she told me she was taking tea to the library. I believed her as that's not an uncommon task at this hour. Or the next several."

Ah.

I see.

"It's where certain young masters go if they've had a particularly unpleasant day."

"Or if they simply can't sleep."

"I got it, thank you," I said when Molly opened her mouth, presumably to drop more hints.

"Good," Molly said.

"Good," Mabel agreed.

"Then our work here is done, isn't it? We're all in agreement."

I hesitated. "I'm not sure if... I mean, it's lovely that you're both trying to help, but I don't want you to get your hopes up."

They could give me all the correct information, and I could do my best to utilize it, but still. There was no guarantee it would work.

"Well, we won't know unless we try, will we?" Molly said quietly.

"And either way, we appreciate you hearing us out, dear," Mabel said as they both stood. "Enjoy the rest of the pastries. We'll pick up the trays in the morning."

"Wait."

They both stopped, looking up at me with identically curious expressions.

"What was the other thing?" I asked Molly. "You said you needed two favors."

According to the tick of Mabel's brows, she didn't know either.

Color bloomed across Molly's cheeks, and she looked down, fixing her apron. "Yes, right, well. I was just going to say... I know you may not be too fond of him, and I can't blame you for it, but..." Her words trailed off as she met my gaze. "He could really use a friend, you know. Someone closer to his own age. Someone not on his payroll."

My heart kicked when Mabel reached for her sister, squeezing her hand. They really did love him, there was absolutely no doubt about it.

I cleared my throat lightly. "Well, the best romantic relationships are based on strong friendships so... if I'm able to do my job, we'll be killing both birds with one stone."

It wasn't what she was asking of me, but I wasn't a fan

of making empty promises. And telling her that I'd try to be Jackson's friend would be exactly that. I had no desire to befriend a man who'd looked me dead in the eyes and told me my occupation was useless.

Also, I was pretty confident that Jackson wouldn't want to be friends with me, either.

Molly glanced down at her feet. "Not every child grows up with the privilege of—" She stopped short, squeezing her eyes shut once in an attempt to rein back her emotions. "He's one person and he keeps a staff of thirty-one, dear. You do the math."

"Come along, Molly," Mabel said. "We've taken up enough of her time."

She pulled her sister out of the room. But not before Molly could shoot me one last pleading look that tugged at a small, cobwebbed corner of my heart.

12

It was war.

I knew I'd promised Molly and Mabel that I would try, but I'd also promised Jackson that I'd make his life as difficult as possible. And there was no reason I couldn't do both.

Jackson's slim gaze was pinned to my face as I peeled away the last piece of broken shell from my hardboiled egg and slowly bit into it while maintaining unwavering eye contact.

His cheek twitched.

In my defense, he'd had smoked salmon for lunch with a side of what had to be the most pungent sauce known to man. And despite its fantastic ventilation system, his office was still an enclosed space and the smell had lingered long enough to make my eyes water.

So, yeah. We were officially at war.

"Don't you have actual work to do?" I asked when I'd polished off the second egg and he was still glaring. He'd done very little else all morning.

"I delegated the majority of my important tasks to

upper management in preparation for your arrival," he drawled, the casual boredom in his tone in direct contrast to the intense sharpness of his gaze. "After our initial meeting, I suspected you might prove to be disruptive."

"I've barely said a word to you all day." I'd been too busy organizing my data and preparing for our first interview, optimizing the questions to ensure they procured as much information as possible while delivering a sufficient amount of discomfort.

I rolled my eyes when he continued to stare.

"And my job's the joke," I muttered dryly before turning back to the stapled stack of papers in front of me.

Client work ethic: abysmal.

My attention remained on my notes as he got up, his hands slipping into the pockets of his tailored trousers while he made his way across the room with carefully feigned nonchalance.

"And what, exactly, have *you* been working on so diligently all morning?"

He bent over a little when he reached my desk, tainting my air with his fresh, masculine cologne. At least it was better than the salmon.

"None of your concern." Not yet at least. It would be in two days when we sat down for the interview. But for now, he'd have to—

My molars scraped when the papers were smoothly snatched from underneath my pen-equipped hand.

"Ah," Jackson mocked. "The dreaded interview questions."

"Early coaching tip number one thousand—"

"I don't need coaching."

"—it's rude to grab things out of people's hands without permission."

My seated attempts at snatching the papers back were futile. He simply walked away as he flipped through the pages, skimming them.

I was pretty sure that Lao Tzu had some sort of profound rule against allowing your anger to flare during battle, but I knew in my heart of hearts that if he'd ever had the misfortune of meeting Jackson Sinclair, he would have understood.

I was on my feet, heels snapping irritably against hardwood as I rounded my desk.

"Give them back," I demanded when he moved the papers out of my reach.

"Per my contractual agreement with Charmed, I'm entitled to review all the material you'll be using over the next month."

I crossed my arms. "Most people would have asked nicely."

He *tsked*. "Miss Paquin," he practically purred, not bothering to take his eyes off the page, "look at all these extra notes and added inquiries."

I could tell purely from his tone what section he was looking at. My shoulders pushed back, my spine pin straight as his gaze meandered to my face, brimming with amused mischief.

"Naughty, naughty." He *tsk*ed three more times. "These questions are *very* in-depth. Are you truly so curious about my sex life?"

I refused to be embarrassed.

This process was meant to make *him* uncomfortable, not the other way around.

"Sexual compatibility is an important factor to consider when looking at overall longevity and health of any romantic relationship."

"Is it now?" he mocked lightly, taking a full step forward.

Even in my four-inch heels, I had to tilt my head back to maintain stubborn eye contact.

"Of course it is." And of course his team had returned that particular set of questions back to us entirely blank, save for the red NOT APPLICABLE stamp on the front page.

Again, "*They've been provided with more than enough data to find me a suitable match*" my ass.

His wolfish smirk was in full tact as his eyes slipped over my features. "Really? You don't think some of these questions and tactics are just a little too invasive?"

"Our clients know exactly what they're getting into when they sign up for our services."

He held the booklet up in front of me. "And you think *this* is a perfectly appropriate set of questions to hit them with."

"Not everyone has the same intimacy hang-ups as you."

His brows shot up and I took the opportunity to snatch the questions out of his loosened grip.

"Oh, so in addition to selling emotional snake oil, you dabble in psychology, do you?"

Deep breaths.

Deep, calming breaths.

"Love isn't emotional snake oil." For fuck's sake. "Just because you don't believe in something doesn't mean it's not real. Contrary to what you may think, Mr. Sinclair, you're not a god."

I sat back down at my desk, picked up my pen.

He should've retreated to his side of the office and left me alone. Tension cracked between us, our egos revving up for a fight. Nothing good would come from pursuing this argument and we both knew it. Instead of backing away, though, he decided to forge ahead.

"But again, you've never actually experienced it." His tone was dry. Mocking.

I didn't understand how he managed to irritate me so much. I shouldn't have cared if he thought I was a con artist or a fraud or whatever the hell else. Why did it even matter? What was it about this man that turned the calm, rational part of my brain into an overactive volcano?

On the bright side, according to the rabid glint in his eyes, the lack of rational control was mutual. I grated his nerves just as violently as he grated mine.

"I've *witnessed* it." My nails dug into my palm as my fist tightened around my pen.

He scoffed, as though I'd just informed him of my latest Bigfoot sighting. Not willing to let it go, he gestured sharply at my desk. "You'd have no problem answering any of these, then? You'd be comfortable with openly sharing intimate information about yourself with a practical stranger?"

My teeth were set on edge, and it took active effort to keep my voice even when I answered him. "Some of the covered material is sensitive, sure. But no, I'd have no issues discussing them in detail if I were a client."

Admittedly, that may have been a teeny, tiny bit of a bluff, and Jackson was looking at me like he knew it.

Sure enough, his eyes thinned. "*Really*?"

"Yes." It wasn't like I could backtrack now.

That cocky smirk of his was becoming increasingly sneer-like. "Prove it, then."

"No." I went right back to ignoring him, hoping he'd leave me alone.

He did no such thing. Metal scraped against hardwood as Jackson dragged a chair around my desk, shoving it a little too close to mine.

I frowned. "What are you doing?"

Sitting, evidently. Close enough that his giant knee brushed my thigh.

He tapped two firm knuckles against the questionnaire. "All right. Let's do this."

"Do what?"

"The interview."

I inched my chair back; he inched his forward. For the love of—"Our first interview isn't until Friday."

We were barely halfway through Wednesday.

Oh god, we were barely halfway through Wednesday. Of week one.

"Nothing wrong with a head start." He reached over to flip the page and damn it, he smelled so good.

I held back the irritated huff crawling up my chest. If he was doing this to get a reaction, he was going to be sorely disappointed.

I was cool as a cucumber.

There was real power in that—not allowing your opponent to see what you're really feeling. Making them think that, regardless of what they do or say, they have no impact on you whatsoever.

Especially when your opponent wasn't accustomed to people being indifferent about him.

He quirked a brow when I remained quiet. "Unless you're not actually as comfortable with this as you claim," he challenged. "I can imagine how awkward it might be to ask some of these questions and hear their answers."

"I think I'll live."

I wasn't afraid of a little sex talk. I assumed that's what

he planned on torturing me with, given that he was currently thumbing the corner of the "Kinks and Compatibility" page.

"Great." His tone was almost too sarcastic to actually be sarcastic. "Let's dive right in then, shall we?"

"The questions aren't ready yet and I'd rather not—"

He rolled his eyes and I had to remind myself that cool, unbothered cucumbers did not have flashes of nuclear rage or thoughts of deriving pleasure from murdering someone via strangulation. Psychopaths did.

"All right, fine," I seethed calmly. "I guess it wouldn't hurt to go over one or two sections now."

Except when I tried to flip the page, he stopped me, jabbing a finger at the one he'd chosen. "Let's start right here. Since you've been paying so much extra attention to this section."

The page was filled from top to bottom with bright red scribbles, none of which he was supposed to have seen. It was part of the whole *I'm gonna make this process as painful for you as possible* thing we were both doing.

I crossed my legs, clicked my pen, and quirked a professionally curious brow. "You seem very eager to discuss your sexual interests with me, Mr. Sinclair. Any particular reason why?"

"Is that a question from your list?"

"I'm allowed to improvise."

His pupils briefly flared, right before his mouth tilted in a sarcastic smile. "It's because I think you're full of shit, Miss Paquin. I don't believe you're nearly as cavalier about any of this as you're pretending to be, and the fact that you're stalling isn't helping your case."

Once again, I could not believe *this* was the man I'd spent eight months comforting broken hearts over. He was quite possibly the most aggravating human being on the planet. I really didn't get the appeal.

Swallowing back the emotionally charged quip biting at the tip of my tongue, I forced another polite, unaffected smile. "When we initially provided your team with a simplified version of the questionnaire covering this topic, it was returned to us blank and marked as 'not applicable.' I'm surprised you're so enthusiastic to get into it now."

"It was marked as 'not applicable' because it's not applicable," he retorted.

"And why's that?"

"Because I don't plan on having a sexual relationship with my wife."

I almost dropped my pen. My fingers went limp with the momentary shock of the statement, and I blinked, wondering if I'd heard him correctly.

"What... like, at all?" I asked slowly. That had *definitely* not been mentioned by his team.

"Not if I can help it." A satisfied smirk toyed with his lips. He liked that he'd surprised me. "And definitely not in any capacity that would require our fantasies and kinks to be aligned. We'll need to produce an heir or two for the family legacy, but that's it. And that can be done via less traditional methods."

My mouth stuttered for a beat as my brain struggled to catch up. He took it as an opportunity to keep going. "I plan on getting my sexual needs met outside of the marriage," he explained, just in case I hadn't gotten the full picture yet. "With her knowledge and consent, of course. I'm sure she'll also have her own arrangement."

What... just... *what*?

"And you think she'll be okay with that?"

"She'll have to sign off on it before the wedding, so yes," he answered simply. "My lawyers are drafting the paperwork as we speak."

My mouth had slighted open, my brows knit so tight it was bound to lead to a headache. "I'm... confused. You're going to make your future wife sign a bunch of paperwork agreeing to your extramarital affairs?"

"Also known as an open marriage. She'll be encouraged to do the same."

Right. That would be a nightmare scenario for me personally, but so would being married to someone who didn't believe in love. The mere thought sent a chill down my spine.

But, you know, as long as all parties were aware of the situation, and it was all consensual. I just... none of this had been shared with us and it was obviously *very* relevant.

"All right," I said, slowly recovering. "Then I guess it really isn't applicable. Anything else I should know about this agreement your lawyers are drawing up? We're going to need to make sure all future matches are comfortable with your requirements." As neverending as they were.

"I'll provide you with a copy when they're done."

Great. Perfect. Except for a pesky little thing called curiosity that was making the inside of my brain itch. "Can I have a couple of examples? Just so our team can prepare a little in advance."

His mouth quirked. "You're stalling again."

"We've already established that this isn't a relevant topic," I said. "We can move on to a different one."

Something to do with emotional intimacy. He'd hate it almost as much as I despised the way he huffed a knowing chuckle. It scraped against my patience, stripping away what little remained.

"Fine," I accidentally snapped. "I guess it wouldn't hurt to have the data on file. In case you end up changing your mind."

"I guess." Again with the mocking.

I was going to make him regret every life decision he'd made leading up to this point.

Every. Single. One.

I clicked my pen, drew a picture on a blank sticky note, and slid it over to him. "Let's start with the basics, shall we?" I said smoothly, matching his taunting tone. "Tell me, Mr. Sinclair, whereabouts d'you think the clitoris might be?"

13

Client's sense of humor: no signs of improvement.

Jackson Sinclair was looking at me like he was trying his damnedest to Jedi mind murder me. You know what he *wasn't* doing? Pointing to the clitoris in my very well-drawn and anatomically correct illustration.

Client's ability to bring sexual partner to orgasm: likely needs work and—

"You really should stop doing that," I said when he snatched the pen out of my hand. "A short fuse is a red flag for a romantic partner."

"The fact that you believe yourself to be anywhere near qualified to give *anyone* advice on how to conduct themselves is astounding to me."

My eyebrows shot up. "Excuse me?"

"Utterly astounding."

I bristled. "Mr. Sinclair, with zero due respect, the fact that *any* of your previous matches willingly wanted a second date with you is utterly astounding to *me*. You are surly, rude, beyond arrogant, and the most unpleasant and unreasonable client I've ever had the displeasure of working with."

He inched closer, giant shoulders hunching as he crowded me. "Why is it that the pot always insists on calling the kettle black?"

Little patches of anger blotted my cheeks. I bit down on my bottom lip to stop from hurling another string of highly unprofessional insults at him. What *was* it about this man that got me so fucking riled up? I was so annoyed it was making the inside of my skin itch.

That wasn't normal.

His eyes lowered to where my lip was wedged tightly between my teeth, and when they eventually resurfaced, you could barely see the ring of blue ice circling his pupils.

"Go on a date with me."

Wait.

My lip sprang free.

"What?"

"Go on a date with me," he repeated evenly.

He couldn't be serious.

"Absolutely fucking not." The itch was spreading, crawling up my chest, over my throat, into my ears.

"Why not?"

There wasn't a spot left on my body that wasn't either blotted in patchy pink or pleading to be scratched. He was fucking with me. He had to be.

"Jamie."

My heart skipped three full beats before it hurled into my ribs. His accent did… a not entirely unpleasant thing with my name.

"I didn't realize we were on a first-name basis."

"Go to dinner with me."

I swallowed, refusing to break eye contact even though I had no idea what the fuck was going on with my insides. "More coaching advice: when someone turns you down, you shouldn't take it as an invitation to keep asking them out."

"That's the thing," he said. "I know I don't need a dating coach, and you're under the false impression I do. I can't think of a better way to settle this."

Oh.

He didn't want to go on a *date* date, he just wanted to prove me wrong and get out of the whole coaching thing. Yes. Okay. That made a lot more sense.

"The answer's still no."

"Why? Because you know I'm right?"

"Because the absolute last thing I want to do is go to dinner with you again." We'd already established this.

His jaw tightened. "Tell you what, Miss Paquin. You allow me the opportunity to prove to you that I don't need coaching, and if afterward you still believe otherwise, I'll play as docile as you want while you torture me with unwanted advice for the next twenty-odd days. I'll listen to whatever you say and stop arguing with you altogether."

Huh.

Tempting.

"You really wanna skip the coaching that badly?"

"I do."

"Why?"

He quirked a brow. "Would *you* enjoy going on supervised dates?"

No. I imagine it would be kind of embarrassing.

I tapped my foot, considering him. "Tell me something first. Why did you agree to sign up with Charmed in the first place if you're so against the idea of being in a relationship?"

"I didn't agree to it."

"What does that mean? How are you here if you didn't agree to it?"

"Blackmail."

I couldn't tell if he was being serious. "Your aunt is blackmailing you?"

"That she is," he said with another dry smile. "Very much so."

"With what?"

"Company shares. When my father passed away last year, she became the majority shareholder."

There it was. The golden carrot she'd been dangling in front of him.

My head tilted to one side. "Your father left his shares to your aunt?"

That didn't add up with what I knew about him and his family. I was very much under the impression that Jackson had practically been bred to take over the company. He'd taken over as CEO well before his father passed.

"Not exactly, no." He cocked his head. "Technically, he left them to her cat."

Not for the first time during this interaction, my mouth popped open.

"It was to make a point," Jackson said, answering my silent question. "Much like you, Miss Paquin, my father also found me to be... how did you put it? Ah, yes, *abysmally inadequate*." He grinned, but it might as well have been a sneer. "The two of you would have gotten along splendidly. You despise me almost as much as he did."

Well.

This was quite possibly the most awkward predicament I'd ever gotten myself into.

I cringed internally. "I didn't... I never said *you* yourself were..." I couldn't even finish the sentence.

Ignoring me, he tossed my pen onto the desk. "My original deal with Minerva was simple. All I had to do was sign up with Charmed and attend whatever blind date I was set up on, the only caveat being that I *try*. Her tarot reader claimed that I'd meet my wife through the service. One year of participation and the shares would have been mine, regardless of the outcome." He rolled his lips, pausing. "Then you happened."

I had so many questions. "And now..."

"And now I have to get married."

But *why*?

Jackson got up, straightening his tie. "Be ready by seven. I'll take care of everything else."

My stomach swooped. "I haven't agreed to anything yet. I've got more questions—"

"Which I'll be happy to answer on our date."

Was the AC still running? Because it was starting to feel uncomfortably warm in here.

"We're going to need something to talk about, right?" he insisted just as I opened my mouth.

He maybe had a point there. It wasn't like we had anything in common. The potential for painfully long stretches of awkward silences was quite high, so saving the questions was probably a good idea.

I crossed my arms as Jackson sat back down at his desk. He regarded me with a conflicting mixture of amusement and mild annoyance as he waited for another round of my objections.

"If I were to agree, where would we go?"

"To dinner."

"*Where*?"

"A restaurant of my choosing."

"You'd expect someone to go on a first date with you blind? They're going to want to know the location ahead of time, for safety purposes if nothing else."

"This wouldn't be our first date," he said. "It would be our second."

Seriously, it was insanely warm in here all of a sudden. My knees were sweating.

"That's a technicality," I said.

He shrugged like that made no difference.

"At the very least, I need to know what to wear. What's the dress code?"

"I wouldn't worry about that either."

What was he talking about? Had he ever met a human woman?

"This is already going terribly," I informed him.

He rubbed a knuckle across his lips, almost like he was trying to hide an incoming smile. "Humor me, would you?" he said. "It's one night."

"I'll give you one hour," I decided. That was the amount of time he'd allocated to all his dates, so it seemed karmically fair.

His mouth twitched. "Sure. Let's start with that. I'll come get you at seven."

My pulse tripped again, which was odd. There was no reason for it to be skipping any beats.

"Fine. I'm wearing jeans."

I was half-hoping that would goad him into giving me a hint about the dress code, but it only made things worse.

"Wear whatever you want," he said dismissively.

"You're not going to be keeping it on for very long anyway."

And if his mouth hadn't twitched again, indicating that he was, in fact, attempting to make a joke, I'd have *noped* right out of the deal and told him to go shove it.

14

As it turned out, my jeans didn't stay on for very long.

The box arrived at five-thirty on the dot, fifteen minutes after we'd arrived back at the penthouse. It was delivered by a suspiciously cheeky-looking Bensen.

"A gift," he explained, placing the sleek package on the oversized vanity.

Before I could ask him for further explanation, six other members of staff waltzed in, each holding a large round container filled with perfectly arranged pink roses.

"What... is happening?" I asked as the arrangements were peppered on various surfaces across the suite.

Toebeans growled when one of the maids stepped a little too close to the armchair he was occupying, and she immediately thought better of making use of the end table behind him. Smart.

Bensen cleared his throat. "Young Master Sinclair would like you to know that he is very much looking forward to your date this evening."

"Oh that's, um, it's not a real date," I explained quickly, on the very off chance that he wasn't already aware.

"Of course." He was really struggling with the whole not-smiling thing. In fact, he looked about ready to burst into a laugh.

Warmth splashed over my cheeks, which only made him lose further control over his (incredibly misplaced and unnecessary) glee.

"We'll leave you to it, then," Bensen concluded with a slight bow of his head. "I do sincerely hope you enjoy yourself on your non-date date, Miss Paquin."

Okay, well, he didn't need to put it like *that*. It made the fake part of the whole thing sound fake. Which, obviously, it wasn't.

This was a very real fake date.

It wasn't until the rest of the staff started filing out of the room that I noticed their expressions. Bensen wasn't the only one miserably failing to mask his amusement. One of the younger maids stole a brief glance at me as she passed, and I heard the distinct sound of a muffled giggle as soon as the door shut behind them. It was quickly *shush*ed.

Weird.

I swiped my palms over my jeans, frowning at the boxed roses.

This was incredibly excessive for an evaluation date. Which, again, was exactly what this was—a one-hour dinner with the client from hell, just so I could reaffirm what I already knew about his coaching needs. Then I could proceed with my diabolical plans of exacting miserable revenge on him, all the while trying to keep my promise to the Harrison sisters.

Plus, professionally speaking, working with the most accurate data available was generally advised. It would be helpful to know what he was like on a date he wasn't trying to actively sabotage.

I made my way over to the gift Bensen had brought with him, a strange, swirly sensation rushing through me. The box was quite elegant—a luxurious midnight velvet with a cream ribbon knotted tastefully around it. An envelope was tucked beneath its lush bow, and my name was swept over it in delicate cursive.

I reached for it, my blood humming with unexpected anticipation.

One night. Just go with it.

I placed the card down, carefully stripped off the lid, and gasped.

I audibly gasped.

Folded neatly underneath layers of silky tissue paper was a blush-pink dress. A gown, actually, which became evident when I gingerly held up the fabric and watched it spill all the way down to the hardwood. It was, without an iota of doubt, the single most breathtaking item of clothing I'd ever seen in real life.

It shimmered. There were tiny crystals sewn into the buttery fabric, and they glistened delicately every time they caught the light.

It was *magical.*

I had to hand it to him. Jackson Sinclair had fantastic taste in personal shoppers. How had they managed to find something like this so last minute?

On a related note, I had to shave my legs. There was a (*very*) long slit running up the side of the skirt that looked like it would cut all the way to my upper-upper thigh.

"What d'you think, cutie?" I turned to Toebeans,

holding the dress against my shoulders for him to see. "Should I wear it and go along with whatever lunacy The Bad Man has planned? One tail flick for yes, two for no."

The shimmer had managed to capture his wide-eyed attention, and after a few entrapped moments, his fluffy tail swept through the air once. Twice.

Three times.

"That wasn't one of the options," I chided, carefully placing the dress back in its box before stripping out of my jeans.

It was one night. What could it possibly hurt?

~

I was twirl-walking in front of the lengthy wall mirror when the knock came, gleefully watching the liquid fabric dance mesmerizingly around my feet.

He was exactly on time.

"Coming!"

My fingers were a little clumsy as they adjusted the dainty straps of the dress and checked the pins holding my loose updo together, but it was just work nerves. The last time I'd gone on a fake date with a client, it hadn't exactly gone according to plan.

Wiping my palms against the shimmering fabric, I leaned in to double-check for lipstick smudges and loose mascara flakes. I'd stuck to pink and neutral tones for my makeup, except for the delicate black liner sweeping across my upper lids, giving their outer corners a sultry lift.

Oh, and I may or may not have dabbed on the tiniest bit of the emergency perfume I kept in my purse. Not for Jackson, obviously. It was all for The Dress.

The Dress was pure magic.

I loved it more than I'd ever loved any nonliving thing in my life. If it were mine, I'd cuddle it to sleep every night. Every. Single. Night.

I all but pranced to the door, my serotonin levels spiking every time I caught a glimpse of my shimmery pink self on a reflective surface. The slit was sexy as all hell, though it would have been even hotter with the right shoes. I hadn't packed for a black-tie evening though, so a pair of my work heels had to suffice.

They didn't do The Dress the ethereal justice it deserved, but they were better than sneakers.

I paused when I reached for the door handle and realized my fingers were still unsteady. Clearing my throat, I took a deep, grounding breath, not wanting Jackson to mistake my excitement about The Dress for excitement about our non-date date.

I was not excited about our non-date date. If anything, I was dreading it. Because, again, the last one had been a nightmare.

I took another breath.

"Jamie."

I blinked. His voice was crystal-clear from the other side of the door. No wonder he'd overheard me talking to Toebeans the other day.

"What?"

"I can hear you."

I narrowed my eyes at the slab of wood. "I didn't say anything."

"You're breathing very noisily."

"I'm breathing normally."

"Are you that nervous?"

My fingers curled tighter around the silver door handle. "Of course not."

"It's okay if I make you nervous."

"You don't make me nervous," I insisted as an odd, fluttery sensation swept up my chest. What was with him? He sounded different.

"Are you going to open the door, or shall we conduct our date like this?"

Very, *very* different.

His voice had taken on a light, playful edge. Almost flirty. Which, combined with the dress and roses, could only mean one thing: this was another battle within our greater war, and Jackson was bringing out the big guns. The soulless heathen was being charming on purpose.

Which, I mean, if he was trying to prove that he really didn't need a dating coach, I guess that made sense. But still. I wasn't going to let him disarm me so easily.

"Jamie."

"Yes?"

"Could you please open the door now?"

I was getting there. Clearing my throat again, I twisted the handle and calmly pulled. "You're very impatient, you... know..." *Oh.*

Ohkay. Whoa.

Jackson Sinclair was standing outside of my suite wearing a custom-tailored tux.

Complete with a bow tie.

Which, you know, was fine. I was fine, the bow tie was fine, Jackson seemed fine. This was all very perfectly great, and it was going exactly according to plan.

I immediately forced my eyes up to his face, deciding right then and there that for the next hour, Jackson did not have a neck. He was neckless. Like Nearly Neckless Nick or whatever.

But, again, everything was fine. It was just a stupid tie, shaped like a stupid bow, looped around his stupid neck. Nothing special about that.

A slow, wicked grin crawled across his face when I met his gaze. "You wore the dress," he murmured down at me softly. "I thought I'd have to fight you on it."

"I agreed to play along for an hour," I said, refusing to allow my attention to flick downward.

His smile touched the outer corners of his eyes. "You look incredible."

I did. I really did. The Dress was working all its magic on me.

"Thank you," I replied smoothly, ignoring the blush trickling up my neck. He was so symmetrically handsome that it was exhausting. I was already exhausted. "I didn't have the right shoes to wear with it, though."

"Ah. This might help." He reached into the dark shopping bag I hadn't noticed he was holding and pulled out a caramel box. "It would have arrived with the dress," he said, fingers hooking underneath the lid. "But I didn't have your shoe size on hand since you didn't leave those at the bottom of my pool."

Then he *winked*. Like the whole pool incident was an amusing, cheeky inside story that we could laugh about now.

My heart did a funny little flip, but I managed to keep my expression as neutral as possible. That is until he peeled back the lid.

All my facial muscles promptly fell slack. Nude heels with an open square toe, wraparound straps, and tell-tale red bottoms. They were perfect. Quite literally *perfect* for The Dress.

"How… um." I cleared my throat. Again. "How do you know they'll fit?"

"I have my methods."

I narrowed my eyes up at him, but before I could voice any accusations, he said, "I assure you that no one has entered this suite without your presence or permission since you moved in. Your privacy has not been breached."

"Then how?"

"Maybe you should just let it go so we can get on with the date."

"No."

His lips pressed into a line. Then, as though we were the best of buds, he gently nudged my forehead with two knuckles. "It's supposed to be a romantic gesture, Jamie. Allow me a little mystery, would you?"

I eyed him warily, then prodded the tissue paper to the side and glanced at the insole. "It's the wrong size."

I didn't know whether to be relieved that he didn't know my shoe size (because that would be kind of weird) or disappointed. They really were beautiful and would have gone perfectly with The Dress.

Again, his personal shopper had incredible taste in women's black-tie fashion.

He quirked a brow. "What's your actual size?"

"Eight."

"Okay."

He slipped the box back into the bag, placed it beside my door, and reached for… an identical one. There were seven identical bags lined up against the wall to my left.

My mouth popped open.

Jackson twirled his finger in a rewind motion. "The

last two minutes don't count. If this were a real second date, I'd already know your size."

I frowned. "What? How?"

"Because your shoes would have been discarded on my bedroom floor by the end of the first one."

My cheeks flared to life. "That's presumptuous, and so weird. Why would you have taken a look at their size?"

He held up the bag as though the answer was obvious. "Gift-giving purposes."

I didn't know what to say to that. My mouth floundered uselessly for a few seconds which seemed to thoroughly amuse him. His pale eyes swam over my features, crinkling in their corners. Then he leaned forward and in a light, teasing tone, said, "Still think I'm predictable, Jamie?"

So, his love language was gifts. As far as giving was concerned at least. Not entirely *un*predictable, given what I'd observed about his relationship with money. "I'm not sure you want my answer—"

I cut off when it happened.

When Jackson Sinclair *dropped to his knees in front of me*.

"You were saying?" he teased with a knowing smirk. The cocky bastard.

"What the fuck are you doing?" I hissed down at him, taking two full steps back as he methodically removed the box from the bag, the shoes from the box.

"What does it look like?"

I didn't fucking know. My brain was shutting down at the sight of him—and his wide shoulders and stupid *bow tie*—on his knees. Had he lost his damn mind?

"Get up," I demanded.

"Isn't the whole point of this evening for you to see how I'd normally act on a date?"

"This isn't how you'd normally act on a date."

"Ah. Yes," he said dryly. "Because you and I are so well acquainted that you'd know that."

"I think it would have come up in at least one of the post-date conversations I had with your matches if *this* was normal behavior for you."

"I wasn't interested in any of those women."

My pulse kicked. "Jackson."

His fingers stuttered over the leather straps when his name tumbled out of my mouth. After a beat, he looked up at me with a challenging heat in his eyes. "Jamie."

I swallowed, my tongue tying itself into an incoherent knot. We really needed to go back to last names.

Without a word, I snatched the shoes out of his hands and walked back into the suite. Sitting down on the bed, I slipped off my work heels. "Let's set a couple of boundaries for tonight," I decided. I should have discussed limits before agreeing to do this, but better late than never. "The primary focus of this evaluation is your attitude and general conduct, so let's keep the physical contact to a minimum, shall we?" I slipped on a strappy heel, barely able to appreciate its elegance, my heart was racing so fast. "Better yet, let's just go ahead and set a firm 'no touching' rule."

From my peripherals, I saw his head slant to one side. "I can't touch you on our date? At all?"

"There's no need." My eyes remained fixed on my feet. "From a professional standpoint—"

"Please," he interrupted, voice laced with all the scorn I'd grown used to. "Any semblance of professionalism was thrown out the window the moment you looked me dead in the eyes and told me I had the personality of a hard-boiled egg. This isn't how you treat your other clients, and it certainly isn't how you speak to them. You wouldn't still have a job if that were the case. You're not here to actually help me and we both know it."

He was back on his feet, stalking into the room as I continued to wrap and knot the thin leather straps over my calves. "You don't *want* my help, remember? And why would you when you believe I sell emotional snake oil?"

He sighed. "Let's rewind again. This isn't how—"

He was interrupted by the low growl coming from his left.

"I'm nowhere near you," Jackson complained, returning the lethal glare he was being fixed.

"*Mreor.*"

"Might I remind you, *Cat*, that this is my home, and that is my chair."

"*MrEAAAARR.*"

Jackson took two rapid steps back.

"He's like this with all men?" he asked me. "How do you bring anyone home?"

"Not all of them," I said. "He's obsessed with Adrien. Turns into a puddly little cuddle slut around him, don't you, cutie?"

Toebeans perked up at the mere mention of the name, his ears twitching attentively. For the life of us, Ria and I could not understand what it was about Adrien Cloutier that had Toebeans so enamored. But every time—*every time*—that man entered the room, it was like Ria and I didn't even exist. He was walking catnip.

He was also highly allergic and had to take medication before every visit, which only made it all the more endearing.

"Who's Adrien?"

I stood up, testing the heels. They were more comfortable than I was expecting, and oh so pretty. I smiled down at them, tempted to twirl again.

When I looked up, Jackson was watching me with an oddly curious expression. My grin died. "What?"

"You like them."

I blinked. "What? The shoes?"

He nodded.

"Of course I do. They're gorgeous."

"And the dress?"

"Probably the prettiest thing I've ever worn." I pulled on the skirt, watching it shimmer with the movement. I was giddy all over again. "I don't know if everyone would be cool with a guy sending them clothes to wear on their date though, so maybe keep that in mind."

There was a lengthy beat of silence. Then, "And what about you?"

I glanced up at him again, the soft curiosity in his tone throwing me off. Why did he keep asking if I liked things? Why did it matter?

I shrugged. "I didn't think I would, to be honest. But most men don't have the country's best stylists and personal shoppers on speed dial, so... I think it depends on both the clothing and the person. Either way, I'll put this in your file. It's useful to know you like giving gifts, and I'm sure—"

"I don't. Normally."

My brows knit together. "What do you mean?"

"I don't normally enjoy giving gifts. It depends, like you said, on the person."

I paused, processing. "Okay. Because the point of tonight is to see how you'd act *normally*," I reminded him for the umpteenth time. "That's what you're being evaluated on."

Something light flitted across his features, almost like an inadvertent reaction to an inside joke. "Ah, right. Yes. Well then, feel free to include it in your observations."

I eyed him with blatant mistrust, and his mouth jerked like he thought it was funny. Then he held out his hand. "Shall we?"

"I already said we should refrain from any physical contact on our... um, during the evaluation."

"You did say that." His palm didn't drop.

My pulse skipped when our gazes locked. A fluttery and weightless sensation swept through my stomach, and before I could think it through, he was closing the space between us, hand still outstretched, eyes still boring into mine.

When he reached me, he raised an eyebrow in a subtle challenge.

One night.

Just go with it.

I swallowed, my mind going blank as my hand moved slowly, timidly, until my fingers had slipped into his open palm.

His eyes visibly softened, their icy blue thawing as his large hand swallowed mine whole. He smiled then, and it tugged at something dangerously deep inside my chest.

"Good girl," he murmured, so quietly that I almost didn't hear him. Wouldn't have if he wasn't standing so close.

But I did.

I definitely heard him.

And I definitely didn't hate it.

Uh oh.

15

Something was off.

Not with Jackson—I knew exactly what was going on with *him*. He was being as polite and charming as he could stomach because he desperately wanted to wiggle his slick way out of being coached by someone he neither respected nor liked.

What I didn't understand was my reaction to the faux persona he'd adopted for the evening. I knew it was fake, was fully aware that he'd snap right back to being an insufferable ass once the evaluation was over, and yet...

To put it bluntly, I was experiencing a concerning amount of *tingling*.

The sensation was stemming from where Jackson's warm and surprisingly soft fingers were threaded with mine, and slowly spreading up my arm, through my chest, and down to the very tips of my toes.

Almost exactly like an allergic reaction.

It explained the tingling, the subtle flush of my skin as his thumb brushed over my knuckles, and the fact that I was seconds away from breaking out in hives. But as soon as I thought to pull my hand out of his grasp, the noise registered.

We'd taken the elevator up to the roof, and Jackson was leading me toward a set of double doors where Bensen was waiting with a secretive smile and two large headsets.

You have got to be kidding me.

The more we walked, the louder the rapid *fwipfwipfwipfwipfwip* sounds became. I stopped in my tracks, gaping up at Jackson. He was feigning as much nonchalance as he could muster while a knowing smirk tugged at the corner of his resisting mouth.

"Something the matter?" he asked in *that* tone. The expectant one that knew exactly what I was thinking.

But I wasn't going to give him the satisfaction. "Nope."

Jackson released my hand and an unpleasant shiver slithered up my arm, protesting the sudden lack of warmth. I never realized contempt could manifest in such vividly tangible ways. Then again, there weren't very many people I actively disliked, so a lot of this was new for me.

"Where are we going?" I asked.

Jackson picked up a headset. "You'll see."

Bensen was—once again—failing spectacularly at keeping his amusement in check. Weren't butlers supposed to be, like, masters of professional stoicism? Wasn't that a thing?

"I'd kind of rather you tell me now."

Instead, Jackson placed the headset over my ears, rendering the world eerily silent. This was about as good as noise-canceling technology could get, I gathered. I couldn't hear a single thing. Not until he switched on his mic.

"Can you hear me?"

As it turned out, I was also highly allergic to his voice. The stark clarity of it through the headphones poured over me like sizzling honey, making my breath hitch.

He heard it.

Heat bloomed over my cheeks as his smirk died, his glacier eyes thawing at an alarmingly rapid pace. Or maybe my brain was making shit up. It did that from time to time.

Jackson blinked away from me and cleared his throat, signaling at Bensen with a wave.

"Come on." He offered me his hand again. "If we don't go now, we might miss it."

I hesitated. Why wouldn't he just tell me where we were going? And why did we need to take a helicopter to get there?

He huffed a semifrustrated chuckle, which... honestly sounded a little erotic through the headset. His voice was just so deliciously deep. I hated it.

"We're just going to a restaurant. I swear I'm not kidnapping you." And as soon as I opened my mouth to ask, he said, "You've given me one hour. I'm not wasting half of it fighting traffic. That's why we're not driving."

All right. Fine. Evening traffic in downtown Toronto was an absolute nightmare, I'd give him that.

His brows pulled together when I still didn't give him my hand. "Do you truly have so little faith in me?"

"Yes."

There was a short beat of silence, and then he smiled. Full-on grinned like this was excellent news. Unsurprisingly, I found that I was also allergic to his happiness. My pulse spiked as the corners of his eyes crinkled with delight.

"You want to know a little secret?" He still hadn't dropped his hand.

"Only if it's relevant to helping me find you a suitable match." I had very little interest in learning anything about him otherwise.

I swear his eyes were twinkling as they slid between mine, his smile jerking. "I kind of like it when you're mean to me."

My eyebrows shot to my hairline. "Pardon?"

Bensen placed one hand on Jackson's shoulder and made a signal I didn't recognize.

"All right, we have to go."

This time, I wasn't provided with the option to hesitate. His fingers slipped over mine, gently pulling me toward the double doors.

My lips parted when we stepped out onto the rooftop. The chopper was way bigger than I'd been expecting. Very black, very sleek, and *very* large. Were all helicopters this huge? I'd never seen one up close before.

Jackson's soft chuckle vibrated through my headphones, and I realized I was gawking. My mouth snapped closed and remained that way… until we stepped inside.

Holy shit.

The cabin looked like it'd been plucked straight out of a compact private jet. I'd never been in one of those either, but I'd seen pictures. It was so roomy in here. And *swanky*. The space was entirely closed off, a champagne-colored partition separating us from the operators.

Speaking of champagne, there was a bottle waiting for us on the table.

Jackson pulled me inside while I continued to gap at my surroundings. Was the concept of luxurious helicopter travel common knowledge? Because the idea had never so much as crossed my mind before this.

I sunk into the plush window seat, biting back my grin as best I could. It didn't work. There was far too much excitement bubbling up my chest. Not for the date—sorry, *evaluation*—obviously. But for the ride. I had to admit, this was pretty cool. Once in a lifetime experience for sure. After tonight, I'd likely never ride in one of these things again.

Jackson took the seat next to mine, even though there was a perfectly good window-adjacent one right across the table. "Is that a smile I see, Miss Paquin?"

"No, it's actually a grimace."

He chuckled quietly, then leaned forward and pulled my seatbelt over my lap, clipping it in place.

A few more items to add to my growing list of life-threatening allergies:

1. Whatever cologne he was always wearing.

2. My body being forced into close proximity with his body.

3. His bow tie (which I was absolutely *not* internally obsessing over).

4. Him clipping my safety belt into place for me.

I was very, *very* allergic to Jackson Sinclair doing a thoughtful thing. Even if it was in fake thoughtfulness and fueled by not-so-secret ulterior motives.

My symptoms were made significantly worse by the fact that he was still—very unnecessarily, might I add—holding my hand. Why was he still holding my hand?

But before I could slip out of his grasp, he lifted our joint hands and guided my fingers to a small circular indent on the left side of my headset.

"If you push this button, it'll activate the intercom

function and you'll be able to communicate directly with the crew." My finger moved again. "This is the one you've got on now. It's just you and me. No one else can hear what we're saying. If you want to mute me at any point, then all you have to do is press this—"

I wasted no time. His voice cut off abruptly and I grinned.

Jackson bit down on his bottom lip, finally releasing my fingers so he could unmute himself.

"Is that really appropriate behavior for a second date, Miss Paquin? Should I be taking notes?"

I lifted a shoulder. "If I've agreed to go on a second date with someone it's pretty safe to assume they have a solid sense of humor."

"Is that what you—"

He was cut off by a sudden *beep*, just before our pilot's voice came on the headset to do a quick pre-flight briefing.

I barely heard her, though. My stomach dipped and swooped as we began to lift, and within a handful of seconds, I understood why Jackson had insisted on rushing us out the door. The sunset.

Damn. Okay. Full points for the pre-dinner part of the evaluation. This whole scene was breathtakingly romantic; I was in absolute awe of the view.

When I finally peeled my gaze away from the soft oranges and bruised pinks of the sky, I found him watching me with a triumphant smirk pulling at the one side of his arrogant mouth. Not only that, but the bottle of champagne had been opened, and two delicate flutes filled with sparkling golden liquid were already sitting on the table.

Smooth. Almost unreasonably so.

Jackson picked up his glass, tilting it toward me, and... um... there was a lot of golden light spilling into the cabin from the sunset and, unfortunately, it kind of complemented his everything.

It wasn't until his victorious little smirk expanded to a full grin that I realized I was staring.

"Like what you see?" he teased playfully as I snatched up my own flute.

"Don't flatter yourself, Mr. Sinclair," I quipped easily, touching the lip of my glass to his. "You don't meet any of the items in my criteria for a partner. Looks included."

I couldn't help the slight bitterness that seeped into my tone during that last part. His criteria had been my hell for eight months. I still wasn't over it.

I sank into the plush comfort of my seat, my attention turning back to the painted skies as I sipped on my champagne. This was nice. Significantly better than crawling through the congested roads of downtown Toronto in a car. He'd done well.

"I see." And then, "What is it about my physical appearance that doesn't appeal to you, exactly?"

Spoken well and truly like a man who was too attractive to have experienced a healthy amount of rejection in his life.

"My preferences aren't relevant to the evaluation or the job I'm here to perform," I said.

"Are you exclusively into women, then?"

I had to bite my cheeks to stop myself from laughing. Imagine the level of confidence you'd need to automatically zipline to that conclusion instead of just accepting that someone simply wasn't attracted to you.

Was *confidence* the right word?

"Again," I said, "my preferences don't matter. Only yours do."

He frowned as he sipped his drink. "And what about Adrien? Does he meet your preferred list of physical attributes?"

It was my turn to frown. That was kind of unexpected.

"Adrien," he repeated, misinterpreting my confusion. "The one Cat likes."

"His name is Toebeans."

"No, I definitely remember you saying it was Adrien."

My eyes slimmed. "And I definitely remember you saying you didn't have a sense of humor."

"That is correct," he said flatly. "I don't need one. I have a lot of money."

He almost got me with that one. I almost laughed. But I didn't want to give him the satisfaction, so I swallowed it back with a large sip of golden bubbles.

I'd add it to his file later—the dry sense of humor thing. Some people were into that.

You're into that.

Thankfully, before I could spiral into an internal argument with myself, we began to dip into a slow and smooth descent. I leaned closer to the window, trying to see where we were landing.

Another rooftop from the looks of it.

I didn't get it. The helicopter ride had been really cool and all, but Jackson was well aware that the evaluation was on his mannerisms and behavior. With the limited amount of time allotted, he would have been better off choosing his apartment as the setting. Especially since we were just doing dinner.

I didn't get it... until I did.

Until we took the elevator down to the twenty-sixth floor and I saw what—or rather *who*—he had planned.

I stopped dead in my tracks when the scene registered, my mouth falling open. I gaped up at Jackson with wide, disbelieving eyes.

"Shut up," I hissed as his grin grew increasingly more triumphant. "Shut. *Up*."

He'd won.

Motherfucker had won the whole night, and I was way too shocked and excited to be mad about it.

16

My borderline unhealthy obsession with the seventh season of *Chef Wars International* started exactly four and a half years ago, and it was all Ria's fault.

I'd been on day three of the godawful stomach bug that had reduced me to a useless, couch-ridden blob of vomit and cold sweat, watching Ria dick around on her phone when it happened. She clicked a video of fresh, still-squirming octopus tentacles being served raw on Yet Another Cooking Show. (Seriously, how many of them did there need to be?)

Under normal circumstances, I'd have been intrigued. But these were not normal circumstances. I was at the cruel mercy of a microscopic bug that considered raw, wiggling tentacles to be about as appetizing as moldy foot cheese.

I'd barely made it to the toilet in time.

Now why would that, of all experiences, create an all-consuming obsession with that particular season of a TV show I couldn't have cared less about until that one defining moment?

Because of *him*.

Daniel Omori.

Seconds before my very life was being violently yanked out of my empty stomach, I'd caught a glimpse of the sexiest dimple to have ever bracketed anyone's chin, tucked just underneath the most endearing, boyish smile to have ever been smiled.

I didn't stand a chance. My inner hopeless romantic immediately took over and, as soon as I could stomach it, I'd binged the whole season.

Three times. In the span of four weeks.

He was the youngest competitor that year, a complete underdog in terms of schooling and experience, yet he'd still managed to win. Oh, and his best friend and the love of his life was Maple, his blind, three-legged golden retriever.

I mean... how could I *not* have fallen into immediate infatuation with him?

To this day, the viral photo of him celebrating his win with Maple in his arms was my desktop background, which... if that was how Jackson figured it out, I also needed to add "impressively observant" to his profile, because it was impressively observant.

I grinned up at Jackson, well beyond the point of controlling my emotional expressions. "How... just... *how*?"

We were quite literally on the set of the show. Or more plausibly, an insanely accurate recreation of it. Everything was here—the cooking stations, the judge's table, the signature branding. The only real difference was the massive Teppanyaki grill set up in the back, complete with two place settings and a very tall, very real Daniel Omori dicing something behind the bar.

He was here.

Not in Tokyo, running his world-famous restaurant.

He was *here*. In Toronto.

Breathing the same air as me.

My heart was pounding inside my throat.

Jackson's shoulders ticked up with cocky pride as he took in my reaction. He stood a little straighter. "You see? Much better as a surprise, is it not?"

Yes. Yeah. Absolutely. This was hands down the coolest thing that had ever happened to me.

"Is it just us here?" I asked quietly, my gaze sliding back to Daniel's tattooed forearms. He'd gotten so many new ones since the show. I couldn't wait to ask about them.

"Yes. We have him for the full night. Or, in your case, another thirty-eight minutes since you insist on ending our date right on the hour."

I was aware that he was teasing me, I just didn't care. I was seconds away from meeting my celebrity crush and, as luck would have it, I was wearing a dress that made me look like a literal princess. It couldn't be more perfect.

Ignoring Jackson's quip, I ran my hands over the front of my dress and adjusted its straps, casting nervous little glances toward the Teppanyaki grill. I was tempted to run to the bathroom, wanting to check my makeup and make sure I didn't have anything stuck in my teeth.

But when I looked up at Jackson again, I found him watching me with less arrogance and more uncertainty clouding his expression.

"What?" I asked.

He hesitated for a beat. "You're a fan of the show, correct?"

"Yes. Sure." The show. Daniel's generously tattooed biceps and chin dimple. Same dif. "Shall we go?"

His fingers curled around my arm, making me pause midstep. "And you have a picture of that guy on your laptop... because he won. And he's a famous sushi chef... and you like sushi. That's all."

I blinked, confused by his tone. Why did he sound like he was trying to convince himself of the reasoning behind my choice of desktop backgrounds?

"Uh, sure. Yup. Can we go now?" I threw another longing look toward Daniel, rapidly running out of what little chill I still possessed.

And oh. My. Fucking. God.

He looked up at the same time I did and *smiled* at me. It was glorious. Heart-throbbingly *glorious*. I beamed back, waving at him—

"Hey!" My grin died when Jackson tugged my arm, pulling me back the way we'd come. "Where are we going?"

"Leaving," he bit out, shoving at the elevator button.

Disappointment weighed on my shoulders, making them sink an inch. My heart dropped. "What? Why? We just got here."

He adjusted his bow tie, a muscle ticking across his jaw. "I miscalculated."

What? I glanced down at my phone. "No, you didn't. We still have over a half-hour left like you said."

For the life of me, I couldn't decipher the look that response earned me. Jackson held my gaze as the elevator doors slid open... and closed again. The allergies were back.

As were the tingles.

I slipped my arm out of his grip. "Okay," I relented, smoothing my palms over my dress again. "Where would you like to go instead?"

He didn't answer right away. Then, "Not sure yet."

Was he serious?

"What's wrong with this place?" I asked. "You very clearly went through a lot of trouble. It couldn't have been easy to get Daniel Omori here on such short notice."

I'd agreed to the evaluation less than eight hours ago. Daniel was a famous chef who lived on the other side of the world. Pulling this off seemed more than a little impossible to me.

"How the hell did you manage to even get him here on time?" I asked. Wasn't the flight from here to Japan like fourteen hours or something? "How did you get him to *agree*?"

"Money," Jackson said simply. "Most people are willing to do anything if you offer them enough of the stuff. And he flew in from New York, it's not a big deal."

That made even less sense. Why was he trying to downplay it?

I crossed my arms. "So, you spent all that money on a celebrity chef, and you want to leave before you even get to taste the food?" I was missing something. What was I missing?

He rolled his lips. "Like I said, I miscalculated."

And since he very clearly wasn't talking about the time, I had no idea what—

"Hey, you guys ready to eat?"

Judging by the way both our heads snapped toward the new voice, Jackson hadn't heard Daniel sneak up on us either. My pulse jumped, my mouth going dry as I struggled to recall the proper cultural protocols for greeting someone you were meeting for the first time.

Because *oh my god*, his accent! It was even more deliciously Australian in person.

Daniel's friendly smile widened as he met my star-struck gaze, the adorable little dimple on his chin digging deeper. I returned his smile, the connection between my brain and my mouth mending as my hand shot out.

"Hi!" Was that my voice? That didn't sound like my voice. It was four pitches higher than I remembered it being. "I'm Jamie?"

Nope.

That was meant to be a statement. Not a question.

"Danny," he said humbly. As if he wasn't Daniel frickin' Omori, internet sensation of my heart. As if his chin dimple didn't have its own Instagram fan account with half a million followers.

"It's nice to meet you, Danny." And it was. It really, really was—

I inhaled sharply, my grin faltering when a large hand slid gently over my lower back. It wasn't the gesture that made me gasp (though that was also rather surprising), but the electric current that shot up my spine in response to the deceptively possessive touch.

Jackson's fingers splayed across the thin fabric of my dress, covering a surface area so impressively large that it made my mind go blank.

It was to the point where I missed whatever was said next. I heard the words, but they didn't register over the swarm of sparks floating through my body, ignited by the gentle stroke of Jackson's thumb.

What the hell?

I blinked, trying to clear the static from my mind as Daniel asked yet another question I actively missed.

No, seriously, what the hell?

What was wrong with my body? I felt flushed, my heart was racing again, and before I even knew what I was doing, my shoulder pressed to Jackson's broad chest, leaning into him for support.

He stiffened when it happened, but as soon as I went to correct my posture, his hand slipped to my waist and pulled me against him.

And *ooohmmkay*. The man was about as soft as marble, and those sparks from earlier? They were everywhere now. My skin was doused in electricity.

Before I could make another feeble attempt at putting distance between our bodies, Daniel turned around with a polite smile and walked away.

What was going on? Were we leaving?

Jackson's palm pushed into my hip ever-so-slightly before I could ask, and my body intuitively followed the silent command, falling into smooth step beside him. I slid into a curved stool as Daniel made his way behind the bar. It was happening. It was really happening.

I mean, my initial excitement had somewhat waned, but that was to be expected. What *wasn't* expected was Jackson hooking his fingers under the edge of my seat and pulling me a foot closer to him in one smooth motion.

"What are you doing?" I whispered, frowning at him.

He wasn't even sitting properly. His body was turned toward me, legs spread shamelessly to accommodate the fact that my stool was all but tucked between his knees.

"You're the relationship expert," he said. "What do you think I'm doing?"

First of all, "I'm a matchmaker, not a relationship expert."

Second of all, "If I knew, I wouldn't ask."

Third of all, his eyes were, um, even more striking up close. They were at least five different shades of winter blue, cutting over one another like thin shards of ice fighting for dominance—

I'm sorry, but what the actual fuck are you talking about? Shards of ice? Fighting for dominance? Are you okay?

No. I was not okay. I was familiar with what okay felt like, and this was not it. Breathing was a lot easier when I was okay.

"I'll give you a hint," Jackson murmured darkly. His pupils ate away at the surrounding color as he leaned to whisper in my ear. "I don't share, Jamie."

The sparks had infiltrated my brain. I couldn't think.

"I'm a selfish, selfish man." His nose accidentally brushed the shell of my ear and I jolted.

"I'll make sure to add that to your profile." My voice cracked.

Jackson leaned back again, a secretive smile toying with his mouth. "Eat."

I blinked down at the twin small plates sitting in front of us. The same ones that had been empty a second ago. When had Daniel—holy shit, I'd forgotten about Daniel.

I blinked again, giving my head a small shake. How was that even possible? What the hell had been in that champagne?

I picked up the small piece of... I couldn't remember what it was.

"Uni," Daniel supplied, reading the impending question on my face. He was working a small serving of rice in his palm, prepping it for the next dish.

"It's delicious." I could barely taste it.

It wasn't the uni, it was me. Daniel continued to place several artfully crafted dishes in front of us, explaining each one in meticulous detail. There'd been well over a handful of them so far and, gun to my head, I wouldn't have been able to recall a single one.

You want to know why?

Because Jackson's knee was brushing mine underneath the bar, his hand was draped possessively over the back of my chair, and he was *still* wearing a bow tie. But at least he wasn't whispering things in my ear anymore—

I started when my alarm went off, indicating our hour was up. I fumbled with my phone and proceeded to miss the Stop button three times before my unsteady thumb finally found it.

"I'm so sorry," I said to Daniel as hot embarrassment sprinted up my neck.

He didn't look impressed. After almost thirty minutes of receiving distracted, half-hearted praises for his world-renowned cooking, my alarm had startled the tin of caviar out of his grip. It'd landed facedown on the grill, sizzling and ruined. "It's fine."

Judging from his tone, it wasn't. I couldn't believe I'd been so rude, or that I hadn't thought to turn off the stupid alarm earlier.

Clearing my throat, I offered him a polite smile as he carefully peeled the lid off a fresh gold tin. "I really am sorry," I pressed. "That was very rude of me. I was just so nervous and excited to meet you that I forgot to turn it off before we sat down."

Jackson's knee pressed to mine. I crossed my legs, effectively breaking contact.

Daniel smiled back. Just a little. "Oh yeah?"

"You have no idea." I leaned in and placed my forearms on the bar, giving him my full attention. When Daniel's shoulders rose an inch, I forced my smile wider.

"You're a fan of the show?" he asked.

"Kind of. Season seven is my favorite. You know that episode where they brought Maple in for the first time?"

His eyes twinkled as he nodded. It was working.

Jackson's knee pressed to my thigh again as he leaned forward. I ignored him; he could have my attention again in a minute. I needed to fix this first.

"Probably my favorite TV moment of all time," I said. It was so sweet. They'd flown the contestants' families in for moral support during the tenth episode of the season, but since Daniel's grandmother —the only living member of his family—was too old to travel halfway across the world, they'd brought Maple in instead. The three-legged, blind golden retriever had trotted onto the set a little nervously at first... until Daniel said her name in shock, a half-second before sinking onto his knees and breaking down into her fur as she whined with uncontainable excitement.

Oh, and attached to her collar was a handwritten letter from Daniel's grandmother.

There hadn't been a dry eye in the room. Any room. Anywhere in the world, probably.

Ria and I had lost it. We'd had to rewind the clip three times to actually hear him read the letter out loud, we'd been sobbing so hard.

"Eating at your restaurant in Tokyo is on my bucket list," I told him, encouraged by his reaction.

He chuckled, sliding two identical sashimi dishes in front of us. "Toro sashimi with beluga caviar."

This time I forced myself to actually pay attention to the flavors and... yeah, okay. "This is genuinely incredible."

"That's Maple's favorite caviar." He was all smiles now.

Also, I loved the way he said *caviar*. His accent made the word sound utterly exquisite.

"Maple has a favorite caviar?"

He shook his head. "She's so spoiled now. The last time I tried giving her dry kibbles she wouldn't even touch it."

I giggled. "Cute."

Jackson cleared his throat rather pointedly, and just as I was about to pull him into the conversation, Daniel gestured between us and asked, "So how long have you two been together?"

"Oh, we're not."

I said it, and then I regretted saying it. Not because it wasn't true, but because it could not have tumbled out of me any faster.

Daniel's eyes slid between us slowly, his smile tilting with confusion.

"I mean... this isn't"—My hand flapped between me and Jackson as I tried to think of the right words—"It, uh, I'm his dating coach."

That one I regretted saying altogether.

I couldn't see Jackson's expression from this angle but the gloomy cloud of disapproval forming around him was making the hairs on the back of my neck rise.

"You're his dating coach?" Daniel gave an entertained, disbelieving laugh. "What does that mean?"

"Oh, it's um... long and boring to explain. Sounds more exciting than it is."

"I doubt that," he said. "Truffle butter lobster sashimi."

It didn't escape me that Jackson hadn't touched his last two dishes. He also made no indication that he was going to try this one.

"Tell me, how close is the real thing to the Will Smith movie?" Daniel asked.

"*Hitch*," I supplied with a polite laugh. "And not close. I actually work at Charmed Elite. It's a matchmaking..."

I trailed off when his expression changed.

"No way." He crossed his arms, soft brown eyes lighting up. "One of my investors met her wife through you guys. She's been pushing me to sign up for a while." Then, "You got a card on you?"

Um. I did. Yes.

But I hesitated as something unpleasant snaked through my gut.

Technically, this wasn't a real date. And even if it was... it wasn't like Daniel was asking for my contact information for personal reasons. Asking for someone's business card because you were interested in their professional services was not the same as asking for their number.

So, this was fine. We were well within respectable boundaries here.

"I don't have any on me. Sorry."

Under the bar, Jackson's knee brushed my thigh gently. A praise.

My cheeks darkened for literally no reason. I'd lost my mind.

"All right, well, take mine." After wiping his hands, Daniel quickly nabbed a sleek white card out of his back pocket and placed it in front of me.

Just like that, I had Daniel Omori's direct contact information staring up at me, ready for use. Ria was going to die when I told her.

"Call me, yeah? We'll set up an appointment at my restaurant if you want, so you can cross it off your list. Janice said you guys are willing to fly out wherever?"

Wherever. Whenever.

It was all covered in the hefty signup fee for members.

I took the card. "Sure. I'm on a full-time case for the next few weeks, but I can connect you to—"

I cut off when he shook his head. "I'm not in a rush."

Okay, but I also wasn't planning on staying at Charmed once the Immersive was over. But, at this point, it felt like more excuses would push things into awkward territory and make it seem like I was actively discouraging a potential client from signing up for our services, which I really shouldn't have been doing.

So, I slipped the card into my phone case with a smile and said, "Cool. We'll be in touch."

On a completely unrelated note, Jackson didn't say anything else for the rest of the meal.

17

THE HELICOPTER RIDE back to the apartment was arguably even more scenic than the first, what with the dark skies and city lights. Unfortunately, it was also excruciatingly more silent.

Neither of us said a word during the entire ride. For Jackson's part, it was likely because the evaluation was over, and he had no reason to engage with me anymore.

For me, it was more... well, I didn't actually know. I just felt weird.

At one point during the flight, Jackson's hand accidentally grazed mine on the armrest and you know what happened? My breath hitched, my stomach flipped, and my pinky twitched like it wanted to do it again. He'd *barely* touched me.

After it happened, I thought I saw him straighten in a way that indicated he was about to say something, but he seemed to change his mind. And by the time we landed, I physically couldn't stand the tension anymore. It was beyond suffocating.

"We can discuss the results of the evaluation tomorrow," I said in what I hoped was a calm, professional tone as we entered the penthouse. "Thanks for dinner. Have a good rest of your night."

And I was so weirdly tuned in to him tonight that I could feel his gaze linger on my back as I retreated, almost like a gentle touch.

The door to my suite banged shut with more force than I intended, making Toebeans sit up in vigilant alarm.

"Sorry," I mumbled, unstrapping my heels.

He yawned before flopping over on the bed, looking at me expectantly. He required belly rubs to accept my apology.

I huffed a small laugh as some of the tension in my shoulders eased. "Give me a minute, I just gotta get out of this..."

What the hell?

I pulled at the zipper harder, my contorted arm groaning with the stretch and added pressure. It wouldn't budge.

"Damn it." I shook out my arm before trying again. And again.

On my fourth attempt, with my muscles strained and my teeth bared, I finally felt it give... then snap clean off.

Fuck me, are you joking?

How did I have such terrible luck with expensive dresses? They couldn't all be like this. It had to be me.

"Okay, I need a strategy," I said to Toebeans, trying not to panic about the broken zipper.

I mean, it was a *zipper*. How much could it possibly cost to replace?

Swallowing down the fresh bout of anxiety telling me I'd go into debt because of a tiny piece of metal, I shoved the straps off my shoulders and tried to shimmy out of the dress. The fabric got stuck around my hips, refusing to be pushed down.

So, then I tried it the other way—carefully bunching the delicate skirt up before attempting to pull it over my head. And it might have worked, had I not made a teeny, tiny, catastrophically fatal mistake. I'd forgotten about the heels. They were off my feet, but instead of tucking them to the side, I'd left them *right there.*

Right in the way.

So, when I took an inadvertent step forward during my struggles with the dress, I, of course, stepped on one of them.

And I, of course, rolled my ankle.

And I, of course, tripped backward, the weight of my body shoving at the vanity behind me until it scraped across the hardwood.

And I, *of course*, did all of this while completely blind because half of my gown was still gathered around my face.

The loud, ominous *creak* was my one and only warning, followed by two full seconds of silence—just long enough to provide a false sense of security.

I started to lower my arms. Right before something hard and obscenely heavy smashed over my head and shattered.

18

Ow.

I blinked against the pink fabric as a throbbing ache bloomed over the crown of my head. My arms lowered carefully, pulling the dress back down so I could see what—

Bang. Bang. Bang. "Jamie?"

Two things. One, that shattering sound had been the vanity mirror. The very large, very broken-into-tiny-pieces vanity mirror. Two, Jackson's knocks startled the shit out of me, they were so aggressively loud.

He was going to be so fucking pissed.

"Yes?" I called shakily, scanning the room for Toebeans. He wasn't on the bed anymore.

"Are you okay? What was that sound?"

I chewed on my bottom lip, assessing the damage. There was glass *everywhere.* All over me, the hardwood floor, surrounding my bare feet.

"Jamie."

I couldn't tell if he really did sound panicked or if I

was assigning him emotions as some sort of coping mechanism. Panic was better than rage in this instance.

"Um... yeah, just fine."

A pause. "You don't sound fine."

"Oh."

That was it. That was all I could come up with.

"Can I come in?"

"Wait, let me just..." What? How was I supposed to clean this all up without help? I couldn't exactly walk over shattered glass with my bare feet to grab supplies.

Also, I didn't know where the brooms were kept in this house, but it probably wasn't in my suite. Either way, he was going to see the mess.

"Okay," I eventually said. "Come in."

The door handle was being twisted before I was done giving shaky permission. Jackson stepped into the room with purpose and promptly froze when he saw me.

"You, um, really need to stop hanging outside my suite like a stalker, w-weirdo."

Jackson's eyes were scanning the situation, sliding between me and the floor. "You have glass on you," he said flatly. It was a statement. There was absolutely no emotion behind it.

"Oh yeah, that's because it fell on my head."

His eyes flared, shoulders tensing.

"I think your house might be trying to murder me," I whispered.

He didn't smile, though. He didn't have a sense of humor.

I cleared my throat softly. "Because, you know, first the whole pool thing and now this," I overexplained. "Or maybe the universe is trying to tell us to stop going on dates. I mean, I know you don't believe in that stuff, but what are the chances?"

Two not-real dates ending in almost-real deaths.

Jackson didn't seem like he was listening. He was just walking toward me slowly, glass crunching underneath his fancy black shoes.

"You okay?" he asked gently when he reached me.

"I couldn't get the dress off. Broke the zipper trying. I'll compensate you for it, obviously, but we might need to arrange a payment plan if it's made from mammoth tusks or something. Either way, you'll eventually get your money—"

"Jamie." He tucked a gentle knuckle under my chin and tilted my face so he could scan it properly. "Are. You. Okay?"

A ball of unexpected emotion lodged itself in the pit of my throat. I couldn't swallow it down. "I think so. I'm not bleeding or anything..."

If I was, I couldn't feel it.

Jackson nodded but didn't drop his hand. "I'm going to lift you now, okay?"

I thought about it, even though there was literally nothing to think about. I couldn't move.

"Okay," I agreed after much unneeded deliberation. "But, um, can you check on Toebeans first? He might be under the bed or hiding in the bathroom or something. I didn't see where he ran off to."

I could tell by the way his brows scrunched that he was about to argue, so I shook my head. "Him first."

"You're being unreasonable. Let me at least—"

I shook my head again. "Need to make sure he's not hurt. There's glass on the bed."

Jackson's lips rolled with blatant disapproval. "All right," he said, sounding not at all happy about it.

More glass crunched under his shoes as he made his way to the bed and peered underneath. Then to the bathroom. And finally, the walk-in closet.

"Hello again, Cat."

I strained my neck. "He's okay?"

Jackson cocked his head. "Physically, yes. He looks rather enraged, though. Fangs bared and all."

Oh. Yeah. "Don't go in there. Just... slowly shut the door so he doesn't come out until I clean all this up." Chances were good he was too spooked to meander out of there anytime soon anyway, but just in case.

Jackson shot me a look, his features pinched into a confused scowl.

"What?" I asked. What did I say?

He shut the closet door and stalked over to where I was uselessly waiting. "Did any of it get inside your dress?"

Great question. I felt around for sharp edges and uncomfortable pokes. "Don't think so."

Then, in one smooth motion, he scooped me into his arms like I weighed less than nothing.

I may have gasped.

I also may have turned a rather telling pink when said gasp drew his attention. For one breathless moment, our gazes locked.

Make that two breathless moments.

Three.

"You can just drop me off near the door," I said. "And if you could please tell me where the brooms are kept, that would be swell."

He was giving me that confused scowly look again, so I

decided to clarify. "Toebeans gets excited when he hears a vacuum cleaner. A broom would be better until he calms down. Also, aren't your arms tired?"

Mine would have given out by now.

Then again, Jackson was really... *muscly*.

"Is Cat okay to be left alone for a bit?" he asked, still peering down at me through surprisingly thick lashes.

"Yeah, he's not gonna want to come out of there for a while, I don't think."

"Good." He carried me out of the room.

"Wait, where are we going?"

"To get you that broom," he replied dryly.

"I can just walk there."

"You don't even know where it is."

My mouth twitched. "Can't argue with that logic."

As it turned out, the broom closet was on the second floor of the penthouse. It was also not a broom closet.

I gave Jackson the most dry, unimpressed look I could muster as he placed me down on the couch... in what could only be his bedroom.

"Stay," he ordered.

I was on my feet the second he disappeared into the ensuite. I didn't know what he had planned, but there was a good chance I'd regret not making my sleuthy escape when I had the chance.

Unfortunately, I didn't even make it to the stairs.

"What do you think you're doing?" I asked when I was, once again, swept off my unsteady feet.

"Ability to follow simple instructions: abysmally inadequate."

I narrowed my eyes. "You can't just grab women without asking permission first."

"Haven't heard any complaints so far."

"I don't know if I've told you this yet, but I swear sometimes you're just one giant walking red flag."

His throat worked with a light chuckle. Bow tie.

"You should put that in my file," he said.

I was placed on the dark leather couch again. This time Jackson took a seat beside me, inserting himself right into my personal space.

"Do we really need to be sitting this close?"

"Where did you hit your head?" he asked, leaning in another inch. His scent was everywhere, lingering on my skin.

"Right... here." I felt around until I found the bruised spot. A bump was already starting to form and there was a bunch of glass stuck in my curls, but at least there was no blood.

"Does it hurt?"

My fingers went still. "Why?" What was his angle?

His mouth slanted into a half-smile. "You really don't trust me."

Not even a little. "We've already gone over this."

"And you're not... impressed by me. At all."

I scrunched my brows as my fingers started to prod at my bump again. It hurt when I touched it. So why did I keep touching it?

"Do you hear yourself when you say stuff like that?" I asked. "Like, do you hear how arrogant you sound?"

His half-smile widened. "And you don't like that, either. The arrogance."

My hand dropped. Why was he acting so weird? "Is this part of the making-my-life-miserable thing?" Or was he still trying to disarm me?

He chuckled, then reached up and plucked a shiny piece of glass out of my hair. "And how did you think our date went?" he asked, completely ignoring my question.

I shrugged, a little distracted by all the strange sensations swirling in my chest as he picked out another little shard, carefully placing it on the coffee table to his right.

"You need to wait until tomorrow for the evaluation results." I fiddled with my skirt as Jackson continued to delicately remove the glass from my loose updo. "How did you think it went?"

I wasn't asking for *me*, obviously. It didn't matter what he thought of me as a date. But he was a client, and client feedback was, um, important.

Ah, yes, because you've been soooo professional during this whole Immersive process. And you've tried soooo hard to listen to his feedback.

I had to stop myself from visibly cringing. There was a slight chance some of my behavior was starting to catch up with me.

Jackson's gaze snagged on mine, his mouth twisting into a wry smirk. "Like I said, I miscalculated."

"I really don't know what that means."

His lips—okay, you know what, I really needed to stop paying so much attention to his mouth before it made things weird.

"It means, Miss Paquin, that I'm not exactly accustomed to competing for my date's attention." Another small piece of the shattered mirror was discarded onto the table. "It didn't even occur to me that you may be more interested in conversing with Damien than me. Not until we got there, at least."

"His name is Daniel." My throat was starting to dry up.

Another twitch of his lips. I was looking at them a lot. It was super inappropriate.

"Right."

His fingers found one of the pins holding my updo in place, lingered there for a moment, then pulled. A small batch of my curls tumbled free, falling over my shoulder. I watched his gaze trace them, his hand frozen in the air.

I shifted on the couch, feeling oddly warm. "If you're unhappy with the level of engagement we had during the evaluation, I'll take that into consideration."

Not that I needed to. He'd definitely passed.

"Or..." Another section of my hair fell loose, and I swear his pupils briefly flared. "We could try it again."

I blinked. "You want to do another evaluation?"

Again with the mouth twitch. "A third date, yes."

My pulse kicked. *Evaluation* was the more correct term; he didn't need to keep saying *date*.

They weren't dates. Charmed had a very strict, zero-tolerance policy against *dates* with clients. It was a huge conflict of interest.

"Something a little more intimate this time," Jackson went on. "So we can actually talk. That way, you'll have even more accurate data to work with."

The last pin was discarded. All of my hair tumbled free.

His lips parted, his eyelids lowering ever-so-slightly. I reached up self-consciously, wanting to soothe and fluff them into proper shape, but he grabbed a hold of my wrist before I could touch even a strand. His grip wasn't hard or rough, but it was definitely... authoritative.

"Let me get all the glass out first. I don't want you cutting yourself."

"Since when do you care if I'm hurt?"

He could probably feel my pulse thundering through my wrist. Maybe that's why he was frowning.

"I'm an asshole, not a monster." He said it softly, no venom in his tone. Then he placed my hand on my lap and returned his attention to the task at hand.

Jackson Sinclair was tenderly running his fingers through my hair so I wouldn't cut myself on broken glass. What was going on? The date was over. There was no need for him to keep up the act.

"Jamie." My eyes accidentally darted down to his lips again. "Have a drink with me tomorrow night. After work."

The oxygen levels in this room had reduced significantly since we'd walked in.

"Shouldn't you wait until you get the results? If you pass, there's no point in another evaluation."

He clicked his tongue. "We barely talked. Your results would be based on incomplete data, and we wouldn't want that, would we?"

"Yes, but I've gone on two fake dates with you so far and they've both ended in some sort of physical disaster for me. The universe is definitely trying to tell us something, and I'm pretty tempted to listen."

He chuckled again. "All right, so let's say this one's a real date instead. You know, just so we can appease the almighty universe."

My eyes narrowed. "You're mocking me."

"I wouldn't dream of it, Miss Paquin. I firmly believe that the cosmos is conspiring against the two of us going on fake dates and is communicating its grievances via gruesome murder attempts. That makes total logical sense to me, which is why I'm saying we should just go on a real one, instead—see if it likes that better."

I crossed my arms. "If I didn't know any better, I'd think you *wanted* to go on a date with me."

"Nonsense." He continued to tease his fingers through my hair, even though they kept coming back empty. "I just want to ensure you have all the data you need to do your job."

"You don't want me to do my job," I pointed out. "In fact, you've done everything you can over the last nine months to make it as difficult as possible for me to do my job."

"Another miscalculation."

What did that even mean? "What does a miscalculation have anything to do with you not taking our personality tests?"

He sighed. "How would you like it if someone was blackmailing you into going on blind dates? How easy would you make things for them?"

My teeth clamped together. He had a point.

"I wasn't trying to make life difficult for you. I was just —" He cut off, scrubbing a hand over his jaw. "I apologize for my behavior that night, but just know I had my reasons. And I'm willing to take some of the responsibility for making your professional life difficult, but your employer was also at fault. I didn't force you to work all that overtime, Jamie."

Again, he had a point.

I dragged my teeth over my bottom lip, thinking. "I'm sorry too," I eventually said. It was only fair. "I've been... burnt out and frustrated, and I think I've put a little more blame on you than is maybe warranted."

He nodded. "I appreciate that."

Look at us, being all mature and civil.

"Cool." And, for whatever reason, Molly's request chose that exact moment to ring through my head.

"He could really use a friend, you know. Someone closer to his own age. Someone not on his payroll."

So, after a strangely dense silence, during which our eyes were locked in another breathless staring contest, I said, "Hey, do you... do you maybe want to tone down some of the, um, animosity we've got going on, and maybe... maybe we could try to be friends or something?"

That was about as eloquently as I could put an idea that had an extremely high chance of being immediately shut down.

Sure enough, Jackson's brow gave a surprised little tick. "You want to be my *friend*."

I didn't understand the emphasis he put on the word, or why his eyes narrowed when he said it, but "I don't know. Maybe."

He didn't respond. Not a good sign.

"I mean, to be honest, this whole hating each other thing is already becoming kind of tiring, don't you think?" As it turned out, my personality was not all that suited for revenge. Being at emotional war with another human was exhausting.

I wasn't convinced I could do a full month of it.

"And so, you'd like for us to be... *friends*."

He clearly hated the idea.

"Well, maybe we could start with just being more civil."

His eyes were razor-thin at this point. "Did Molly put you up to this?"

My head tugged back. "What? No. Of course not. Why would you... even..."

He knew. He was looking at me like he definitely knew.

"Maybe..." I admitted with a sigh.

Jackson pinched the bridge of his nose in clear exasperation. Although it did kind of look like he was also trying to bite back a smile. Before I could talk myself out of it, I took the shot.

"It's okay, no one is surprised that you don't have any friends."

A chuckle burst out of him, though his eyes remained closed. "Fuck me. What am I going to do with those two?"

I grinned. "They care about you a lot. It's honestly sweet."

When he finally dropped his hand and opened his eyes, they were sparkling. "I have friends, Jamie," he claimed, a subtle hint of color spreading over his cheeks.

"Of course you do, buddy."

"I do," he insisted.

My smile widened, digging into my cheeks. "Is that a no, then, to being my friend?"

He studied me for a beat. "What would it entail, exactly?"

I raised a brow, but before I could settle on an appropriately clever quip, he said, "I lied, I don't have any friends. You're going to have to hold my hand through the whole thing."

A giggle spilled out of me before I could stop it. *Damn it*. Jackson's eyes crinkled in their corners as he watched me laugh.

"I think I can do that," I eventually agreed. "I'm already your dating coach, so why not?"

"Then I guess we have a deal."

My heart was doing a *lot* of stuttering over the prospect of earning Jackson Sinclair's friendship. It was excessive. "Cool."

He cleared his throat lightly and sat up straight, palms

sliding over his knees. “So, what now? Do you want to hang out, or…”

“Sure, okay. But first thing’s first,” I said. “As my friend, I officially need you to make good on your earlier promise and get me out of my clothes.”

He stiffened. Blinked.

“No, seriously,” I said. “I’m stuck.”

19

JACKSON CURSED UNDER HIS BREATH, his grip on the fabric tightening as he—unsuccessfully—tried to rip down the broken zipper.

"Told you," I said. "It's really stuck."

He released me. "I'm cutting you out."

"What—no!"

He rounded the desk tucked in the corner of his room and snatched a pair of scissors from the top drawer.

"Turn around."

My arms wrapped around my chest protectively. "Absolutely not."

"Why? What's the issue?"

"Have you *seen* this dress? I'm not letting you anywhere near it with that thing."

His eyes raked down my body, taking their time. "Yeah, it's a shame." He rolled his lips. "Guess I'll just have to buy you a new one."

He snapped the scissors threateningly as his long strides swallowed the space between us. When my back hit the wall, his head slanted to one side. "Would you rather I rip it apart using my hands again?"

The sudden flash of the memory made my stomach swim, a spark of heat igniting in my core. When I didn't answer, he tossed the scissors onto the bed. "Hands it is."

I pressed tighter against the hard protection of the wall. "No, wait. Tell me how much it cost first."

He frowned. "How would I know?"

Right. What was I thinking? "Ask your shopper."

His frown dug deeper. "How would any of them know?"

"Don't they keep the receipts to, like, send to your accountants or whatever?"

"They would if they bought it."

"Did they not buy it?"

"No."

"Then who did?"

"Me."

I blinked up at him, then down at the dress. "Wait, you picked this out?"

"Yes." And then, "Was that not clear?"

I shook my head slowly. "The shoes, too?"

He nodded. "What else did you think I was doing on my computer this afternoon?"

"Your *job*."

He scowled at me with disgust. "It was after *lunch*, Jamie."

"Okay, you know what, you went from having no sense of humor to straight-up too much of it."

He chuckled, twirling a finger. "Turn around."

Another deep, quiet command.

I swallowed. "Okay, real talk since we're now friends, I might not be able to pay you back right away if this thing costs anywhere close to what I'm imagining. It would have to wait until the rest of my bonus comes in at the end of our thirty days. Or maybe even longer depending on how much the mirror also costs to replace. Is that okay?"

The more I talked, the deeper his scowl dug.

"You're not paying for a mirror that fell on your head because it wasn't properly secured. If anything, you should be lawyering up." He nudged my temple with his knuckle like I was being a knucklehead. "And the dress was a gift. Do friends usually pay each other for the gifts they receive?"

"I mean, no..."

"Great. *Now* may I tear it off you?"

Really, that should have eased my hesitation. But instead of dropping my arms and allowing him to Hulk me out of yet another gown, I tightened them around me, feeling protective of the fabric for a whole new set of reasons.

"I definitely can't let you touch it now."

Jackson let out a heavy sigh, though it was accompanied by a reluctant smile. "And why's that?"

I raised my chin. "It was a gift from a friend."

His tongue darted out to wet his twitching lips, and I accidentally looked. On an unrelated note, he was still wearing a bow tie. "Jamie, we've been friends for a total of, like, six minutes."

"Don't care."

"I'll buy you ten new ones. Two in each color."

Wait, The Dress came in four more colors? Which ones? Were they all pastels or—you know what, no.

"This one's got sentimental value."

"How about we revert back to hating each other for a second? Will you let me tear through it then?"

I pressed my lips together and shook my head. "Sorry, bud. That's not how this works."

"Then I'm all out of ideas."

I chewed the inside of my cheek, eyeing the scissors again. "How good are you at following instructions?"

It took eight minutes, a handful of hot, breathy curses tickling the nape of my neck, and a very specific set of instructions, but Jackson managed to carefully cut through the zipper seam without accidentally snipping the dress.

I held my breath through the whole thing.

"There," he murmured. "All done."

I didn't know how close he was standing, exactly, but I kept having to stop myself from tilting back and leaning into his warmth. The man was a whole space heater. And he smelled positively divine—I could not stress this enough. I'd never met a better-smelling human in my life.

"Thanks." It came out a lot quieter than I'd intended.

Jackson stepped away.

I knew this because he took all the warmth with him.

"Come with me."

Fighting my way out of another mental fog, I followed Jackson into... *whoa*. "This is your *closet*?" It was twice the size of my studio apartment, and *way* nicer. There were three couches in here. Three! And two chandeliers. Two!

The walls were lined with crisp suits, floor-to-ceiling shelves filled with shoes, and glass display cases housing watches, ties, and cufflinks.

"Here." While I'd been gawking at my surroundings, Jackson had retrieved a large sweatshirt and was holding it out to me. I wouldn't have pegged him for a sweatshirt guy. Interesting. "The dress is spilling off of you, so..." He stopped to clear his throat. "Better if you wear this."

"Thanks."

Was it just me or was he doing everything he could to avoid eye contact? "I'll just... be outside, then," he muttered.

Once I'd changed (and gawked a bit more), I trotted back out to Jackson's bedroom, hugging my neatly folded dress to my chest. "I don't know if anyone's ever told you this, but your closet is what dreams are made of. How many suits d'you think you have? Just ballpark."

He chuckled, slipping out of his jacket. "I can give you an exact number, one of my shoppers keeps a spreadsheet with—" He cut off when he saw me. Blinked.

"What?" I asked, peering down at myself. His sweatshirt had swallowed me whole. There was literally nothing to look at.

Even in the limited light, I swear I could see a hint of color dash over his features. For a second, I thought it might be anger, but his eyes were a little too glazed for that.

He said nothing.

I shifted on my feet, tucking a ringlet behind my ear self-consciously. My brain chose that moment to remind me of Jackson's preference for taller women.

He snapped out of buffering mode with a blink, right before his eyes shot up to the ceiling and decided to stay there. He shoved his fists into the pockets of his trousers (rather roughly, I might add), and turned his torso away from me.

"It's getting late," he told the light fixture hanging

above his head. "Do you remember how to get back to your suite?"

Okay, so I guess he didn't want to hang out anymore.

"Um... yup," I said, confused by the sudden awkwardness. And here I thought we'd been making such good progress. "I memorized the whole floor plan after that time I got lost, so... should be fine."

His only reaction was a curt nod.

Message received.

Ignoring the strange and unexpected pangs of disappointment, I made my way over to the double doors. "Wait, can I get that broom first?"

His shoulders were so stiff I was surprised they didn't creak when he shoved an irritated hand through his hair. Without giving me an answer, he stalked into the ensuite and didn't come out again. Not even to hand me a stupid broom.

So much for the whole friends thing.

"Good night to you, too," I grumbled under my breath.

There was no broken glass in the suite when I walked in. It was all gone.

20

Day one of being Jackson Sinclair's friend was going about as unexpectedly as I should have expected. And not in a good way.

"Jackson," I chided while keeping my eyes on my laptop screen, "we've talked about this."

He swiveled lightly in his chair, gaze still stuck to my face. "Have we?"

My fingers didn't stop moving. "Just because you have nothing to do doesn't mean you can just sit there and stare at me all day."

I didn't know what he was being paid to run this company, but I could say with full confidence that it was too much.

"We're friends," he said.

"Friends don't sit around and stare at each other all day."

He cocked his head skeptically. "That doesn't sound correct. Then again, I have no frame of reference so you might be right."

And that—that right there—had been the entirety of my morning.

"What else do friends not do?" he pushed.

I tried ignoring him again as I finished typing my email to Alice and Mitch, requesting that they add *highly sarcastic* and *dry sense of humor* to Jackson's profile immediately. My silence backfired.

I ground my teeth as Jackson dragged his chair all the way across the office. I ground them harder when he plopped down beside me, tainting my personal bubble with all his warmth and dizzying scent. Again.

He leaned in. "What are you working on there, friend?"

I wasn't an innately violent person, but there was a reasonably good chance Jackson's office was going to be a crime scene by lunch.

"My job," I said. "Some of us have to actually work to get paid."

"I thought your job was to pay attention to me."

You know what this was like? This was like when Toebeans got into one of his extreme cuddle moods. He'd sit on my chest and yell his demands for attention right in my face.

"That's not my job." It very much was my job.

Unable to take the hint, Jackson leaned even closer so he could peer over my shoulder. My allergies flared up in an instant—elevated heart rate and body temperature, pebbled skin, difficulty breathing, nausea.

"Oh, that's nice," he murmured approvingly, adding chills and shudders to my ever-growing list of symptoms. "You're emailing your coworkers about how funny you think I am."

I had been. Past tense.

My fingers weren't moving anymore.

Honestly, if my future partner smelled half as good as Jackson Sinclair, I'd probably spend the majority of our relationship with my face stuffed into the crook of his neck. Especially if he had a nice neck.

I'd probably make him wear bow ties a lot, too.

"Jamie."

Since we're making a future boyfriend wish list, let's add Jackson's voice, too. And his accent.

"What now?" I'd meant for that to come out a lot more curt and exasperated than it did. Why was my voice so breathy again?

"What else do you like about me, friend?"

Oh my god. I'd never regretted befriending someone so quickly. "Literally nothing," I said, biting back a smile. "Now would you please go back to your own corner?"

"I think I'm good right here." He shifted closer, practically crowding me.

"Jackson," I warned.

"Yes, friend?"

I had to swallow back a laugh. "I'm going to murder you if you don't stop."

He grinned. "Ah, yes, a friendly jest between two pals. I've seen this on television."

That one got me. It was the delivery more than anything. He said it with so much earnest excitement that my composure crumpled, a defeated giggle escaping as the heels of my palms pressed to my eyes.

Jackson let out a low, victorious chuckle. He'd gotten exactly what he wanted.

Damn it.

"I hate you," I said unconvincingly.

"Just a reminder that you brought this on yourself."

“In my defense, I did not know you’d be like this.”

“Why? Is this not how friendship works?”

“Please stop.” My cheeks were starting to hurt.

“Can you be more clear with your directions? I’m really out of my element here.”

“Jackson! Go away!”

“No, see, you’re still not being very clear.”

I folded over my desk, face buried in my arms as a defeated laugh burst out of me. At least ten percent of my tears were from frustration.

I’d created a monster.

When the giggles finally subsided, I straightened again, wiping at my cheeks. There was a good chance I had makeup smeared all over them.

“It wasn’t that funny,” Jackson said, a smile in his voice.

“I cry pretty easily when I laugh. It’s a curse.” I owned an ungodly amount of waterproof makeup, none of which I was wearing today.

“Is my makeup smeared?” I swiveled in my chair, presenting my face to him for inspection. What were friends for, after all, if not this?

Jackson’s light gaze slid over my features slowly, his smile dampening a touch as he brushed a knuckle over my cheekbone, wiping away a lingering tear. The caress was so feather-light and gentle that I barely felt it.

So why did sparks trickle down my spine when he did it? Why did it make my toes curl?

“You’re good.” His hand dropped.

An oddly misplaced emotion tugged at the base of my ribs, and I realized I was tilting forward, shortening the already limited distance between our bodies.

I stiffened, hoping he hadn’t noticed.

“Thanks,” I muttered as I straightened again. It was his

damn cologne. It was like catnip to me. I wanted to roll around in it.

Was that weird? I'd never had the desire to roll around in someone's scent before. Then again, I'd never met anyone that smelled so intoxicatingly incredible.

"Jamie."

Damn it, I loved how he said my name, too. His stupid voice was just as seductive as his stupid cologne.

"Are we still on for drinks tonight?" he asked.

What did he mean *still*? "I never agreed to drinks."

"You also never disagreed."

My mouth twitched. "We don't need to do a third evaluation. You pass. We can axe the coaching and supervised dates."

I expected him to throw at least one I-told-you-so smirk in my face (and then hopefully leave me alone). Instead, he said, "What? Friends can't have drinks together?"

That was it?

That was his reaction to being told he didn't have to do all the coaching he'd been fighting me on all week?

My eyes narrowed as I studied him. This was the official cherry on top of his weird-behavior cake. "What's going on with you?"

His shrug was almost *too* casual. "Nothing. Why? What's going on with you?"

"Allergies," I muttered without thinking. My mind was busy formulating an experimental test of sorts. One that I decided to conduct right away. "You know what, though? In my professional opinion, I still think you'd really benefit from coaching. Just because it's not mandatory, doesn't mean—"

His brows scrunched together. "What allergies?"

Huh.

"Did you hear what I said?"

"Yes. Why were your allergies not disclosed to me before you moved in? Is it the roses?"

What? "No. That wasn't what I meant."

"What are you allergic to, then?"

"Nothing."

"Jamie, we're going to be living together for another three weeks. You should probably tell me what you're allergic to."

"I'm not allergic to anything." My cheeks were on fire.

"But you just said—"

"That wasn't what I meant," I repeated.

"Okay, then tell me what you meant."

My heart was fluttering all over the place. "Nothing, just—go back to your corner," I said. "I can't think when you're—"

Fortunately, I caught myself just in time.

Unfortunately, it was still too late.

I saw the exact moment it clicked for him; watched his eyes flare with awareness. "When I'm what?"

My throat must have moved when I swallowed because it snagged his attention. And he could probably see my pulse pounding out of my neck. Maybe that was why his lips were parting like that.

"Jackson."

His eyes snapped back to mine. They were unrecognizable, there was so little blue left.

I swallowed again. "You know how you asked about what friends don't do?"

No answer.

"Because this would be pretty high up on that list. Friends don't, um, sit this close to each other."

Hypocrite. You're leaning in more than he is.

Yet I made no moves to correct it.

"Are you sure?" Jackson teased lightly, the one corner of his mouth lifting.

"Pretty positive, yeah."

He didn't move. "And do friends normally evade each other's questions the way you keep evading mine?"

The sultry tilt to his tone made the air grow thick. As if I wasn't already having a hard time breathing.

"I can't do drinks tonight," I said. "Toebeans is still pissed about the glass incident and needs a solid four hours of cuddling to get over the trauma."

This was all lies. He'd gotten over the whole thing pretty damn quickly. I mean, he'd half-sat on my face while he licked his butt bright and early this morning but, you know, it could have been a lot worse.

"Why can't the pet sitter do the cuddling?" Jackson asked, not sounding at all like he was joking. "Adrien, I think you said his name was."

I huffed another laugh. "My god, you're obsessed with him."

"Isn't everyone?"

"He *is* quite dreamy."

Jackson scoffed. "You know, most women—and even some men—would say the same about me."

"That doesn't sound correct."

His eyes practically twinkled when his grin reached them. He chuckled.

Wow, he really *did* like it when I was mean to him. Weirdo.

"Adrien's not the pet sitter," I clarified, even though he already knew this. "He's a friend."

There was a short pause. "Like how you and I are friends?"

My pulse kicked. No. That was absolutely nothing like this.

"He's married to my best friend," I explained, not sure how else to answer him. "So, he's kind of like my brother-in-law."

"Ah." His mouth quirked with what my brain was trying to convince me was relief. "And why does Cat love him so much?"

I shrugged. "Your guess is as good as mine. It might be a scent thing? Also, Adrien spoils the shit out of him, so the love has grown over time."

The two of them were ridiculous together.

"Spoils him how, exactly?"

"You know how spoiled Harry the hairless cat is? Diamond collar and all?" When he nodded, I said, "Child's play. You haven't seen shit."

Jackson huffed a laugh. "Oh yeah?"

"The day after the two of them met, Adrien bought him the biggest, most elaborate cat tree you've ever seen. It had a literal throne and *multiple* hammocks." I held up a hand when he opened his mouth. "I haven't even gotten started. Toebeans has had his own room in Adrien's penthouse since before him and Ria were even engaged. It's bigger than my current apartment and a lot nicer. It also has a throne."

"That's nothing."

"His food is made in Switzerland and custom-tailored to his preferences. It took two weeks of testing to perfect the recipe."

"That's it? That's all it takes?"

"Okay, you know what? You not getting it isn't my fault."

"Do you even know what spoiled means?" His brows were all tangled like I'd somehow insulted him.

That did it. My eyes flicked to the ceiling as I rolled my chair back a foot. "Okay."

"Swiss food, Jamie?"

"All right."

"*That's* your pinnacle of fine feline dining?"

"You're being very rude. Go away now."

Shockingly, he didn't argue this time. Even more shockingly, he dragged his chair all the way back to his desk, sat down, and started to type away at his keyboard.

And for the next six hours I genuinely believed that, for the first time since I'd started to shadow him, Jackson Sinclair was actually getting work done.

I was not correct.

21

"BEHOLD!"

Looking slightly more wild-eyed and unhinged than I'd thought possible for him, Jackson threw the set of double doors open to reveal...

"Oh. My. Fucking. God," I breathed, frozen stupid.

"I know."

"Jackson..."

"I know."

"This is..."

"I know."

I gaped at the colossal... palace. It was a full-on *palace* stuffed into the empty suite down the hall from mine.

A palace made out of cardboard.

"Oh. My. Fucking. God," I said again. Toebeans was going to lose his fucking mind.

"Yes," Jackson purred. "She's exquisite."

My mouth was still hanging open. "How did you..."

"Money."

"In less than six hours..."

"Money."

"This is... holy shit, that's a throne." Which meant that by the end of today, Toebeans Maguire would have sat on three separate thrones, all of which had been custom-made just for him.

Jackson strutted into the suite, all arrogance. "Adderall might have built Cat a room full of intricate toys and accessories, but if Cat is anything like Harry, then he's significantly more interested in the boxes those toys come in."

"You know his name is Adrien."

Jackson frowned at me. "Then why did you tell me it was Toebeans?"

I pinched the bridge of my nose as the laugh escaped. He had a very specific brand of humor—one that *should* have annoyed the hell out of me—and it was growing on me at an alarmingly rapid pace.

"I can't believe..." I trailed off, unable to think of the right words.

It was incredible. There was a clock tower (with an actual working clock that doubled as a treat dispenser), stables (housing horse-shaped scratch posts), a dungeon (with cardboard mice trapped behind steel bars), and... and just *so much* more.

There was even art! Images and shapes that had been carefully carved into the cardboard walls, arched windows with stained glass, and a colorful little outdoor garden with battery-operated butterflies!

It was fucking magical.

"When did you even have the time to make this happen?" I asked.

"I was at my desk all afternoon. What else would I have been doing?"

I blinked up at him. "*Working*."

"Don't be ridiculous, Jamie."

Jesus Christ. I really could not with this man.

But also, like, how genuinely sweet was this? I was trying really, very hard to stop my heart from melting over it, but I couldn't help it. I wanted to hug him. I didn't, but I wanted to.

Jackson rubbed his hands together. "Shall we bring Cat in? See what he thinks?"

I held up a palm to stop him. "A few questions before we do that." Although I was honestly a little afraid to ask. "One, why does it smell like you in here?"

It was like someone had rubbed him all over this room.

"Ah, yes, you're going to love this."

I bit down my smile.

"You said Cat likes Adrien because of his scent, right?"

My heart skipped a beat. "That's just a theory. We're not actually sure..."

He waved a dismissive hand. "Either way, having my scent associated with all this is probably going to help him warm up to me."

I crossed my arms over my pounding chest, like that would help protect it. "What about the pictures?"

Along the walls of the palace were framed pictures of Jackson's face, all in varying sizes and expressions.

"Brilliant, no? Same idea as the scent."

"You're unhinged. This"—I flapped a hand around—"is unhinged."

He grinned. "Would you like to hear the best part?"

I guessed it immediately. It was the emphasis he put on the word *hear* that tipped me off.

Jackson clapped his hands together twice.

"Hello, Cat. This is Jackson Sinclair, your favorite male human. You love me, and you love my voice. You do not hiss when I am near, especially not in my home—"

I clapped, cutting the recording off. My chest couldn't handle much more. This was... I was just... Every single piece of data we'd accumulated in Jackson's profile was incorrect. *None* of this aligned with the information we'd been provided by his team.

He was so much more... Honestly, I'd never met someone quite so...

"What do you think?" he asked before my thoughts could fully form. His expression was slowly sobering. "I know it's unhinged, but do you... like it?"

He stepped closer. I meant to take a step back.

"It's..." I trailed off, my blood thrumming as his gaze met mine and softened. "I don't... really understand why you did this."

There was a long, dense pause. "I want Cat to like me."

My fists dug into my ribs as my pulse scrambled for purchase. "And why's that?"

"Because." His head slanted to one side. "I've decided that I like... him."

Whatever response my brain pieced together died in my throat when Jackson tilted my chin up, thumb caressing my skin.

"I find Cat intriguing," he murmured, and I was convinced my heart was going to beat out of my chest. "I've never been outwardly loathed like that before. People always pretend."

Willing my voice not to crack, I said, "So... you only like him because he doesn't fall at your feet like everyone else?"

Jackson dropped his hand.

"You have no idea how rare—how fucking *refreshing*—that level of honesty is when you've spent your whole life not knowing whether the people around you are there because of *you*, or your money." His throat worked with a rough swallow, eyes sliding between mine. "I like that he doesn't put up with my bullshit just because of my family name. That he refuses to be bought with my money."

We were still talking about Toebeans.

Yup. We were definitely still talking about my cat, so if my heart could stop trying to beat itself into cardiac arrest now, I'd sincerely appreciate it.

"You want to know the real reason I was so rude to you on our first date, Jamie?" His voice dipped to a low gravel, snaking through me like ivy. "I was trying to see how far I could push before somebody finally told me to go fuck myself."

My breath hitched when his thumb caressed my chin again, my lips drawing his gaze when they peeled apart.

"Sixty-seven matches," he said, hooded eyes locked on my mouth. "Every single one of them wanted something from me—wealth, status, connections—but none of them wanted *me*."

Every time I thought of something to say, the words would melt away before they reached my tongue.

"I could have gotten away with murder on those dates. They would have helped me bury the body in exchange for a ring and no prenup."

My lips twitched. "You're so cocky."

The corners of his pale eyes crinkled a touch. "It's not just women, either," he whispered. "Why do you think Molly is so concerned with my lack of friends?"

"I assumed your lack of friends was largely due to your personality," I teased lightly.

His teeth tugged at his smiling lower lip, and a fresh wave of heat washed over me. "I told you I like it when you're mean to me. I'm starting to think you're doing it on purpose."

"That's because your ego truly knows no bounds."

He was still holding my chin, still caressing it. And I was still letting him.

Why was I still letting him?

My tongue darted out to wet my lips and, again, it immediately drew his attention. This time, his gaze darkened, his smile fading.

I saw the signs. All of them. The glazed look, the slack mouth, the lean-in.

And I still didn't see it coming.

I still gasped when his lips brushed mine, featherlight. Still blinked in surprise when tiny little sparks traced that exact spot. But I didn't pull away.

Jackson waited, drawing back just an inch to see if I would bolt. But I stayed rooted on the spot, utterly transfixed. He did it again—the lightest brush of his lips along mine, and when my eyes fluttered shut, he...

Oh.

Oh, whoa.

The first press of his lips was soft, testing. The second pulled a frail whimper from my throat. My hands moved, tracing his biceps as they curled around me. I was pulled flush against him, right before my feet were lifted off the hardwood.

My arms snaked around his neck, every last semicoherent thought in my head melting into shapeless putty when his tongue traced the seam of my lips. Another helpless sound escaped as my lips parted. I clutched onto him tighter, my core clenching as my whole body sparked to life. He tasted like mint and molten sugar, and when I teased his tongue with a shy lick, his chest vibrated with a pleased groan.

I couldn't breathe. Between the fiery sparks racing through my lungs and Jackson crushing me to him, I couldn't get enough oxygen. And I couldn't seem to care.

Was this what kissing was supposed to feel like? Because *holy shit* had I been doing it wron—

"Oh!"

My eyes flew open.

"Oh, what now, Mabel? Surely you—oh!"

Shit.

Shit shit shit shit shit.

My heart stopped beating when the voices registered. I tried pulling back from Jackson, but he wouldn't budge. Also, my bottom lip was currently wedged between his teeth.

Fuck me.

"Out. Out out out out!" one of the sisters hissed as I wriggled in Jacksons arms. The man was built like a marble fucking statue. He'd lifted me no less than a foot off the ground and was showing exactly zero signs of physical exertion.

"Jackson!" I hissed when his mouth moved to my jaw. I mean, it did make my eyes roll to the back of my head, but only a little... until he licked at that one spot just underneath my earlobe. A piece of my soul died then. "Jackson, we should, um, I need... should stop. There's... people here."

That was about as coherent as I could be with him nipping at my earlobe like that.

His embrace only tightened. “Go away,” he grumbled unhappily, even though I was pretty sure the sisters were long gone by now. “We’re busy.”

He sounded very growly and a little drunk.

“Jackson,” I tried again. The fact that I could even form the word was a miracle. He was very, very, *very* good with his tongue. Very excellent.

“You taste like peaches.”

“That’s... anatomically... impossible,” I panted.

“Tell that to your skin,” he said before licking my jaw again.

I clenched around nothing, my core burning. “Jackson… look at… me… please.”

Reluctantly, he peeled his mouth away from my neck and glared at me with hazy, melted-blue eyes. The man was pouting.

“Molly and Mabel... saw us,” I explained, still fighting for air.

“Okay.” His eyes locked in on my lips again. He leaned forward.

My palm pressed to his mouth before he could kiss me, which made his eyebrows crumple. Like he truly didn’t understand what the problem was.

“What are…” My lungs were all but heaving, yet none of the hoarded oxygen was able to reach my brain. “You kissed me. Why would you do that?”

He cocked his head and quirked a brow, my hand still pressed to his mouth.

Little by little, the realization seeped into my skin.

Little by little, I started to panic.

“Why would you…” Did he have *any idea* what he’d just done? How something like this could impact my career? “We’re supposed to be friends!”

His brows slammed together at that, then he nipped at my fingers. I kept them secure over his mouth, my eyes narrowing. My senses were returning bit by bit, the gears in my head groaning to stiff motion.

"Put me down."

His arms tightened around me for a single stubborn beat before he gently placed me back on the carpet. He did not look happy about it.

"Listen to me very carefully," I said, still not having peeled back my hand. My confusion was very quickly morphing into hot panic, nipping restlessly at my skin. "This—whatever it was—never happened, okay? I'm going to go to my room and finish prepping for our interview tomorrow, you're going to go explain to Molly and Mabel that this was just a misunderstanding, and then we're never going to talk about it ever again."

Then I made the mistake of pulling my hand back.

"No."

My fingers dug into my palms. "I wasn't asking."

"And I'm not going to pretend like we didn't just make out," he said. "You know what we should do instead? Talk about it."

"That sounds like the worst possible course of action."

"Effective communication is the cornerstone of any healthy relationship," he pointed out.

The tips of my ears tingled. I was in so much fucking trouble. "You and I are not in a relationship."

He tutted. "We've got a professional relationship, not to mention a budding friendship that requires nurturing—"

"*Jackson.*"

"You kissed me back."

I stopped short, my throat constricting.

He took a step forward, eyes searching mine. "You didn't push me away; you didn't pull back."

My mouth stuttered uselessly for a beat. "I can't... you have no idea what..."

This wasn't about losing my job at Charmed. If word got out that I'd kissed Jackson Sinclair, my professional reputation would be scorched. I'd be blacklisted.

The industry didn't fuck around with stuff like this. Getting romantically involved with a client was a massive conflict of interest. I knew of exactly two people who'd been caught doing it, and neither of them worked in the industry anymore.

Not to mention the gossip, the rumors, the unkind labels, and general shaming they'd had to endure...

"What?" Jackson asked when I remained silent.

But I couldn't tell him, could I? If he knew how big of a deal this was, it would give him a *lot* of leverage to use against me if this whole friendship thing didn't work out.

Protocol dictated that I report the incident to HR and take myself out of the situation immediately. Except I'd also royally pissed off my boss, who was a PR genius. She, too, could very well use this against me.

I had no idea what to do.

"Why... just *why*?" Why had he kissed me? We'd been making such good progress. I didn't understand.

"Judging by your reaction, I'm not sure now's the time to—"

"Just tell me! What the hell were you thinking?" He couldn't be *into* me. I wasn't sure he could be *into* anybody, based on the conversations we'd had about romance and love.

Was it just an attraction thing? If so, why the hell would he act on it, knowing we'd be stuck together for another three weeks? Did he not realize how fucking awkward it would be?

"All right, I guess I'll just spit it out." And then Jackson Sinclair, the absolute *bane* of the last eight months of my existence, looked me dead in the eyes and said, "I was thinking that you and I should get married."

22

WHAT?!

Stunned silent seconds turned into minutes, then hours, probably. Was he joking? He had to be joking.

He was so sarcastic, his humor so dry, that I genuinely couldn't tell. But Jackson Sinclair was not proposing to me right now. Even the notion was laughable. So I opened my mouth to laugh.

What came out was: "Is this a joke?"

"No," he said. "It is, however, the most clear-headed conclusion I've come to in years. It makes so much sense."

My heart was hammering inside my mouth. "What?"

"You process this however you need to."

What the actual fuck was he even talking about?

"What the actual fuck are you even talking about?"

"Think about it." And then he just stopped speaking. As though the reasoning was so abundantly clear, it didn't require an explanation.

"We can't get *married*, Jackson." It was unbelievable to me that it even needed to be said. "We barely even know each other."

"We've got three weeks left in the Immersive. That's plenty of time."

My head was spinning. "What the hell type of mental gymnastics... How the hell do you imagine you and I could fall in love in the span of three weeks? Or *ever*?"

His features pinched in confusion. "What does love have to do with it?"

I took a deep breath, centering myself. "I swear, if this is your idea of a joke—"

"It's not."

My arms were deadweight at my sides as I stared up at him, failing to fit the pieces together. I'd spent the better half of a year trying to find this man a wife. Two matches per week for eight months, all of whom checked off every single item on his long list of requirements.

Me? I didn't even check off one.

Not *one*.

I was too short. Too young. Too blonde.

I didn't have a master's degree from an Ivy League school, didn't own my own seven-figure business, had never competitively played any of the sports on his list, didn't speak a second language. And that was just the tip of the iceberg. I wasn't even close to what he wanted in a wife.

"Explain this to me like I'm a child," I tried. "Break it down to a molecular level."

Jackson slipped his hands into his pockets and considered me for a moment. "I have to get married," he said. "If I want to keep my position as CEO, which I do, then it's no longer optional. Minerva isn't giving me a choice in the matter."

"Okay." So far, I was with him.

"Problem is, I very much don't want to get married, and being cornered into it isn't exactly helping."

I huffed a breath through my nose. "Why don't you just... I don't know, hire someone to marry you? Aren't contractual marriages a thing in your tax bracket?"

I didn't need to ask because they definitely were. Charmed had a package to cater to those clients, but it was all very discreet. I wasn't senior enough to take on any of those cases, so I had no idea what they actually entailed.

He cocked his head. "If I offered you fifty million in exchange for one contractual year of marriage, would you do it?"

"Absolutely not."

His face split into a heart-stuttering grin. "A hundred million."

"No."

"Two hundred."

"*No*."

A low chuckle rumbled out of the depths of his chest. "Then that idea doesn't work. What else do you have?"

The back of my neck was growing increasingly damp. "I didn't mean *me*. Find someone willing. It shouldn't be very hard." Not with a dollar amount that hefty. "Better yet, why don't you make that offer to one of the *sixty-seven* women we'd set you up with before this?"

I knew his deal with Minerva had changed after the whole pool incident; back then he'd only been required to attend the dates. But it wasn't too late. He could probably arrange something with one of them now.

"Finding someone willing may not be difficult," he said carefully, "but finding someone I could stand to spend that much time with is damn near impossible."

"You hate having me around."

I didn't understand why this conversation was so amusing to him. His stupid grin kept twitching.

"You've grown on me." *Twitch*. "We are friends after all, are we not? They do say that the happiest marriages stem from solid friendships."

Valid point, minus the part where, "We've been friends for *one day*."

"And yet it's felt like a lifetime, no?"

My teeth sunk into my bottom lip. Punishment for smiling. "I hate you."

"So you claim." His eyes dropped to my mouth.

The wicked temptation to lick my lips and add fuel to whatever fire was burning in his gaze struck me like lightning. Then came the stark realization that I very much wanted him to kiss me again.

I didn't even notice we'd moved until my back hit the wall. Didn't notice how close we were until the tips of his shoes nudged mine. His hand was braced beside my neck, my head was slanting ever-so-slightly to one side, and I could feel the heat of his breath on my skin, but I couldn't remember how we got here.

I needed to push him away.

"Then there's... this," Jackson murmured. He tipped my chin up, and my breath hitched. "I definitely think we should explore this."

"You're full of horrible ideas today," I breathed.

He was caressing my skin again. It was so confusing.

"You're not curious about this?" His thumb brushed my lip and *fuck me*. I was drowning in butterflies. "That was a damn good kiss, Jamie."

Shut it down.

SHUT IT DOWN.

"I've had better," I said as evenly as I could manage. That was a blatant lie, meant to discourage further flirtation. It failed spectacularly.

"Mean." He was positively beaming. "I don't believe it for a second, but still mean."

"God, you're arrogant." And damn it, the breathiness of my voice made it sound like I was fawning. I glared up at him defiantly, hating the way his eyes thawed with warm amusement.

"This could be fun, don't you think?" he teased. "You, me, the blistering sexual tension, and twelve months of a marriage neither of us wants."

"*Blistering* is a bit of a stretch," I said as the fire reached the tips of my fingers, consuming me whole. "I'm not going to marry you, Jackson. We'd make a horrible fake married couple and you know it."

"I know no such thing. We'd be great together. I'm even starting to like you, and I don't like anyone save for my household staff."

"You don't like me," I said firmly.

"Oh, but I do. I might even *like* like you."

Incorrect.

"Jackson, listen to me. You don't like me. You just think you do because I don't want your money and I'm a little mean."

"That's not all of it."

"If I flipped the switch and started kissing your ass and showing interest in your money, you'd revert right back to hating my guts."

"Shall we test it out?" His smirk was so cocky, it was almost lewd. "Say something nice to me."

"Well *now* it won't work. Not if you know what we're doing."

He shrugged. "Try it."

"You just want me to pay you a compliment."

"Perhaps." His smile grazed his eyes. "But if your theory is correct, then at least some of the attraction should dwindle. On my end, I mean. You'll continue to find me irresistible."

I almost took the bait. The mean little quip made it all the way to the tip of my tongue before I caught it. Being outwardly unimpressed by him was what'd gotten us into this mess in the first place. Reining in my desire to sass his ego back in check, I batted my eyelashes up at him instead.

This already felt stupid.

"I'll admit you aren't... *un*attractive."

His throat worked to suppress a chuckle. "That's significantly more generous than I thought you were going to get, to be quite honest."

"Did it work? Are you disgusted by me yet?"

"You're marginally less desirable than I found you a minute ago, so yes."

Only marginally? "How many compliments before my face makes you want to retch, do you think?"

Jackson stepped around me and leaned a muscular shoulder against the wall. Even covered in a three-piece suit, you could tell the man was ripped.

"Let's try four more," he said. "See how we feel."

Four?

"I don't think I can come up with—" I cut off when his eyes got all lusty, blowing out a breath. "All right, fine. You have... a somewhat pleasing voice."

"*Really*?" Jackson teased lightly. "How revolting."

I sucked on my cheek, my hands folding delicately behind me as I leaned against the wall. My shoulder inadvertently brushed his chest, and he took it as an invitation to move closer.

"And don't even get me started on your eyes," I said. "Because I wouldn't know what to say. They're blue, which I guess is better than, like, beige."

"You're being far too kind, Miss Paquin. It's making me ill."

My mouth expanded into a smile against my direct orders. I felt light; fluttery.

"You smell adequately clean," I told him.

"You disgust me."

I giggled as the lightness spread, bubbling under my skin. "There *is* one very particular thing about you that I find exceptionally sexy, though. Should I tell you what it is?"

His pupils flared. "I may vomit if you do."

Having fully forgotten about the purpose of this exercise, I rose to my toes and whispered, "I'm sorry to say, Mr. Sinclair, that you look like the type of man who'd be packing a remarkably impressive set of forearms."

He didn't even try to hold back his grin.

"Makes my toes curl just thinkin' about it." I dropped back to my normal height. "How was that?"

"Perfect," he said. "I may never experience another erection ever again."

I burst into a laugh.

"You've likely rendered me well and truly flaccid for the rest of my sexless days, Miss Paquin. Well done."

My hands came up to cover my face. I was dying.

"You know what will make it even worse? If you demand that I take you shopping for our third date. I'd positively detest buying you things while you talk about how sexy my forearms are."

"Shut up," I laughed.

"Theory successfully confirmed. Now we just need to properly execute. I'll have Savannah set up an appointment with my shoppers tomorrow."

I wiped at the wetness trailing down my cheeks. "That's not happening. We're going back to my original plan. You go talk to Mabel and Molly, I'll go prep for our interview, and we'll forever pretend like this never happened."

"No."

"Why the hell not? You said you wanted to talk about it, and we did."

He shrugged. "You can pretend all you want, but I'm not doing it."

I wasn't laughing anymore. "Are you... going to tell people?"

He frowned. "I wasn't planning on it. Not until you and I come to an agreement, at least."

So, if we never came to an agreement, he wouldn't tell anyone? That could work.

"But you *will* talk to the Harrison sisters, right?" I asked. I'd also have to pull them aside at some point and ask for their discretion.

What a mess.

"Yes. I suspect I'll have no choice."

My eyes slimmed. "And what are you going to tell them?"

"The truth," he deadpanned. "That I very much wanted to kiss you, so I did, and that you did not react violently like I thought you might."

"To be fair, I thought about it."

He chuckled. "If you'd like, I can also let them know that you're not interested. That this attraction is strictly one-sided." He waited for a beat before adding, "Would that be an accurate assessment?"

There was only one correct answer to that question. I didn't need to hesitate or pause or think about my response.

Yet I stood there, holding his gaze while he patiently waited for my rejection.

"I… I'm never going to marry you."

With that, I made my swift exit out of the cardboard palace Jackson Sinclair had built for my cat.

23

"EVERYTHING ALL RIGHT?"

My shoulders scrunched even tighter, reaching for my ears.

Jackson took a seat beside me at the small conference table. Within seconds, the masculine notes of his cologne swirled into my lungs, making me lightheaded.

I clicked my pen and flipped the interview booklet open. "Everything's fine. Why?" I'd been perfectly amicable with him all morning.

Warmth trickled over my skin as he eyed my profile. I kept my attention bolted to the questions in front of me.

"Well," he started gently, "It's almost noon, we've been attached at the hip since five a.m., and you haven't looked at me once."

He only knew that because he'd been doing enough staring for the both of us. I didn't say this out loud though, knowing my irritation was misdirected.

I was mad at myself, not him.

"I'm just tired," I said. "Didn't get a lot of sleep last night."

He shifted in his chair like he was going to probe further, but after a short pause, he picked up his phone and began typing away.

"Are you ready to get started?" I continued to scan the papers, even though it wasn't necessary. I had the questions all but memorized at this point. "And just a reminder that, per your aunt's request, this session will be recorded and subject to review by—"

"Since when?"

"Since you signed the contract and agreed to it."

"Your interview is not the standardized one I signed off on being recorded," he argued. "You've got questions in there about my past relationships and sexual preferences."

"Because that information wasn't provided to us by your team, and we require the data to do our jobs." I kept my tone calm and neutral, sticking to the facts. To be honest, I agreed with him. I couldn't imagine my answers to some of these questions being shared with a member of my family.

In fact, the more time I had to digest Jackson's situation, the ickier I felt about it. This whole process must have been incredibly invasive for someone who'd been thrust into it against their will.

Consent was the key thing here. All our other Immersive clients agreed to have someone follow them around for fourteen hours a day and observe their every routine, habit, and interaction. Not only did Jackson *not* want that, but he was also being forced into the end result.

And I was playing a major part in it.

My inability to sleep last night had given me a lot of time to think. And thinking had led to a whole lot of guilt.

"I don't agree to this interview being recorded," he said simply.

I knew he expected me to ignore his request because when I reached for my phone and hit Pause, his posture stuttered, and he blinked.

Which, in turn, made me feel even worse.

"Any other concerns?" I asked.

He let out a breath. "Yeah, you still won't look at me, Jamie. Is it because of yesterday? Were you—"

He was interrupted by Savannah poking her head into the room. "Your order has arrived, sir."

He'd ordered more food? But we'd just had lunch—*oh*.

The seductive aroma of fresh coffee filled the room when Savannah walked in. She placed a steaming cup of heaven in front of Jackson, along with a side of cream, honey, and macarons.

Caffeine and sugar. My sleep-deprived brain drooled at the sight, and I cursed myself for not having thought to grab a cup before we'd sat down. The small Americano I'd had early this morning was on its last legs.

"Thank you," Jackson said. "That'll be all."

She disappeared with another smile, and I shifted my attention back to the booklet, my mouth watering. "If you don't have any other immediate concerns, we can get started."

Instead of answering, Jackson slid the hot cup of temptation toward me. "For you."

My gaze flew up to his, my heart stammering when I met their piercing blue. How was he more attractive every time I looked at him? Where was his ceiling?

"Thank you," I half-croaked as my fingers wrapped around the warm, inviting cup. It was delicious. Rich and dark with a slight hint of cocoa.

His thoughtfulness didn't help the guilt I was drowning in.

Jackson snatched up a purple macaron and bit into it, waiting as I took my time, savoring the first few sips of my coffee. The sharp edges of my mood were already starting to soften.

"All right, so... because there was so much pertinent info missing from our original dataset, I want to start by filling in some of those gaps," I eventually said, placing my cup down. "I'll need to combine your answers with my own observations—which we'll also go over—in order to create a new, more accurate profile for you. After that, we can move on to the standard check-in. Any questions?"

He shook his head.

Fiddling with my pen, I decided to go off-script for a second. "I realize that your current situation isn't exactly ideal, but I think... if you can give me some honest answers, I could really help you. Getting married might not be so bad if I can find you someone you like—someone you're really compatible with, you know?"

I risked a glance up at him but couldn't decipher his expression.

"How does that sound?" I tried. It was my way of letting him know I was on his side; but I wasn't sure it translated.

Unsure of what else to do or say, I chose to interpret his unblinking silence as a *yes*.

"Great." My eyes scanned the first question on the first page... three times.

I placed my pen down, picked it back up, sipped my coffee.

"Are we going to get started?" Jackson asked.

No. Yeah. Of course. My first meeting with Minerva was tomorrow, so this needed to get done.

I opened my mouth, meaning to voice the question I'd been staring at. Instead, I accidentally went off-script again. "You mentioned earlier this week that some of these topics felt invasive to you. If that's the case—if I ask you a question that makes you uncomfortable—then you don't have to answer it."

He didn't need to be in my direct line of sight for me to feel the shift in his demeanor, the curious tilt of his head.

I cleared my throat.

"I thought my compliance was mandatory," he said.

Yes, well, "I've been given creative control over the process and I'm saying you don't have to answer any question you're not comfortable with. I'll just work with the data I have."

After a short pause, Jackson leaned in. Again.

I sighed. "We really need to work on your aversion to respecting personal bubbles."

"Tell you what. I'll provide an honest answer to whatever question you ask."

I raised an eyebrow at him. "But..."

"But some of those sections were left blank for a reason. So how about I give you all the answers, and we keep the private ones just between us."

Damn Jackson Sinclair and his sultry voice. I swear I could get tipsy just by listening to him talk. Especially on zero sleep.

"And what am I supposed to do with the information if I can't use it to find you a wife?"

"I'm sure you'll figure it out." He winked and my whole chest exploded into a tornado of butterflies.

My eyes snapped back to the questionnaire. Permanently, this time.

~

"Okay, last question for this section. You didn't list any instruments on your original form, but you own multiple grand pianos. Do you play?"

Jackson tapped the strawberry macaron I'd placed in front of him. That was our system—green for the record, red for my knowledge only.

"I do," he said. "I've played since I was six."

I frowned. "Are you sure you don't want that included? I still don't have much to work with regarding your hobbies and interests."

Jackson liked to make money. And then he liked to spend it.

That was basically all I had.

"It's not relevant. I don't play for other people."

"All right. Fine." I flipped the page, only to flip it right back and make sure I hadn't skipped forward. We were already at the Past Relationships section? That was fast.

Jackson reached for the red macaron as soon as he saw the header.

I sighed. "Any chance there's a single question on here I can use?"

"I doubt it."

Tossing my pen onto the table, I stretched my arms above my head. We'd been sitting here for over five hours. My whole body was stiff.

"Let's just skip it, then," I offered.

Only because I didn't want to waste any time. Not because talking about Jackson's long line of impressively accomplished exes was about as appealing to me as chewing on a handful of thumbtacks.

My stomach clamped when he reached over me to peek at the booklet. With his attention on the pages, my rebellious eyes decided they were free to roam over his features and shamelessly drink him in.

He was undeniably perfect. Even with the afternoon stubble covering his sharp jaw and the light shadows etched underneath his eyes, he was *devastating*. I understood why so many tears had been shed over him. Now that the anger had ebbed and the burnout wasn't so overwhelming, I could understand how he could be so easily destructive.

The urge to push myself away warred with the one begging for touch. I wanted to run my fingers over his cheekbone, his jaw... wrap his tie around my fist and force him to look at me.

I did neither—just lingered in the in-between like an indecisive coward.

An indecisive coward who loved her career and couldn't justify risking it for a kiss.

"I don't want any of these on the record," Jackson muttered in his smooth accent, blissfully unaware of the havoc he was wreaking on my insides. "This section or the next two."

"Then we just have the check-in... left..."

My words died when he met my gaze. It was like my brain shut off and I couldn't find the switch to bring it back online.

Alarming.

On so many fundamental levels, this was alarming.

"I still think we should go over it." He said it quietly. Like that, too, was only meant for me.

"Why?"

"You can still use it. When you're... picking my next match, you can still keep this stuff in mind. I just don't want it fed to a machine."

I couldn't even tell if that made sense, I was so distracted. As soon as he mentioned being set up with someone else, my fingers balled into fists and my gut clenched again as something in the deepest depths of my soul snarled possessively.

Extremely alarming.

"All right," my mouth said as the snarling Thing grew bigger, developed claws, fangs, and the ability to spit fire. "I'll just... you share whatever you want me to keep in mind for your next match. Since, um, you've already read over the questions."

My voice lost the last bit of professionalism I'd tried so hard to maintain when it quivered. Then again, the proximity of our faces wasn't exactly respecting any professional boundaries. Neither was the way he was looking at me. Like I was something to be devoured.

"And what about you?" he asked gently. "Are you comfortable getting into all this?"

"It's my job." I'd spent years discussing these topics with clients. This shouldn't have been any different.

"How about this." His head tilted to where the red and green macarons were sitting on the table, though his gaze never left mine. "If at any point you want to stop, just say 'strawberry.'"

A whole lot of the muscles south of my professionalism clenched. "You're assigning me a safeword?"

More clenching.

"I don't care if it's your job. You want to stop, we stop."

"Okay," I whispered back.

And that was the moment my brain chose to remind me that it'd been a year since I'd had sex. I slipped my hands underneath my thighs and cleared my throat, indicating that he should go ahead instead of staring at me. He took the hint.

"As far as my relationship history is concerned, blank is accurate." He paused. I blinked. "I've never been in one."

Maybe I shouldn't have been surprised.

Maybe that should have made sense, given what I knew about his distaste for romantic love.

Still, it caught me off guard and, for a single deer-in-the-headlights moment, my face went slack. I'd dealt with other clients who'd been single all their lives, of course. It really wasn't as uncommon as you'd think. However, that information was disclosed at a very early stage in the process.

And also, none of those other clients had been Jackson fucking Sinclair.

"Okay." I managed to school my expression with impressive reaction speed, considering how close he was still sitting.

His stupidly handsome face split into a stupidly handsome grin. "Come on. I know you have questions."

So. Many.

I didn't even know where to start.

"You think romantic love is emotional snake oil. This checks out."

At some point over the last little while, my chair had swiveled in his direction and his chair had swiveled in mine. We were face to face, our legs all but tangled.

"What about you?" His knee gently nudged mine. "When was your last relationship?"

"This interview isn't about me."

"I'd still like to know," he said. "If you're willing to share."

Was I willing to share? It felt like we were dangerously close to crossing yet another professional boundary and I wasn't sure how many more we could get away with before this whole thing blew up.

"It's been just over two years," I said.

Unsatisfied with my lack of detail, Jackson said nothing.

"He wasn't ready to be in a committed relationship, so we decided to part ways." Simple, standard stuff. Nothing too exciting. Oh, except, "He did get engaged to someone else like six months later, so..."

"You haven't dated since?" He seemed genuinely surprised by that.

"I haven't exactly had a lot of spare time over the last eight, nine months. And before that... I don't know. There was no one I was into, I guess."

"What was his name? The ex?"

"Lee."

"Lee's an idiot."

"Oh please." I huffed a humourless laugh.

"I'm being genuine." His shoulders straightened, mildly offended by my reaction.

I rolled my eyes. "Right. The man who thinks my entire profession is a joke and doesn't believe in relationships *also* thinks my ex is an idiot for breaking things off with me."

"Because he is."

The look I gave him was so dry, it made him visibly bristle.

"All right, look." He ran a hand through his hair,

nudging closer to me. "I apologize for what I said about your job. Truly, it was impolite and out of line. I regret it. To be clear, I do *not* actually think your profession is a joke."

I snorted.

It only added fuel to his fire. "Jamie, I asked you to marry me yesterday."

My pulse jolted. "That doesn't count."

"How?"

"Because one, you definitely didn't mean it. And two, it was for convenience, not love."

His features contorted as he grew increasingly insulted by my accurate judgment of the situation. "I did mean it," he insisted. "And, again, I'm not quite sure what love has to do with us getting married."

I threw my hands up. "It has everything to do with it, are you kidding? Do you have any fucking idea how horrible it is to be trapped in a loveless marriage? Honestly, I'd kind of rather die."

His brows slammed into each other. "You'd rather die than marry me."

"Not, like, *literally*. I just mean... You know what I mean."

"I do not know what you mean."

I sighed. "You and I don't want the same things. We don't view relationships the same way. I *love* love, Jackson. So much so that I've made it my whole career. If I ever get married, it'll be because I love that person enough to want to share my life with them. That's it."

It was the one thing I'd wanted for myself since I was old enough to know what it meant. He still didn't get it, though, judging by the way he was frowning at me.

"Let's just move on," I tried.

There was a stubborn edge to his posture I'd come to learn meant he was going to see the battle through to the end. "I'm not sure you understand what a marriage between us would entail."

"Off the top of my head? I'm thinking loneliness, regret, boredom, discontentment, lack of fulfillment." *Loss of career.* "What am I missing?"

The pointed lack of enthusiasm in my voice was meant to deter him. It had the opposite effect.

Amusement shimmered in his eyes, toyed with his mouth. "Let's paint you a slightly more accurate picture, shall we? Just so you're able to make a more informed decision."

"If I tell you that nothing you say will make a difference, will you listen?"

"Not likely."

"Then I'll make you a deal." I tossed my pen onto the table, crossed my arms, and leaned back in my chair. "I'll listen to your offer, so long as you listen to my answer."

"Fine, but let's make it more interesting, shall we? I get to pursue this until you use your safe word. If you say 'strawberry,' I stop. Anything else I take as a green light."

"Why can't I just say 'no'?"

The unsubtle glint in his eyes told me everything I needed to know. "The former can be much more fun."

He was a dom, then. Figured.

"Fine." It made no difference to me what word I had to use to get him to stop, just as long as he stopped. "You've got yourself a deal."

Famous last words.

24

JACKSON INSISTED we continue the conversation back at his home office, over drinks. He said he "needed time to gather his thoughts and solidify his arguments."

I called bullshit. He knew exactly what his arguments were, he just wanted to change the location to somewhere more comfortable and whiskey my inhibitions away—make me more agreeable.

It wasn't going to work. But it was 7 p.m., I was exhausted, and a drink didn't sound so bad. So, I agreed.

That was my first mistake.

My second was letting him sit beside me on the couch instead of quite literally anywhere else. I should have known better. He smelled so good it made me stupid.

"Here."

"What is it?" I eyed the cloudy liquid in the tumbler he'd handed me. It had an impressive layer of smooth foam on the top.

"The best whiskey sour in the country."

Really, truly, the man's ego knew no bounds. I took a small, doubtful sip.

Damn it.

He chuckled, presumably reading my mind. I didn't know if it was the best whiskey sour in the country, but it was the best one I'd ever had. He'd perfected it.

"A pretty solid point in my favor, wouldn't you agree?" he teased as he settled beside me—*way* too close. "Think about it, you come home at the end of a long day, exhausted, and your husband makes you a fresh cocktail while you vent."

I wouldn't have a job to come home from if I married him, but all right, sure. I nodded.

"And if I'm not here, your staff will be."

I raised a brow. "My staff..."

"You really haven't thought this through, Jamie." He twisted on the couch to face me, arm slung over the backrest. "One year of marriage and you'd never have to lift a finger again in your life."

I turned so that we were face to face. "Quick reminder that I've turned down all of your previous monetary—"

"I'd stop reminding me of that if I were you."

"Why?"

He leaned in to whisper his answer like it was a secret. "Because you've managed to awaken something rather odd in me. The more you turn down my money, the more... *inclined* I become to want to spend it on you."

I blinked. "That's incredibly irrational."

"I'm aware." He sipped his drink. "You wanted a list of my kinks? There's your first one."

My third mistake was asking, "People rejecting your money is a kink for you?"

"No, Jamie, *you* rejecting my money is a kink for me."

Fireflies infiltrated my chest. My oxygen levels tanked. "That's..." *Nonsensical. Inappropriate. Probably a lie.* "A quick FYI—friends don't have kinks centered around their friends, and if they do, they keep that information to themselves."

He cocked his head. "Do friends kiss the way we did yesterday?"

"I thought we weren't going to talk about that anymore."

"Tell me you didn't like it and I'll never bring it up again."

I opened my mouth. Closed it. "Whether I liked it or not isn't the point."

"Ah, but you see, it very much is the point—my next one, in fact." He gestured lightly between us. "This works."

"*What* works?"

"Our bodies. They're quite into each other."

Were hot flashes in your late twenties a cause for medical concern? Because I'd been experiencing a noticeable number of them lately. "I'm not sure that's accurate."

One good kiss was just that—*one* good kiss. It didn't mean every subsequent one would be earth-shattering.

With a cheeky smirk, Jackson polished off his whiskey, got rid of the empty tumbler, and held out his palm. "Give me your hand."

"I think I'm good. Friends don't really hold hands."

He chuckled. "Just humor me for a moment, would you?"

With a strangely nervous sip of my drink, I placed my fingers in his palm.

That was my fourth mistake.

His hand engulfed mine, sending a buzz over my skin that had nothing to do with the alcohol. Then he did something I wouldn't have predicted in a million years.

Jackson Sinclair guided my hand forward and pressed it to his chest. Over his heart.

Over his rapidly beating heart.

"Now feel what happens when I do this." Without warning, he leaned in and brushed a kiss over my cheek.

My body went up in flames.

His pulse jumped under my palm.

"You feel that?" His hot breath grazed my skin, making me shiver. "It likes you."

I went rigid. Blinked. "I... pardon?"

He didn't know what he was saying. He didn't understand what "my heart likes you" could be interpreted as, surely.

"My whole body likes you."

"Jackson..." This was officially too much. We'd crossed another line, and I really didn't see how we could find our way back from this one.

"Use your safeword, Jamie." My lashes fluttered when he brushed his lips over my jaw.

I meant to use it, I swear. It was *why* I opened my mouth in the first place. But he nipped at my earlobe just as I was about to thread the correct letters together, and what came out was a ruptured whimper.

"Say it," he demanded unreasonably. "Tell me to fuck off."

I would if he'd just stop nibbling on my skin like that for a second. It was so... distracting. And pleasant.

So, so, so pleasant. Why was it so pleasant?

Before I knew what'd even happened, my half-empty glass was discarded, Jackson had looped a muscled arm around my waist, and I was seated comfortably on his lap.

Oh, and my hand was still clamped to his racing chest.

"Is this so bad?" he teased. "Would a year of this be so horrible, Jamie?"

"This is... so inappropriate."

"You know how to make it stop." His nose brushed over the shell of my ear, and I quivered against him.

I should've insisted we had this conversation back in his office. So many mistakes had been made in such quick succession.

"Tell me some more about how you don't want my money, so I can tell you exactly how spoiled you'd be as my wife." He placed a searing kiss on my neck, then nipped at the spot with his teeth. "You wouldn't have a choice. I'd put it in our marriage contract. You wouldn't be allowed to say no to me buying you things."

In my defense, I hadn't meant to break him like this.

"Jackson—"

"I'm not done." His eyes were black when he pulled his head back to look at me, his heart pounding against my hand. It was fucking intoxicating. "You'd have your own staff, I'd gift you apartments, clothes, company shares. You'd be financially secure for the rest of your life. What more could you possibly want?"

"I..." I had nothing.

"See?" His midnight gaze dropped to my mouth. "It's a fantastic deal, so take it."

I swallowed. "No."

With a frustrated growl, he pulled me flush against him—pressed me right to his raging erection. It drenched my brain in charged static.

"What else do you want?"

"Nothing. I'm not going to marry you."

I was panting. He was panting. There was no breathable air left in the whole house.

He licked his lips, cheeks reddening with… either lust or rage. I couldn't be sure. "Then say the word."

"No." The rebellious little quip slipped out of me before I could stop it. There was something so unbelievably thrilling about not giving Jackson exactly what he wanted.

It was like standing at the very edge of a cliff with no harness on. Or toying with fire.

His gaze was borderline feral. Still, he couldn't fully hold back his smile, no matter how hard he kept trying. "You like being a little tease, Jamie?"

Without waiting for an answer, his hand slipped a little too high up my skirt, edging up the fabric.

Whoa, okay.

Now would have been the seventh most perfect time to put a stop to the destructive path we'd set ourselves on.

"I asked you a question." His fingers inched up and up, ruining me with gentle caresses. "Do you enjoy teasing me?"

"I don't know what you're talking about."

"No?"

"Mm-mm." I shook my head innocently, desperately clinging on to his shirt. My nails were going to leave permanent bites in the crisp fabric.

"Telling me I have the personality of a hardboiled egg… calling me *predictable*… refusing to obey the simplest commands…"

"You're a dom, I get it," I panted. His fingers were dangerously close to discovering just how much I didn't hate this.

"Am I?"

"Typical, seeing as how you're such a control freak."

He chuckled darkly. "You're so fucking mean."

I'd have laughed too if he hadn't chosen that exact moment to brush the edge of my soaked panties with his finger. I swallowed back the moan that tore through my chest, stopping it just in time.

"Spread your legs a little wider for me, Jamie. I'd like to tease you properly." His fingers kept brushing the seam of my underwear, dousing me in dark lust and liquid fire.

This was it. If I listened to him, it would be a clear indication that I wanted it. I'd be saying it without actually saying it.

"Come on. Show me what a good girl you can be."

Fuck me.

Who the hell would have guessed that Jackson Sinclair, of all people, was into dirty talk? And teasing?

My thighs inched open for him, my last bit of rationality melting into need.

"That's it," he purred approvingly. "It's going to feel so good when I finally touch you properly, isn't it?"

I whimpered when he drew a knuckle up my seam and mercilessly pressed it into my clit. Even through the cotton fabric, the shock of pleasure hit hard enough to make me shudder.

Jackson *tsk*ed. "Needy little thing. You'd need to be fucked regularly if we got married, wouldn't you?"

I wanted to point out that he'd very specifically told me that he wasn't going to have a sexual relationship with his wife, but the words withered into a desperate whimper when he pinched my clit over my panties.

Then he did it again—harder this time.

I choked on a gasp. "Ohmygod."

"Let's go over the rules again, shall we?" His fingers teased my slick inner thighs, tracing fire over my skin. "What do you say if you want me to stop what I'm doing?"

"Strawberry," I managed.

"And what happens if you tell me 'no' instead? What if you beg me to stop without using your special word?"

I swallowed, my thighs quivering. "You keep going."

"Do you agree with those terms?" he teased, trailing kisses over my jaw.

I shouldn't have wanted it. Not only was he a client, but his "terms" probably should have freaked me out, made me want to push off his lap and run. He really was one giant walking red flag.

Yet I'd never been so turned on in my life. "Yes."

His heart raced against my hand, a harsh breath shoving out of him. "Good girl."

My lashes fluttered.

"You know what I've been wondering since the first time you insulted me?" His fingers continued to explore my inner thigh, teasing the sensitive skin with featherlight touches. "Take a guess."

I was not nearly lucid or coherent enough for that. "Just tell me."

He licked his lips again and I almost blacked out. "I've been dying to know if your pussy is as pretty as the rest of you."

His accent was so sexy, his voice so deliciously deep. I couldn't handle it.

I had to close my eyes for a moment to gather myself. When I opened them again, he was watching me with that evil, knowing smirk pulling at his gorgeous mouth.

"Will you show me?" he murmured.

He couldn't be serious. He wanted me to... actually, I didn't really know what he wanted me to do.

"Stand up," he ordered softly.

"Someone might walk in."

"I've instructed the staff to stay out of this wing and security cameras have been turned off. I told you I don't share, Jamie. You're for my eyes only. Now... stand up. Show me how good you are at following instructions."

My heart was pounding so hard it was making me dizzy. After a few seconds of hesitation, I gently pushed onto my shaky feet and stood between his knees.

"Good girl." His throat worked with a hard swallow as his gaze raked over me. He cupped his generous bulge. "Pull up your skirt."

His commands were starting to push a very specific button in the back of my subconscious, and the resulting rush was unlike anything I'd ever experienced. I did as I was told, bunching up my skirt with trembling fingers, until the fabric was gathered around my hips.

Jackson squeezed himself over his pants, his gaze heavy, chest rising and falling with effort. Like he was just as affected by all this as I was. It was quite possibly the hottest thing I'd ever witnessed.

"Now... pull your panties aside and show me how pretty you are."

Non-horny Jamie was going to hate me for this. I'd cringe and kick blankets over it for the rest of my fucking life. I knew this for certain, and I still went ahead and did it.

With a shaky breath, I pulled the dark, damp cotton to one side.

His eyes went black.

I was pretty sure he'd been expecting me to say no, to fight him on it. My compliance pulled a pleased rumble from the depths of his chest, and he tugged on himself, tongue darting out to wet his lips again. "Show me properly, Jamie. Let me see that sweet little clit."

This had gotten so out of hand. I had no idea what I was doing, or why I was doing it. I just knew that it felt incredible. There was real power in this—in having someone look at you like... like *that.* Jackson may have been the one giving out instructions, but he was just as helpless against this as I was. He looked lost, dazed, fully focused and entirely out of it all at once.

And when I delicately pulled myself apart for him, he groaned, shifting on the couch as a small spot on his tailored trousers darkened with lust.

My knees were seconds away from crumbling.

Like your career.

I blinked, panic blooming in my chest. Yet my feet stayed firmly rooted in place.

"You're being such a good fucking girl." His voice was dark, crisp, breathless. Almost like he was in pain. "Shall I make the rest of my case while you stand there and pretend like it's not everything you want? Or do you think your pussy will give you away?"

I was well beyond forming even one word, let alone a full sentence.

"I'd like an answer. Shall we discuss just how spoiled you'd be as my wife? How I'd buy you diamonds just so I could fuck you in them?" If he licked his lips one more time I was going to go into cardiac arrest. "I'd make you the envy of every woman in the world, Jamie, even if it was against your will. And with a clit that sweet... the ways I would torture you. You'd look so fucking pretty all tied up for me, blushing and begging for mercy with all those diamonds wrapped around your neck. I'd ruin you."

I clenched. Visibly, according to the evil smirk it earned me.

"Would you like that? Would you like being tied up

and at my mercy?" When I didn't respond, he said, "What if I forced you to pick out the toy you'd be tortured with every night? What if I made you wait for me on my bed, kept you on the phone while you edged yourself and begged your husband to come home early from work?"

Another whimper. Another clench. I was dripping down my thighs.

He noticed.

"Should I give you a little preview of what it would be like if you were my wife? What do you think?"

Every time he said *wife*, my stomach clenched. He kept putting a possessive emphasis on the word, and it pleased the lusty little monster he'd awakened in me.

Then he leaned forward until his face was inches away from my throbbing clit. "God, just fucking look at you, keeping yourself spread for me. You really are pretty everywhere, aren't you?" There was enough awe and praise in his voice to last me a lifetime. "You're dripping all the way down your thighs, sweet girl. You must be in agony."

My brain was drenched in enough flammable static to reduce my comprehension levels to a bare-fucking-minimum, but I was pretty sure he'd just called me *sweet girl.*

I was even more sure it made me clench again. My core was scorched.

Jackson ran two knuckles up my inner thigh, gathering the slick evidence of my lust. "What I'd do to see myself spilling out of you like this… you have no fucking idea. It's very quickly becoming another one of my kinks."

The visual slammed into me like a ball of fire, making my head spin.

"What do you think, sweet girl? You want to know

what it feels like to take a full load of my cum in your perfect pussy?" He cocked his head to one side when I whimpered, running his knuckles over my slick skin again. "If you keep making those noises, it'll be two loads, darling. My cock likes them a little too much. You think your pretty little cunt can handle being fucked twice in one night?"

Before I could even think to talk myself out of it, my mouth was moving. "I'm on birth control. Tested and everything." Translation: *YES. PLEASE.*

He didn't need to give me his answer. Charmed required their clients to be tested every three months. Jackson's results were in his file; clear as of two weeks ago.

"What if I was rough with you?" he pushed. "Do you think you could handle being held down and fucked hard? Could your pussy take it?"

It was like I was see-through. He was smashing all my secret buttons one by one. "Yes."

"Good girl."

What little oxygen my lungs had managed to retain rushed out of them when he slipped his knuckles into his mouth and licked away my arousal.

He fucking *groaned* when he did it, eyes shutting momentarily with ecstasy.

"Fucking peaches," he muttered darkly, going back for more.

Was I going to die here? Because it kind of felt like it.

"Fuck, I want to lick your little clit so fucking bad." He adjusted himself as his tongue flicked over his fingers, cleaning them off again. The little spot of precum seeping through his pants had spread. "You're all swollen and glistening for me, darling, practically begging to be tortured."

Perfect.

Great.

So why wasn't he doing it?

"Do you want that? Do you want my tongue on your pussy, giving you a little taste of how fucking spoiled you'd be as my wife?"

I hummed instead of answering—wasn't entirely confident I could speak anymore.

Jackson *tsk*ed. "You need to answer my questions if you want to be touched again."

I swallowed in an attempt to stop my voice from cracking when I answered him. "Yes."

"Yes, what, darling? What is it you want? Tell me."

In what world did he imagine I could weave that many sentences together while he was looking at me like that? I tried to focus, gathering my thoughts so I could create something coherent out of them, but there were so many different things my body wanted. He'd broken some sort of kinky dam in my soul and the flood was overwhelming.

I wanted too much, and I didn't know how to communicate it.

So why don't you show him?

That... I could do that.

Chewing the inside of my cheek, I lowered to my knees in front of him. He released a breath as he watched me, his gaze heavy with desire.

"Can I show you instead?" I whispered.

He tipped my chin up, the one side of his gorgeous mouth slanting up. "You can do whatever you want. Spoiled wives don't hear the word 'no' very often, Jamie. We might as well get you used to it."

It was like I'd crossed some sort of invisible barrier into an alternate reality sometime over the last week. Not only was Jackson Sinclair trying to convince me to marry him, but it was starting to turn me on.

Like... *a lot*.

My tongue darted out as I ran my palms over his hard thighs, when I reached his abs, I gave them a little push. It was like trying to nudge a boulder. He chuckled, obeying my silent command. When his back hit the cushion, I leaned in and placed a soft, innocent little kiss at the base of his bulge.

A low, pleased sound rolled out of his chest. He brushed a stray curl away from my forehead and slid closer, giving me better access.

My confidence grew and I continued placing kisses over the fabric covering his impressive length, until I reached the little wet spot of desire. Then I licked it.

His inhale was sharp, startled, *empowering*.

He gaped down at me, brows pulling together like he couldn't believe what I'd just done. So, I leaned forward again and kissed the same spot, before parting my lips and suckling on the fabric.

"Oh, fuck..." His head fell back, then immediately snapped up again, like he'd realized he didn't want to miss a single second of the visual.

My fingers itched to unzip him. I wanted to take him into my mouth and blow his mind through his dick, but... what if I teased him just a little more first?

With a cheeky smirk, I ran my mouth over him again, giving him little kisses and licks along the way until he was panting, gaze drunk with need.

"Okay, enough, just—" He cut off with a loud, vibrant groan when I turned my head and grazed my teeth over his full length, teasing him through the fabric. "*Fuuuuck*."

When I reached the tip and gave it a little extra attention, his hips bucked. His fists were white against the dark velvet couch.

This hadn't been the plan. I hadn't thought about teasing him for this long; the point of doing this was to show him what I wanted, not melt his brain. But... what if I kept going until he broke? How much could he take before he snapped, pinned me on the couch, and fucked me into the cushions with unforgiving vengeance?

My core purred at the thought, a thrill swirling up my torso.

I reached for his belt, continuing to kiss him as I unbuckled it. His thighs were tense under me, his breathing shallow. It hitched when I unzipped him, and again when I pulled his briefs down, and—*oh... my god.*

His cock was beautiful.

Yup. I officially knew what Jackson Sinclair's cock looked like, and it was *beautiful.* Long, thick, perfectly curved, and topped with a regal crown. Like the rest of him, it was also huge. I'd never been with someone this big before. It was probably going to hurt.

With that exciting thought, I grabbed him with gentle fingers and delicately angled him toward my mouth. I didn't have a grip on him—wouldn't even give him that much. Just the smooth touch of my fingertips to keep him where I wanted.

"Jamie."

Ignoring him, I pressed a sweet kiss to that one sensitive spot right under his crown, then stroked it with the tip of my tongue.

His lungs deflated. He was leaking so much already; it was incredibly satisfying.

"I know what you're doing." His voice was barely human, it was so charred and thick.

"What am I doing?" I asked lightly, mesmerized by the pearly precum trailing down his shaft. Not wanting to let it go to waste, I licked it off his skin, practically purring when his salty, masculine taste caressed my tongue.

I was so far gone—didn't even recognize myself anymore.

More precum. This time, I went straight for the source and gently suckled it out of his gorgeous, angry tip.

"*Jesus.*" He bucked instinctively, trying to get more of himself in my mouth. I didn't allow it, but I did tease his leaking slit with the tip of my tongue. The noise it earned me hit me right in the primal, lizard part of my brain.

What little reservation I had left about what we were doing snapped like a stale cracker. I started spoiling his cock with soft licks and open-mouthed kisses, making sure to capture every last drop of precum I teased out of him. When my focus shifted to his balls, his patience unraveled.

"Enough." It was a command.

"I thought you said I could do what I wanted," I teased. "This is what I want."

His groan shattered into breathless pieces when I gently suckled him again. It was so fucking addicting. Jackson Sinclair, one of the wealthiest, most powerful men in the world was breaking in front of me, and all I was doing was teasing him with feather-light flicks of my tongue.

"Jamie..." He was fraying at the edges. His cheeks were flushed, eyes completely out of focus, and every time I licked him, he leaked a little more for me. Hottest experience of my life.

"Please don't make me stop," I begged delicately. "I like tasting you like this."

"Then open your mouth and do it properly."

Nah. This was more fun for me.

"Is this how you really want to play this?" he asked.

Yes. Yes, it was.

"Last chance. Open your mouth." His voice had grown dangerously dark. It was delicious. "I'll even shoot down your pretty throat as a reward and fuck you extra hard as punishment."

Nope.

I gave him a slow lick before tracing the tip of my tongue over the protruding vein running raggedly over—

With a fractured growl, Jackson fisted my hair and lifted my head off his dick. It didn't hurt, but it was firm enough to make me vibrate.

I was on the couch before I could so much as blink, pinned to the cushions the way I'd wanted. But instead of shoving my panties to the side and thrusting into me with revenge, he yanked them off, hooked his arms under my thighs, locked me in place, and dove in tongue-first.

I gasped, my back arching at the shock of sensation. He wasted no time. *None.*

There were no teasing licks or promising kisses. He went straight for my clit and roughly sucked it into his scorching mouth, groaning with angry satisfaction when he got what he wanted.

I was panting and squirming against him within seconds, spiraling up to the edge of orgasm at breath-taking speed. I needed him to slow down. "Jackson, I—"

His growl of pleasure vibrated against my clit, making my vision sway. He was licking and sucking me like a man starved, and… it took less than a minute. I screamed when the orgasm hit, my fists tightening in his hair as my spine curved and the world spun.

Holy shit. Holy fucking shit.

I saw stars. They twinkled and danced and nipped at my skin and I'd never flown so high or crashed so hard in my life. My entire body shook with the release. My lungs seized, my throat constricted, my stomach quivered, and *THIS* was what an orgasm was supposed to feel like? How the fuck had I been doing them so wrong for so long?

And why the fuck wasn't Jackson stopping?

He didn't slow down, didn't come up for air, didn't even stutter. His arms remained locked around my thighs, keeping them wide open so he could continue to eat me out without interruption.

The oversensitivity kicked in within seconds.

"Oh, f—Jacks—shit—*stopstopstop*."

He did no such thing.

And it... I loved it. This was officially my favorite game.

He fucked me with his tongue, groaning like he was enjoying it far too much to ever relent. At some point during all of this, he'd moved off the couch and was now kneeling in front of it, angling my hips to give his mouth better fucking access.

I tried to nudge him away, but it was like trying to move a brick wall. Even when he was kneeling like this his frame was so intimidating, so imposing, so unbelievably powerful and sexy.

His eyes were on my face, drinking in every bit of pleasure and agony his mouth was inflicting as I whimpered and mewled my complaints. It played to my deepest, darkest desires, knowing he wasn't going to relent until I used my safeword.

Soon, the pain morphed back into pleasure, and my half-hearted attempts at pushing him off turned into my fingers fisting his hair again, pulling him closer as my hips ground against his mouth with shameless need. He was so good at this. I'd never been with a man who was so enthusiastic about oral.

"Oh god, Jackson, that feels... I'm gonna... again."

The tingles were already spreading, nipping at my everything as I fought for air. It hit me just as hard as the first, forcing my limbs to curl and contort with excruciating ecstasy.

I could not believe how much I'd been missing out on. I needed better toys.

I was chanting his name, panting and shuddering through the incessant aftershocks his tongue was tormenting me with.

But again, he didn't stop. He lapped at my pussy, unwilling to let a single drop of my orgasm go to waste.

I tried again to push him off, half because I physically could not take the torture, and half because feeling helpless against his unyielding hold turned me on even more. I was really into the whole power imbalance thing, apparently. Who the fuck could have guessed—

He bit my clit.

Sucked on it.

Bit it again.

Flicked it with his tongue, groaned, and I was done.

I cried out, tears springing to my eyes as my muscles seized—a little painfully this time. It felt fucking amazing. Even the pain was incredible. It amplified the pleasure, melted my insides into quivering goo, made me choke and gasp and beg for mercy.

The pleading only encouraged him. It made him more ruthless and starved, not less. So, obviously, I kept doing it.

"Jackson, please. Pleasepleaseplease. Fuck. Please. I can't." I couldn't.

Yet I did.

Another orgasm slashed through me, making me cry out in more pain, more pleasure, and *oh my god*, I really was going to die tonight. Willingly and from too many orgasms inflicted on me by Jackson Sinclair's wicked, ravenous mouth.

I wasn't even tempted to use my safeword. There was something so seductively pleasurable about this that it made all the agony worth it. Maybe because I wasn't the only helpless one.

Jackson was eating me out like he *needed* it. He was about as out of control as I was, and that's what made it so seductive.

I blinked down at him, willing my vision back into focus. He was watching me with such intense, feral concentration that it stole my breath. My teeth sunk into my bottom lip, tugging at it as my hips began grinding again.

I'd be picturing this exact scene every time I reached for my vibrator for the next... for the rest of my life. Jackson Sinclair on his knees, biceps bulging as he kept my thighs splayed wide open for his licking and sucking pleasure.

I moaned his name, reveling in its subtle impact on his physical demeanor. He worked me faster, watched me more closely, forced my thighs wider. I didn't have the words to describe how desired and attractive it made me feel. I was drunk with it.

Lost in the overwhelming intensity of the moment, I reached down and used my fingers to peel myself open for him like before. I did it without thinking, wanting to please him and let him know how good this was. That he could take as much of me as he wanted.

He fucking *lost* it.

His hips bucked into the couch, shoving it back as a vicious growl ripped out of his lungs. Something clattered, something else smashed, he didn't seem to notice. His tongue thrust into me with feral need, his grip becoming rough enough to leave a few delicious bruises on my skin. Well-fucking-worth it.

"Jackson..."

He shuddered with a deep, soul-crushing groan, and shut his eyes for a beat, his movements becoming increasingly wild and desperate. It was so hot. I was close again... so, so close. Just... a little...

I came against his searing tongue with a broken cry, and he bucked again, his muscles tensing as he licked me into permanent incoherence. And then he was shuddering against me, choking out groans while he shook and shook and shook.

It went on forever.

Until, finally, it stopped, and he peeled his mouth away.

I was liquid. A whimpering, blubbering puddle of numb liquid.

"Fuck..." he breathed, his grip finally loosening as his head collapsed onto my stomach. He was heaving. "Jesus..."

We stayed like that for minutes. Or maybe it was hours. I couldn't tell the difference anymore; didn't really care to.

"Jamie."

"Mmmm."

"You all right?"

No. He'd broken me. How was I ever supposed to have sex with another man, knowing it would never—*could never*—live up to what I'd just experienced?

An unpleasant shiver snaked through my limbs when Jackson lifted himself, selfishly taking all the heat with him. I was too sore and sensitive to close my thighs, so they stayed wide open as he cupped one side of my face and tilted it in his direction. "You okay?"

I blinked sleepily up at him, the sight slow to register. My slick arousal was all over his mouth and chin, his hair was ruffled, eyes hooded and glassy.

So sexy...

"Jamie. I need to know if you're good."

I was getting there, damn. Gathering every last molecule of energy I had left in this lifetime, I forced myself to swallow. "So good."

A slow, devastating grin spread over his evil, talented mouth. "You liked that, did you?"

"Mmnmhm," I confirmed. There was a chance I'd never be able to move or speak ever again.

"C'mere, sweet girl. Let's get you cleaned up."

Yeah, I wasn't gonna be able to move for—*oh*. Never mind. He was doing all the work for me, gathering me in his arms, lifting me from the couch. How nice. I'd thank him in my next life, just as soon as I regained the ability to speak.

I was curled up against him like a drowsy kitten as he carried me upstairs, keeping me pressed to his chest while he whispered sweet little praises in my ear.

I was such a good girl.

A sweet girl.
I'd done so well.
He was so pleased with me.
He was going to take such good care of me now.
I deserved it.

25

"JAMIE."

I kept my eyes shut, kept my breathing even, my body limp.

Jackson brushed a piece of my hair away from my face, his fingers caressing my temple as he pressed a soft kiss to my shoulder. Our legs were tangled under the sheets, my back locked against his chest thanks to the possessive arm he had wrapped around me.

I hadn't gotten dressed after the bath he'd given me last night so, unlike him, I was fully naked. It was heaven, and as soon as I opened my eyes, it would have to end.

"I know you're awake." Another sweet, gentle press of his mouth. This one on my neck, right over my fluttering pulse.

"You know no such thing. S'just a theory."

The warmth of his laugh dripped down to places it shouldn't have been able to reach. With a deep, satisfied sigh, I pressed my ass to the raging erection he was sporting under his sweats.

He hissed; I smiled. He nipped at my earlobe; I pushed harder and wiggled—

I was flat on my back in an instant, giggling as Jackson pinned my wrists, shoved my thighs open with his knee, and attacked my neck.

"Open your eyes," he demanded gruffly. "We need to talk."

"Five more minutes," I pleaded quietly.

My wish was granted. I kept my eyes shut as he spoiled my skin with tender kisses, tracing them over my neck, across my collarbones, down my breasts, stomach, thighs...

"Jamie." Right on the five-minute mark. I was sure of it. "You're splayed out naked in front of me and I only have so much self-control. We need to talk before I dive tongue-first into your sweet pussy again."

My fingers curled around fistfuls of buttery Egyptian cotton as his tongue traced a teasing line across my hip bone, making me shiver.

"I don't see the problem," I breathed.

"We don't have time. Minerva's expecting us soon."

My eyes snapped open.

Shit. Shit shit shit shit shit. "What time is it?"

I'd set an alarm. Why hadn't it gone off? Where was my phone?!

I bolted upright so fast it made my vision sparkle and darken. I blinked and blinked, trying to clear it. "What time is it?" I asked again. And why was he being so slow to answer?

My first progress meeting with Minerva was at nine and there was a lot of sunshine spilling through those windows. It was alarmingly bright.

"Half past eight," Jackson said just as my vision

cleared. I barely even heard him over his ridiculously handsome face. How was he *more* beautiful this morning than he had been last night? Stupid oxytocin.

The air was sucked out of the room when I met his gaze. He was fully clothed and crowding me on the bed, I was fully naked and vulnerable...

Again with the power imbalance thing. My libido really loved that shit.

No, that was a lie. My libido loved that shit *with Jackson*. There was a difference.

"Tonight." His voice was a dark, promising gravel. "I'll fuck you right after we come to an agreement."

"About?" I sounded weirdly out of breath.

"The marriage contract you'll be signing. I assume you'll want to negotiate a decrease in your compensation, given your visceral distaste for financial security and comfort."

My heart stuttered.

"I'm not going to marry you. Last night didn't change that." Last night shouldn't have even happened. Tonight certainly wasn't going to.

"Save it for the negotiations."

No.

Not a chance. Entering into a contractual marriage with Jackson Sinclair would be a catastrophically horrible idea that would end in nothing short of disaster for me. It wasn't going to happen.

Breaking my gaze away, I snatched a pillow from behind me and held it up to my chest. "Can you close your eyes for a sec?"

A pause. "Seriously?"

"Seriously." I needed to get dressed and run back to

my suite, and I knew for a fact that I didn't look good while folded over and shoving on a skirt.

He smiled but complied, shutting his eyes so I could scramble out of his bed.

"Keep them closed 'til I say."

The meeting was being held at Minerva's home, which was around a fifteen-minute drive. I had exactly eleven minutes to run back to my suite, feed Toebeans, brush my teeth, tame my sex-tangled hair into a semipresentable bun, and get dressed. It was tight but doable, so long as I didn't get distracted.

"The marriage only has to last a year, but I'm thinking the contract should have a flexible-term clause, just in case Minerva decides to pull something last minute."

Wait, where were my clothes? I spun around, trying to locate where Jackson had put—ah, the ottoman.

"We also have to argue about your compensation. I'm thinking fifty million as the base pay, plus another fifty for each produced offspring, if any. It'll be up to you."

I reached for the clasp of my bra again. It had snapped out of my clammy grip when Jackson said the word "offspring."

Was that what he expected? That I'd be able to marry him, have his child, and then just... walk away from it all after one year?

"You'll have all the negotiation power here, though," he went on. "I'd suggest using it to your advantage."

I shoved into my skirt, ignoring him. We could have this argument when I wasn't rushing out the door.

"I'm taking your silence as a positive sign."

"You shouldn't."

He chuckled like I was joking. "Can I open my eyes now?"

"Go for it." I was halfway buttoned up anyway. My focus remained fixed on my working fingers as Jackson rose to his feet. "Can you do me a quick favor? I don't know where my phone is, can you call me a cab?"

He stepped right into my bubble. "Why do you need a cab?"

"Because you refused to give me garage access, so I left my car back at my place."

"No, I mean, why wouldn't we just go together?"

"Where?"

"My aunt's. I don't see the point in taking two separate cars."

What was he talking about? "Why would you go with me?"

"Because she emailed yesterday morning and demanded that I accompany you."

"What? Why?" I thought the whole point of the meeting was to provide her with honest and unfiltered progression updates. How was I supposed to do that if Jackson was there, supervising the whole thing?

"I've stopped trying to make sense of Minerva's whims," he said. "But if you wanted my best guess, I'd say her decision was prompted by Imogen, seeing as how she called me right after her bi-weekly reading."

I frowned up at him.

"Imogen is her tarot reader," Jackson supplied.

"No, I know who she is." That wasn't why I was confused, but we didn't have time to talk about why I was confused. "Fine, yes, let's just go together. But we can't be late, so I'll see you downstairs in..."

"Eight minutes?"

"Eight minutes."

I went straight for the door, threw it open, and yelped

as my spine folded in half, my hand shooting out to prevent the incoming crash.

"Oh!"

The black ornate trolley rattled with the shock of my weight, and my face halted less than an inch from the steaming pot of coffee, but I managed to steady myself just in time.

"Are you all right, dear?" Molly—or maybe it was Mabel—placed a gentle hand on my shoulder while her sister helped me straighten.

"Yes, sorry." I blinked down at the trolley I'd almost knocked over. Two cups, two sets of cutlery, two silver lids covering two breakfast plates...

Ah, crap.

My hands moved to my skirt, subtly checking to make sure it was on straight—something I should have done before opening the door.

"Good morning, Molly, Mabel." I kept my voice as collected as I could, considering the circumstances. If I acted like I hadn't been caught engaging in highly inappropriate and unprofessional behavior, maybe they'd believe it.

Then *he* happened. Jackson appeared behind me, choosing to stand close enough for his chest to brush my back. I saw it happen in real time—the pure, unfiltered glee that flashed across the twins' faces.

"What's all this?" Jackson asked, head bending over my shoulder to look. He was pressed right up to me now.

I didn't know if he noticed how glassy and soft Molly's eyes were getting as she watched us, but I sure did. The guilt was going to eat me alive when it sunk in.

Mabel was the one to respond. She seemed to be holding it together more effectively than her sister. "Just a bit of breakfast. Back in you go. We didn't mean to interrupt."

She used the trolley to herd us back into the bedroom, talking over my every attempt at getting out a protest.

"We were going to just leave it outside, but this is much better. We wouldn't want the food to get cold now, would we? Sit, sit. Molly and I will be out of your hair in a moment."

The distance between me and the door grew with every backward step I was forced to take. As much as I appreciated the gesture, I really, really didn't have time for it. "Mabel, I'm so sorry, but I have to—"

"Sit."

I was not given a choice in the matter. She simply gripped my shoulder and pushed me onto the couch I'd been backed into.

"Mabel, we've got to get going," Jackson tried. Unlike me, he was still standing. She couldn't reach his shoulder without a step stool.

"Nonsense. It's a Saturday, is it not?" She propped her fists against her plump hips and frowned up at him like a chiding mother. "Whatever you've got going can certainly wait until after you eat. Now *sit*." She snapped her fingers.

He sat.

"Good." After a firm nod of approval, she turned and marched away, grabbing a starry-eyed Molly on her way out.

I stared blankly at the closed door, guilt and anxiety clawing at my chest. This was my fault. I'd created this mess.

"Hey."

I blinked over to Jackson. "Did you talk to them

already?" I asked, knowing how little time we had left. "What did you say?"

"Later." He glanced at his watch. "We've got six minutes to get out the door. Tell me what you need to do before then."

"Brush teeth, wash face, get dressed, feed Toebeans, fix my hair, grab my laptop," I recited. "Oh and find my phone."

"All right." He stood and gestured toward the ensuite. "All your grooming stuff can be done in there. There's spare everything in the cupboards to your left when you walk in. Your phone's probably in my office. I can grab it."

Wait, "But—"

"It'll take you three minutes to run to your suite, and another two to make it to the front door. And that's if you're not intercepted."

Damn it. "But Toebeans—"

"His breakfast will be two hours late; he'll live. If you don't want the maids to know you spent the night, I'll run and grab your clothes for you as soon as I change. Just tell me which ones."

When I hesitated, he glanced at his watch again.

"Fine. Okay. Yellow blouse and light jeans, both hung in the closet. Oh, and fresh underwear, please. Top bedside drawer." I froze, *remembering*. "Don't... don't look in the bottom drawer."

I knew I'd fucked up before he even grinned.

He was definitely going to look in the bottom drawer.

26

We made it.

Barely, but we made it.

And, apparently, so had Imogen. Minerva had invited her tarot reader to our meeting, which meant that Jackson's theory regarding his own attendance likely wasn't that far off.

"You're late," Minerva said as soon as we were guided into her home office. She was sitting on one side of a square oak table, a purring Harry cradled to her chest. Imogen occupied the seat beside her, shuffling a deck of black cards. She paid us no attention.

We weren't late, but I wasn't going to argue with her.

"My fault," Jackson said as soon as I opened my mouth to apologize. "I was taking care of an urgent work matter and lost track of time."

My heart did a breathless backflip when he pulled out a chair and gestured for me to sit with a secret wink. I took it with a whispered *thank you*, warm goo dripping down my chest. He didn't have to take the blame for me like that.

"Really?" Minerva's tone was so sharp it was borderline sarcastic. "Because from what I hear, you haven't been doing much work at all this week."

Jackson said nothing as he took a seat next to me. My smile died.

That wasn't information she'd gotten from me.

"Do correct me if I'm wrong, Jamie, but isn't the whole point of you shadowing him at his office to observe his regular schedule, habits, and interactions?"

"It's part of it, yes."

"And? Has he been cooperating?"

I shifted in my chair as I shot a quick glance to my left. Jackson's expression was blank.

When I didn't immediately answer her, Minerva said, "Let me rephrase. Has Jackson conducted a single in-person meeting at work over the last week with you in attendance?"

Damn. This wasn't how I thought this meeting would start.

"No," I eventually said. "But it's fine. I've been able to gather the information I need to satisfy that dataset regardless."

Beside her, Imogen's mouth quirked. She hadn't said anything—or even looked up—since we'd arrived. She was just sitting there, shuffling and flipping her cards.

"How so?" Minerva asked.

I shrugged. "He's taken meetings over the phone, and I've looked at relevant, publicly available corporate data." That all counted. "More importantly, I've witnessed how he is with his household staff. It's told me almost everything I need to know about who he is as a boss. I assume most of the data I'd gather from a regular workweek with him would likely be redundant, though I could be wrong."

I could feel Jackson watching me from the corner of my eye, but I kept my attention fixed on his aunt.

"What corporate data?" she asked curiously.

"Namely turnover rates and other publicly available information pertaining to employee satisfaction with the CEO. The year before Jackson took over the position, Sinclair Group was grappling with a whopping turnover rate of 27 percent, up 1 percent from the previous year. There were reported issues of widespread dissatisfaction among employees regarding management, company culture, and opportunities for internal growth. Eight months after Jackson took over, that number went down to 20 percent. The year he did an in-depth review of the leadership teams within the organization and removed individuals who had an overall negative impact on culture and morale, it dropped to 14 percent. Last year, he managed to bring it down to 8 percent."

All three of them were looking at me now. Minerva with her thin brows arched all the way up, Imogen with that amused, knowing smirk still toying at the corner of her painted mouth, and Jackson—I wasn't sure about him, actually. I could feel his eyes on me but that was about it.

I cleared my throat and straightened my spine. "I did initially question his lack of productivity at the office. I couldn't wrap my head around how the CEO of an investment company this large could hand off all his work for a full month just because he felt a little inconvenienced. However, after learning about the initiatives Jackson has taken to retain talent and prioritize employee well-being and satisfaction, I'd say it's impressive. Most companies struggle to cover a month of work for their regular employees, let alone the responsibilities of a CEO. Effective delegation of duties and ensuring there are no gaps in workflow when an employee is indisposed are highly valuable skill sets. I don't think it's laziness, I think he's just incredibly good at his job."

I was starting to sound defensive even to my own ears. The way Minerva had accused Jackson of slacking over the last week made it seem like she was questioning his abilities to lead the company. I may not have seen him actively work, but those numbers didn't lie.

Her attention slid to Jackson, lingering, assessing. I wondered what she saw that made her brows tick like that. Unless my peripherals were wishful little liars, he hadn't taken his eyes off me once during my whole speech.

It was a little distracting. I wanted so badly to look at him.

"If I may." It was Imogen who spoke. Her voice was husky, curious, and surprisingly serene. "What exactly does all of that have to do with finding him a wife?"

Her hands stopped shuffling when a card jumped out of her deck. She flipped it over and placed it next to the one already on the table. A crowned man holding a sword, a crowned woman holding a cup. From where Imogen was sitting, the man was upside down. To me, he was right-side up. Handsome fellow. Great authoritative scowl.

Her mouth twitched again.

I smoothed my palms over my jeans. Something about her secretive amusement was making my stomach squirm. "Jackson is a caretaker at his core and significantly more nurturing than our original data suggested, though I'm not sure he recognizes these qualities within himself." If he did, then he was actively attempting to hide them from people he didn't trust. Actions didn't lie, though. "His first focus as CEO was correcting a culture that had resulted in widespread employee dissatisfaction. His household staff are all extremely well taken care of and most of them have been working for him for well over a decade. That's all in addition to my own experiences with him over the last week. In my professional opinion, he's more likely to thrive in a relationship where the quiet nurturing side of him is recognized and appreciated, but not taken advantage of."

That last part was imperative.

"Your own experiences," Minerva repeated slowly. I couldn't tell whether it was a statement or a question.

"That's correct."

"Elaborate."

Imogen was all but laughing to herself now as she flipped card after card, and it was clawing at my confidence. What the hell was so funny? What was she seeing?

"Um..." I blinked away from the table, pulling my thoughts back together. I wasn't really sure I believed in tarot—or anything occult-related—so her behavior shouldn't have bothered me so much. "There was an incident last week with some broken glass," I said, keeping it as vague as possible. "The way Jackson handled the situation, how quick he was to jump in and help, reaffirmed my observations."

There. A short summary of what had happened without going into any intimate details. Minerva didn't need to know that he'd carried me out of the room and gently plucked shards of broken glass out of my hair.

My chest squeezed and leaped at the memory, and I had to fight back a smile.

Minerva didn't look satisfied with the lack of details in my story though, and before she could push for more, I tried to derail her by blurting the first thing that popped into my head. "He's also significantly more playful than we'd—"

Imogen burst into a throaty laugh, cutting me off. She muttered something to Minerva in a language I didn't recognize, her voice brimming with pure glee.

I scanned the cards in front of her again, trying to get even a speck of meaning from them. But all I saw were the people in crowns, two dogs howling up at a moon, a young man with a small sack slung over his shoulder, and two gold chalices. There were no labels, no descriptions, no words. I had no idea what any of it meant.

"Keep going," Minerva said, pulling my attention back to her.

Suddenly, I couldn't wait for this meeting to end. I wanted out before Imogen saw a whole bunch of things that I didn't want her to see. How humiliating would it be if the cards showed her all the secret things I wasn't supposed to be feeling? Oh god, what if she *said something*?

It wasn't even a big deal.

Everything was under control.

Just a stupid little crush that would go away in no time.

I cleared my throat again. The sooner I gave Minerva the information she needed, the sooner I could bolt. "All I'm trying to say is that Jackson's original profile was so heavily flawed that it was actively working against us, which is why we had such a hard time finding him a suitable match. A new one has been set up and will be updated frequently as I gather more data over the upcoming weeks. For now, our focus will be to find someone compatible with what we currently have on file for him and, more importantly, someone who either shares his views on romance and relationships, or is at least open to them."

Jackson was not going to be happy with someone who believed in fairy tale endings, soulmates, or any of the more idealistic notions of romance and relationships. Forcing him to fall in love was never going to work. He would be much better off with a great friend, a partner in crime that he enjoyed spending time with—someone who shared his beliefs and didn't hold any long-term expectations that wouldn't be met.

Jackson marrying someone who *did* believe in those things would be nothing short of a living nightmare. He was charming, attractive, funny, caring, and so many other secret, wonderful things. It would be so easy for his wife to fall in love with him, and to develop a foolish, desperate hope that one day, if she tried really hard and showed him just how good she could be to him, he'd maybe love her back.

Then their one-year contract would end, and she'd be forced to leave him. Or worse, she'd beg and plead and convince him to stay married to her, and he'd force her to sign a postnup agreement, detailing his plans to get "his needs met elsewhere." Because twelve months was long enough for the lust and attraction to wear off. Twelve months was long enough for him to get bored of her.

He'd shatter her heart and step all over it, and she'd have no one to blame but herself. Because he'd told her exactly who he was and exactly what he wanted, and when people did that, you were supposed to listen.

You couldn't force someone to change for you.

I wasn't a fool.

"I think that's the most important part," I reiterated. "Because he has such specific and unconventional views of romance, the two of them need to be on the same page about their expectations and what they hope to gain from the relationship. Otherwise, we'd be setting them up for disappointment in the long term. It wouldn't work."

Jackson was drilling holes into the side of my face with the intensity of his gaze. My eyes may have been on Minerva, but I could only see him.

I was aware of his every movement, the harshening rise and fall of his chest, the way his fingers had slowly curled into fists on his lap. I couldn't decipher the expression he was wearing though, and it was becoming excruciatingly difficult not to look.

"All of this is detailed in the weekly progress report I've drawn up, a finalized copy of which will be emailed to both your team and Jackson's first thing Monday morning. But there is one other pressing matter I'd like to discuss in person," I went on. "I realize that my original recommendation was for Jackson to receive intensive coaching on how to conduct himself on dates, however, I no longer believe that's warranted or necessary. There are a few things we'll need to go over, but they're brief and can be covered in under an hour. I strongly suggest we hold off on anything further until after his first date."

Minerva rolled her lips, studying me. "And what then? We'd discussed supervised meetings for him to ensure he doesn't... That everything runs smoothly."

Babysitting. She was concerned he'd intentionally throw the dates again.

"I can accompany him to the first one." I really didn't want to, but I'd do it. "If it goes the way I suspect, he won't require further shadowing unless he specifically requests it. In fact, if my presence continues to be a distraction to Jackson at the office, we can also cut back on the work shadowing a week early, and I should be able to move out by—"

"No."

I looked at him then. His tone demanded it.

"Pardon?" Minerva said.

Jackson held my gaze, eyes narrowing. "No. I want the coaching, the shadowing, and all of the handholding I was threatened with when this whole nightmare started. You're not moving out until the agreed-upon thirty days are over."

Shocked. Silence.

Imogen had stopped shuffling and flipping her cards, Minerva was gaping at her nephew like he'd produced lightning out of thin air, and I couldn't so much as breathe. He wouldn't let me.

"You... you *want* her to stay?" Minerva asked.

"You're forcing me to get married." He made no effort to temper the bitter resentment dripping from his voice as he peeled his gaze away from mine. "You're forcing me to then *stay* married for a year, and I'm relatively certain that, at some point, you'll also force me to produce a child to secure the precious familial line you're so concerned with. I no longer have a fucking choice in the matter, so my only option is to, at the very least, find someone that doesn't make me want to set myself on fucking fire. The more information Jamie has, the higher her chances of success are going to be. Wouldn't you agree?"

That was the bar he'd set. *That* was his expectation of marriage. He simply wanted someone that wouldn't make him want to set himself on fire.

I ripped my eyes away from him, ignoring the painful throbbing in my chest.

"Oh, stop being so dramatic," Minerva scoffed with a

barely contained roll of her eyes. Harry stirred in her arm, ears twitching. "You have lived a life of sheer privilege, and I simply don't care what it is you *think* you are further owed without sacrifice. You've studied under the best tutors, attended the best post-secondary institutions money could buy, and been provided with every material thing you could ever want. Millions of people would sacrifice a hell of a lot more than a single year of marriage to switch lives with you. It is not unreasonable for me to ask that you also produce an heir and—"

"I can have a child without—"

"You are not having a child out of wedlock," she snapped. "You of all people should know what happens when the men in this family attempt to raise children without the aid of a proper, loving mother. The cycle ends with you, Jackson. I will not have you repeating what that vain, repulsive *bitch* and Richard—"

"I am not my father!" Jackson roared. His voice ripped through the air, making it ring. Every muscle in his face and neck was taut, his lips rolled back in pure rage.

Imogen *tsk*ed. "Naughty, naughty," she cooed happily, grinning down at the table.

Minerva blinked over at her. "I'm sorry?"

"The cards," Imogen answered. I couldn't tell whether she was unaware of the crippling tension in the room, or simply unaffected by it. "They want to play. I'm starting to see why your nephew's presence today was so... *encouraged*."

Minerva's shoulders eased an inch, her interest piqued. "What does that mean? What are they saying?"

Jackson leaned back in his chair with a deep sigh, scrubbing a hand over his face like he couldn't believe his life had been reduced to such nonsensical bullshit. My fingers itched to reach out and smooth out his frown, so I curled them into fists and shoved them underneath my thighs.

Imogen hummed noncommittally, which only made Minerva more desperate for answers. "What is it? Am I wrong about this?"

"They don't want to talk about that," Imogen said, placing one deck down only to pick up another. "They don't want to talk about you. They don't want to talk about him." She paused, she grinned. "They only want to talk about *her*."

All eyes were on me again.

"Me?" Why me? I had the least interesting energy in this room right now.

"You."

A card jumped out of the deck she was shuffling, landing smack in the middle of the table. This one did have a label on it. In bold white letters etched into a matte-black background, the card screamed: DEATH.

Oh good.

"Would you like to hear what they have to say?"

"Are they going to tell me how little time I have left to live?" Because I'd rather not know.

Her smile widened. "No. It's about your love life."

That snagged Jackson's attention. His body went rigid for a moment before he forced it to relax again.

"I'm not sure if my love life would be an appropriate topic of conversation at a client meeting," I tried.

Another card slid out of the deck. PAGE OF SWORDS, it read. The page had no swords on it, though. It was as black as the DEATH card, with a few grey lines scribbled in the background.

"You'll want to hear it," she said. "There's nothing here

indicating that you'll feel otherwise once the message has been relayed. I'm not channeling any regret." Her mouth twitched again. "Not from your end, at least."

"We don't mind." Minerva nudged to the edge of her seat, eyeing the cards. Though her interest in the reading was likely more geared toward an explanation as to why Jackson's presence had been so "encouraged."

"You can tell me to stop whenever you wish," Imogen offered. "Though, again, I really don't see that happening here."

I shifted in my chair. My knees were starting to feel weirdly clammy. "All right," I agreed slowly. The peer pressure and curiosity had won.

Honestly, as long as she didn't reveal my teeny, tiny, not-at-all-a-big-deal crush on Jackson, we were golden. And if the whole tarot thing wasn't a hoax, then maybe I'd get some answers as to why I'd had such relentlessly terrible luck in—

"Your luck has turned, but you're not seeing it." She tapped an untitled card with a mauve fingernail. It depicted a woman tying a blindfold around her own eyes. "The universe is trying to give you exactly what you've been asking for, but you're turning it away because, on the surface, it's not what you expected. Either this has already happened or it's about to."

The tension in my shoulders relaxed a touch. That was just vague enough to make my bullshit meter *ding*. I'd always suspected that tarot was more about reading the client than the cards.

So, I nodded politely and listened.

"You've met a man recently," she went on, "certainly within the last month or so, though the cards are indicating that you knew of him for quite a while before that."

That... was a bit more specific.

"He's going to come to you with an offer... or maybe he already has. The timeline isn't being made clear to me." Her head tilted to one side, amber eyes gliding over the cards spread out in front of her. She hadn't looked at me once since she started, so either my theory about reading the client was wrong, or her peripheral vision was excellent. "It's interesting. Almost like they're being intentionally vague about it. What I am being shown clearly is that this man will come to you with a proposal of sorts, and it's going to lead you to everything you've always wanted. However, the presentation is... it's almost as though the package is deceiving and will veer you off the path you had your sights set on. It does not *look* like what you want because it's not... but it will lead you to it. There is no doubt about that here. The doubt all lies within you."

My heart was pounding against my skull. Jackson's whole body was slowly starting to twist in Imogen's direction, and I swear he even leaned forward at one point, trying to sneak a proper glance at the cards.

"If there's any confusion as to who this might be, or if you'd like some signs to look for when you do meet him, there are a few very... *specific* things I'm channeling." Her impish smirk returned as she met my gaze. It made the hairs on the back of my neck rise. "He's tall," she said, and my throat went tight. "I'm hearing an accent..."

I should have stopped her right there. This was the exact direction I'd been hoping she wouldn't go in.

But I said nothing. My tongue was swollen deadweight.

"There's also an emphasis on food... seafood specifically. Either sushi or something very niche within that type of cuisine that you'll enjoy together. And I'm being shown a pet. A well-loved one... quite spoiled by the man. It could be his or yours." She stopped for a moment, her gaze flicking over to my left. Whatever she saw made her smirk again. Almost like this was a game to her. "He'll have a bunch of tattoos... or perhaps some sort of scarring that's oddly shaped. Around a dozen of them. Maybe more."

Wait. Did Jackson have any tattoos? He hadn't taken his shirt off last night or this morning, so I couldn't be sure...

"I'm also seeing the letter D being significant in terms of initials or... hmm, perhaps a sign of some sort."

I frowned. Jackson Parker Sinclair. There wasn't a single D in his name, and I was pretty sure that if he had a dozen tattoos, I'd have—

Oh.

Ohhh.

She wasn't talking about Jackson.

27

Jackson Sinclair may not have any tattoos, but Daniel Omori sure did. Two full sleeves of them, in fact. Maybe even more. He was also tall, had a spoiled pet, an Australian accent, and worked as a sushi chef.

Oh, and I'd definitely known *of* him before we met. Very much so.

"It's not him." Jackson shoved himself into the backseat of his town car, sliding right up against me as the door shut behind him.

"I've always wanted to live in Japan," I sighed wistfully. I may have been poking the bear a bit, but he was so cranky about the whole thing that I couldn't help myself.

Jackson glowered down at me, and I pouted up at him, pretending like I'd drank the Kool-Aid. "Do you have any tattoos?" I asked.

His brows drew together all unhappy-like. He hesitated for a beat. "No."

"A name that starts with a D I don't know about?"

His jaw locked.

"Then it has to be him because I haven't met anyone else in the last month that fits that exact description."

"It's *not* him."

I cupped his cheek. "And to think you introduced us," I said softly, forcing my lower lip to wobble. He had murder in his eyes. "We'll always be grateful, Danny and I. You'll get a toast at our wedding for sure."

Hot air shoved out of his nostrils. This was so much fun.

"Over my dead fucking body, Jamie."

"You don't even believe in tarot or anything occult-related," I reminded him, letting my hand—and the ruse—drop. "Why are you so worked up?"

"You believe in it."

"I never once said I believed in tarot. The details she gave were kind of freaky, though. She described him to a T."

"It wasn't all accurate. Last I checked, Omori didn't come to you with an offer that would veer you off whatever path you had your sights set on."

"Wrong. I was going to look for another job as soon as the Immersive was over. If I accept Daniel as a client, I'd have to stay at Charmed. There's your veered path right there."

He was going to challenge me every step of the way on this, I could see it in the stubborn set of his jaw. Not that it mattered. I didn't care who Imogen had been referring to in her reading, or what the details were. I was never going to end up with Jackson.

I wanted love, connection, a partner I could share my life with. Jackson needed a temporary wife who'd sign a contract, maybe give him a child, and happily walk away from it all when the term of their agreement was over. He couldn't do an ever-after, and I couldn't do without one.

We'd make each other miserable.

I held up a palm when he opened his mouth again. "I'm not going to argue about this with you. We have more important things to talk about."

"Somehow I doubt that."

"Supervised dates, Jackson? A full coaching package? Suddenly you're on board?"

For the first time since he'd stomped out of Minerva's office without so much as a goodbye, his scowl eased a touch. "I changed my mind."

"*Really*?" I folded my arms over my chest. "You *want* me on all your dates, critiquing every little move you make?"

"Yes," he said simply. "If I must suffer through them then so do you. Plus, you did say that if I had any personal areas of concern, you'd help me work through them."

He was up to something. There was no doubt about it.

He nudged closer to me, his massive thigh pressing to mine. "We can go over the details later today. But first, we need to feed Cat."

We? "Why would we do that?"

He frowned at me like I'd asked a stupid question. "Because he hasn't had his breakfast yet."

That wasn't what I meant, and he knew it.

"I don't know what you're scheming, but I can almost guarantee it'll end with a bite mark," I warned. "And blood."

He smirked to himself. "We'll see."

Toebeans was perched beside his empty food bowl when I opened the door, simmering in hanger-induced rage. He growled when he saw me, because how *dare* I?

"Hi, cutie. I'm sorry we're so late—"

Jackson snatched my wrist as soon as I stepped into the suite, stopping me in my tracks. How could one person generate so much electricity? One small touch and every inch of my skin buzzed with it.

"Where's his food?" he asked.

"Um... bottom cupboard. Far left."

"Can I do it?"

I hesitated. "I mean... you could try." But why would he want to?

"Thanks."

Normally Toebeans would have been entangled between my ankles by now, noisily screaming about how neglected and famished he was while simultaneously making it as difficult as possible for me to get to his food bowl.

Then again, normally I didn't have a Jackson Sinclair accompanying me to his mealtime.

His tail stopped flicking as Jackson stepped closer, a warning growl rumbling from his chest. This wasn't going to work. Jackson wouldn't even make it to the cupboard before being forced to back off.

"Watch your ankles," I warned.

Jackson came to a stop around six feet from his target. Then he slowly, carefully, crouched down.

Wrong move. Toebeans bared his sharp fangs, ears flattening as his pupils flared.

Uh Oh. "Jackson—"

"Hello, Cat."

Toebeans froze. His fangs retreated. His ears flicked.

"That's right," Jackson murmured, "you recognize my voice, don't you?"

I bit into my lower lip as Toebeans and his one brain cell tried their best to slot the puzzle pieces together. Why did the half-giant crouching in front of him sound like his palace overlord? It made no sense!

"Here's the deal," Jackson went on, daring a small step forward. Toebeans watched him warily but didn't show any new signs of aggression. "I am going to use this hand right here to reach into the cupboard beside you, and I'd very much appreciate it if my skin wasn't shredded in the process."

Another step forward.

I couldn't decide which was more amusing—my wide-eyed, dumb-struck cat, or the duck-walking half-giant at his mercy. I did, however, know which one was more endearing. How could I not, when it was making my heart want to burst?

"You may sniff me if you'd like." Jackson held out a cautious hand with his next step, but Toebeans didn't move.

It took almost a full minute of patience and stillness, but it... it worked. My lips peeled apart as Toebeans took one tentative step forward. Then another. *What the hell?*

"Come on, little one. It's all right." The coax was so soft, so gentle, that it made my chest ache.

My lungs seized when Toebeans leaned his head forward, but instead of sinking his teeth into Jackson's outstretched arm, he carefully sniffed his fingers.

"Good boy. Well done." Jackson smiled and it broke a piece of my heart clean off. "You see? I'm not so bad."

While Toebeans was busy trying to decipher why this man sounded and smelled exactly like his new favorite place on earth, Jackson reached over with his other hand, opened the cupboard I'd referenced earlier, and successfully retrieved a small silver tin of cat food.

"Here." He peeled back the lid while Toebeans watched, keeping his movements smooth, slow, and steady.

Toebeans eyed him, trying to gauge his exact level of threat as his breakfast was served. Jackson didn't push him, though. Instead, he lowered into a seat right beside the food bowl, stretched out his legs, pressed his back to the cabinets, and feigned focused interest in the content labels of the empty can.

Toebeans watched him cautiously, waiting to see what he would do. When Jackson remained disinterested in further engagement, he chirped a soft, questioning "Meowr."

"Bluefin tuna, mussels, and quinoa, huh?"

"Meowr."

"Sounds rather foul. Is that why you're not eating it?" Jackson turned his attention to me. "Has he ever tried Wagyu beef?"

I pressed my twitching lips together and shook my head.

He held up the tin and frowned down at Toebeans. "This isn't gourmet anything, Cat. You've been duped by Adolf."

"Adrien," I corrected. "And that's not why he's not eating."

"Why aren't you eating?"

"Meowr."

I walked over and took a seat beside Jackson's feet, facing the two of them. "Go on, cutie. I'm watching."

He continued to hesitate, still somewhat unsettled by

Jackson's presence. Eventually, though, the hunger won. He ate slowly at first, not taking his eyes off the potential threat. But once it was clear that Jackson had no interest in stealing any of his mashed-up tuna, he munched faster, bushy tail swishing happily.

"Can't believe you pulled it off," I said to Jackson. "This is honestly impressive. Other than Adrien, we've never been able to get him to warm up to a man before. Not even my dad." And it hadn't been for a lack of trying.

"Send me a recording of his voice. I'll have Cat obsessed with him in no time."

I huffed a laugh as Toebeans crawled onto my lap for his mandatory post-feeding cuddle time. Scratching his neck and ears, I began asking him a string of nonsensical questions in between head kisses.

Smooch. Who was the most handsomest boy in the whole wide world? *Smooch.* Who had been such a good and patient boy while waiting for his breakfast all morning? *Smooch.* Who was the most majestic kitty king with the most majestic kitty palace anyone had ever seen? *Smooch. Smooch. Smooch.*

It was all fine and great until, from the corner of my eye, I saw Jackson's hand twitch. And damn it to hell, another piece of my heart snapped off.

With a small sigh, I held out my palm. "Give me your hand."

He didn't even attempt to mask his excitement as his massive palm landed in mine. I bit back my own smile, guiding his fingers forward so Toebeans could sniff them again. When he didn't hiss or swipe, I said, "Try scratching behind his left ear."

It worked.

It frikkin' *worked.* Toebeans was allowing a practical

stranger to pet him, and all it took was a massive cardboard palace drenched in Jackson's scent, a recording of his voice on an endless loop, and... ah, yes, the portraits. How could I forget about those?

"He's so soft."

I hummed in agreement. He was super soft. A total cuddle slut too when he was in a snuggly mood.

"I can't believe he's actually letting you touch him."

"Just wait," Jackson murmured. "By the end of next week, he'll be all snuggled up on my lap, purring away."

A hurricane of butterflies erupted in my chest when I pictured it. The air was stripped right out of my overinflated lungs. My pulse stuttered.

Maybe it wouldn't be such a bad idea to give Daniel that call he'd asked for, since he'd given me his business card and everything...

"You okay?"

"Huh?" Meeting Jackson's curious gaze was a mistake. It only made the fluttering worse. "I'm fine. Why?"

"You very suddenly stopped moving," he pointed out. "And breathing."

Had I? "I was just trying to remember where I put the business card."

His fingers slowed their scratching, his eyes slimming dangerously. Almost like a predator locking in on its prey. It made my clit flutter.

I cleared my throat and tore my gaze away from him. It messed with my thinking when he looked at me like that, and the quicker we could have The Talk, the better.

"Listen, about last night..." I trailed off. Why did I trail off?

My hesitation provided him with just enough space to

say, "I'd like to do the coaching orientation as soon as possible."

Okay, sure, "But first we should... I really think..."

The statement was at the very tip of my tongue, short and simple: *it can't happen again*.

That was it. That was all I had to say.

If I didn't end it here—if I allowed this... *thing* between us to escalate any further, I'd end up getting hurt. I knew what I felt, and I knew where it was all headed. It would be really, very stupid of me to keep going down this path.

Both for my emotional well-being and my career.

Jackson waited for me to say it, watched quietly as I struggled to get the words out. The silence stretched and stretched... until it started to feel like a dare.

I licked my drying lips. "What I'm trying to say is that last night really shouldn't have... and we can't—"

I was going to say it that time, I swear. But just as I was about to get the words out, an overstimulated Toebeans twisted in my lap and sunk his teeth into my hand.

"Ow," I noted flatly. That was, uh, definitely a lot harder than he usually bit. Normally it was a playful little nip or a quick swipe of his paw to let me know he was all done.

Normally he didn't break skin. Or growl like that.

"What's happening?" Jackson's fingers had gone still, a frown pinching at his handsome features.

"Nothing. He's just letting us know he's done being petted."

Jackson lifted his hand right away and another corner of my heart melted. Toebeans leaped off my lap and trotted toward the door, tail swishing as he licked his lips, satisfied. It was palace time.

I stretched my hand as Jackson pushed to his feet. "I

swear he's somehow become both more cuddly *and* more grumpy with age. It's almost—what are you doing?"

He rattled the small first-aid kit he'd grabbed from the linen closet before sinking down beside me again. "Give me your hand."

Th-thump. "I'm fine."

"You're bleeding."

"It's not a big deal." It was the teeniest, tiniest bit of blood you'd ever seen. I might as well have accidentally poked myself with a pin.

... Okay, maybe it was a little bigger than that, but not much.

He gently grabbed my wrist anyway, and then I had to sit there and watch him carefully clean and disinfect the small cut, apply ointment, and cover it with sterile dressing. Massive overreaction. I'd barely needed a Band-Aid.

But the damage was already done. My heart squeezed and sang as I watched him, sparks nipped at my soul, and it felt like I was floating.

"There." Jackson smoothed a thumb over the applied dressing, then kissed it. "All better."

... He *kissed* it.

I was lightheaded, couldn't breathe, and I swear if I didn't tackle him to the floor and permanently fuse our mouths together for eternity I was going to burst into a fluttering swarm of butterflies and die.

I snatched my hand out of his grip and all but flew to my feet. "Excuse me for a moment."

Fight or flight kicked in; autopilot took over. I scooped up Cat—no, sorry, *Toebeans*—and marched out of my suite.

I was in so much trouble.

28

I DROPPED Toebeans off at his palace, lingering for long enough that it was probably suspicious. But I needed the space to think.

As it turned out, my receiving love language was very, very, *very* much acts of service. My heart was so inflated, so full of air and sparks and fireflies and warmth and... and... a lot of other things that were triggering all my internal alarms. I really needed to gather my thoughts and remind myself of a few cold, hard facts.

A part of me hoped Jackson wouldn't be there when I got back to my suite. A much larger, much more prominent part of me soared when I found him on the couch, scrolling through his phone.

"You're being very confusing," I accused, storming inside.

He cocked his head. "How so?"

"This"—I held up my bandaged hand—"and all the gentle tenderness that went with it? Absolutely unacceptable levels of confusing."

"I'm afraid you're going to have to be a lot more specific."

"You kissed my hand better!"

"I was under the impression it would help."

Well, it hadn't.

I snapped my fingers and pointed one at him. "You know what, we're about to have our first coaching session."

"Fantastic." He tossed his phone on the table as I plopped down on the couch beside him. "I have so many questions—"

He wasn't given the chance to finish. The moment my ass hit the cushion, his beautiful face was in my hands and his insufferably pretty mouth was captive against mine.

The plan was simple: teach Jackson Sinclair a lesson by kissing his soul straight out of his gigantic body. And that was exactly what I did. I shoved the crippling fear and doubt aside and gave in to the hunger, the need, the incessant *craving* I had for him.

I craved him with every fiber of my soul and didn't know how to make it stop. It was horrible, and wonderful, and terrifying, and all his fault, so I shoved my tongue into his mouth as punishment.

He groaned and... it was over. He snapped out of his initial state of shock, and whatever leverage I'd started with crumpled with a broken whine when he wrapped his arms around me and effortlessly pulled me onto his lap.

My gut fucking purred. I was exactly where I belonged, straddling Jackson as he touched me, kissed me, and made filthy, *filthy* promises with that wicked tongue of his.

Absolutely unacceptable. I bit his bottom lip and pulled away.

"Lesson number one," I panted, pushing him back when he tried to chase the kiss. My palm was kept firm against his pounding chest as I glared into his dazed eyes. "There's a big difference between lust and affection. *This* —" I fisted his shirt and yanked him forward for another hard, frustrated kiss before shoving him back again. "This is lust. That's all it is. You and I have had the extremely inconvenient misfortune of being physically attracted to one another and were stupid enough to act on it."

Was he listening? He didn't look like he was listening.

"Stop staring at my mouth like that," I snapped. "I'm saying things."

"I'm quite aware of what lust is, Jamie," he told my mouth. "I'm suffering through the affliction as we speak." In case there was any confusion whatsoever around his meaning, he grabbed my thighs and jerked me forward. He was rock-hard, his grip punishing.

My clit hissed.

"So you agree that's what this is," I said, barely managing to keep my voice even. "Just lust."

Genuine surprise flicked over his features. He faltered for a moment, then blinked himself back into focus. "Of c —yes."

I knew that would be his answer—I *knew* he was going to say yes—yet my stomach still dropped, my throat still ached, and my fist still tightened around his shirt as I held up my bandaged hand. "Then this has to stop."

He was silent for a moment. "What?"

"There is lust, and then there's affection," I repeated slowly. "One is purely physical. It's driven exclusively by attraction and wants one thing, and one thing only: sex."

"I already said I know what lust—"

"Affection is not that," I interrupted. "Affection is about emotional intimacy and connection. The two have very different natures, objectives, and psychological impacts. Showing genuine and consistent affection to someone who isn't closed off to emotional intimacy like you is *confusing*, Jackson."

It led to hope. To longing and desire and, eventually, crushing disappointment.

His eyes slid between mine as his grip on my thighs softened. After a long pause, he asked, "Which part are you confused about?"

My own fingers loosened around his shirt. I swallowed. "All of it." Everything about him confused me. "You're not allowed to be sweet and tender with me anymore, understand?"

"No. Explain," he demanded. "In detail."

How much clearer could I get?

"It's called a boundary," I said, "and I'm officially setting one. Lust, I can do. That'll burn out in a week or two if we just... give it what it wants. But no displays of affection before, during, or after."

"Meaning?" he pushed.

Fuck's sake. "Meaning you can bend me over and fuck me as rough and hard as you want, but you're not allowed to clean me up afterward." I slipped his bottom lip between my teeth and softly pulled, then licked. "*Meaning*, Jackson, that you can tie me to your bed and use me like your own personal fucktoy all night, you can leave your marks and your bruises on my skin, but you're not allowed to soothe them when you're finished. Is that more clear?"

His breathing stopped abruptly when I got to the

personal fucktoy bit, his pulse slamming harder against my fist.

"Is that really what you want from me?" he asked.

What I wanted was for this burning need for him to subside before it consumed me whole. And if he had to fuck it out of me, so be it.

"Yes."

The silence that followed wouldn't have been so nerve-wracking if I could read the slow change in his expression as he studied me. I had no idea what he was thinking.

"Don't you think we'll both feel better afterward?" I tried. "Even if it's just once... don't you think it'll at least take the edge off?"

His pale eyes thinned, his lips rolling back unhappily. *That* expression I recognized right away. War was being declared.

My heart bounced. I bit back a smile.

"Did last night help take the edge off for you, Jamie?"

"It would have if you'd stuck to your word," I retorted. "All that talk about holding me down and fucking me hard, filling me with your cum... so disappointing."

I was playing with fire, and I knew it.

"*Disappointing*," Jackson repeated dangerously. His mouth ticked up, eyes knife-sharp. "Is *that* how you'd describe last night?"

If I lied and said yes, there'd be consequences.

"Yes."

His palms trailed fire up my thighs, fingers hooking under the waistband of my jeans. A tremor ripped up my spine.

"And what happens when I fuck you as hard as you want, and you realize once isn't enough?" He thumbed the button of my jeans, igniting a swarm of sparks in my core. "What then?"

"Then we'll do it a second time." The lust would have to fade eventually.

But when I reached for the top button of his shirt, he grabbed my wrists.

"Stand up," he ordered.

My vagina practically melted. I pushed to my feet.

"Strip" was his next command.

My fingers fumbled their shaky way through buttons, zippers, and sleeves, until I was standing next to a puddle of fabric, wearing nothing but my underwear.

"All of it," Jackson commanded when I hesitated.

My stomach tightened as I reached behind my back and unclasped my bra, letting it fall to the floor. Then, with a shaky breath, I slowly peeled off my panties.

I swear if this didn't end with him pinning my body to the bed and shoving into me, I was going to lose my goddamn mind. I'd never wanted someone this badly before, and I needed it to stop. I needed my muscles to not quiver when his eyes moved over my body like that. I needed my heart to not skip and dance for him, and my gut to not purr every time he walked into a room.

"So beautiful." He unbuckled his belt, dark gaze glued to my breasts. "You're so fucking beautiful, Jamie. I can't fucking handle it."

And I couldn't fucking handle him looking at me like that. My knees were going to melt.

"Calling me beautiful counts as affection," I breathed. "Don't do it again."

His jaw twitched, his throat working as he bit back the argument. "Back on my lap." The command was molten and rough. He ripped his belt free and twisted it over his large hands. "Wrists behind you."

I did as I was told, placing a knee on either side of his muscular thighs before clasping my hands behind my back. The leather belt was looped and secured around my wrists with effortless ease and efficiency. "You really would make the perfect little fucktoy, wouldn't you?"

My lungs emptied, and I was pretty sure he could see my pulse hopping out of my neck. It got worse when he hooked a finger under my dainty gold necklace and used it to pull me forward. Like a collar. He licked at my bottom lip. Nipped it with his teeth. Kissed it.

Fire teased my core, my skin, my everything.

"Pull your pants down," I said. We were wasting too much time. I needed him to be fucking me like I needed air.

Jackson tutted at me like I'd misbehaved. "Is that how good little fucktoys speak to their owners, Jamie?"

That one... that one did something to my brain. Itched another deep, hidden scratch that had been dormant and unrealized until that very second. Goosebumps raced across my skin. I shivered.

He tugged on my chain again and grazed his lips over mine. "I asked you a question."

I swallowed, refusing to answer. He smiled against my lips before giving them a soft, tender kiss. "I see."

"You're being affectionate again."

Another sweet kiss. "Unfortunately, your little rule isn't gonna work for me."

"It's not really up for negotiation."

"Affection is one of my major areas of concern. I'm afraid you're going to have to coach me on it."

I called bullshit. "*Jackson*."

He shut me up with a deep, toe-curling kiss. It scorched through me, lit the very thread of my soul on fire. When he tried to pull back, I chased the flames with my tongue.

His chest rumbled with pleasure, and when I teased his tongue with a seductive little lick, his fingers shoved into my hair. They weren't being gentle anymore.

He wasn't being gentle anymore.

With a tortured curse he crushed my body to his, hard enough for it to hurt.

It was perfect.

"You shouldn't feel so fucking good, Jamie." His mouth moved to my jaw, my neck. Everything was fire.

I felt good? *I* did?!

He pulled back and peered down at me, his hand slipping between my thighs with no warning. I gasped.

His eyes were locked on mine as his fingers ran over my slit, my entrance, my inner thighs. Anywhere and everywhere, with one exception—they wouldn't touch the little ball of oversensitive nerves begging and fluttering desperately for their attention.

Judging by his sinister smirk, it was on purpose.

"Do you want to know what my second area of concern is?" He teased my weeping entrance again and pulled a broken, shuddering breath out of me. "Remember that little diagram you drew for me?"

The what? "What diag—" Oh.

Oh, *fuck me*.

He grinned. "Where oh where could it be, the elusive little clitoris?"

Oh my god. He was going to tease me until I cried.

"I hate you," I panted. Begging would be futile. I could see it in his vicious, heartless eyes.

"You drew the picture but never bothered to show me where it was."

"No. Seriously. I hate you."

That shit-eating grin told me everything I needed to know about how much fun he was having with this. What a monster.

"As my dating coach, I think you would agree that it's your responsibility to make sure that I can at least pleasure my future wife."

"You said you didn't plan on sleeping with your wife, remember?"

He wasn't listening.

"Is this it?" He stroked a spot that made me whimper. Out of frustration, not pleasure. "Or is it maybe this one?"

"Karma's a bitch, Jackson. Watch your back."

"Is that a yes? Have I finally found it?"

I huffed a small laugh. Couldn't help it. "You're so annoying."

He pressed his smiling lips to mine in yet another tender kiss. "And you're incredibly fun to tease, anyone ever tell you that?"

There was a beat of silence, both our brains a little too slow to process what he'd just asked.

It hit him first. He pulled back. "Scratch that."

But it was too late. My evil brain had formed its evil plan, and the evil words were already tumbling out of my evil mouth. "Yes. I've been told that *so* many times by *sooo* many very attractive men tha*mphnmnn.*"

I'd never kissed someone while we were both laughing before. It felt dangerously right. Like I'd been kissing the wrong people my whole life.

Whatever panic was supposed to follow that realization was swept away by the tender strokes of Jackson's tongue. I couldn't feel anything except for the deep, burning desire simmering at the very pit of my core. Didn't even realize he'd lifted me until my ass hit the mattress and Jackson pulled away.

"On your stomach."

Finally.

Finally, finally, *fin*—

My reaction time was too slow for his liking, so he decided to flip me over himself. And... yup. I definitely had a big thing for being manhandled; shuddered and moaned when he grabbed my hips, yanked them into position, and kneed my thighs an extra inch apart. I was fully exposed to him then, entirely at his mercy with my hands tied behind my back, my ass in the air, and half my face pressed to the mattress.

I fucking loved it. Apparently, I was a tad kinkier than I'd led myself to believe up to this point.

"You're fucking dripping, Jamie." My thigh quivered when he grazed a finger over my skin, tracing the slickness running down my inner thigh. "You need to be fucked and used that badly?"

I buried my face into the duvet and stifled a moan.

"You really are a perfect little sex toy." His hands slid over my ass cheeks, spreading me wide open. "Look at these pretty little holes. They're just begging to be fucked, aren't they? They need it."

I choked against the duvet when he pressed the thick, sizzling pad of his tongue against my clit and slowly, slowly, slowly licked all the way up.

ALL. The way. Up.

Then he pressed a sweet little kiss to my trembling lower back.

"Slight problem, though," he murmured darkly. "I like

to take good care of my toys. I enjoy that part almost as much as all the playing. Without it, the process wouldn't feel quite as complete. And what good will all the playing be if we don't reach completion, wouldn't you agree?"

I knew exactly where he was going with this and I wasn't having any of it. I wasn't changing my mind.

"Not necessarily," I panted. "I can't orgasm just from penetration but that doesn't mean it's not fun or pleasurable."

A long pause. Then, "You've never come from just penetration?"

"No." It wasn't uncommon, and I swear if he was about to tell me it would be different with his miracle-working magic dick—

"So I can fuck you as much as I want, and you won't be able to come until I allow it?"

My heart stopped beating for a second. "That's... one way to look at it."

He cursed under his breath, and then I heard the unmistakable sound of his zipper ripping open. My muscles were vibrating.

"What's your safeword?"

"Strawberry," I panted. "Can we stop talking about it now and—"

The air was slammed out of my lungs, my muscles clenching against the unexpected sensation of suddenly being filled. It hurt just enough to make my clit sing.

He hadn't been kind or gentle about it, and he was so big that it... it... I moaned, squeezing my eyes shut. It was so fucking *perfect*.

I wasn't the only one in agony. The groan that ripped out of him echoed in my ears, making my everything curl. I'd made him feel good.

"Fuck." His hands were back on my hips, his unforgiving fingers digging into my skin. "You've got a tiny little fuckhole, don't you?"

No. He was just massive, but I was not coherent enough to argue with him.

He moved his hips, pushing deeper. I moaned again. How was there *more* of him? Another half-inch and I choked. I couldn't do it. He was too big. It felt too good. It hurt too much. I wanted it too desperately.

"Jackson..." I was out of breath, unable to get enough oxygen. "I can't..." Breathe. Think. Take it. "You're too... I *can't...*"

"You can." His voice was dark and utterly tortured. "You'll take every last inch like a good little toy."

He pulled out, eased back in. Pulled, eased. Pulled, and shoved.

I didn't know who cried out harder, me or him. My vision shimmered with stars, danced with ecstasy. The rest of me was burning from the inside out.

Holy.

Fuck.

Jackson let out a string of curses under his breath, keeping himself buried all the way to the hilt. "You okay?"

"So okay. So good." *Please keep going.*

"Still want it rough?"

Yes. So badly it burned. "Please."

The plea had barely escaped before it was met. Jackson pulled out, shoved back in, and did exactly as I'd asked. He kept his grip on my hips unrelentingly firm as he slammed into me over and over again, fucking me hard until a familiar pressure began to build and coil in the depths of my core.

It wouldn't spill over, but that didn't stop it from

feeling excruciatingly good. It didn't stop me from gasping and moaning every time his balls smacked my clit and sent an arrow of pleasure blazing through me.

I was in heaven.

And the more vocal I was about it, the more ruthless and punishing his thrusts became. It didn't hurt at all anymore. I was just a moaning, quivering mess of pure need.

"Fuck, Jamie. Look at how fucking well you take cock. Your pussy fucking loves it."

How was he able to form full sentences? I was dying.

The only thing I could do was keep my legs open and take the assault, knowing he wouldn't let me come right away. Or maybe not at all. Maybe he'd keep me begging all day. The thought made my toes curl. "So good... oh god, *Jackson*..."

He'd been holding back. Because the second his name slipped out of me, drenched in sugar-sweet ecstasy, his movements became more harsh, jerky, and erratic.

I choked out more moans, more whimpers, more mewls and cries and praises for how good he was fucking me. I'd never experienced anything this intense before; didn't want it to ever end.

"Fuck, Jamie. Fuckfuckfuc*kfuck*—" He cut off with a final bruising thrust and a deep, guttural grunt. I felt every jerk and spasm as his cock emptied inside me. He groaned and trembled through the orgasm, his fingers digging into my flesh like they were intent on leaving permanent bruises.

I was wound so tight that my body was trembling.

Eventually, his breathing began to even out and his grip on me loosened. He didn't let me go, though, and he didn't pull out. Instead, he ground into me, teasing my clit until I let out a wounded whimper.

"How was that?" he asked gruffly. "Did that take the *edge* off for you? Shall I untie you and leave?"

If he did, I would cry.

He moved his hips again and a tremor ran down my thighs. "God, you were just made for fucking, weren't you? Look at how well you're behaving."

"Jackson..." It was barely a whisper. I didn't have the strength to use my full voice. "Please."

He knew exactly what I was asking for. His semihard cock twitched inside me, giving him away. He enjoyed the pleading, the consensual imbalance of power, just as much as I did.

"Didn't you come enough last night?" he teased. "Don't you think it's my turn?"

I swallowed, clinging on to the very last thread of sanity I possessed.

"Sorry," I muttered.

There was a long pause before he said, "Why are you sorry?"

"Because... I don't know if you got to finish, and I should have checked before passing out." I mean, I was *pretty sure* he'd gotten there, but I couldn't know for certain.

A low, dark laugh rumbled out of his chest. "I definitely finished. That's how fucking good you taste, Jamie. It made me spill in my pants like a teenager."

Heat flooded my cheeks, and I bit my lip, stifling another moan.

"You should put that in my file." It was a dare. "When you pick out my wife, you should let her know my favorite kink is eating you out. Tell her I love the taste of your pussy so much that it's all I'll be able to think about whenever I get my *needs met*."

What was he doing?

And why did it make me throb around him?

"Tell her that if you'd agreed to marry me, you'd have woken up with my head buried between your thighs every single fucking morning. Let her know that while she has to beg for me to touch her, you had to beg for me to stop. That's how maddeningly attracted to you I am, how much I fucking loved eating you out, and I want to make sure she knows it."

He was fully hard again which, up until that moment, I didn't realize could happen. My fingers curled into fists as he slowly slid out an inch, then back in.

"Do you think she'll understand, Jamie? That the reason I won't lick her pussy is because I know she won't taste like you?"

Oh my god. I shut my eyes, my heart pounding in my chest. Foolishly, I wanted to believe him. Selfishly, I wanted to be the only one he desired. Logically, I knew how incompatible we were.

Still, I loved hearing him say it.

His next thrust was much harder. It might have even hurt if I wasn't so wet and dripping with his cum. "I want to fucking do it again. I want to tie your wrists to my bed and lick your sweet pussy until you're begging and pretending like you don't want me to keep going. I'm fucking rabid for it, Jamie."

My muscles tensed as he picked up speed, fucking me harder and harder, until we were both fighting for air again.

"How's this, darling? That edge you were talking about gone yet?"

I hated him. So much.

He had no idea what he was doing to me. How good he felt. How confused I was. How easily his words could be misinterpreted.

"Shut up," I breathed, which only made him laugh.

"Fuck. Jesus. I'm already close." His hammering sped up, and no matter how tight the tension in my core twisted, it wasn't enough to push me over the edge. I was in agony.

Sweet, torturous agony that had me close to tears by the time Jackson twitched and spasmed and groaned through his second release. I loved every bit of it.

Hot liquid spilled out of me when he slowly pulled out, and I whined, protesting the sudden emptiness. It felt strangely foreign and hollow, and I wanted him to fix it. Instead, he zipped up and set my hands free.

No. I wasn't ready.

"Look at you." He ran the tips of his fingers over the curve of my ass and huffed a dark, amused chuckle when I quivered. "Two full loads of my cum and your greedy little fuckhole's still pulsating for more. Who knew my sweet girl would turn out to be such a needy slut?"

My freed fingers curled into the duvet as I bit back an embarrassingly loud cry. There was a good chance I'd climax if he just kept talking. It was like he had a roadmap of my secret buttons and was intent on smashing them all, one after another.

The bedside drawer opened, and I knew. He'd looked this morning.

"Get on your back."

I rolled over as gracefully as one could with trembling muscles, my knees melting inward at the sight of Jackson towering over me.

The fact that I was fully naked while he was still fully dressed added an extra layer of vulnerability I enjoyed way too much.

"Do well behaving fucktoys close their legs before they're done being used, Jamie?" He turned on my studded purple vibrator; turned it off again.

A threat.

This was officially out of control. I was so out of my depth. It was overwhelming, and scary, and oh so thrilling.

"Spread your thighs," he commanded. "Show me what a good little slut you are, how badly you need to be fucked again."

My pulse kicked. So insanely out of my depth.

Still, I listened, splaying my thighs open for him, watching his eyes go dark and his throat work with a rough swallow.

"Do you have any fucking idea how pretty you look with my cum spilling out of you like this, sweet girl?" The vibrator clicked on again and he stepped closer. "The sins I would commit if I could have a full year of this?"

And what if the year ended up not being enough? What if I wanted a lifetime? What then?

"I'm not going to marry you." Out of all the times I'd said the words, that one sounded the least convincing. My voice was shaky, uneven, full of air.

"You sure about that?" His palm curved over my right knee, forcing it wider before he nudged at my entrance with the vibrator. I moaned. He grinned. "I've got three weeks to convince you to sign the contract. By the time our thirty days are up you might be begging for another twelve months of my cock."

"And then what? How many people do I get on my list?"

He frowned. "I'm not following."

"You said you'd encourage your wife to get her needs met elsewhere, right?"

So many of his facial muscles ticked in such quick succession that I had to bite back a laugh.

"Well?" I teased. "How many more men are allowed to tie me up and—"

My mouth fell open when he pushed the vibrator in, but no sound came out. My eyelids fluttered, my fingers curled, and if Jackson hadn't pushed onto the bed and positioned himself between my thighs, my legs would have snapped closed.

"Say that again."

"Holy shit."

"Say it again."

I blinked his scowl into focus, my chest heaving. He'd twisted the vibrator so that the protruding clit stimulator couldn't do its job. Asshole.

"I bet one of them would let me come," I panted. "Maybe if I make use of that business card and called my soulma—"

His lips crushed mine, shutting me the hell up. He punished me with his tongue, bit me, and pressed the vibrator deeper. I moaned into his mouth, my hips wiggling. When he broke the kiss, his icy-blue eyes narrowed down at me. "For the last time, you're not for him. And just so we're crystal-fucking-clear on this, you won't be fucking anyone else with my ring on your finger."

His hand had started to move, slowly pulling the studded vibrator out, pushing it back in. I was going to lose my fucking mind.

"No one," he said. "No one but me."

I whimpered, my back arching slightly. He was going too slow. I needed more.

"You'd be mine, Jamie." He twisted the toy, edging the stimulator just a little closer to my clit. "You'd only ever come for me—*because* of me."

Another little twist and I choked out a broken cry. He was so close. I just needed him to turn it one more time.

I was heaving, trembling like a leaf as he loomed over me, a hand braced beside my head.

"How many hours of fucking do you think you can take?" He bent down and nibbled on my bottom lip. "Should we test it out?"

The toy twisted again.

The wrong way.

I whined, my will cracking straight down the middle.

"Please no. Please." I couldn't take it anymore.

"You're so fucking pretty when you beg. I can't handle it." His gaze roamed over my face, drinking in every ounce of the pleasure and suffering he was inflicting. "Would you like to know another secret?"

No. The only thing I wanted was for him to twist the damn vibrator.

"Every single one of my kinks—all the ones we've talked about—are exclusive to you. I don't want to do any of this with anyone else; never have. Why is that, Jamie? What the fuck did you do to me?"

I didn't know, couldn't stop choking out moans to answer him.

"So fucking pretty..." he murmured. "You want to come, sweet girl?"

"Yes." I didn't know if the word actually made it out of

my mouth, but I really tried. "Please... please... I need it so bad—"

He kissed me right as he twisted the toy, swallowing my every cry and moan as the vibrations shot fire and electricity through my clit, up my torso, down my legs.

The orgasm slammed into me so hard that I couldn't stop shaking, couldn't breathe, couldn't see anything over the bright white and red dots dancing over my vision. It was never-ending. It just kept going and going, soaking me in lust and fire.

It was incredible.

He wouldn't stop kissing me, even after the vibrator was discarded and the aftershocks had relented. And instead of pushing him away, I'd shoved my hands into his hair and was gripping onto it for dear life as our tongues tangled and played. He touched me everywhere, palms roaming all over my body like he simply couldn't pick which part he liked best.

I didn't get it. Didn't understand how I could possibly need more of him after all that.

I also couldn't stop.

We rolled around on the bed, devouring each other until Jackson was fumbling with his zipper again.

The third time did not take the edge off. It sharpened the damn thing.

I was fucked. Both literally and figuratively, I was well and truly and thoroughly fucked.

29

I'D LOST control of the situation, the week, myself. I'd lost control, period.

I thought I had it. I thought that if I just gave the lust what it wanted, it would eventually subside and leave me alone. That wasn't what happened.

It'd been a full week, and the "edge" had not worn off. It'd grown into a voracious, all-consuming Goliath, and I was helpless against it. Jackson couldn't stop touching me, and I couldn't stop wanting it, needing it, *craving* it. It was every night, every morning, and still not enough.

On Monday, I'd barely had a chance to close his office door after lunch before he pushed me up against it and dropped to his knees. I was instructed to be "quiet like a good little toy" while he shoved up my skirt, hooked my leg over his shoulder, and ate me out like it was his final day on earth and I was his last requested meal.

Tuesday, he placed me on his desk, wrapped his belt around my wrists, his tie around my mouth, and sucked and licked my breasts until I was a squirming, helpless puddle of need, entirely at his mercy. Then he tortured three orgasms out of me with his fingers before thrusting into me to finish.

Wednesday, he pinned me to the wall, pulled up my skirt, and fucked me from behind. Twice.

Thursday and Friday were the worst offenders.

We didn't even make it to the office before giving in on those days. I straddled him in the backseat of his town car and took what I needed. There was no kink, no dirty talk, no binding or teasing or torment. My arms were looped around his neck, his hands roamed over my back, and it was... *tender*. Deep kisses, gentle caresses, shared breaths, fluttering heartbeats, and an alarming amount of eye contact.

Sunday, it all started to catch up with me.

ALICE

Hey.

Can you talk super quick?

Sorry. I know it's early.

I squint-blinked at the too bright screen, my fingers slow to draft the response.

I'll call you in five

I locked my phone and, very slowly, attempted to slip out from underneath Jackson's arm without waking him up. I was unsuccessful.

He grumbled incoherently into my hair and hooked a heavy, muscled leg over my hip, effectively locking me in.

"I need to make a phone call," I whispered. "It's for work."

"Do it here," he mumbled.

"I can't. My phone only works on speaker."

"It does? Why?"

"The pool."

He hummed but didn't loosen any part of his hold on me. "I'll get you a new one."

"Jackson."

"I'm sleeping. Won't listen."

I sighed. It was a little hard to pretend like I wasn't smiling, but I think I managed it.

Any sensitive info being discussed? People are around

ALICE

No, all good. I'll codename existing clients.

I cleared some of the groggy rasp from my throat before hitting the Call button.

She picked up right away. "Hey! So sorry, I know it's Sunday."

"It's okay. What's up?"

"A couple of things. First, we've already got four candidates lined up based on Ripper's new profile. Great job on that, by the way. Even Vivian didn't have anything negative to say when we reviewed it. And your report was so detailed, I actually think it pissed her off a little."

"Thanks," I mumbled awkwardly. It didn't help that the compliment made Jackson smile into my hair before placing a kiss on the crown of my head. Almost like he was proud of me.

We needed to have the affection talk again. He hadn't been listening at all.

"She wants you to confirm a time and place for his first

date by tomorrow morning, and says it needs to be on, or before, Wednesday this week. Ripper's aunt called and demanded it. I think her spiritual something-or-other gave her the timeline."

"Will do," I said, ignoring the painful jab that arrowed from my gut to my chest. "I'll need to brief him on the candidates first, but you'll have the info by the deadline."

Jackson wasn't smiling anymore.

"Great. Second, do you know a guy named Daniel Omori?"

My heart stopped beating for a second as Jackson stiffened to stone against me. "Say that again?"

It was possible we'd both misheard her.

"Daniel Omori," she repeated. "He's like a famous sushi chef based in Tokyo? His restaurant is a celebrity hotspot, it pops up on my feed all the time."

"What about him?" My chest was hammering against Jackson's bicep. Meanwhile, he'd stopped breathing.

"He called and asked to meet with you."

I blanked—couldn't think of what to do or say for an awkwardly long amount of seconds. When the gears finally decided to start turning again, I tried to wiggle out of Jackson's hold. It was no use.

"Hello? You there?"

"Uh, yup. Still here." I was staring at the ceiling so I couldn't see Jackson's expression, but I swear I could feel the lethality of it.

"Do you know him?"

I licked my lips, fully alert at this point. "We've met."

"Okay, yeah, sounded like it," she said. "Anyways he called and had a bunch of questions about the Immersive program and asked if you were available."

Could humans growl? Because Jackson's chest was vibrating against my arm and emitting a rumbling noise that sounded very *predatory*. His muscles were starting to flex too, cutting off a good chunk of my airflow as he pinned my body to his.

"What did you tell him?" I asked, pretending like I could still breathe just fine.

"I didn't speak to him, Vivian did. She told him you'd be available next month."

I should not have taken this phone call here. If I'd been more awake, I'd have thought better of it. Jackson's mouth was pressed to the top of my head like it was the only thing keeping him quiet.

But before I could talk my way into hanging up and calling her back, Alice said, "He's insisting on meeting with you sooner than that, which is why I'm calling. Are you available tomorrow night? He's in New York reshooting a commercial, but if you're free he's willing to fly out after filming wraps up—just needs to know right away so he can book his flight."

"He wants to fly to Toronto just to talk to me for a couple of hours?"

"*Right*?" Her voice lit up like she was sharing a particularly juicy piece of gossip. "We offered to set up a virtual meeting, but he kept pushing for dinner. Claimed it'd be easier to discuss the specifics of you relocating to Tokyo in person."

My head was spinning, struggling to come up with an excuse to get me out of it.

Except... why? Technically, this didn't mean anything. Technically, it was just a work meeting, and if I *did* decide to take him on as a client, nothing could happen between us anyway. Not to mention a second Immersive would look pretty solid on my résumé. There was no real reason for me to say no.

Except maybe for one.

"I'm in the middle of an Immersive already. I can't accept a meeting with a new client." I was being paid to focus solely on the Sinclair file. That was kind of the whole point.

"Vivian's making an exception."

Damn.

"She is?"

"Minerva allowed it from what I gather, so if Ripper gives you a hard time you can direct him to her."

I tried, I really did. My only other excuse was that I planned to quit at the end of this month but, again, a second Immersive would elevate my résumé and a second bonus wouldn't hurt, either. I'd have some financial breathing room for once.

My desire to say no was driven by my feelings, not my head.

"Okay," I said. "If they've both cleared it, then sure, I'll meet with him."

"Great. I'll reserve something close to whatever hotel he's staying at and send you the details."

We hung up.

My eyes remained glued to the ceiling as my pulse raced. Guilt gnawed at the base of my chest, unwarranted. I was allowed to agree to business meetings. And even if it wasn't just a meeting, Jackson and I weren't together, so it shouldn't have mattered either way.

I waited for a few minutes, hoping he'd break the silence so I could at least get a sense of what he was thinking. When he didn't give any indication that he was going to speak, I gently cleared my throat again. "So... I think our plans for today just changed. We'll need to go over the candidates together and discuss some of my observations over the last couple of weeks. I'll need a bit of time to prep first, though."

He didn't respond. He also didn't loosen his hold on me.

"Can we meet up again at around noon?" That would give me enough time to finish my work and get an hour or two of extra sleep. Jackson hadn't allowed much of that over the last week. I was exhausted, sore as hell, and could tell just by the minimal amount I'd moved so far that my joints would creak the second I attempted to get out of bed.

It'd been so worth it, though.

I chewed my bottom lip, giving him another minute before asking, "Does that time work for you? If not we can—"

"Why do you like him so much?"

My mouth stuttered and I blinked. What was I supposed to say to that?

"What is it about him?"

I couldn't remember. I also couldn't place the shift in his tone. It was new.

"Is it because he has a dog?"

I couldn't remember.

"Is it his tattoos?"

I couldn't remember.

"Is it because he's a sushi chef?"

I still couldn't remember.

It must have been a combination of all those things at some point, but for the life of me, I couldn't recall the exact reasons. I hadn't even known the guy. It didn't make sense.

"Do you truly believe Imogen was talking about him?" he asked.

"You don't think any of that stuff is real, remember?" I reminded him gently. "Tarot and spirituality aside, you don't believe in soulmates or romantic love. You claim it's all bullshit." My fingers curled around the duvet, my mouth moving silently for a beat. "Or has your opinion on any of that changed?"

And then I held my breath.

For a few foolishly optimistic seconds, I thought his silence meant he was considering it. Maybe even grappling with it. I didn't need him to be on the same page as me, or to feel any of the things I was starting to feel for him. I just needed to know that there was a possibility, no matter how small, that one day he'd—

"No."

It was firm. Finite. He left zero room for interpretation.

Stupidly—*hilariously*—my throat thickened, a crack running down my chest. As if his answer hadn't been entirely expected.

Hope was such a viciously miserable thing sometimes.

When people tell you who they are, when they tell you what they want, believe them. Always believe them.

"Then it doesn't matter, does it?" I said.

It was official. Going to dinner with Daniel would be a good thing for me—it was exactly what I needed. If nothing else, it would be a much needed reminder that there were men out there that wanted the same things I did.

This time Jackson didn't stop me when I tried to slip out from underneath his limbs. The crack spread, and I had no one to blame for it but myself. Keeping my head down, my eyes averted, I quietly gathered my clothes and put them on.

"I'll see you at noon."

I didn't wait for a response from him. I just left.

30

I HOPPED onto my laptop as soon as I was showered and dressed, and threw myself into work, hoping it would distract me. Except I'd been staring at the screen for just under an hour, and the only thing I'd done was open Alice's email and click on her first listed candidate.

Miray Kaya.

Thirty-four years old. Former gymnast and current CEO of Counter Couture—the largest vegan, cruelty-free, and sustainable clothing brand in the country. She had an MBA from Cambridge with a concentration on sustainable business, had won numerous innovation and ethical fashion awards, and was quite possibly the most beautiful human being in existence. She was *stunning*.

Like, her photos straight-up did not look real.

Under the Consultant Notes section, Alice had written:

> Shares client's views on the romanticization of romance itself (though not as strongly). Much more interested in compatibility than love. Would consider an open

marriage under the right circumstances but would prefer to maintain a sexual relationship and sleep in the same bed as primary partner, as both activities heavily promote bonding between mates, which strengthens the foundation for raising and co-parenting future children. She is well-read on the topic and is happy to discuss the science behind it at length.

Overall compatibility score of 90.3 based on available data. Higher-than-normal error margin is expected due to limited/ undisclosed information pertaining to client A's: childhood and upbringing; interpersonal relationships; attachment style; conflict resolution style; sexual preferences.

Under private notes, she'd written:

Nope, pictures aren't photoshopped. Believe it or not, they actually don't do her justice. I've got major hair/face/body envy. I don't think even Ripper would turn her down.

I felt a little sick to my stomach, to be honest. I knew I had to keep it moving and open the next profile but couldn't bring myself to do it. This was exactly why Charmed (and almost all other reputable matchmaking services) had such strict policies and guidelines prohibiting their consultants from getting physically or romantically involved with their clients.

The conflict-of-interest bit was a very real thing. I was living it.

I shut my laptop, stood up, and started pacing. There were only two possible ways this thing with Jackson could end—with me agreeing to sign the contract, or him marrying someone else. There was no third option.

If I didn't sign the contract, our little affair would have to end in two weeks.

If I did sign the contract, it would have to end at the one-year mark, *and* I'd lose my career over it.

Again, there was no magical third option. I wasn't going to delude myself into thinking that, somewhere along the line, Jackson would change his entire belief system and confess his undying love to me. I also didn't trust myself to not fall for him and definitely didn't hate myself enough to—

I halted when my phone *ding*ed.

UNKNOWN NUMBER

Oh, there we go.

UNKNOWN NUMBER

Did you do it?

UNKNOWN NUMBER

I think so.

UNKNOWN NUMBER

How do you know?

UNKNOWN NUMBER

I'm in the next room, Molly. You can just come talk to me.

MOLLY

Well that wasn't the plan, was it?

UNKNOWN NUMBER

Hush.

MOLLY

She hasn't even joined yet.

UNKNOWN NUMBER

She has.

MOLLY

How do you know if she hasn't said anything?

UNKNOWN NUMBER

It's all automatic, isn't it? I did exactly as Bensen's boy said.

MOLLY

I don't think it worked, Mabel. It would have told us so.

MABEL

It did tell me so.

MOLLY

Well, why didn't it tell me so?

MABEL

How should I know that?

MOLLY

Call the boy back and ask.

MABEL

All right.

Biting down a smile, I typed out a response.

ME

If it helps, I'm here

MABEL

I knew it.

MOLLY

Well, why didn't you say something earlier, dear?

Sorry. Didn't want to interrupt

A handful of minutes ticked by without a response, though Mabel's typing indicator kept flicking on and off. Then:

MABEL

That's quite all right. We were just wondering if you've had a chance to visit the library is all.

Not yet, no

To be honest, I'd forgotten they'd even mentioned it. Eons had passed since the night they'd snuck over to my suite. Two lifetimes' worth of orgasms had been experienced.

MOLLY

That's too bad. Are you busy now?

We've got new matches for Jackson. I'm going over their profiles.

MABEL

Oh, well that can wait, can't it?

MOLLY

We're feeling a bit under the weather, you see, and were wondering if you'd be willing to run a few errands for us.

At the library.

I'd never met two people so relentlessly entertaining. They'd really grown on me. Before I could respond, Mabel started typing again.

MABEL

It's a bit urgent, I'm afraid. We'll need it all done while the Young Master is preoccupied.

Wait. I thought Jackson would be at the library. Wasn't that what they'd been insinuating before?

What's he doing?

MOLLY

No time for that now, dear. First things first, you'll need to grab the key.

There's a key? To the library?

MABEL

Jackson started locking the door when you arrived.

That probably means he doesn't want me going in there.

MOLLY

Well, he doesn't need to know, does he? We'd go ourselves if we weren't so terribly ill.

Tell me the truth, how much trouble will I be in if he catches me?

MOLLY

We're not exactly sure.

MABEL

Apart from Jackson, Molly and I are the only other people who have ever been allowed in.

MOLLY

Not to worry, though, dear. We just need you to grab a couple of books for us, nothing nefarious.

MABEL

We're bedridden and wasting away, aren't we, Molly?

MOLLY

If the illness doesn't take me, the boredom will.

You're terrible liars.

MABEL

The key has been tucked under the vase to the left of your suite. Avoid the main kitchen area at all costs.

More instructions to follow.

~

The silver skeleton key was, in fact, tucked under the very large, very irreplaceable-looking vase to the left of my suite. It was also looped through one of those rainbow twill necklaces kids made at preschool. The colors were worn, and the fraying twill had been tied in three separate places—but not as a method of repair. Trapped above each knot was a bright blue plastic pendant in the shape of a letter. J, M, and M.

I should have taken it as a warning.

I didn't think I'd ever been as unprepared for something as I was for what was on the other side of that door. Then again, if Molly and Mabel had tried to describe it to me, I wouldn't have believed them.

I hadn't moved in a very long time. I'd unlocked the

door, stepped through what must have been an invisible portal, and promptly froze.

It was *beautiful*. In every sense of the word, Jackson's library was breathtakingly and awe-inspiringly *beautiful*.

It also made no fucking sense whatsoever.

The only things that sort of checked out were the floor-to-ceiling bookcases that lined three out of the four walls... but even those had been drawn and painted on. *Everything* had been drawn and painted on. There were tiny little flowers and leaves and stars and candy-colored critters etched into every wooden surface in the room.

It was nothing like the rest of the penthouse.

There was color *everywhere*, and so much sunshine. How could there be so much more light spilling through these windows compared to the rest of the penthouse? It was like I'd been trudging through perpetually grey weather and hadn't realized it until I'd stumbled onto a field of flowers on a clear summer day.

And this room actually looked lived-in. There was a red blanket thrown haphazardly over the side of a dented, wrinkly leather couch, a forgotten mug left on top of the drawing-covered coffee table, and a handful of dog-eared books with bent covers lying around in various unkempt positions.

Even the Persian carpet was faded and aged.

I loved it. All of it. It was homey and cozy and beautiful, and had I known it existed, I would've spent a hell of a lot more time in here over the last couple of weeks.

Did Jackson know his library had been vandalized by a group of children of varying ages and drawing skill levels? Because if not, he was going to throw a fucking fit when he found out.

The mug user hadn't even bothered with a coaster. It was *bad*.

What is this place?

Was it a setup? Had I been sent here as bait because they needed someone to blame for the mess? Ria always said it was the innocent-looking ones you had to watch out for.

MOLLY

It's the library, dear, we've talked about this.

Okay, well, at least now I knew where Jackson got that specific aspect of his humor from.

No, I mean what's with the drawings on everything?

MOLLY

Oh.

Yes, well, the old Master Sinclair wasn't all that happy with Jackson's interest in art, you see, so we had to get creative.

MABEL

He didn't leave us much of a choice in the matter, I'm afraid.

MOLLY

Not after he tore up the sketchbooks we bought Jackson and left the wee little love weeping in our arms on his fifth birthday.

I blinked down at the screen.

His dad had done what?

MOLLY

And he didn't stop there.

MABEL

Went as far as to ban sketchbooks, coloring pencils, and all painting supplies from the whole house. Staff's quarters included.

MOLLY

But he never did say anything about fabric dye, did he?

MABEL

He did not. And there was no mention of wood or furniture or books or makeup brushes, either.

MOLLY

So, we went out and bought as much dye as we could carry, gave Jackson a little tutorial, then set him loose in our quarters.

MABEL

Fantastic at keeping secrets, the Young Master. Always has been.

MOLLY

We still use the bed frames he painted on, but the rest of the furniture is housed safely in the library.

MABEL

We insisted he keep it all.

I looked around again, paying closer attention. Sure enough, there were a couple of dressers tucked between bookcases, a side table, and a small vanity I'd missed during my initial scan of the place.

Jackson did all this?

MABEL

Quite wonderful, isn't it?

I walked over to the closest bookshelf and knelt down to study the paintings at the very bottom. The progression of Jackson's age was clear. The farther up I moved, the more detailed and advanced the art became.

It was so, so lovely.

The big, clumsily painted flowers gradually morphed into intricate vines snaking around meticulously detailed dragons and Monarch butterflies. The oversized stars with shaky lines became vibrant patches of a starry night sky. There were mystic forests with animated trees and talking gnomes. Woodland creatures playing in moonlit waterfalls.

It was brilliant. Every inch of wood told a different story, and I lost track of how long I spent going around the room, drinking it all in.

Then I decided to pull out a random book off the shelf and open it. I gasped, my mouth falling open.

At some point in the later years, Jackson must have managed to get his hands on some real art supplies, because I didn't think you could sketch anything with this level of detail using a normal pen or pencil. It was fucking *magical*. Castles and crows and lions and lilies and pirate ships and swordfights sketched over the words, interacting with chapter titles and depicting underlined passages.

Anything and everything he'd ever drawn or painted was probably preserved in this room, etched into an item or a piece of furniture. I'd never seen anything like it.

Molly and Mabel had been silent over the last... however long I'd been here. Not by accident, I suspected.

Which books did you need me to grab?

MABEL

Oh, darn. I can't seem to recall the title of mine.

I couldn't help the smile that tugged at my mouth as I typed out my response. Of course she didn't.

Do you remember anything about the cover or spine? Or an approximate location?

MABEL

I think it had a dark green cover. Try the small bookcase beside the baby piano.

What baby piano?

I definitely didn't see one of those in here.

MABEL

It's down the steps, dear.

What steps? I walked around the room again, checked underneath some of the bigger pieces of furniture, but nothing. And just as I was about to ask, my phone *ding*ed.

MOLLY

Try rubbing the genie lamp.

Again, what genie lam—oh, never mind. It was on the bookshelf to my left, perched beside a leather-bound version of The Arabian Nights.

I rubbed it. I still don't see any stairs.

MABEL

Try again. Make sure you give it a good scrub.

Still nothing.

MOLLY

You might have to use one of your wishes to make them appear.

My grin widened slowly.

Molly and Mabel Harrison, are the two of you fucking with me right now?

MOLLY

We wouldn't dream of it, dear, would we Mabel?

MABEL

Certainly not.

MOLLY

Try opening the lid.

Done. Still nothing.

MABEL

Now say the words: open sesame.

They were one hundred percent fucking with me, and I two hundred percent didn't give a damn. This was kind of fun.

"Open sesame*ohmygod*."

I half tripped on my own feet when the shelf moved, my palm flying up to my chest.

Because, again, it fucking *moved*—slid three feet back, then rolled aside to reveal a small set of stairs, leading to a *secret room!!!!*

Holy fuck. YES!

I'd always, always, always wanted to partake in secret room shenanigans. This was amazing. Ria was going to lose her mind when she found out.

OMG!!!!

MOLLY

It is rather whimsical, yes.

MABEL

We never could keep up with Jackson's imagination, could we?

MOLLY

We tried our best, Mabel. That's what counts.

Honestly if he kills me for sneaking in here tell my parents I said it was worth it

MABEL

lOl.

MOLLY

I don't think that's the expression, Mabel.

lol

I officially loved those two. Almost as much as I loved this magical library.

Tucking my phone into my back pocket, I hopped down the five steps, my heart fluttering with giddy excitement. There were only a handful of bookshelves down here. The rest of the space was peppered with even more art-covered furniture—chairs, desks, bedside tables, and, yup, there it was... the sweetest little kids' piano. It was adorable.

Found the piano.

MOLLY

That one was a bit trickier to keep under the radar, wasn't it, Mabel?

MABEL

Very much so. We had to coordinate with Mikey on that one.

Mikey? Like Jackson's driver, Mikey?

MABEL

The very one. Though he was Richard's driver back then.

MOLLY

We could only allow the Young Master to practice when his father wasn't home. Mikey would provide us with that information.

MABEL

Richard would've had our heads otherwise. He was convinced that music and art would make the boy "soft" as he put it.

Who taught Jackson how to play?

MABEL

Bensen to start.

Rahul's daughter-in-law took over when Bensen was fired. He's the barber, dear. I'd imagine you've met him by now.

Something severely unpleasant tugged at my chest. The reason why Jackson kept so many members of staff—the reason why he had "a person" for everything—wasn't because he was useless and incapable of self-sufficiency. It was because they were *his people*. His family. He kept them around out of love, not necessity.

My heart inflated, a thick wad of cotton forming in the pit of my throat. In hindsight, I could see why they were so insistent I'd misjudged him.

Why was Bensen fired?

I assumed Jackson had rehired him at some point, likely when he'd been old enough to get a place of his own.

There was no immediate response, which gave me time to meander around and take in more details. Like the framed picture Jackson kept on an old desk tucked in the corner of the room. He must have been twelve or thirteen at the time, sporting a Santa hat and a mouthful of braces. Embracing him were Molly and Mabel, and the Grinch smiling evilly behind them was... a much younger Bensen, I was pretty sure.

It was far more precious than it had any right to be, and definitely wasn't helping the tightening in my throat.

MOLLY

Do you see a bedside table with a big cactus drawn on one side?

Yeah

MOLLY

The book I need you to grab for me is in there. Second drawer.

Okay, so they weren't going to tell me why Bensen was fired which, of course, only made me more curious. I opened the drawer she was talking about, but there was no book inside it. There was, however, a journal.

It was bookmarked in multiple places.

If this is Jackson's diary I'm not touching it with a ten-foot pole.

I drew a hard line at reading another person's most private thoughts without their explicit consent. And I wasn't willing to steal it for Molly, either.

MOLLY

It's not his, dear. It's mine.

Oh. Fair enough.

Okay. I've grabbed it. I'm looking for your green book now, Mabel.

MOLLY

Actually, can you check a few things for me first? I need to make sure it's the right journal.

Okay what should I check?

MOLLY

Why don't you flip to the first marked page.

A fair warning though, dear...

31

In her defense, Molly warned me about the content before I opened the journal. I just... I didn't realize how hard it would hit.

On one hand, I now knew why Bensen had been fired, and had a pretty solid theory to explain Jackson's aversion to romantic love. On the other hand, my heart had been shattered into a million pieces and I hated everything.

Bensen—poor, wonderful Bensen—had been fired for taking Jackson to the hospital after "the boy showed up to music lessons wincing with pain, unable to focus on a single thing. It took ages of convincing to get him to show us the cigarette burns. He'd done his damnedest to hide it for months, judging by some of the older scars. Mabel threw a fit, but Bensen insisted on taking the bullet. He thinks Jackson needs the two of us more, but I can't be so sure."

It didn't get any better after that.

Jackson's so-called mother? Vain, selfish leech of a woman who'd had affair after affair after affair, drilled into Jackson's head from a criminally young age that any married couple that claimed they were "in love" and that their relationship wasn't "simply a transaction," were lying to both themselves and to everyone else, "and if you ever tell Richard you saw me with Uncle Ross, I'll make sure to tell him *allll* about the doodling you've been doing with Fatty One and Thing Two."

The threat had been made in front of Molly. Beatrice Sinclair wasn't all that fond of acknowledging "the help" as she referred to them. Most of the time, she liked to pretend they weren't in the room.

According to the journal entries, she'd celebrated her husband's death by moving to Paris. Without telling Jackson. But at least she called, right? Not on his birthday or any major holidays, it was only when she wanted something from him (money) *but at least she called.*

I hated everything.

And I *really* hated Richard and Beatrice Sinclair—fucking *loathed* them with every fiber of my soul. I was shaking with it as I continued to flip through Molly's journal.

The second one.

There were four of them, according to the last set of texts I'd received from the sisters, each hidden in a different location. I'd been granted permission to read all of them, as long as I promised to stop when it became "too much."

I'd broken that promise around a hundred pages ago. I couldn't stop even though I knew I had to get back to work. I still hadn't prepped for my meeting with—*crap. What time is it?*

I snatched my phone off the floor, tapped the screen, and... nothing. It was dead.

Shit.

I scrambled to my feet, quickly put the journals back, and hurried out of the room. Then I realized I didn't know how to shut the secret door.

I tried putting the lid back on. Nothing.

"Close sesame." Nothing.

I rubbed the lamp in case the sisters hadn't been messing with me and there was a sensor or something that would trigger the door. Nothing happened.

Okay, it's okay. Don't panic, because if you panic, you won't be able to think, and if you can't think, you won't be able to—

"The command is 'ten swords, twelve lies,'" a male voice said from behind me. "But you have to open the lid for Genie to hear you."

Without looking back, I tentatively opened the lid and muttered the command. Sure enough, the shelf moved, smoothly sliding back into place. I swiped at my cheeks before turning around, not wanting him to see any of the residual wetness still lingering on my skin.

Bensen stood at the arched doorway of the library, hands clasped professionally behind his back, spine straight as ever.

"Thanks," I said quietly.

He dipped his chin. "Of course."

I shifted on my feet awkwardly, fiddling with the edge of my phone case. "Are you going to tell him I was in here?"

He considered me for a moment. "The staff was given explicit instructions prior to your arrival to report any suspicious activity directly to the Young Master."

I nodded. "Okay. That makes sense."

"I would be going against his direct orders if I kept quiet about this."

"I understand." This wasn't his fault. He was just doing his job.

"He's quite protective of this space, you know. It's off limits to all members of staff, save for the Harrison sisters."

"I get why—wait. Then how do you know the command to close the secret door?"

His mouth quirked. "You'd be surprised at how much one picks up in a position such as mine simply by... being present. It's also the name of a bedtime story I made up for the Young Master when he was a child; not something I'd easily forget."

Damn it, I was going to start tearing up again. "You've really never been in here?"

"Not once." He glanced around the room, and I swear his eyes, shoulders, posture—everything about him visibly softened. "It's lovely. I haven't seen his drawings in — This brings back a lot of memories."

And then, to the utter detriment of what little emotional stability I had left, Bensen choked up.

"My apologies, Miss Paquin." He fished a cloth handkerchief out of his breast pocket and gently dabbed at his eyes while my own overfilled with fresh tears. "I wasn't expecting... Regardless, we should take our leave." He folded his handkerchief back into a neat square and sniffled. "The Young Master is expecting you in the main kitchen for your meeting. I was tasked with fetching you from your suite which, I'm sure you can agree, is exactly what I've done."

I wiped my eyes as I made my way to the door. "So, you're not gonna tell him?"

Bensen sighed. "You are not to blame for the scheming of the Harrison twins, Miss Paquin, though I suggest keeping your phone on the next time they send you out on an adventure."

"It died," I muttered, waving the useless brick in the air.

Bensen shut the door behind us. I locked it.

"Shall we?" he said.

I fiddled with the rainbow twill in my hands, twisting it over my fingers. "Before we go... I'm gonna do something and I need you to not be weirded out by it."

He blinked. "What exactly—"

I threw my arms around his shoulders and pulled him into a tight hug.

"You're a good dude, Bensen," I said, my throat clamping over the words. "For real."

After a moment of hesitation, he patted my back. "Thank you, Miss Paquin. For what it's worth, I think you, too, are a good dude."

~

We took the long route, making sure to enter the open kitchen area from the direction of my suite. Not that it mattered. Jackson barely noticed when we walked in. His head was tucked, hands working, features tight with concentration.

I couldn't tell what he was so focused on though. He was standing behind a split-level kitchen island and I couldn't see over the upper slab of white marble.

He still didn't look up when Bensen excused himself, but when I tried to walk up to the counter, he held up a hand. "Wait."

I slowed to a stop.

"You're late," he said. "And now they're falling apart and... just hold on."

I raised my chin, trying to peek over the top counter. "What are you doing?"

His attention remained zeroed in on his work. "Lunch. I'm hungry."

"You cook?"

"Not usually, no. It's tedious, boring, and a blatant waste of my time. However..." His lips pulled into a sinister grin as he made the finishing touches to his dish. "Today I have a point to prove."

He lifted what I initially thought was a minimalist charcuterie board and placed it on the top counter. That wasn't what it was, though. It was a slab of wood topped with sushi. Sloppily made, unevenly cut sushi.

My mouth slighted open as Jackson beamed down at his creation with pride, like it was the most perfect thing anyone had ever created with their own two hands.

"You... you *made* that?"

"It's not that hard, Jamie," he said just as a strip of sticky rice began to peel away from its nori. Two more followed. "Anyone could do this for a living, but not everyone—what the hell?"

I blinked away from the board to find his eyes on me. His smile died.

"What?" I said.

"What's wrong with your face?"

"Excuse me?"

I stumbled back as he rounded the island and advanced toward me, all frowny and intense. He grabbed my face and tilted it for closer inspection.

"What the hell?" he said again.

"Your hands smell like fish."

"Have you been crying?" His thumb brushed my cheek, wiping away a phantom tear.

I swallowed. "Remember what I said about affection?"

"Why were you crying, Jamie?"

"It's not a big deal."

"Did something happen?"

"People cry for no reason all the time."

"That's bullshit. Tell me what's wrong."

"You're being real dramatic about literally nothing and your hands still smell like fish."

His thumbs brushed over my cheeks again. Quietly, gently, he said, "Tell me what it is so I can fix it."

You know how sometimes you manage to convince yourself that you're fine and that everything's under perfect control when, in reality, you're barely hanging on by a frayed thread? And then something really small happens, or someone says something seemingly insignificant, and it makes you break in half?

Well, I broke in half.

Panic flared in Jackson's eyes when the first little sob escaped, despite my best efforts to swallow it back. Then the tears were leaking, streaming down my face, and I couldn't catch a hold of them no matter how hard I tried.

Within seconds I was a sobbing, blubbering mess, and poor Jackson had exactly zero idea what to do with me. He kept trying to ask me what was wrong, but I was one missed breath away from hyperventilating like a hysterically crying child, so I couldn't even babble out an excuse.

The more I didn't talk, though, the more flustered he seemed to get.

"Stop it," he demanded at one point, sounding like he was in genuine pain. Unfortunately for him, it wasn't a switch I could just turn off.

When I didn't obey, he wrapped me in his arms, lifted me up, and gingerly placed me on the counter. Then, because the man was dead set on ruining my life, he cupped my face again and started to kiss away my tears as they fell.

Obviously, that made everything much, much worse.

Because how the fuck could he be this sweet after everything—all the neglect and abuse—his disgusting parents had put him through?

How many times had we joked about him not having any friends when... had I known the truth behind it—had I known how isolated and alone the poor thing was for so long—I would have never teased him about it.

How could a parent not allow their child to have any friends growing up? How could they *punish him* for attempting to make some?

"Tell me what's wrong."

Everything was wrong.

He'd made us handmade sushi and it was adorable, and his dad had forced him into homeschooling when he was eight and he wasn't allowed to have birthday parties with kids his own age and I was a *wreck* over all of it.

"Darling, breathe."

And it made sense. It made *so much* fucking sense, you know? All his dad cared about was money. The only reason his mom ever contacted him was for money. And every single person who'd ever shown him any real love or affection had been under his or his father's employ.

Did he think they wouldn't still be in his life if he wasn't paying them? Did he think they'd love him any less? Or was I just a little too deep into my emotional spiral?

"Jamie." He pressed his forehead to mine.

I understood why Molly and Mabel were so worried. It was burning in my chest, sharp and biting. What *was* he going to do when they were gone?

"Whatever it is, it's going to be okay. Just breathe."

It took a handful of concentrated minutes but, eventually, my sobs began to subside. Eventually, my lungs stopped shaking and my breathing evened out. Eventually, I regained enough control of myself for the embarrassment to kick in. And it kicked hard.

"S-sorry," I stuttered. "That was... a lot."

He swiped at my cheekbone with a knuckle, unaware of the tingles his touch left behind. "Tell me what happened."

"Nothing." I sniffled. "Except for the fact that my face smells like fish too now, which is a real bummer."

The smile tugging at his mouth was reluctant, but it was still there. He pushed away from me and stepped over to the sink to wash his hands.

"I bet Daffodil always smells like fish. Occupational hazard. Is that really what you want to be coming home to every day?"

I huffed a laugh as I wiped away at my cheeks, grateful for the change to a lighter topic. "Worth it if *Daniel* makes me sushi all the time."

"I can make you sushi all the time."

"You just said you don't enjoy cooking."

"Hate it. It's a complete waste of time." He tossed the towel he'd used to dry his hands and wedged himself between my dangling knees again. "But if it made you happy, I'd do it."

My heart threatened to burst at that, expanding to four times its normal size. Then he said, "We can add it to the contract," and it deflated like a cartoon balloon, puddling lamely in the pit of my stomach.

Right.

Of course.

I sniffled and wiped at my cheeks, blinking away from him. I was so raw that the mere mention of the stupid contract made my chest ache all over again.

"Jamie, please just tell me what's wrong."

"It's nothing. I'm just having a bad day."

When another tear escaped, he leaned forward and kissed it away. It was horrible. I was fighting a losing battle, and it was only a matter of time before I ripped my heart straight out of my own chest and voluntarily presented it to him, knowing he'd crush it.

"Remember what we said about the whole affection thing?" I tried.

"You also said we were friends," he murmured with another soft press of his lips against my skin. "Am I not allowed to comfort you when you're upset?"

My throat worked as I tried my best to contain the emotion clawing at it. "I know... I know you think that the whole friendship thing with us is a joke, I know you don't take it at all seriously, but just so *you* know, I don't think of it that way." And right now, right here, it was really important to me that he understood that.

"I care about you, okay?" I said, my voice wobbly. "Very much. And I want you to be happy and fulfilled and... honestly, I think you're really awesome. Like you're funny, and you're charming, and *kind*. You try to hide it but you're all of those things, and I'm sorry I misjudged you at the beginning. I'm sorry for how mean I was, which —oh, and for the whole disguise thing. That was really unprofessional and not nice, and I completely understand why you acted the way you did on the date. I also never thanked you for saving my life even though, like, you could have pushed me into the pool, and I don't know if I'd even blame you for it? Because no one should be forced into a marriage they don't want, and I'm also sorry that's happening to you, but I can promise that, as your actual friend who cares about you, I will do my best to find you someone great."

His eyes were sliding between mine, his frown ever-so-present. He opened his mouth to speak, but I shook my head. I wasn't done.

"I really think, like, if she has your sense of humor and a compatible lifestyle, it might not be so bad. But she'd also have to be on the same page as you about the whole romance thing, because otherwise it really wouldn't be fair to her, and would probably create a big emotional mess for you by the year-end mark because, honestly, I think you're a lot easier to fall in love with than you realize, and we really just need to make sure that we do our best to avoid any hearts being broken... and... you know..."

I trailed off, realizing what I'd just said. Nothing good ever came out of my mouth when it started running ahead of my brain, and I should have stopped when I'd noticed I was rambling. On the bright side, I'd said so many words in such a short amount of time that there was a good chance he'd missed—

"You think I'm easy to fall in love with?" His voice was husky, quiet.

My cheeks flamed, sparks tingling over random patches of my skin, making it itch. I was tempted to laugh it off, punch his arm, and call him "buddy" so he knew how Not A Big Deal this was.

But what if... like what if that was something he

genuinely needed to hear? What if there was a part of him that believed otherwise? What if he just needed someone who wasn't on his payroll or interested in his money to tell him exactly how great and awesome and loveable he really was?

What was more important? That or my stupid pride?

"Very," I said. "You'd be insanely easy to fall in love with, Jackson. For all the reasons I said and so much more. Just look at how thoughtful you are. Look at this." I pointed at the sushi. They were messy, unevenly cut, and slowly falling apart, and it was *killing* me. "Do you understand how adorable this is?"

He wouldn't look at it though. Wouldn't take his eyes off me.

"Listen to me so carefully right now." I grabbed his face and pulled it closer, pressing my forehead to his. I needed him to pay extra close attention to everything I was about to say. "You are about as loveable as it gets, Jackson Sinclair. You're *perfect* exactly as you are right now, in this moment. I. Was. Wrong. I admit it with my whole heart. I was so wrong about you that it's fucking embarrassing. And you want to know what else? If you ever end up changing your mind about this whole romance thing, I think it's really important that you understand how stupidly easy it would be for you to find someone who'd love the shit out of you for the rest of your life. That's how loveable you are, Jackson.

"And just to be extra fucking clear on this, absolutely *none* of it has anything to do with how much money you have or what your last name happens to be. I mean, you gifted my cat a whole palace made out of cardboard! He's *obsessed* with it! And you put in all that effort just to make him more comfortable around you! And you *listen*. You pay attention. You're thoughtful. Smart. Witty. Fun. Beautiful. And that's just the tip of the iceberg, isn't it? I've known you for less than a month. Imagine how many more wonderful things there are about you to discover!" I stopped to catch my breath for a moment, running my thumbs over his cheeks like he'd done to me. "And as your friend—because I *am* your friend, Jackson—I think it's imperative you know all of that, okay?"

He said nothing. His shoulders were tense, and his jaw was locked tight, but his grip on my waist was kept gentle and caring.

"I think you're really awesome," I whispered. "And I promise I'll try my best to find you someone you like. I'm sorry Minerva's putting you through this, and I'm sorry your dad left the shares to her stupid cat in the first place. You said before that you thought he and I would get along, and I... I'm sorry I ever called anything about you abysmally inadequate. That was so mean and untrue."

He'd gotten it all the time from his dad, according to Molly's journal. Nothing he ever did was good enough for Richard Sinclair and the consequences he'd suffered as a result had been cruel. I'd unknowingly rubbed salt into a major wound and I felt horrible about it.

Jackson wasn't breathing very much anymore. His whole body had gone stiff, and I started to wonder how long it'd been since someone had just... held him. Hugged and soothed him the way everyone sometimes needed. He'd been so quick to comfort me, but when was the last time someone had comforted him? When was the last time he'd *let* someone comfort him?

Slowly, I slid my arms around his shoulders and neck. Slowly, I pulled him into a gentle hug and closed my eyes.

"Remember how you wanted a bit of coaching on

affection?" I whispered after a little while, smiling into his neck. "Well, usually when someone wraps their arms around you like this, you'll want to do the same."

Maybe that had been his way of asking for affection back. Maybe it was something he'd wanted but wasn't sure how to voice. I wondered what his other "areas of concern" were.

"Other acceptable options include shoving them away or simply telling them to fuck off," I offered.

He didn't do either of those things, but he did move.

His arms wrapped around my back, pulling me closer. And when I placed a soft kiss against the shell of his ear, he buried his face into the crook of my neck and let out a pleased rumbling sound.

The more I showered him with gentle affection, the more he seemed to melt in my arms. It was addicting. I played with his hair, ran my fingers through it and told him just how soft it was. I kissed his head, his cheek, and whispered a never-ending string of compliments into his ear. It didn't matter what the compliment was, how much it bruised my ego, or compromised my defenses. If it came to me, I said it.

By the end of the hour, he knew exactly how handsome and witty I thought he was, how unbelievably good it felt when he touched me, how genuinely charmed I was by him. I also told him I thought he was brave. That I hadn't appreciated how hard it must be to carry a whole company on his shoulders while simultaneously dealing with all the bullshit he was being dragged through.

He didn't seem to mind, either. Just hugged me back and nuzzled my neck while I repeated it all over and over again, until I was sure every single word was permanently carved into his long-term memory.

"Jackson, we really should go over the candidates now."

He'd been communicating mostly via rumbles and growls since I started pampering him an hour ago, and this one was, by far, the most displeased sound he'd made.

"Come on. I gotta get your pick to Alice so she can set up the date."

He tightened his embrace.

I sighed. "I skimmed over one of the profiles this morning. She's really gorgeous, really smart and accomplished, and doesn't do the whole love thing. I don't know about the others yet, but I think you'll like her."

That one earned me a full glare. He actually pulled back to glower down at me, all grumpy-like. "We don't need to go over the candidates. You're signing the contract."

"That's absolutely not going to happen."

"Sixty million for the year."

"That's an insane amount of money. You should've started a lot lower."

"Seventy."

"I like you too much, Jackson. Our marriage would be a disaster. I'd become so invested and emotional. You'd be so annoyed with me."

His jaw was doing that ticking thing again. He hated everything I was saying. "One hundred million dollars. You'll have your own driver and staff, access to my jet, yacht, properties, and whatever else you could possibly want. I'll teach you how to play the piano."

That last item was the most enticing offer he'd made yet. Still, "No, thanks."

More ticking. "You're being incredibly irrational."

"I'm aware."

"No one in their right fucking mind would turn down nine figures for one year of playing mild pretend."

"I don't want your money."

His eyes narrowed. "And I already told you, the more you tell me you don't want it, the more I want to spend it on you. It's very irritating."

"*You're being incredibly irrational,*" I parroted.

He really wasn't in the mood. Didn't even pretend like he found me amusing.

"Pick whoever the fuck you want for my dates. It won't matter since you'll be the one signing the marriage certificate."

I cupped his face again. "Jackson, listen to me, I *will not* enter into a contractual marriage with you. We can continue being friends after the Immersive is over, but that's it."

"I don't accept."

"Then you're going to be wasting your own time."

Not that he was listening. His blue eyes sharpened as they studied me, looking for a weakness. Then he handfed me the sushi he'd made (which was incredibly delicious, by the way), aggressively pampered me with kisses and thinly veiled threats, and once he was satisfied with how much I'd eaten and how many times I'd turned his marriage proposal down, he locked himself up in his office.

32

I SNUCK BACK into the library again that night, once it became apparent that Jackson wasn't going to be visiting.

For the life of me, I couldn't come up with a single justification for my decision. I knew it was wrong, I knew it was a massive violation of Jackson's privacy and trust, I knew how upset he'd be if he found out, but I still went ahead and did it anyway.

After three full hours of staring at the ceiling, unable to sleep, I slid out of bed, put on a pair of yellow fuzzy socks (for stealth-walking purposes), and quietly crept to the other side of the penthouse.

After checking to make sure there was no light leaking from beneath the door, I unlocked it and slipped inside. This time, without the initial element of surprise, I could absorb more of the art, take in more details, open more books.

It was unbelievably endearing, watching the growth in artistic skill and sophistication from the books targeting younger kids to middle schoolers, YA, and beyond. I loved the sketches he'd done inside the pages, his highlighted passages, his little notes and annotations (which became increasingly rare as he grew).

It was a bit like peering into his soul, and he was so breathtakingly beautiful it made me ache.

When I'd had my temporary fill of the creative stuff, I opened the secret door, slipped into the secret room, and grabbed the two journals I hadn't read through yet. Even though I knew it wouldn't get better. Even though I knew it would wreck me.

By the time I was done with the last one (which ended when Jackson was nineteen), my throat hurt, my eyes were swollen, and I had some very concrete plans to visit Richard Sinclair's grave and spit on it.

He was so vile, so evil and cruel, that I couldn't bring myself to feel even an ounce of sympathy for him when Molly noted how desperately in love he'd been with his wife; how deep in denial about her unending affairs.

According to Molly, Jackson was forced to watch his father throw countless rage-induced tantrums, agonizing over his wife's whereabouts late at night. He'd smash things. Throw vulgar insults at anyone within his line of sight. And go on extremely destructive drinking binges that made him even more violent.

When Jackson's mother finally did come home, all it would take was a single one of her smiles and a purred excuse to calm Richard down. She'd charm him into utter submission, kiss away his anger, and when he wasn't looking, tell Jackson exactly how pathetic she thought her husband was.

A week or two later, the cycle would repeat.

Jackson witnessed his father's friends whisper about Beatrice's affairs behind his back. He witnessed how easily the man could be manipulated by his wife. How he bent to her every mood and whim. How destructive he became when he thought he was losing her.

Every time he found out about another one of Beatrice's lovers, he'd take it out on Jackson. He couldn't control his wife, so he tried his damnedest with his son.

That was what romantic love looked like to Jackson growing up. Pain. Humiliation. Abuse. Lying and manipulation.

It was horrible.

I was drained and exhausted by the end. So much so that it took genuine effort for me to put the diaries away and quietly sneak back to my suite instead of passing out on the very inviting couch I'd been curled up on.

I was out before my head even hit the pillow, right as I was about to make another false promise to myself about never going back to the library ever again.

33

KARMA CAME for me the very next morning in the form of a freshly shaven, already dressed Jackson Sinclair knocking on my door at 6:47 a.m., less than two hours after I'd fallen asleep.

"What are you doing?" I croaked, squinting at him as he stalked toward the bed.

Instead of hissing at the intrusion, Toebeans got up from where he was sleeping (on my neck), did a big stretch (again on my neck), and swished his fat tail expectantly (in my face). The giant servant had arrived to bring him pets; this pleased him greatly.

Jackson immediately went for the ear scratches, smiling when Toebeans leaned into his touch. "Good morning, handsome."

My heart flipped and fluttered. "What's going on?" I asked again, barely managing to keep my voice even. "Why are you here so early?"

"I'm taking you to work with me. You should get dressed."

I blinked. "I'm only supposed to shadow you at work for the first two weeks."

"And I'm requesting an additional day." The soft smile that tugged at his mouth when Toebeans started to purr would be burned into my memory for eternity. He was almost as enchanted by my cat as I was by him. "You wanted to see me actually work, so come see me actually work."

I really would've appreciated a heads-up on the change of plans. Maybe I'd have thought twice about sneaking into the library last night and opted for some actual sleep instead.

(This was, obviously, a lie I was choosing to tell myself.)

I slid out of bed, rubbing my eyes as I dragged my feet to the bathroom. It took maybe twenty minutes for me to get dressed, dab on a light layer of makeup, and tuck my curls into a somewhat neat bun, but that was enough time for Jackson Sinclair to obliterate me.

When I walked back out, he was sitting on my bed with a *very* satisfied-looking Toebeans loaf purring on his lap.

"Um…"

Jackson beamed up at me. "He'll growl if I try to cuddle him, but this is already pretty great."

My heart burst.

It inflated, took out my lungs, and fucking burst into heart-shaped confetti and circus music.

It was me. I was the clown.

"We should go." I was done. I could *not* with the two of them like this.

Jackson frowned like asking him to move was the craziest, most nonsensical thing that could have possibly come out of my mouth. So I turned around and ripped open the cat food cabinet.

Toebeans immediately unloafed and hopped onto the floor, and I didn't need to look at Jackson to know how unhappy he was with my betrayal. I kept my back to him as I watched Toebeans munch away at his breakfast, my arms crossed and my shoulders bunched.

Everything was fine, I just needed to refocus. As skeptical as I was about Imogen's premonitions, they were starting to feel like a lifeline. Maybe Daniel wouldn't come on as a client. Maybe we'd hit it off and... I don't know, but anything would be better than the current path I was set on.

I was dangerously close to falling for the most unattainable man in the world, getting my heart shattered, and never recovering from it. I'd never get over this man if I allowed myself to fall in love with him. I knew that to be a fundamental, irrefutable truth. Water was wet, the Earth was round, and if I, Jamie Paquin, fell in love with Jackson Sinclair, I'd never get over him.

Daniel was officially my best-case scenario, and since my meeting with him was in less than twelve hours, all I really had to do was not fall in love with Jackson before then.

Totally doable.

I had this. Everything was fine.

Nothing was fine. Not *one* thing.

Listen, I knew I'd messed up with the library thing. I knew it was wrong and that I deserved some sort of punishment for violating Jackson's privacy, but this... this was genuinely unfair.

I gritted my teeth, willing my stupid, *stupid* heart to stop flip-flopping and allow enough oxygen to reach my brain so I could actually fucking *think* for one stupid second.

The problem was, of course, Jackson. Instead of sitting in his office all day, we'd hopped from boardroom to boardroom, with little breaks in between so he could take calls and respond to urgent emails.

It was fucking lewd, how disgustingly competent he was at leading these meetings. He had this calm, firm confidence about him, and actually *listened* when his employees contributed, regardless of their age or job title or level of seniority. In fact, I'd sat through six of these stupid things so far today, and he hadn't made a single decision until he was sure no one else had anything more to contribute to the topic.

It was so fucking sexy. I hated it so much.

I glanced at the clock behind Jackson's head for what must have been the tenth time within the last five minutes, not thinking much of it. I really didn't think he'd notice.

While I'd spent the whole day watching him, he'd spent it ignoring me. That was not a complaint—it was what we encouraged our clients to do when we shadowed them. If they forgot we were there, it increased the accuracy of our data. The point was, I'd grown so used to being invisible that when my gaze landed back on Jackson and found him glaring at me, my pulse kicked.

I didn't look at the time again after that.

When the meeting was finally over, he didn't so much as spare me a glance before storming out of the room, didn't say a single word as I struggled to keep up with his long strides. Once we were tucked into the private elevator leading up to his office, I started on my apology.

"Sorry. I swear I was paying attention." And I had four pages of detailed notes to prove it. When he continued to stare straight ahead, I reached for his sleeve. "Hey, seriously, I didn't mean anything by—"

I barely had a chance to process the fact that he'd smashed the red emergency button before I was lifted off my feet and pinned against cool metal, my legs pulled around his waist.

His lips crushed to mine, stealing my breath. And instead of pushing him away, instead of telling him that this needed to stop like I'd promised myself I would, I threw my arms around his neck and kissed him back. Our tongues tangled, our teeth clashed, and my whole existence erupted into sparks.

I'd been lying to myself all day. I didn't want Daniel to be a lifeline. If I got to choose, I'd choose Jackson over and over and over again. I swear, if there was even a small chance he'd ever allow himself to love me back, I'd never look at another man again.

A pathetic, whimpering whine ripped out of me the second he broke the kiss. But I didn't have the energy anymore to care.

To my immediate relief, he placed a tender, soothing kiss on the corner of my mouth.

"I've been wanting to do that all fucking day," he murmured, pressing his hips tighter against mine. I bit back a moan at the rock-hard feel of him, my core clenching around nothing. "All fucking day, Jamie. While you've been stealing glances at the clock, counting down the minutes until your date, all I've been able to think about is this."

I shivered when he moved his hips again, grinding against me. My pulse was thundering, heat simmering under my skin.

"I'm tempted to take you to my office, lock the door, and make you get on your knees for me." His fingers dug into my flesh with promise. "I want you sucking me off before your date, and I want you swallowing every last fucking drop so if he tries to kiss you, you can let him know exactly what he'll be tasting."

Holy shit.

That was... so filthy I didn't know how to respond. But *holy shit* did my body like it. His words washed over me like liquid fire. The ache in my core was bordering on unbearable.

"You're driving me out of my fucking mind. You want to talk about red flags? I'm fucking *territorial* over you." He traced his lips over my jaw, all the way to my ear. "I should have fucked you last night. I should have made you beg and scream until you forgot about him."

"Why didn't you?" I'd waited for him, even though I shouldn't have. And the longer I'd waited, the stronger the urge to go to the library had become. The craving had been for him. The closeness and intimacy I would have gotten if he'd come to my room.

"I needed to finalize our agreement with my lawyers. It took longer than I thought it would."

My chest squeezed. I couldn't muster the energy to argue with him this time. Instead, I lifted my chin and allowed his mouth better access to my neck.

There was a good chance there was at least one security camera in here. There was an even better chance I didn't care.

"When do you have to leave for your date?"

"You should maybe stop calling it that," I breathed. "It's a business meeting."

"Don't go."

"I have to. It's a business meeting."

"If I stopped you from going, would you hate me for it?"

"Probably, seeing as how it's a business meeting."

"Might be worth it." He nipped at my skin, then licked it soothingly. "He wants to fuck you."

I bit back a smile. "We're not allowed to sleep with our clients. It's a massive conflict of interest." At this point, it didn't really matter if he knew. Or maybe it did, and I just didn't care.

"You think he's your soulmate," he argued.

"I didn't say it, Imogen did."

"You weren't listening properly."

"Spoiled pet, the letter D, tattoos. Pretty sure I got it all."

There was a beat of silence before he pulled his head back. "She didn't *just* say tattoos."

My amusement slowly waned. "What? What else did she..." A scar. She said it could be a bunch of tattoos *or* prominent scars.

Hope—pure, unfiltered, *foolish* hope—tore through me, slashing my heart open. My eyes flared, scanning his face, his jaw, his neck. "Do you have any? Scars?"

It didn't help that he'd always kept his clothes on during sex. I'd assumed it was another kink; part of the power imbalance thing we both enjoyed. It hadn't occurred to me until now that there may have been another reason for it.

He opened his mouth, closed it, opened it... and said nothing.

I blanked. Every thought I had running through my head vanished in an instant, and all I could do was stare up at him, my lips parted, my lungs frozen.

His hands ran over my thighs, his steel length hot and prominent through the layers separating us. I remained silent while he continued to struggle. Sometimes people just needed a bit of time to put their words together and that was okay. He could take however long he needed. I'd still be right here.

And then it happened. I saw the change in his eyes when he made the decision. He took in a breath and—

"Sir? Is everything okay?"

You have got to be kidding me.

The emergency button had been pressed like ten full minutes ago! They couldn't have had worse timing if they'd tried.

Jackson sighed and tapped his forehead lightly to mine. "Everything's fine."

"Would you like to start moving again, sir?"

No.

"Yes."

"Right away."

The elevator started its smooth slide upward just as my feet hit the floor. Goosebumps spread over every inch of my skin, my body protesting the loss of heat as he stepped back.

It was a severely unpleasant sensation.

"What time do you have to leave?" Jackson asked, sobering.

I didn't want to answer him. "A few minutes, probably. If I don't want to be late."

He nodded. "I've arranged for a driver to take you there and bring you back. She's waiting for you downstairs."

The elevator came to a smooth halt; the doors slid open; Jackson didn't move. His gaze was stuck to mine, his jaw and throat working silently, almost like he wanted to say something but didn't know how. Then he blinked away from me, his chin dipping as he scrubbed a hand over it.

"I'll see you later, then," he said.

My stomach sank, disappointment tugging hard enough at my chest to make it ache as he walked out of the elevator. The doors began shutting behind him... right before a hand shot out and stopped them from closing all the way.

The second they reopened, Jackson stormed back inside, cupped my face, and kissed me until my toes curled, my knees wobbled, and my head spun.

"It's not him," he whispered against my lips. "It's *not* him. Come back to me, Jamie."

And it broke my brain in half.

34

"COME BACK TO ME, JAMIE."

"Come back to me, Jamie."

"Come back to me, Jamie."

It was all I could hear, see, think.

I'd been sitting across Daniel Omori for the better part of an hour, and my brain was on autopilot.

It was polite smiles, polite chatter, polite answering of questions, and polite explanations of the services we offered at Charmed. I was going through the motions, but I wasn't really here. I couldn't pull myself to the present no matter how hard I tried.

I couldn't remember how or why I'd crushed so hard on this man just a few weeks ago, because I felt none of it now. I felt absolutely nothing.

We shook polite hands after dinner, exchanged polite goodbyes and polite promises to keep in touch regarding the Immersive program. He'd be enrolling in July.

"Come back to me, Jamie."

How dare he?

How *dare* Jackson put the weight of those words on me knowing he'd never truly own them?

"Come back to me, Jamie."

Why? So in twelve months when I was desperately in love with him and he was thoroughly bored of me I could cry and beg him for the same thing?

A hundred million bucks said he wouldn't do it. He'd let me go and I'd have to put all the pieces of myself back together so *how dare he*?

I could barely breathe on the car ride back. I was antsy, restless, jittery. It didn't help that we were crawling through traffic.

What should have been a ten-minute ride took ten years off my life. Impatience clawed at my sanity, and I had to actively stop myself from ripping the car door open in the middle of the road. I was convinced walking would be faster.

My bones were itching by the time we turned onto Jackson's street, and I was out of the car before it'd come to a complete stop. I ripped through the lobby and bounced on my heels as I waited for the longest, slowest elevator ride of my life to end.

I was in such a fucking hurry that I didn't even see him.

My legs were moving before the chrome doors had fully opened, and I would have smashed headfirst into Jackson's chest had he not captured me in his arms before it happened.

"Come back to me, Jamie."

His lips smashed to mine, setting my whole world on fire. I snaked my arms around his neck and fisted his hair, our tongues colliding as he carried me inside. Doors flew open, they banged shut. His hold on me was savage, his kisses starved, merciless, almost... angry.

No, not almost. He was definitely angry.

Furious, from the feel of it.

The moment it clicked, he released me. I hit the cushion with a gasp, my stomach lurching from the unexpected drop. It took a few seconds for the blurry reds, warm chocolates, and bright colors of my surroundings to come into focus. There was only one place on his end of the penthouse that wasn't all right angles and sterilized shades of grey.

The library.

My jaw snapped shut when I met Jackson's seething, icy glare. He was towering over the couch I'd been dumped on, waiting for me to explain myself.

Shit.

Before I could even sit up (let alone string together a valid excuse), Jackson was on the couch, pulling my thigh over his lap until I was straddling him. His grip was unforgiving as he pinned my hips to his, and I had to keep a hand on his chest to allow an inch of necessary distance between our faces.

"How was your date?" His jaw ticked, barely prying open enough to allow the question.

"It was a business meeting."

"Are you going to see him again?"

"Potentially. For work." Was that really what he wanted to talk about? I felt like there was a much more pressing topic we needed to discuss. "How did you find out about... this?"

"Molly couldn't take the guilt. You're not hopelessly in love with him, then?"

"It was a business dinner."

"That doesn't answer my question."

I sighed. "No, Jackson. I did not fall hopelessly in love with Daniel Omori over the two-hour business meeting we had where we talked about business."

His withering glare thawed just a touch, some of the tension in his shoulders easing.

"Come back to me, Jamie."

"Shouldn't we be discussing how much trouble I'm in?" I asked.

"Do you still think Imogen was talking about him?"

No.

Both my palms were resting flat against his chest now, one right over his hammering heart. "Does it matter?"

Jackson's throat worked as he studied me. The taut anger in his features had slowly started to wane, giving room to... uncertainty, maybe. "Molly said you read through her journals."

Damn. She'd told him everything then. I chewed the inside of my lip, nodding.

He paused for a beat. "What did you learn?"

When I didn't respond, he said, "I wasn't aware she kept diaries and now she won't tell me where they're hidden. I have no idea what you know, and I need you to tell me. All of it."

"I'm not sure if—" I swallowed, hesitating again. It didn't feel right for me to start listing out all the abuse he'd suffered as a kid.

"It's the least you could do after sneaking in here *twice* without my knowledge or permission, don't you think?" he said bitterly. "The first time I could excuse. I'm fully aware of how cunning the Harrison sisters can be. They look homey and innocent, and they're clever enough to utilize it to their full advantage. When I say that Molly couldn't take the guilt, I mean she planned this all out and then pretended like she couldn't take the guilt. She knew full well I'd never bring you in here, and that you'd never confess to your crime, so she forced our hands."

Somehow, I was both surprised and not surprised by that. The sisters had to be cunning to get away with years of hiding everything they had from Richard—all of it regarding his only child, no less.

"However," Jackson went on, "you weren't tricked into the second trip. You did it willingly, knowing that if I wanted you in here, I wouldn't have locked the door. So, tell me what you know. I've spent a good hour searching for the cursed things with no luck, and she won't tell me where they are. It doesn't matter how many times I threaten to fire her." He paused to look around again, eyes squinting with suspicious displeasure. "She probably snatched them before confessing. Clever little witch," he grumbled.

He had every right to be angry. He had every right to kick me out and fire the twins. I understood what their intentions may have been, but if Jackson hadn't wanted me to know about his past, his trauma and abuse, that was well within his right.

"I'm very sorry," I said. And I meant it. "I shouldn't have snuck in here the first time, let alone a second." It wasn't about being "tricked" into it, either. "You're right. The door was locked, and I knew that meant you wouldn't want me in here. I'm really, very sorry, Jackson."

He was silent for a long moment. "Just tell me what you know. I'm owed that much, am I not?"

"Fine," I agreed, even though the mere thought of reciting any of it made my stomach lurch. "I know... I know that..." I trailed off, my gaze dipping down to where my fingers had started fiddling with the crisp collar of his shirt.

Where was I even supposed to start?

"I, um... I know that you're good at art." Nope. No. That didn't even come *close* to the truth. I cleared my throat as I fought to contain the emotions swirling through my chest. "Scratch that. I know that you're *incredible* at it, because this—" I gestured to my surroundings. To the furniture and books and every other thing that had a piece of his soul etched into it. "This is quite possibly the most beautiful thing I've ever seen, Jackson."

He was so, *so* beautiful. I couldn't get over it.

I also couldn't look at him anymore.

"I know that Richard was a monster and that you deserved better than both him and Beatrice. Hatred doesn't even begin to describe what I feel toward them."

I was tempted to tell him how glad I was that his father was dead, but that seemed just a tad insensitive.

Mabel had promised me that they'd buried him a few feet deeper than needed, ensuring a smoother, shorter trip down to hell. He fucking deserved it.

"I know how helpless Mabel and Molly felt when Bensen was fired. I understand that, no matter how hard he tried and what evidence he provided, no one would do a damn thing to protect you. Not when they found out who your father was."

It was so cruel and unfair that it made me want to scream.

Richard had made one phone call—*one*—and Jackson had been dismissed from the hospital and sent home. Law enforcement and CPS had been instructed by their supervisors to close the case, and that had been that. Bensen had fought for weeks, until Richard had served him the legal papers.

He'd been given two options: continue screaming into the void and go bankrupt, or shut up. I couldn't blame him for giving up, for choosing to protect his own family, even though Molly had mentioned how much guilt he still held onto.

"I know how sorry I am," I continued. "I regret so many things I've said to you, knowing what I do now. I judged you too quickly and was so insensitive about your situation, and I'm honestly so angry at myself. I don't care what Minerva's reasoning is, no one should be forced into a relationship or a marriage they don't want. *No one*. And I would've seen it earlier if I hadn't been... I was just so burnt out. I couldn't see or think straight, and... I can't blame you for what you did or how you acted. I would've rebelled too, if I'd been in your shoes."

For the first time since I'd started talking, I braved a glance up at him. His jaw was still tight, but his eyes were pure glass. My throat thickened painfully. I cupped his cheek and stroked it soothingly with my thumb. If he cried, I'd *lose it*.

"It wasn't all your fault," he managed quietly. "I didn't have to be such a dick."

I continued to caress his cheek, and when he put his hand over mine and turned his head to kiss my palm, my heart cracked in half.

"Keep going," he whispered.

"I know why you don't believe in love," I murmured. "Better yet, I *understand* it. How could you, after everything you witnessed between your parents?"

How could he, when his own mother had told him outright that she didn't love him? That she wouldn't have given birth to him if she hadn't needed to? Jackson was a sacrifice she'd made to secure the lifestyle she wanted, and she hadn't allowed him to forget it.

I couldn't imagine.

The amount of respect and gratitude I had for Mabel and Molly, for Bensen and Mikey, and for every other person who'd cared for him and shown him love was overwhelming. They'd banded together to protect Jackson as best they could, especially after Bensen was fired.

A good chunk of their scheming had been detailed throughout Molly's journals. They had secret phones and pagers, a guy on the security team who monitored the cameras for them, and various methods of distraction and hiding spots for Jackson to utilize when his father was throwing one of his rage fits.

No wonder Jackson had kept every last one of them around.

"I know all of that, and I know about the abuse you suffered, but please, *please* don't force me to say it out loud. I'm sorry I snuck in here and looked at things you didn't want me to see. I take full responsibility for it, but... don't make me list it all out."

Maybe one of the reasons Molly didn't want him reading the journals was because she hoped he'd forgotten some of it, and I didn't want to remind him.

He swallowed roughly. "Fine, then we'll just talk about the one."

The one? Which one? "What d'you mean?"

"You said the journal talked about Bensen getting fired."

I nodded, watching him carefully.

"Did it say why?" he asked.

"You showed up to your secret piano lessons in pain from... an injury, and he took you to the hospital."

His jaw twitched under my palm. "And what was the injury?"

My eyes searched his, my heart stuttering as something softly clicked into place in the back of my head. "Cigarette burns," I muttered.

He said nothing, just held onto my gaze and slowly reached for the buttons of his shirt.

I knew. Before his fingers had worked through the buttons, before they pulled the fabric apart to bare his chest, I knew.

My heart crawled inside my throat. Slowly, I dropped my hands. Slowly, I allowed my eyes to travel down. There, on the left side of his chest, were the small circles of marred skin. A dozen of them, at least. Etched right above his heart.

They were spaced out and organized to form a structurally perfect ***D***.

35

Some of the scars were more prominent than the others, as though they'd suffered overlapping burns. Some of them were white, others tinted just a little pink. But all of them looked stretched out, like they'd grown with their owner.

That was the part that made my breath catch—the evidence that they'd once belonged to a child. Without thinking, I reached for them. Jackson tensed when the tips of my fingers brushed his skin, but he didn't pull away.

My throat ached, my heart heavy as I traced the dots. How bad did the original burns need to be for their scars to last this long? And why the shape?

As though he'd read my mind. Jackson cleared his throat. "It's not an initial, doesn't have anything to do with anyone's name. The D stands for discipline, something I severely lacked at thirteen, according to my father."

I tried to swallow the emotion lodged at the base of my throat, tried to blink back the wetness blurring my eyes. "They look... they must have been deep."

After a short pause, he said, "I earned one whenever

he thought I was slacking off... or if he'd had a little too much to drink and decided that the way I was breathing wasn't to his liking."

I brushed my fingers over the ones at the beginning of the curve. They were noticeably worse than the others. Bigger, deeper, more marred.

"Sometimes he completed the D before I'd had a chance to fully heal, so he'd just start going over them again."

My lips wobbled, the aching mass in my throat swelling. Even if I'd known what to say, I wouldn't have been able to get the words out without dissolving into tears. I dropped my hand and rolled my trembling lips. The urge to lean forward and kiss his pain away kicked at my chest, but it would only make this next part harder.

"I told you she wasn't talking about him," he said.

"I didn't think—" My voice split into an uneven half, opening the dam. "You didn't have to... I'm sorry."

A harsh breath rushed out of him, his pale eyes sharpening. "Stop crying," he demanded.

"Okay." I took a sleeve to my face. "Sorry."

"Jamie." The skin underneath his left eye feathered unhappily. "Stop it."

"I'm trying!" My god. If he'd just give me a minute.

"This wasn't why I showed them to you." He quickly buttoned up his shirt, his brows pulling into a deep frown.

"I know."

"I was just trying to—damn it, Jamie." To his utter dismay, I'd hiccuped. "I had a plan."

"So-orry." I was a broken record of apologies, and I didn't care.

His thawing gaze slid all over my blotchy face, and his

thumb brushed away a rogue tear that had slid down to my bottom lip. "I fucking hate it when you cry."

"Sorr-ry."

"Stop that, too."

"Okay."

He gave me a minute, soothing away my tears as they fell. Once I'd gathered the pieces of myself into a somewhat solid pile again, he murmured, "Do you have enough proof now? Can you sign the contract or do I need to—"

"Okay."

"I... what?"

"I'll do it. I'll sign it." He didn't deserve to be forced into a relationship, and if this was the only way I could really help, so be it. "But I've got a few conditions and they're nonnegotiable."

"Anything," he said, voice light with disbelief. "Whatever you want, just tell me. The agreement I had drawn up has a two-hundred-million dollar—"

"I won't do it for money," I said firmly. "Or any sort of material gain. That includes properties, cars, company shares, or whatever else you're thinking of compensating me with."

His forehead pinched. "*Jamie*—"

"No." I shook my head. "I won't budge on it. You're my friend and I care about you. So I'll do this for you as a favor, or I won't do it at all."

His eye twitched. "As my *wife*—"

"On paper." Which was a perfect segway to my next condition. "I will be your wife on paper for exactly one year, just until those shares are legally yours."

The tension in his forehead eased, his eyes searching mine.

"I want the same relationship terms and boundaries that you had in the original agreement. Separate bedrooms, separate lives, an open marriage, all of it. We will be husband and wife on paper, and we can maintain a friendship outside of our contractual obligations, but I can't offer you any more than that, Jackson."

He swallowed roughly, eyes continuing to slip between mine, studying them.

"And I can't... have a child with you. If you need an heir, then you'll have to figure something else out."

He said nothing, so I cleared my throat and moved on to my last condition. "But before all that, you have to complete the Immersive program and go on the dates I set you up on. If you still haven't found someone you like by the end, I'll sign the agreement."

I couldn't think of a more reasonable solution than that. It gave him what he needed and reduced the chances of me getting my heart shattered. Plus, I needed time to figure out how I'd handle getting married to a client without scorching my reputation in the industry and never landing a job in it again.

I shifted on his lap, my pulse restless under his gaze. It didn't help that I couldn't quite decipher his expression. "And I also think... with all that going on, it's probably best if we stop sleeping together right away. We should go back to being just friends."

"We were never *just* friends," he ground out.

"Fine, but we can start now, can't we?"

"Why? Why the boundaries?"

"Well, for one, if it got out that you and I were sleeping together, I'd not only lose my current job, but I'd also be blacklisted from the entire industry. I'm thinking we should stop before that happens."

His brow ticked. "What do you mean *blacklisted*?"

"I mean I'll never be able to find a job at a matchmaking firm again."

"That would never happen."

"I don't think you understand just how taboo—"

"Let me rephrase," he interrupted. "I would never allow that to happen."

I sighed, but before I could piece together a reasonable argument, he said, "We have an understanding now, so why can't we carry it into the marriage? We get along great, the sex is fucking phenomenal, and we... this *works*, Jamie."

"Those are my conditions."

"Why?"

"Because..."

"Because *why*?"

Fuck's sake. "Because if we keep this up, I'm going to fall in love with you, Jackson."

There. I said it. I'd alluded to it a bunch of times, but he hadn't seemed to—

"You won't."

It took me a second. "I'm sorry?"

His fingers dug into my thighs, his words firm and unwavering when he said, "You won't fall in love with me."

I blinked back at him. "No... I definitely will."

Were we really about to have this argument?

"You won't."

Yup. We were really about to have this argument.

I grabbed his stupid, lovable face as my eyes narrowed. "Jackson, if we keep sleeping together—if I marry you and you don't stop with all the affection—*I'm going to fall in love with you.*"

It wasn't even a question. It *would* happen.

"You can't know that for sure."

"I do. I'm going to fall stupidly, madly, head over heels in love with you, and you're going to end up resenting me for it."

"That's never going to happen."

"It is."

"I don't think—"

"I'm already halfway there, okay?" I snapped in utter exasperation. "We *need* to stop. It will never just be sex for me with you. I mean, just... *look* at this place!" I released his face and gestured to our surroundings, to everything he'd created. "Look at how beautiful you are!"

I didn't stand a chance.

I wished he could see himself through my eyes. He'd have no choice but to believe me then.

"It'll be a nightmare," I said. "Full stop. We'll be married and I'll be in love with you and you know what'll happen then?"

He swallowed. Shook his head.

"I'll start to *hope*, Jackson." The path ahead was clear as day, and it was drenched in a whole lot of darkness, heartbreak, and despair. "Every time you kiss me, I'll *hope* it means to you what it does to me. Every time you show me affection, I'll *hope* it means that you're starting to love me back. And I won't be able to help it. So, unless..." My fingers pressed into my palms as my stupid heart skipped and stuttered. "Unless there's like a chance you'll... We should stop, if not."

He stayed so silent for so long that it became suffocating.

I couldn't handle it.

"Is there a chance that if... if we kept going and I fell in love with you... is there even a small chance that you could ever... feel that way about me, do you think?"

I didn't know how many times I needed to hear it for the truth to sink in, but I promised myself this would be the last. I held my breath, waiting. It didn't take long.

"No."

To his credit, he said it quite softly. The fact that it landed like a punch to the gut wasn't on him, it was on me. I'd asked for it.

"Okay." I shot him a wobbly smile. *Stupid, stupid, stupid.* "Okay." I didn't know why I said it twice. He'd heard me fine the first time. "Can I just... It's going to sound silly, but can you maybe say it? I think I've misread some of the signs and I need to hear the words for it to sink in, if that's okay."

His throat worked as he hesitated. I understood how ridiculous and unfair the request was, but I knew that if I didn't hear the words for myself, I'd always cling on to the *What If*.

"I'm never going to fall in love with you."

That punch didn't go for the gut, it went straight to my heart. I winced.

"Jamie..."

"No, it's okay, don't worry about it, you really don't have to explain. Thank you for your honesty, seriously. I just... misinterpreted our chemistry and you kissed my hand and it—not that it's your fault. You couldn't have been more clear with me from the beginning. So it's fine. I'll be fine."

He grabbed a hold of my wrist when I tried to slip off his lap. I couldn't look at him anymore though.

"Wait, just—"

"No, like, it's okay," I assured him, nodding aggressively. It would've been more convincing if a whole lot of tears hadn't already started streaming down my chin and neck. "It's okay. I get it, I really do. It's fine. But let's maybe try to avoid any unnecessary physical contact while I get over you, okay?"

Slowly, reluctantly, he released my wrist.

"I know you have some thinking to do, so... I'll see you later then. And seriously, don't worry about this, I'll get over it—you, I mean. With a bit of time, so... yeah. Okay. I'll see you later. At some point."

Thankfully, I managed to hold the first sob until the door was shut and I was completely out of earshot.

Or maybe that was just another lie I chose to tell myself.

36

THE HARRISON TWINS were permanently banned from speaking to me about Jackson, his parents, his upbringing, or any personal experiences they may have had while working for the Sinclairs. Molly had sent me a long message outlining the new restrictions (sounding rather chastised over the whole thing), and I hadn't seen or interacted with either of them since.

Jackson had also been avoiding me.

He hadn't looked at me once all week; wouldn't speak to me unless I initiated the discussion or directly asked him a question, and even then, his responses were kept polite, short, and impersonal.

Oh, and Ria still didn't have any reception, so I couldn't call her and tell her about all the ways I'd fucked up when Wednesday rolled around.

I couldn't talk to my best friend about how I'd had to sit there and watch the man I was halfway in love with have dinner with another woman. Her name was Lola Tan, she kissed his cheek when she greeted him, and it had ripped my heart in half.

On Thursday, it was Abi. On Friday, Parisa.

I wished I'd never met him.

I wished I'd never met him, but I was so fucking glad I had, you know?

I was at constant war with myself. Part of me—the part that was desperate and bleeding—kept trying to convince me that a contract was enough. He didn't need to love me back.

Maybe it's just you he can't love. Maybe with Lola or Abi or Parisa it would be different. If you don't stop this, you'll have to watch him fall in love with someone else.

Is that what you want? So what if he'll never love you back? Wouldn't having just a small piece of him be better than not having him at all?

I was falling deeper and deeper into my personal pit of hell and couldn't map my way back to solid ground.

He had another date tonight, and I didn't know how I was going to get through it without breaking apart. I tried swallowing back the clump of misery lodged in the center of my throat as I finished applying my mascara, but the wretched thing wouldn't budge. It was there every morning when I woke up, and it was there every night, keeping me awake.

I twisted the mascara cap back on and tossed it into the vanity drawer with a soft sigh. Not like anyone would be looking at my lashes tonight, but the restaurant was fancy enough to require a restrictive dress code. It didn't matter how drained or tired I was, the effort was required.

I twisted my hair into a low, elegant bun and pinned it into place, then slipped into my dress—black, simple, and perfect for blending into the background. I still looked a little pale despite the bronzer and blush, and my puffy eyes were rimmed a bruised pink, but this was as good as it was going to get.

Not that it mattered. While I'd been forced to watch him for hours on end, Jackson hadn't looked at me once all week. I was invisible.

I slipped into my heels, grabbed my clutch, and took a deep breath before leaving my suite.

At least I knew exactly what to expect. We'd fallen into a quick, unexciting routine: Jackson would meet me in the car, I'd brief him on his date while he scrolled through his phone or stared out the window, and then I just had to make it through the next hour.

If the date lasted any longer than that, I was free to make my way to the bar. A perk I'd taken advantage of three times so far.

"Good evening, Miss Paquin." Mikey dipped his head as he opened the car door for me.

"Hey, Mikey." My smile felt stiff, but it was better than nothing. "We're headed to Rouge this evening."

"I'm aware," he said before I could give him the address. "Young Master Sinclair will be meeting you there."

Wait, what? "Where's he now?"

"At the restaurant. I drove him there just over an hour ago."

"Why?"

Mikey shrugged. "I didn't ask."

Weird. I tried calling him once we'd merged into traffic, but it went straight to voicemail. I was getting really sick of that happening, to be honest.

I hung up with a sigh and decided to text him the briefing instead. His date was with Miray Kaya—sustainable fashion icon and the most beautiful woman on the planet. Out of all the candidates, her and Jackson had the highest overall compatibility score.

Maybe that's why my bones ached so much today.

Not two seconds after my briefing went through, it switched from Delivered to Read. Frowning, I started to type again. But then he reacted to my message with a thumbs-down emoji.

That was all. He didn't say anything else.

What does that mean? Which part isn't to your liking?

Another thumbs-down emoji.

Why? What had I said?

Can you talk super quick?

Thumbs down.

Can you respond with actual words?

Hedgehog emoji. Dentist emoji. Broken heart emoji.

Okay, so Jackson's phone had been stolen. I scrolled up to the text containing Miray's personal information and deleted it.

JACKSON

:(

I left it alone and slipped it back into my clutch. Jackson Sinclair had never used an emoji in his life. I wasn't even sure he knew what they were.

"Name?"

"Sinclair. We have a reservation for two separate tables at... seven..." I trailed off, confused by her expression.

With a tight, forced smile the hostess aggressively snapped her leather folder shut and said, "Follow me."

I wasn't sure what I'd said or done to earn that tone, but maybe she was just having a rough day. Maybe it had nothing to do with me.

People were allowed to have bad days.

But did she have to walk so far ahead of me, and so fast? I was half-jogging just to keep up with her. And just as I was gearing up to politely say something, she stopped, turned, and pointed a finger toward the bar.

"We had tables reserved," I said. No way we'd all be sitting at the bar.

"Mr. Sinclair instructed us to take you to him when you arrived," she said tightly. "Your tables are ready whenever you are."

Right. Okay. Except Jackson wasn't at the bar. It was just a bartender and some guy slumped over the—*oh, shit.*

I ran over to him when recognition hit, my pulse kicking. Jackson was fully slumped over the bar, his cheek pressed against it. His suit jacket was slung over another stool, and he was... he was petting the decorative hedgehog figurine beside him.

Oh my god.

"Jackson?" I whispered as I approached.

Please don't be drunk. Please, please, please don't be drunk.

"D'you see? I'm even hearing her voice," he slurred at the hedgehog.

Oh god. He was wasted. No wonder the staff was pissed.

"Are you the date or his Jamie?"

I blinked at the bartender, my stomach tightening. "Pardon?"

"Are you the date," she repeated slowly, "or his Jamie?"

Uh... "I'm Jamie."

His *date* was going to be here any minute now, which meant... I had to get him out of here. Like *now*.

"I'm Mallory." She shook my hand, a secretive smile tugging at her lips.

"Mallory the dentist." He was still speaking to the hedgehog. The man was gone.

"Studying to be a dentist," Mallory corrected. She didn't sound nearly as annoyed about his state as the hostess. "Not quite there yet."

Okay, well, the hedgehog and dentist emojis were starting to make a little more sense.

Mallory nudged her head in Jackson's direction. "You might wanna get your man out of here before his date arrives."

My cheeks flamed. "He's not my man."

Wrong thing to focus on but her misunderstanding required correction. It was very important.

She grinned. "I hate to break it to you, Jamie Paquin, the prettiest little matchmaker with the prettiest smile and the prettiest heart he's ever seen, but this idiot is your man."

I didn't have time to argue with her so I just placed a hand on Jackson's shoulder and kept my voice as soothing as I could manage. "Jackson? We gotta go. Are you able to stand up for me?"

With a low, frustrated sigh, he shoved upward and twisted around.

His cheeks were pink.

His eyes were glazed.

And he was pouting. Full. On. *Pouting*.

"Hey," I said. Could he see me? His eyes were pinned to the middle of my chest, but they were so heavy and glazed, I couldn't be sure. "It's Jamie."

His blinks were slow and incomplete, and it took a handful of seconds for him to respond. "Jamie," he whispered. Then, just as I was about to ask him to stand up again, he looped an arm around my waist, pulled me to him, and pressed his cheek to my chest.

Mallory quirked a brow at me. *I told you so*.

"Don't you guys cut people off after a certain point?" I asked her. And wasn't that point well before conversations with inanimate objects were being had?

"Not if their last name is Sinclair. We're not allowed to say no to his tax bracket—" She straightened very suddenly, her gaze darting to my left as she cleared her throat.

No. Nononono.

I ripped out of Jackson's sticky embrace and tripped back at least five steps before my hand flew out to grip the bar. Ignoring his confused scowl, I twisted on my heel, pushed back my shoulders, and plastered on the most convincing smile I could manage.

It faltered when I saw her.

She floated into the room... *floated*. I'd never seen someone walk with such elegant confidence. Everything about the way she held herself demanded attention.

She was mesmerizing.

I gulped lightly as the hostess led her straight to us. I needed an excuse for Jackson's state, and I needed one fast. If I let him go on the date like this, Vivian would have my head. More importantly, I didn't want him doing or saying anything he'd regret tomorrow.

I braved a step forward and shot out my hand, hoping to keep as much of Miray's attention on me as possible. I had no idea what Jackson was doing but if I looked at him now, so would she. Fingers crossed he was at least still upright.

"Hi, you must be Miray. I'm Jamie." *Please don't look behind me.*

"Hello." She grinned as she shook my hand, and damn it. Babies—literal *babies*—didn't have skin as soft as hers. "It's nice to meet you, Jamie. Your team mentioned that you'd be... monitoring our date this evening. Is that correct?"

Her tone insinuated that she found the idea more than a little silly, and I couldn't exactly blame her.

"I promise it's not as invasive as it sounds." The other women had forgotten about my existence in minutes. I didn't think she'd be any different. "But I'm afraid we'll have to reschedule. Jackson isn't feeling well, and I don't think—"

"I'm fine."

My shoulders went rigid when I felt his presence grow behind me. How was he even walking?

Miray's mossy green eyes slid to my right and up, up, up. Her long, curved lashes fluttered for a moment before her heart-shaped face split into another grin.

And, just like that, I was invisible.

"You must be Jackson," she purred. He shook her hand and a small, bitter part of me hoped he was too drunk to notice how devastatingly beautiful she was.

"And you must be Miray."

He remembered her name.

My stomach twisted as I watched them. Two gorgeous, successful people, who'd make a gorgeous, successful couple, and go on to produce more gorgeous, successful humans. Everything was as it should be.

I was going to be sick.

"Shall we?"

Jackson said it. His voice was slightly huskier than usual, his words slightly more slurred, but he was coherent. I'd never seen someone sober up so fast. He must've really wanted to go through with this date.

Miray's attention reluctantly moved back to me. "So how does this work? Will you be joining us for dinner?"

My smile faltered, embarrassment prickling at my ears. "I'll blend into the background," I assured her quietly. "You won't even notice I'm here."

~

I was given a small, two-person booth in the back corner of the restaurant. It had a full view of almost every table, but all I could see was them.

I didn't know what sins I'd committed in a previous life to deserve this level of torture, but they must have been bad. With a shaky finger, I tapped my phone to life again. Another eight minutes to go before I could run to the bar.

Or just run, period.

He was going to marry her. I could see it in the way they were leaning into each other, the way they chatted and laughed. She'd had her hand resting on his arm for the last four minutes and he'd done nothing to move it away.

He'd confessed to being drunk as we'd made our way to our separate tables, and instead of being put off by it, Miray had laughed it off. And judging by the way she was smiling at him, she was also charmed by his everything else.

Seven minutes left.

Miray threw her head back with laughter at something Jackson said, and he rubbed sheepishly at his chin, chuckling along with her.

"Would you like anything else to drink?"

I hadn't even heard the waiter approach.

Without looking away from Jackson, without even thinking, I said, "Gin. Neat."

The drink was placed in front of me less than two minutes later, and I downed it, cringing against the overwhelming burn. My tongue tingled, then went numb.

Burn was good. Numb was good. They were distracting.

Four minutes.

I gestured at the waiter, silently ordering another. It wasn't until I'd shot back the second drink that I noticed Jackson staring. My pulse tripped when I caught his gaze, my lips parting. It'd been so long since he looked at me—*really* looked at me. So long since he'd talked to me, laughed with me.

I missed him.

I missed him so much that this tiny morsel of his attention made my chest squeeze. Except... what was he doing? Why was he looking at me like that?

He wasn't laughing anymore. His brows were pulling into a sad frown, his throat was working with one rough swallow after another, and his fingers were curling into fists.

I tried my best to offer him a small, reassuring smile, but it was unsteady and unconvincing.

He shifted in his seat and gripped the edge of the table

like he was going to stand, but I was so busy staring at him, and he was so busy staring at me, that neither of us saw it coming.

Not when she reached for his face.

Not when she turned it back to her.

And not when she leaned in.

37

I FUMBLED my way into the private bathroom with a rough shoulder, half-blind. But at least I managed to keep the tears from falling until I'd yanked on the tap to drown out their accompanying sobs.

The pain was physical. I was shattered. My heart had been ripped in half and left to bleed out.

I tried to convince myself that this was all for the best; that I should've been happy for him. He'd finally found someone he liked.

Their compatibility scores were solid. They had similar lifestyles, wanted similar things, shared agreeable views on core issues, and Miray was beautiful, successful, and highly intelligent.

As his friend, I should've been happy for him. I wasn't.

Selfishly, I didn't want him to be with anyone else. Illogically, I hated her. Unreasonably, I wanted to march up to their table and politely ask Miray to take her hands off my man.

But I couldn't do any of that. Because I'd still wake up

tomorrow morning wanting love; and he'd still wake up tomorrow morning not believing in it. The best thing I could do for myself was to let him go. My heart was bleeding, and my stomach was twisting, but the pain was temporary. It wasn't like I'd still be pining after him in fifteen years. Not like I was going to regret not listening to my gut.

Oh god.

I was going to vomit.

Every last one of my internal alarms was blaring, screaming at me to go get him. This felt... so fucking wrong. Like I was making a huge mistake and—

Knock knock knock.

I sucked in a sharp breath, jolting upright. How long had I been in here for?

Knockknockknock knock knock.

"Just a sec!" I should've cleared my throat first, that crack in my voice had been very telling. I shut off the tap and made quick work of swiping away my tears. My mascara was smudged, my eyes puffy, my cheeks blotchy, but it was as good as it was going to get.

Now all I had to do was sneak out of here without running into Jackson.

I had no idea how he'd reacted. The second she'd leaned in, I'd shot to my feet, ripped my gaze away, and ran straight out of the—

Knockknockknockknockknockknockknock.

Wow, what the hell?

Frowning, I threw open the bathroom door... and immediately attempted to close it again. But Jackson's hand shot out just in time.

My heart had gone from dead to racing, a swarm of

angry bees buzzing over my skin. I'd done my best to clean up, but the evidence of what I'd been doing was pretty damning, and it was all over my face.

His eyes were drunk and hazy as they swept over my features, gathering data, and just as I was about to twist away from him and hide the extent of my misery, I noticed the shadows clouding the skin under his eyes. The somber set of his mouth.

My stomach flipped.

I meant to ask him what he was doing. Where was Miray? Why was he here and not with her? And why was he looking at me like I'd ruined his life? But I couldn't seem to find my voice.

Not when his half-blinks slowed to a complete stop. Not when he reached for my arm and pulled me into the dimly lit hallway. And not when he traced a jagged line down my cheek and neck with the pad of his finger.

I guess I'd missed a tear stain or two.

"Again," he whispered, and my cheeks flared bright crimson. I was aware of how much I'd cried in front of him, he didn't need to point it out like that. But then he said, "My fault. Again."

What? No it wasn't. He was allowed to kiss whoever he wanted; how I felt about it wasn't on him.

He swallowed, cupping my face with his palm. With a delicate sweep of his thumb across my cheekbone, he said, "I am not worth your tears, Jamie."

With that, my throat clogged up and a fresh bout of tears sprang to my eyes. How *dare* he? But before I could string together a semicoherent argument, disproving his very incorrect theory about how much he was worth, he said, "I stopped it. She didn't... we didn't kiss."

The rush of relief was so instantaneous and heady, it made my knees weak. I released a breath, my lashes fluttering as the crushing weight lifted from my chest.

"That's... too bad," I said quietly. "I thought you guys were really hitting it off. In my professional opinion—"

"Stop. Just... *stop*." His voice was gruff with exasperation as he stepped forward. "Does this feel right to you? Does seeing me with someone else feel right? Because I'm losing my fucking mind over here, Jamie. It's fucking horrible."

"How I feel about it shouldn't matter."

He was holding my face with both hands now, tilting it up as he moved even closer, crowding me. I should have told him no; should have put some distance between our bodies. But I'd missed him so much that I couldn't bring myself to do it. Instead, I stupidly leaned into his touch.

"How can you stand it?" His voice was raw, anguished. "How is it fair that you're only halfway there, but I can't fucking breathe anymore, Jamie?"

I blinked, on the brink of a heart attack. "You're drunk."

"Why can't I breathe? What did you do to me?"

"I don't think you know what you're saying."

"I know exactly what I'm fucking saying. I know exactly how much I fucking miss you. I know *exactly* how fucking wrong it feels with these other women, and what just happened out there was the last fucking straw. I don't care about the—"

FLASH.

Awareness tugged at my gut, and I knew, before I tripped back a step and swiveled toward her, I knew. There, at the end of the short hallway was Miray, phone in hand, expression contorted with pure rage.

She'd heard everything.

Shit.

38

Once again, I knew it was coming. Yet, once again, I flinched when the crimson leather folder slapped the oak table.

I'd never get used to it.

"Open it."

My chin remained tucked as I did, unsurprised to find the photo of me and Jackson from last night. The evidence was irrefutably damning. I had no way of explaining why we were standing so close, why he was cupping my face so tenderly, why I was gazing up at him with so much love and devastation and heartbreak.

It was painfully obvious. A major line between me and Jackson had been crossed, and Vivian was going to skin me alive for it. She was pacing back and forth, seething silently while she plotted her revenge.

I didn't blame her.

If Miray made good on her threats, then by noon today, this picture will have circulated through every circle that mattered in high society, and the outcome wasn't going to be pretty. Becoming physically or emotionally involved with a client was sacrilege; Vivian had a PR nightmare on her hands, and it was all my fault.

Oh, and since my actions were in direct violation of my employment contract, there was also a good chance I'd be served with a lawsuit. Maybe that's why she wasn't saying anything. Maybe her counsel had advised against it.

I'd made one poor decision after another, and now it was time to pay the piper.

When she finally stopped pacing and twisted on her heel to glare at me, I braced myself. But before she could start to curse and shout and berate, her assistant knocked on the door.

The Sinclairs were here.

I kept my eyes cast down as the crisp taps of Minerva's heels entered the room; I lowered them even farther when Jackson walked in behind her. We hadn't talked much last night after... everything. He'd tried, but I just couldn't. I knew I was about to lose everything, he was still drunk, and I just needed to cry and spiral in peace. So, I'd left the restaurant and hopped into a cab back to my own place.

I also may have ignored all of his calls. And texts. And emails. They'd still been coming in periodically by the time Vivian's email hit my inbox at 4:49 a.m.

I'd arrived at the office by 5:30, per her request, then waited for over four hours until she stormed in with the folder.

From the sneaky texts Alice had sent me, Vivian had been in back-to-back meetings with the heads of PR, HR, and Legal all morning. Apparently, she'd also intended to meet with the Sinclairs privately before speaking to me, but Minerva had insisted on my presence.

Not five minutes after Alice had sent the last update, Jackson had texted again.

Don't say anything to anyone, especially if lawyers are present. Wait for me. I'm coming.

I hadn't responded then, and I couldn't look at him now. If I did, there was a chance I'd start to cry again. I was a fucking mess.

"Minerva, Jackson." Vivian's tone was curt, professional, and laced with rage. "I'm glad you could make it. Please, have a seat."

There were eight chairs placed evenly around the table, yet Jackson chose the one to my left, nudged it way closer than necessary, and took a seat beside me. My shoulders, spine, heart—everything went stiff.

I could feel the holes Vivian's wrath was boring into the side of my face. As though I'd made Jackson's seating choice for him.

She cleared her throat and pulled out her own chair. "Firstly, I'd like to offer you both a sincere apology for everything that has transpired." Her fingers intertwined on the table, her lips pressing together once to form a thin line of disappointment. "I'm embarrassed by the lack of professionalism displayed by certain members of my team, and I'd like to assure you that appropriate measures are being taken to hold the involved parties accountable."

Okay, so her plan was to talk about me like I wasn't in the room—got it.

"Regarding the most recent allegations, an internal investigation is being conducted as we speak. Jamie will be meeting with HR shortly after this meeting, as well as—"

"What allegations?" Jackson cut in coolly. His knee kept nudging mine under the table like it was attempting to communicate with me through Morse code, and every time I tried to twist my leg away, he corrected it by moving closer. At this rate, he'd be fully pressed to my side before the meeting was over.

Vivian hesitated, but Jackson wouldn't let it go. "What is she being accused of, exactly?"

That protective tone wasn't doing me any favors. I nudged his thigh with my knuckles in silent warming, but it backfired catastrophically. The second he was presented with the opportunity, he snatched my hand, threaded his fingers through mine, and gave me a comforting squeeze before loosening his grip.

If I wanted to, I could've easily slipped away. Instead, my fingers lingered. I was emotionally drained, stressed as all hell, and it felt... honestly it was really comforting. Almost like we were in this together. A team.

I squeezed his hand back and, in response, he caressed my skin with his thumb.

Vivian's expression was strained as she regarded Jackson. "Miray sent me a photo of the two of you last night at Rouge."

"I'm aware," Jackson said. "What I'd like to know is what, exactly, Miss Paquin is being accused of."

"Is this it?" Minerva reached for the leather folder laid open in front of us, careful not to disturb Harry, who was peacefully asleep in her other arm. "I'm not sure what she's doing wrong, either."

Vivian's mouth stuttered, clearly at a loss. "We have very clear-cut and strict policies regarding our consultants engaging in any sort of inappropriate behavior with our clients, and *Jamie*—"

"She's not even touching him," Minerva pointed out before pushing the folder aside.

I mean... yeah, my arms were loose at my sides, all sad and defeated, but he was cradling my face in his hands like it was something precious. Everything about our body language and the way we were looking at each other screamed inappropriate workplace conduct. There was no defending it.

"That's because my affections for Jamie have been unrequited," Jackson said. "She's likely turning down another one of my proposals in the picture. I can't quite remember. I've asked her to marry me so many times, it's becoming difficult to keep track."

WHAT?

Vivian blanched. "I'm... I'm sorry?"

He didn't miss a beat. "She's turned me down on every occasion. It's been a very upsetting experience. I'm rather crushed over it, to be honest."

I gaped up at him. Was he seriously doing this?

Vivian's initial shock quickly morphed into disbelief. "Mr. Sinclair, as admirable as it is that you're trying to protect Jamie, I can't just let this slide. She should have reported the situation to HR—"

"From my experience, employees tend to shy away from reporting issues that could be turned against them to HR, especially if they suspect that management is looking for an excuse to fire them."

"Disclosing a breach in our guidelines regarding a consultant's relationship with their client is not optional, Mr. Sinclair." Vivian wasn't going to back down on this. "The employment contract Jamie signed made that abundantly clear. A scandal of this caliber has the potential to sink a company's reputation in this industry. Regardless of whether or not Jamie herself crossed any boundaries, the situation should have been dealt with internally to prevent this exact outcome."

She was right. And I didn't feel great about Jackson downplaying my level of participation in all of this. But before I could jump in or figure out how to silently ask him to stop, Vivian said, "However, there is a way to make this problem... go away."

Something about the way she said that grated against my soul like talons on a chalkboard. I narrowed my eyes.

"And what's that?" Minerva asked.

"Miss Kaya has agreed to refrain from distributing the photo... if Jackson agrees to the arrangement they discussed over dinner last night."

Silence.

Even though I saw Minerva's mouth move, there was nothing but silence and the roar of fire unfurling in my chest.

Again. He was being blackmailed into a relationship he didn't want *again*.

What the fuck was *wrong* with these people? What was it about the money and power that made their souls rot? My fingers were numb, either because I was squeezing Jackson's hand like it was my last lifeline, or because he was squeezing mine like it was his.

"Miray won't be making good on any of her threats," he said calmly. "I've fixed it."

Vivian's brows shot up. "I spoke with her less than an hour ago."

"And I got off the phone with her shortly before we arrived. She won't do anything with the photo, because if she does, I'll leak this."

Minerva placed her phone on the table, tapped at the screen, and sat back again. Harry didn't so much as stir in her arms. I had to squint my eyes and focus for a second to make sure he was breathing.

And then, it happened.

"I have a bone to pick with you," Jackson's slurred, gruff voice said on the speaker. "I was fine before her. I was *fine*, but nobody wanted to believe it. Not you, not Molly, not Mabel, not Bensen or Mikey or Rahul or anybody else. But I was fucking fine! And now? Now I'm... She fucking broke me, Minerva. I've well and truly lost my mind. When I go to bed, it's her. When I wake up, it's her. When I blink or breathe or dare to merely *exist*, it's her, and... and I never understood how Beatrice managed to sink her claws so deep into Richard's skin. It never made sense to me. She turned a god into her fucking lapdog and put him on an electric leash, *and he fucking let her.*

"It was a disease with the two of them. He could only see what she wanted him to see, believed every lie she told him, and whenever she did something to piss him off, he took it out on me. That's how fucking terrified he was that she'd leave him—he couldn't even properly confront her about any of her affairs. She thought she'd trapped him by giving birth to me, but to him, it was always the other way around.

"He was fucking pathetic. Even as a kid, I could see it. And I swore—*I swore*—it was never going to be me. If *that* was love, then the whole world was being lied to. But it wasn't, was it? That was a cancerous mix of deceit, and manipulation, and greed, and whatever the fuck else, but it wasn't love. You know how I know? Because my Jamie would never manipulate me like that for anything, and I would never—*could* never do it to her. Miray tried to kiss me during our date and my reaction to it was fucking visceral. I had to stop myself from shoving her off of me.

Everything about it was wrong and *that's* how I know what my parents had wasn't love, because even the thought of being with someone else makes me physically ill, Minerva.

"I'm done. Eight billion people in the world and my Jamie's the best fucking one. It's her, or it's no one. I won't be blackmailed and manipulated into making the single biggest mistake of my life, so fuck you, fuck the shares, and fuck the family legacy. I choose Jamie."

Click.

Dead silence.

I was lightheaded; hadn't breathed in almost ten minutes, afraid that the sound of my lungs would interfere with my need to memorize Jackson's every word. I desperately needed to hear it again from the very beginning to the very end, just to be sure I'd understood him correctly.

Jackson cleared his throat as I continued to stare at nothing, dazed, my pulse racing toward the nearest heart attack.

"I informed Miray that if she shared her picture, I'd share my audio. Turns out she's not keen on people knowing that her displays of affection made me feel ill, nor does she want to enter into any sort of arrangement with a man who's publicly known to be desperately in love with someone else."

I felt nothing and too much all at once. That time I hadn't misheard him. I was ninety-nine-point-nine-nine-nine-nine-nine percent sure of it.

Vivian wasn't saying anything, and I couldn't bring myself to look at her. Or Minerva. Or Jackson. All I could focus on was Jackson's voice and the feel of his fingers interlaced with mine.

"If she hasn't made another attempt to reach you already, she will," he finished.

"Vivian, a word?" Minerva said.

I barely heard her, barely registered Vivian's response, or the fact that the two of them were already leaving. My mind was busy... processing.

"You okay?"

Slowly, I let my gaze drift up to meet his. Had I mentioned how painfully beautiful his eyes were? I could stare at them for hours, memorizing every last stroke of harsh winter blue. They were breathtaking and exquisite. I loved them.

And he loved me.

It took active effort to pry my jaw open, and then I realized I had no idea where to even start.

"Um" was the first thing that came out of my mouth, and "you were drunk" was the second.

Thankfully, he knew exactly what I was trying to say. "Wasted, actually. Couldn't see straight when I left the message. Walking felt like a game of liquid Tetris. It was rather distressing."

I'd have been amused by that if I wasn't dying.

"So, you didn't mean any of it," I said.

"Not correct."

Literally dying. "But you regret it."

His gaze melted. "Not even close."

"You told Minerva, and I quote, 'fuck the shares,'" I reminded him.

He hummed. "Alcohol and adrenaline made my speech disorganized and clumsy, but the sentiment was there. Are the shares really what we should be focused on right now?"

"You're just going to give them up? After all that?"

"Again, I really didn't think that would be your biggest takeaway—"

"You said you could never love me back." He'd said those words. Told them right to my face.

The light amusement in his expression went out. "I did."

My breathing had gone from non-existent to embarrassingly heavy. It was a wonder the whole room hadn't fogged up yet. "Okay, so... make it make sense."

"I lied."

"*Why*?"

"Terror," he said without hesitation. "Sheer terror of the consequences if I admitted the truth to you or to myself. I can't... you have no idea what it was like in that house, what curse she had him under. Turning into either of them is—*was*—my biggest fear, just until I realized that if I couldn't get my head out of my ass, you'd walk away, find someone else, and never look back."

My comprehension levels were at an all-time low, but I was pretty sure I got most of that. "Okay, so then—"

"I love you, Jamie."

My heart burst. I couldn't... *wow* that was a rush.

A wicked smile spread over Jackson's lips as he took in my reaction. "I don't remember how or when it happened, exactly, but I've developed an unacceptable amount of love for you and I very much plan on holding you accountable for it."

Delight, pure and overwhelming, unfurled in my stomach, releasing a horde of butterflies. I grinned and his posture eased.

"You broke me," he chided. "It's been a very traumatic experience. Do you know butterflies in your stomach refer to actual butterflies in your actual stomach? And my heart's been very dramatic about you. It's unsettling, to say the least, knowing how many years you've shaved off my life."

"If it didn't mean getting blacklisted, I'd kiss you right now." The glass walls of the room were opaque, but Vivian had left the door open. Not by accident, I presumed.

"That's not going to happen." His mouth twitched. I so badly wanted to kiss it. "Minerva made a call this morning. If there aren't ten jobs lined up for you by now, there will be by the time we leave."

"What?"

He shrugged. "I made myself clear with her. If it's not you, it's no one. I reckon she'll do just about anything to keep you happy from this point on. You're officially the only hope she has left for securing an heir to the Sinclair throne. Whether it be now or in ten years."

I had so many questions. "What if I don't want kids? What if I can't have them?"

He shrugged like it was inconsequential. "She's going to have to deal with it."

"And what about *your* job? What about the company? Is she giving you the shares back?"

"No. Her original deal stands. If I don't get married, I lose the shares and she'll fire me."

He said that way too casually.

"Jackson—"

"Go on a date with me. A real one."

My stomach swooped. "You're giving up? After all that? How?"

"I asked him the same thing."

My attention snapped to Minerva as she walked back into the room; alone. She cocked her head, studying me as she sank back into her chair. "Shocking, isn't it?"

Heat raced across my cheeks, my shoulders squaring. I, too, had a bone to pick with Minerva Sinclair. "Just so we're clear, had I been made privy to the fact that Jackson was being blackmailed into a relationship he didn't want —had I known even a morsel of what I do now—I would've never agreed to participate."

The reaction I got wasn't the one I'd steeled my spine for. Instead of taking offense to my statement, Minerva looked... pleased. "Good," she said.

Clearly, she'd misunderstood my meaning. "I don't agree with what you're doing. I think it's manipulative and outright cruel. Jackson deserves better."

Her slow grin pushed at the corners of her eyes, made them sparkle. "What else? Be honest with me; no sugar-coating."

Was she hearing the words coming out of my mouth? "You should be ashamed of yourself for putting him through all of this. He has every right to be angry, and I don't blame him for trying to make my job impossible before you forced his hand *again*. I'd have reacted the same way."

Minerva nodded with what could only be interpreted as delighted approval. "Agreed."

What? "Then you'll give him the shares?"

"Oh, no. That won't happen unless he gets married by the end of next month."

Exasperation gnawed at my upper back, pushing me forward in my chair. "Why? If you agree with me then *why* are you still trying to force him into a marriage he doesn't want?"

"This isn't just about him, nor is it about me. I have a legacy to protect, Miss Paquin. And the cards were very clear with their message. Jackson *must* get married—"

"And you believe them?! You're playing with his life based on what one person interpreted as a spiritual message being relayed through a bunch of cards?"

I was really starting to understand Jackson's aversion to Charmed using tarot in their program. It was what'd gotten him into this bullshit mess in the first place.

"Imogen has never been wrong when she's read for me. I have no reason to doubt her in this."

I eyed her carefully, thinking. "Is there anything I could say that would change your mind?"

"I'm afraid not." Her tone left little room for argument. "However, if it makes you feel at all better, I've fired Charmed. He won't be required to attend any more blind dates."

"You didn't have a choice," Jackson interjected smoothly. "I wouldn't have shown up to them anyhow."

"It's her, or it's no one."

The soft skin around Minerva's eyes crinkled again, her mouth twitching. "Regardless," she said, "I do also feel obligated to apologize to you, Miss Paquin. I understand the impact this experience has had on your career, and I'd like you to know that if things don't work out with you at Charmed, Oscar Mijares is looking to expand his team and would love to talk to you about joining RUMI." She slipped a pale blue business card out of her purse and got up to hand it to me. "Call him whenever you're ready. I think you'll like what he has to say."

My jaw went appropriately slack. RUMI was small but growing rapidly. It probably topped the list of upcoming competitors for Charmed. Better yet, rumor had it that Oscar was big on company culture and a great boss. We'd lost a few really talented people to him over the last year, and we weren't the only ones.

As far as a new job went... this was about as ideal as it could get. Still, I didn't immediately reach for it. I didn't want her to think this would earn my forgiveness. It wouldn't.

"Vivian is currently on a call with Miray. She'll be back to speak with you shortly. She said it shouldn't be more than fifteen minutes." Her gaze slid to Jackson.

He squeezed my hand one last time before releasing it. "Text me when you're done, okay?"

"Okay."

The good thing about Vivian breaking her fifteen-minute promise and leaving me alone in the conference room for just shy of three hours was that it gave me lots of time to think.

Lots and lots of time to think.

39

THE BOX KEPT SLIDING out of my grip, and I kept having to shove it back up with my knee.

I hadn't realized just how much random stuff I'd acquired over the last few years; plus all the clothes and daily necessities I'd kept in my desk for when we'd had to work through the night for that one pain-in-the-ass client.

I'd texted Jackson after talking to Vivian, letting him know I'd quit. He'd responded with a single heart emoji, neglecting to mention that he was still outside of the building, waiting for me. The second I made it through the glass doors, the box was out of my hands.

"What're you still doing here?" I thought he'd left like five hours ago.

"We weren't done talking." He handed the box off to Mikey then turned to me again. "You okay?"

"Think so. You?" It couldn't have been easy for him, deciding to give up his job and everything he'd worked so hard to build. All for someone else.

All for *me*.

The crippling guilt would set in right after my heart

stopped fluttering with pure joy. His slow, knowing grin wasn't helping. Neither was the fact that, somehow, we were holding hands again.

"I'm great. Come on."

He tugged me toward the town car and slipped in after me. I was straddling his lap before Mikey had shut the door. Not by choice.

"Jackson!" A blush crept up my neck. He couldn't have waited another two seconds before grabbing me?

"I lasted that entire meeting without you on my lap. I only have so much self-control." His gaze darkened when it reached my mouth. "The partition's up, it's soundproof, and Mikey's been instructed to leave the car as soon as we're in the garage. He won't be opening the door."

My body was already melting into him, the air growing thick. "Could you have made it any more obvious?" I chided lightly.

"I don't care. I fucking missed you. It's been unbearable." He swallowed as his hands circled my waist, pulling me closer. "What did you do to me?"

My palms slid up his chest, settling on his shoulders as I gently pressed my forehead to his. "I missed you, too."

His breath hitched. "Yeah?"

"So much."

"Is this what it's supposed to feel like? Because I swear I can't fucking breathe anymore. I can't think, I can't... I'm barely functioning."

I pressed a gentle, smiling kiss on the corner of his mouth. "It's supposed to get easier... so I hear."

"No wonder Richard went mad with it."

And on that note. "Jackson... we need to talk about the shares."

"I already tried. She won't budge."

I licked my lips. "That's not what I'm... I *did* say I'd marry you if you didn't find someone you liked."

"As a friend," he retorted unhappily. "Living separate lives and getting our *needs* met elsewhere."

"In my defense, those were your original conditions."

"They were never meant for you."

I took a deep breath, the knot in my stomach growing jittery and restless. "Okay, so let's say, hypothetically, that we were starting over and laying out fresh terms for the agreement. If that were the case, what would your new conditions be?"

He studied me for a few silent moments. Then, "Are you sure you want to know? You're going to hate them."

My blood was rushing, my fingers bunching over the collar of his shirt with anticipation. "Start with the nonnegotiable ones."

"They're all nonnegotiable."

Maybe if I wasn't somewhat distracted by the thick, raging hard-on pressed against my stomach, I would've argued instead of just nodding.

"To start, there would be no paperwork, no predetermined end date, and no contractual restrictions on our relationship as husband and wife." He grazed a pair of knuckles over my cheekbone and my lashes fluttered. "You would be my *wife*, Jamie. In every way that matters, not just on paper. You would be mine, and I would be yours. I'm not willing to share."

The flutter in my chest had spread, a good portion of it settling between my legs. I shifted on his lap, reveling in the low, tortured growl the friction earned me. "What else?"

He released a breath through his nose and laid his head back. "You'd get your own staff. Driver, maids, the works." I frowned, but before I could respond, he said, "I'm not done. If we get married, I want all the privileges that come with having you as my wife, and that includes spoiling you rotten, darling." His mouth twitched. "Even if it is against your will."

"I don't—"

"Before you finish that thought, just know that your incessant resistance to letting me financially take care of you is what got us into this mess in the first place. It's bordering on becoming a fetish for me, Jamie. I wasn't joking when I said I've started fantasizing about buying you diamonds, tying you up, and fucking you until you're too incoherent to argue with me about it."

"That's... like the third time you've mentioned that."

"Because I can't stop thinking about it. I want to do it so fucking badly."

My whole lower half had melted to sizzling goo. "Just as long as you know it's not your money I'm after."

"You've made that abundantly clear. But if you've got my ring on your finger, the gifts are nonnegotiable." His fingers dug into my waist hard enough to leave marks (one could only hope). "Speaking of kinks, I think it's important that you know exactly what you'll be getting yourself into with me as your husband, because my self-control is currently hanging by a fucking thread, if that. I'm not sure I can keep holding back."

I'm sorry. "That whole week was you *holding back*?"

"You know what's worse?" His hand circled my throat and my panties all but melted. "All of these new depravities of mine are just for you. You broke me, Jamie, and I think it's only fair you pay the price for it, don't you?"

My breathing was becoming increasingly shallow. I would've given anything for him to squeeze his fingers, just a little. Just to make it clear that I was at his full mercy.

"I need you to be a little more specific than that."

He pulled me closer, using the grip he had on my neck. I shivered when he nipped at my bottom lip with his teeth. "You can't have a clit that pretty and expect your husband not to worship it every night, darling. Even if it means making you come until it hurts." He kissed me with deceptive softness. "But you already knew that. There's one particular kink that's new, and it's so much worse than the rest. It's truly depraved, and all because you haven't been allowing me to take care of you properly after I'm done fucking you."

I almost laughed when it clicked. "*Aftercare* is your new kink?"

A smile tugged at his deliciously plush mouth. "You've done me so dirty with that, Jamie. I've started to fucking fantasize about giving you another bath. I've been getting off on the idea of showering you with affection without you telling me 'no.' It's sickening. The aftercare isn't up for debate anymore."

I huffed a laugh, kissing the corner of his mouth. "Anything else?"

His gaze melted as his palm slid to the back of my neck. "I meant what I said on the voicemail... you're my best friend."

Oh god. My heart.

"Yeah?" My cheeks were going to fall off, I was smiling so wide.

He was grinning right back. "Is that sad?"

"No. Not even a little."

"Good. I want the friendship thing to stay."

I clicked my tongue, teasing. "Friends don't torture

each other's private parts, Mr. Sinclair. They play much nicer than that."

He chuckled. "If you've got any nonnegotiables, you should probably say them now. I'm taking you upstairs the second we're home and you won't be able to pry my mouth from your pussy until I've had my fill. It's been a long fucking week."

I squirmed on his lap. "I'm not sure if I've mentioned it yet, but the dirty talk really does it for me."

His smirk turned a touch dark. "Eating you out is what does it for me. It's at the top of my kink list."

"You have no idea how hot that is," I breathed. Or maybe he did. Maybe he knew exactly what he was doing to me.

"Tell me your conditions. I need the distraction."

There was one topic we needed to discuss that would sober us right up.

"Kids," I said. "We need to talk about that whole thing."

Sure enough, the heat in Jackson's eyes went out with a blink. It was replaced with uncertainty.

I cleared my throat. "Obviously, your aunt wants to secure an heir... but that's a massive decision, and I need a lot—and I mean *a lot*—of time to think about it. And I can't promise anything right now one way or the other."

He didn't hesitate. "Okay. That's more than fair."

I released a breath. "Really?"

"Really. If you decide to do this with me, we can talk about it in a year or two... see how we both feel about it."

He said it with firm, unwavering confidence. Like there was no doubt in his mind that we'd still be together, just like this, in a year or two.

"But what if Minerva—"

"Jamie." He tipped my chin until I didn't have a choice but to meet his gaze. "It's *you*, or it's no one. We can talk about the rest whenever you're ready, but I'll never push you to have a child if it's not something you want. I don't care what Minerva decides to threaten me with next. Fuck her. Fuck the company. Fuck the shares. It's me and you, okay? We're in this together."

Relief washed over me. I sighed. "We would make a pretty good team."

His grin was devastating. "Best friends for liiife," he teased in a shocking, sing-songy voice. Like a dork. And when I was done giggling over it, he murmured, "I love you, Jamie."

The man was dead set on sending me straight to an early grave, I swear.

"I love you, too," I whispered back.

His breath hitched, the smile falling off his face. "Yeah?"

"Hell yeah."

"You're the full way there?"

"I'm the full way there."

This time when he kissed me, he didn't stop. Not until we'd arrived at the penthouse, he'd kicked his bedroom door shut, and my half-naked body was splayed out on his bed.

And the only reason he stopped was to make good on all the threats he'd made about what he'd do with his tongue if I were his wife. Every. single. One.

40

It took another eight days for me and Jackson to finalize the terms of our non-agreement agreement, partly because he insisted on being unreasonable (in what world did I need a personal bodyguard???), and partly because we couldn't be alone in the same room for more than ten minutes before I attacked him mouth-first, or vice versa.

We were insatiable. It was honestly exhausting. Thirty percent of my muscles were sore at any given time and in seemingly randomized batches. Still, no matter how many times I had him, it never seemed to be enough.

Most of the household staff had learned to steer clear of whichever section of the house Jackson and I were hanging out in, and all the security cameras he'd installed before my arrival were disconnected.

Oh, and the Harrison sisters were losing their actual minds over the whole thing. The two of them were ticking tear bombs. You never knew when one of them was going to break into sobs of inconsolable joy.

The first time Jackson told me he loved me in front of Molly, she burst into tears and did not stop for a solid thirty minutes. They were over the moon—kept baking me treats and offering to help me shop for a dress. You know, for the wedding ceremony.

... The one I still hadn't told Ria about.

She was going to murder me when she found out. So... in less than ten minutes. But hey, at least my parents knew. They'd been skeptical at first, just until Jackson had turned on the charm. I was kind of hoping tonight would go the same way.

I was restless, my fingers fumbling with the zipper of my jacket as I watched the city lights blur by from the back of the car. When Jackson noticed, he gently slipped his hand over mine.

It helped. Always did.

"Can I ask you something?" he said.

"Please." I needed a distraction.

"Why is Cat coming with us?"

Toebeans was currently loafed up on Jackson's other side, purring softly as my soon-to-be husband (!!!) scratched the sweet spot behind his left ear.

"He hasn't seen Adrien in two months," I said. "If he smelled him on us when we got back, he would... I don't know, actually. This is the longest the two of them have been apart since they met. Plus, Adrien asked me to bring him."

He'd already taken his allergy medicine and everything. The two of them were ridiculous together.

"I don't know if I ever told you the story, but Ria lost her mind the first time Adrien and Toebeans met." I bit down a smile as the memories rushed back.

"Why?"

"Her and Adrien absolutely despised each other. And

Toebeans... well, you'll see." It was the strangest thing. I still couldn't make sense of it.

When the car finally slowed to a stop, I scooped Toebeans up into my arms (he still wouldn't let Jackson hold him) and practically bolted into the building, a fresh rush of nerves and excitement going straight for my knees.

I was bouncing on my heels by the time the elevator doors finally groaned open, and before I'd even had a chance to step into Ria and Adrien's foyer, Toebeans had wiggled out of my hold and sprinted. He knew exactly where we were. There was no stopping him.

"*Jamie?!*"

"Ria!"

Where was she? I stumbled out into the foyer trying to locate where her voice had echoed from. Fucking Adrien. There were so many goddamn plants in their penthouse that I couldn't—

She tackled me.

It came from my left, and I hit the rug with an *oomph* as Ria squealed with utter delight, squishing all the air out of my lungs.

I may have also squealed.

There was a *lot* of squealing.

"Hi!" she exclaimed as I giggled through the tightest hug to have ever been hugged. It was going to cost me a couple of ribs for sure. Well worth it.

"Hiii." I'd forgotten how good she always smelled. Like my best friend. Like *home*. "I missed you, Ree."

"Missed you, too, angel." She gave me one last squeeze before pulling away.

"Holy shit, you're *so* tanned." I grabbed her freshly freckled face for closer inspection. Her skin was perfectly sun-kissed, making the slash of honey-gold cutting through her left iris even more striking. Pride bubbled up my chest as she grinned. My best friend was so beautiful. I'd missed her so much.

"I look *great* tanned," she said.

"You totally do," I agreed. "Did you have so much fun?"

"It was fucking incredible, Jams. Some of those islands were surreal—and the *diving*. Honestly, I'd take it up as a hobby if we lived somewhere that allowed it. I'll take you next year when I'm on break, I swear you'll love it. I wasn't expecting to become so obsessed with it, but the *sharks*, Jamie. It's insane! Oh, and have you ever tried—" She cut off, blinking up at something behind me that made her grin falter.

I twisted on the floor to find Jackson hovering a few feet away, his posture somewhat stiff and awkward, as though he wasn't quite sure what to do with himself.

He was *nervous*. Adorable.

I gave him a small, comforting smile as he cleared his throat. "Hello, you must be Ria. I'm Jackson." He held out his hand, but since we were sitting and he was standing, he had to sort of bend to do it. "Jackson Sinclair."

Her eyes flared as they darted to me, then narrowed. She didn't take his hand.

Uh oh.

"Ree, let's go sit and chat for a few, yeah?" I suggested softly.

"What's going on?" Her gaze slid between us, trying to piece it together.

Before I could respond, Adrien rounded the corner through a whole bunch of exotic plants I couldn't begin to name, holding a very purry, *very* cuddly Toebeans Maguire. My slutty cat was rubbing his head all over his favorite human's chin, eyes closed. He sounded like a fucking motorboat.

"Hey, Jams," Adrien said, shooting me a dimpled grin. I barely heard him over the purring.

Jackson had gone still, his mouth hanging open as he watched the two of them. Poor guy. The amount of effort he'd put in just to be allowed within touching distance of Toebeans.

"Seriously, what is going on?" Ria asked again, whispering this time.

"I'll tell you in a bit, just—"

PPPPRRRRRRRRRRRRRRRRRRRRRR.

Oh my god. I couldn't hear myself think.

After quickly introducing himself to Adrien, Jackson helped me to my feet. The gesture—the exchanged private smiles and too-close proximity of our bodies—did not go unnoticed by Ria. Her eyes flared with understanding, her jaw falling slack.

I helped her up before she could comment, slung my arm around her shoulders, and guided her to the living area. She continued to gape at me.

"In my defense regarding the conversation we're about to have, just remember, you haven't had proper reception in almost two months," I whispered.

"You're *sleeping* with Jackson Sinclair?" she hissed back.

"It's not as inappropriate as it sounds," I assured her. "He's not my client anymore. I quit my job."

"What?"

"Oh, don't worry, I start my new one next week at RUMI. I'm pretty excited about it, actually. Great pay, great benefits... a boss that doesn't believe I should be blacklisted from the entire industry for accidentally falling in love with a client..."

"What?!"

I couldn't remember why I'd been so nervous. This was fun.

"Yeah, I know. He even went as far as to send us flowers to celebrate the engagement, and I haven't even started there yet. Vivian would never." I flashed her my ring. White gold, princess cut. Mabel and Molly had helped Jackson pick it out. "Pretty, no?"

"*What*?!"

"It's not what it sounds like, I swear." I gave her a reassuring smile. "We're only getting married so we can date. Like that movie with Sandra Bullock and one of the Ryans."

"Gooseling," Jackson supplied from behind us.

"Yup. Sandra Bullock and Ryan Gooseling. Except our situation's actually realistic. Even Jackson's aunt's psychic agreed it was the best course of action. We're all set."

"*WHAT?!*"

EPILOGUE

One year later.

I yelped as my back hit the petal-covered bed. Jackson was on top of me in an instant, pinning my wrists as he buried his face in my neck.

"God, you look good in white," he growled into my skin before nipping at it. "I'm tempted to buy you a full line of wedding dresses just so I can fuck you in them."

I hummed. If I'd learned one thing over the last year, it was that arguing with Jackson over his extravagant gift ideas only made things worse. I could almost guarantee that if I said no to him now, I'd go home after our honeymoon to a penthouse full of wedding dresses.

My husband was the most unreasonable man on the planet.

I loved him so fucking much.

"We could make it an annual tradition." He began bunching up the buttery silk of my skirt, pushing it up to my waist. I moaned, spreading my thighs so he could settle between them. "What do you think, Mrs. Sinclair? One year ago today I fucked you in that pretty little lace dress you wore to the courthouse, and I'm about to do the same now. I can't think of a more enticing tradition."

I grinned up at the ceiling. "I think two weddings is enough for one lifetime."

He lifted his head, eyes glazed with lust as he looked down at me. "The first one didn't count. You wouldn't even let me get us a venue."

"I think this one more than made up for it, don't you?" I couldn't think of a more luxurious or extravagant wedding venue than the rooftop patio of the flagship Cloutier Toronto. The hotel's wedding spaces were booked out years in advance. Luckily, the CEO's wife was my maid of honor.

Jackson frowned in that tell-tale way. "Fine. We'll compromise. No annual ceremony but I don't see why you can't get a new wedding dress every year so I can tear it off you. What better way to celebrate our anniversary?"

It was a genuine question. He didn't hear how ridiculous that sounded.

"Have I told you how much I love you recently?"

His grin sent a familiar flutter through me. I'd never get used to how painfully handsome the man was. "We exchanged vows this afternoon, but I'm not opposed to hearing it again, *wife*."

There was a reason for his emphasis. He knew damn well how much it turned me on when he called me that.

"I love you." I whispered, shivering when he pinned me down with a firm press of his hips. Hearing me say that was *his* turn-on. "I love you, Jackson. So fucking much."

He groaned, thrusting against me as the tips of his

fingers dug into my wrists. Anticipation swept through me. If I pushed him enough, he'd snap, hold me down, and fuck me with no mercy.

Like he *needed* it.

"It hasn't gotten easier for me," I said. "I love you even more than I did a year ago. It's so overwhelming. I don't know how to fucking handle it."

The best part of this game? All I had to do was just tell him the truth.

He wasn't grinning anymore.

"I'm so glad I married you. Best decision I've ever made. You make me so happy, baby. I'm borderline obsessed with being your wife."

Another thrust and I whimpered. My limbs were shaking.

"Keep going," he commanded roughly. His expression was half-feral.

"I'm yours," I panted. "I belong to you, Jackson. I'm so in love with you, it's hopeless. You've ruined me. I wouldn't be able to breathe without y—"

Snap.

He kissed me, deep and relentless. And when my spine tried to curve with pleasure, he pressed into me, securing me in firm, unforgiving place.

I purred.

"You did that on purpose." He bit my bottom lip, punishing it. "Here I was, planning on fucking you nicely on our wedding night, but that's not what you need, is it, *wife*?"

"And what do you want? You wanna be gentle or leave a few bruises I'll still be thinking about the next time I wear a wedding dress for you?"

His chest rumbled, pleased with my answer. "How did I get so fucking lucky with you?"

I smiled. "Good thing you didn't let me drown that first night, huh?"

"I thought about it."

"Shut up," I giggled. "And here we are, thirteen months later. Who would've thought?"

His eyes sobered just a touch. "Best year of my life."

"Same. Without question." Huffing another small giggle, I sang, "Best friends for liiife."

"Best friends for liiife," he sang back. "I love you, darling. More than anyone, more than anything."

I craned my neck, brushing his lips with mine when I whispered, "Prove it. Flip your wife over and give her what she wants."

I didn't have to ask twice.

A Note From Kyra

You made it!! Thank you so, so much for reading *Failure to Match*. I couldn't wait to share Jamie's story with you after how much love Ria and Adrien got in *Bossy Devil*. It was so unexpected, overwhelming, and genuinely humbling. I'm more grateful than you'll ever know! Thank you, thank you, thank you. *Insert all the heart emojis*

As always, here are some extra goodies just for you.

- Bonus STEAMY epilogue from Jackson's POV (exclusive to newsletter subscribers)

- Free steamy novella (exclusive to newsletter subscribers)

I'd also be incredibly grateful if you would take a minute and leave a review of this story on Amazon,

Goodreads, or wherever else you like. Every single one goes a long way to helping other readers discover the book.

Wishing you the happiest of ever afters!

Until next time,

Kyra

Also By Kyra Parsi

A Deal with the Bossy Devil (Adrien and Ria)

> Enemies to lovers

> Fake relationship

> Forced proximity

Fool Them Once

> Fake relationship

> Friend's older brother

> Accidental roommates

In Love And War

> Enemies to lovers

> Office romance

> Forbidden love

Printed in Great Britain
by Amazon

56052718R00243